# THE KILL ZONE

KU-050-864

Central Library
Y Llyfrgell Ganolog
☎ 02920 382116

ACC. No: 02516386

# THE KILL ZONE

Chris Ryan

**WINDSOR**
**PARAGON**

First published 2010
by Hodder & Stoughton
This Large Print edition published 2011
by AudioGO Ltd
by arrangement with
Hodder & Stoughton Ltd

Hardcover  ISBN: 978 1 445 85479 3
Softcover    ISBN: 978 1 445 85480 9

Copyright © Chris Ryan 2010

The right of Chris Ryan to be identified as the
Author of the Work has been asserted by him in
accordance with the Copyright, Designs and
Patents Act 1988

All characters in this publication are fictitious and
any resemblance to real persons, living or dead, is
purely coincidental

All rights reserved.

**British Library Cataloguing in Publication Data available**

Printed and bound in Great Britain by
CPI Antony Rowe, Chippenham and Eastbourne

# ACKNOWLEDGEMENTS

To my agent Barbara Levy, publisher Mark Booth, Charlotte Haycock and the rest of the team at Coronet.

**Kill Zone (noun)**

1. The area of a military engagement with a high concentration of fatalities.


2. An area of the human body where entry of a projectile would cause death.

# GLOSSARY

| | |
|---|---|
| AQT | Al Qaeda Taliban |
| CAT | counter-attack team |
| CO19 | Specialist Firearm Command branch of the Metropolitan Police Service |
| Det (the) | 14 Intelligence Company, a covert surveillance unit trained by 22 SAS for deployment in Northern Ireland |
| det cord | detonating cord |
| FOB | forward operating base |
| frangible ammo | soft rounds that break as they hit walls, reducing ricochets |
| GCHQ | Government Communications Headquarters |
| gimpy | general purpose machine gun (GPMG) |
| green zone | the fertile area surrounding a river or wadi |
| Hesco | flat-packed containers that are infilled with dirt or sand to create protective barriers |
| Icom | intelligence communication |
| ICU | intensive care unit |
| IED | improvised explosive device |
| IR | infrared |
| JSIW | Joint Services Interrogation Wing |
| JTAC | Joint Terrorism Analysis Centre |
| klick | kilometre |
| LASM | light anti-structures missile |
| LTD | laser target designator |
| LZ | landing zone |
| MoD | Ministry of Defence |
| MRE | meal, ready to eat |

| | |
|---|---|
| NBC suits | nuclear, biological and chemical warfare suits |
| OP | observation post |
| PE | plastic explosive |
| PIRA | Provisional IRA |
| REME | Royal Electrical and Mechanical Engineers |
| RPG | rocket-propelled grenade |
| RUC | Royal Ulster Constabulary |
| RV | rendezvous |
| SBS/shakyboats | Special Boat Service |
| SOCO | scene-of-crime officer |
| SOP | standard operating procedure |
| UAV | unmanned aerial vehicle |
| UMP | Universal Machine Pistol, a Heckler and Koch submachine gun |
| wadi | a dry riverbed |

All warfare is based on deception. When able to attack, we must seem unable; when using our forces, we must seem inactive; when we are near, we must make the enemy think we are far away; when far away, we must make him believe we are near. Hold out baits to entice the enemy. Feign disorder, and crush him.

Sun Tzu, *The Art of War*

# PROLOGUE

*Iran. Somewhere near the border with Afghanistan. 1980.*

A fire crackled at the mouth of a cave.

It was not a large fire, because it was not a large cave. Just big enough for the four black-robed people who used it as a dwelling place: an old man, an old woman and two children, nine and eight. And even though it had been scorching that day, the fire was as welcome for its heat as for its light. These desert-dwellers knew that the temperature could drop to below freezing as the night wore on.

The orange flames danced in the blackness. And as they danced, they reflected on the metal of a gun. It was not a new gun, nor a particularly expensive or desirable one. Just an old AK-47, its wooden butt burnished and worn. The old man would tell people it was Russian-made but in truth it was as much a mongrel as the wild dogs that ran in packs around these parts, a gun cobbled together from different weapons made in different countries. Hungarian, Chinese . . . It lay on the lap of the old man, who sat cross-legged by the fire, one gnarled finger placed gently—tenderly, almost—on the trigger.

He spoke. Stories of war and death that somehow suited his harsh, weather-beaten face. And as he spoke, the two boys listened, the reflection of the flames flickering in their wide, dark eyes.

'*Az sheytan-e bozorg bar hazar bashed,*' he announced in his native Farsi. 'Beware of the

1

Great Satan—America. And beware its lapdog, Britain. These are the homes of the infidels and the ungodly. It is your duty, as Muslims and followers of the Prophet, may peace and blessings be upon him, to fight a righteous and holy war against these sinners. The time will come when all who are true to the Prophet will be called to rise up and fight against them. My time on earth is not long, but you . . .'

He looked at each of the boys in turn.

'*You* must be ready to answer that call.'

A clattering noise. The old woman placed a pot near the fire and stirred its contents with a spoon. 'You should not fill their ears with such things,' she said. Her skin was leathery with age, her voice croaky. 'They are too young.'

The old man scowled. His eyes were flinty under his bushy eyebrows. 'You don't know what you say,' he rasped. 'No one is too young to understand their purpose.'

'*Your* purpose,' the woman mumbled. 'Not theirs.'

'*Silence!*'

His hands trembled slightly on his Kalashnikov. It took a moment to subdue his anger.

'What would a *woman* know of such things?' he said after a while. 'It is men who understand the ways of the world.'

'*They* are not men,' the old woman insisted in a low voice. She sounded both scared to speak and compelled to do so. 'They are children.'

The old man rose instantly to his feet, letting the rifle fall to the ground. He stepped towards his wife, raised his hand and, with the force of a much younger person, dealt her a sharp blow across the

2

side of the face. The woman cried out, but the man hit her again. She tumbled to the dusty floor, a trickle of blood oozing from her nose. As she lay there, her husband spoke in a firm voice.

*'As for those women from whom ye fear rebellion, admonish them and banish them to beds apart; and scourge them!'*

Holy words from the holy Koran, and familiar to the old woman's ears. She'd heard them enough times throughout her life. Keeping her head bowed, she pushed herself to her knees and dabbed away the blood, then picked up her spoon and continued to stir the food in the pot while the man turned back to his grandchildren.

'Will you be ready to answer the call?' he demanded in a loud voice.

'Yes, Grandfather,' the two boys said in unison. 'We will be ready.'

Young Farzad sat close to the fire. He and his brother had seen their grandmother beaten before. Many times. He admired his grandfather. Admired his strong words. Admired his devotion. Grandmother was always interfering. Whenever she overstepped the mark, she was punished, as was right and proper. She had been beaten before, and she would be beaten again. Farzad was more interested in what his grandfather had to say. In what he had to show them. Like the Kalashnikov that lay in the dust by the fire. And he could tell his brother felt the same way.

The old man gave an approving nod and sat down next to them once more. He picked up the gun and started to dismantle it, carefully laying each of the parts on the ground in front of the two boys. First, the magazine. When this was detached,

3

he pointed the gun out of the cave mouth and pulled back the cocking lever, making sure there was no round left in the chamber. Satisfied it was empty, he removed the cleaning rod, the receiving cover and the recoil spring. He noticed with pride that his grandsons were watching and absorbing his every move. With expert hands he removed the bolt carrier and gas tube, and when the weapon was fully stripped down he handed the shell of the Kalashnikov to the elder of the two.

'Farzad,' he said. 'You are nine years old. I was your age when I first learned how to manage a weapon. You will rebuild this for me now.'

Farzad felt a quiet thrill. 'Yes, Grandfather,' he said and, following the old man's quiet, patient instructions, started to reassemble the rifle. The clunky noise of the metal pieces slotting together echoed around the cave. In only a few minutes, the AK-47 was reassembled and ready to fire.

'Good,' the old man said, and his hard eyes turned to the younger boy. 'Adel,' he announced. '*You* will shoot first.' And he led the two boys out of the cave.

The desert night was already beginning to grow cool. In the distance they could see dots of light— dwellings much like their own, scattered around the foothills of these mountains and the plains beyond. He placed the Kalashnikov in Adel's hands and helped him press the butt firmly into his bony shoulder and aim out into the blackness. 'There are three positions,' he explained to the boys, and he moved the selector lever from safe to the middle position. A tinny click. 'Automatic. The weapon will continue firing until you release your finger from the trigger, or you fire all the rounds

4

from the magazine.' Another flick of the selector lever, down to the lowest position. 'Semi-automatic,' he announced. 'The weapon will fire only once. You need to release the trigger and pull it again to fire a second shot.' With a sharp tug, he pulled back the cocking lever, knowing that it would be too hard for Adel. Then he stepped back. Twenty metres from where they stood there was a low mulberry bush, no more than a couple of metres high, and they could just make out its outline in the darkness. 'Aim for the bush,' he said, 'and fire when you are ready.'

Some children might have been hasty, but not Adel. He was careful. Meticulous. He breathed calmly and did not shoot until he was ready.

The noise of the discharge echoed across the desert. In the distance, a frightened yelp—a wild dog, scared by the sudden bang. The recoil was strong for the small boy, but he absorbed it well before lowering the weapon and handing it wordlessly to his brother. Farzad took the AK-47 confidently and did not need his grandfather's assistance in positioning the gun and firing a round into the black night.

'Good,' their grandfather announced once Farzad had lowered the Kalashnikov. 'Very good.' He walked up to them and put his arms around their shoulders. For a moment they were silent, just standing there, looking out into the darkness. 'Who knows what war will be like when *you* are men,' he murmured. 'When you are called upon to fight—and do not doubt that you *will* be called—it is important that you know your weapon, and that you know it well. But remember this. Your weapon is not the most important thing.'

The old man tapped on his skull with two fingers and the boys watched him attentively.

'It is with your weapon that you win the battle,' he stated, 'but with your mind that you win the war.'

A silence.

And then, prompted by his grandfather, Farzad raised the weapon once more. This time, he flicked the selector lever to automatic. He adopted the firing position and squeezed the trigger. As many novices do when they first fire an automatic weapon, he gripped too hard. The recoil threw the barrel of the gun upwards and to the right; the night air filled with the thunder of rounds being quickly discharged. As he released his finger, a huge grin spread over Farzad's young face.

In the years that were to follow, Farzad never forgot the events of the next few seconds. He wanted to know if the end of the barrel was hot, so with the butt still pressed into his shoulder, he stretched out his left hand to touch the metal. It *was* hot, and his discovery pleased him. He turned, ready to explain to his grandfather what he had learned.

But his grandfather looked alarmed.

'*The safety!*' the old man said harshly. '*Make it sa—*'

He never finished his sentence.

Farzad's thumb was still over the end of the gun barrel when his finger slipped; the gun was pointing just to the left of his grandfather. There was a short burst of fire as the 7.62 mm rounds blew his thumb away and, as the gun lifted to the right, pumped into his grandfather's stomach and ripped a seam along his chest.

Farzad screamed in pain. His brother cried out. *'Grandfather!'*

The old man opened his mouth too, but no sound came out. Just a sudden gush of foaming blood. He collapsed.

Farzad fell to his knees, blood oozing fast from his own hand, and in the confusion he could sense Adel doing the same. Adel shook their grandfather, as if that would do something to bring him back from the brink.

It did nothing, of course.

His final breath was long and choking; blood seeped from the wound in his belly, saturating his robe and oozing on to the ground.

The boys fell silent. Farzad's body was shaking.

'Is he dead?' Adel whispered finally.

Farzad laid his good hand on his beloved grandfather's head. 'Yes, Adel,' he managed to say, gritting his teeth through the pain. 'He is dead.'

And then he started to moan as blood pumped from his wound.

Suddenly their grandmother was there. She took in the scene and started to scream—a panicked, hysterical scream.

Farzad looked towards her. She was silhouetted against the flames. Her shrieks had silenced his own, and now they filled the air. His lip curled, half because of the pain in his hand, half because he felt a burst of uncontrollable anger towards her. 'Silence!' he said, doing his best to imitate his grandfather. But the old woman failed to obey him. Instead, she strode up to where he and Adel were crouched and, seemingly unaware of the dreadful wound to his left hand, started to rain blows down on him, her frail old fists surprisingly forceful.

Farzad stood up and raised his bloodied hand to protect himself from his grandmother's anger, but still she swiped at him.

'What have you done? *What have you done? What is this wickedness? You are an evil child! I saw it in you when you were born. There has always been something wicked about you, and now . . . now *this*!'*

Adel strode the few paces to where the old lady was beating his brother, stood behind her and pulled her roughly away. She tripped and hit the ground, but the screaming didn't stop. If anything it grew louder and more desperate.

'Be quiet!' Farzad hissed, pressing his wounded hand against himself in a vain attempt to stem the bleeding. 'People will come. They will see what has happened.'

*'What have you done? What have you done?'*

Farzad was now shaking with anger rather than pain. He looked at his grandmother and then back at his brother.

Something passed between them. Nothing spoken; just a silent agreement that there was something they needed to do. If their grandmother continued to scream, people from all around would come to see what had happened. They would find their grandfather, and they would learn that Farzad had killed him. The local mullah would try them and they would be stoned to death. As males, they would be buried only up to their waists—it was customary for women to be buried up to their shoulders so their arms were not free— but then the locals would hurl rocks at them. The tradition was to let a family member cast the first

8

stone, to try to knock out the victim so that he would suffer less. But grandfather was their only male relative and he wouldn't be throwing stones at anyone.

*The time will come when all who are true to the Prophet will be called to rise up and fight against them.*

Farzad knew his duty: to keep himself and his brother safe so that they could fight their holy war, just like their grandfather had urged them. Satisfied that he had his brother's approval, he didn't hesitate. Their grandmother was standing between him and the fire, no more than three metres away, with her hands pulling at her hair in anguish. He pointed the AK-47 at his grandmother's head. Her eyes, closed with grief, noticed nothing, and she continued her desperate howling.

There was only enough ammo in the magazine for a short burst of fire. But it was enough to silence her.

The rounds slammed into her head. Farzad watched with detached curiosity as it collapsed in on itself, as her limbs twitched for a few short seconds before falling still. He barely noticed that part of his grandmother's brain matter had spattered on to their faces, warm and sticky.

They stood there, surrounded by the sudden silence of the desert, and the bleeding corpses of their own flesh and blood.

*It is with your weapon that you win the battle, but with your mind that you win the war.*

Farzad and Adel had to think carefully and clearly. It would be stupid to leave the corpses there, ready to be identified by anyone who passed. Their grandparents were well known in this area. Unanswerable questions would be asked. The brothers made their decision with only a few brief words.

First they needed to attend to Farzad's hand. Their grandfather had once taught them how to cauterise the wound of an injured goat, rather than let the precious animal die, and now they could think of no other way of stemming the frightening flow of blood from Farzad's fist. They crouched by the fire together, Farzad with a wild look in his eyes, Adel gripping his wrist firmly.

'Are you ready?' the younger boy asked.

Farzad nodded, biting his lip in preparation, before allowing Adel to thrust the bleeding stump into the red-hot embers.

Farzad had expected to scream, but he didn't. The pain was too searing for that. He was almost unable to breathe, but he kept the wound against the heat for five seconds.

Ten seconds.

He pulled it out, gasping breathlessly, then plunged his hand into a small pot of water by his side. If anything, it made the fierce, burning pain worse, but he still managed to master his desire to shriek with pain. When he removed it, he looked at his four-fingered hand with something approaching horror.

Adel looked horrified too, and Farzad suddenly felt responsible for him. He put on a brave face.

'We must do it now,' he whispered.

Adel nodded.

They moved their grandmother first, each of them taking an ankle and dragging her towards the fire. When they were close, Farzad moved to the head end and together they flung her on to the pyre. The bulk of her body deadened the flames for a moment, but they soon returned—a bigger blaze than before as her clothes caught fire. Strange smells filled the cave. First, a dry, acrid smell as the old woman's wispy hair curled and shrivelled into nothing. The clothes burned brighter as they soaked up the melting body fat from underneath; and now there was a new smell—a thick, greasy aroma like fatty mutton burning on a spit.

'We need more wood,' said Farzad, and he was right. Although the body was burning, it was not reducing in size. It would take longer to destroy the bodies than they thought. The wood supply was at the back of the cave. They selected small logs first, to get the fire roaring again. The mutton smell grew stronger, and now they fed the fire with larger logs.

Their brows were sweating by the time they turned to their grandfather.

His death was painful to them. While their grandmother continued to burn, they stood by his side and whispered prayers for the dead. But the prayers couldn't last forever.

'He would want us to be safe,' Farzad said, and Adel nodded.

They bent down and dragged him towards the fire. He was heavier than the old woman, but not so heavy that they couldn't lift him and throw him on to the blazing remains of his wife.

The skin peeled from his face, and the smell of burnt flesh filled their senses for a second time.

All night they fed the fire. By dawn they had exhausted the wood supply. The bodies were like long, charred stumps, each a metre and a half long. It surprised them that even after all these hours, they had not yet reduced to embers. And so they poured water on the ashes and Adel took a shovel from the cave while Farzad carried the stumps to the mulberry tree. Adel dug a hole, and they placed the remains of their grandparents inside.

'We must leave this place,' Farzad said when it was done.

Adel nodded a little uncertainly, and Farzad realised that he looked scared.

'Remember what Grandfather said,' he whispered. 'It is our duty to prepare ourselves to fight. And it is my duty, Adel, to take care of you. I swear to the Prophet, may peace and blessings be upon him, that I won't let anyone hurt you.'

Farzad stood up, and walked over to where the AK-47 was still lying on the ground. He strapped it over his shoulder, returned to his brother and held out his good hand. Adel took it and stood up, but they kept their hands clasped firmly.

'Brother,' Farzad whispered.

'Brother.'

And without another word they turned and walked into the steel light of dawn, leaving the remains of their family, and of their former life, behind them.

# THIRTY YEARS LATER

# 25 JUNE

# 1

*Helmand Province, Afghanistan.*
03.00 hrs
An enormous dome of light shone in the Afghan desert.

It was visible from miles around, a pulsating hub surrounded by flat ground and sand. If anyone were brave enough to approach it by foot, they would soon hear the low rumble of armoured trucks getting ready to go out on patrol; they would be almost deafened by the sound of military aircraft taking off and landing. Come close enough and they might hear the sound of Coalition personnel shouting instructions at each other. It might still be night-time, but this place was alive with activity 24/7.

No Afghan locals would dare come near it without an invitation, though. Not Camp Bastion.

Jack Harker hurried through the British base. Two hours before dawn and he was already sweating. The mercury was reading twenty-five degrees. Come noon it would be double that and everyone on the base would be guzzling water. One clear piss a day was the aim, according to the medics, but that was a fucking joke. Jack hadn't managed a clear piss in five months.

Bastion was huge. Four miles long, two miles wide, it was home to 4,000 troops and was getting bigger by the day. Its hospital was as advanced as anything back home, its infrastructure as complex. Feeding, cleaning and caring for that volume of personnel was a massive operation in itself. Jack hurried past the Pizza Hut in the centre of the camp—a taste of home that was meant to make them feel better about the fact that they were stuck out in this shithole of a country surrounded by heavily armed militants. It was closed now, but some of the lads were sitting outside, smoking and taking advantage of the relative cool. They were having an argument about something—animated, but good-natured.

On his way to RV with his unit, Jack passed all the machinery of war. Marines were carefully servicing their beige Jackal patrol vehicles. Good bits of kit these—drive a Jackal over one of the Taliban's IEDs and you might just live to tell the tale. Until they made the IEDs bigger, of course, and that was just a matter of time. He passed engineers tinkering with one of the Yanks' unmanned aerial vehicles, armed with a full complement of Hellfire missiles. Half these UAVs were controlled from the Nevada desert, but that didn't make them any less deadly. In the distance there was the noise of an aircraft coming in to land—a C-17 transporter by the deafening sound of the four jet engines screaming in reverse. Jack could hear it, but he couldn't see it because most landings were made under the cloak of darkness with the aircraft's lights switched off. Better for the pilots to guide their planes down using night vision than to let the enemy's rockets do the job for them.

Regular green army boys were everywhere, their skin tanned and their eyes a bit wild, preparing to go out on patrol, none of them knowing if they were about to earn themselves a free ride through Wootton Bassett. Only two days ago they'd repatriated an eighteen-year-old kid who'd caught the shrapnel from a Taliban RPG near Lashkar Gah. Half his face had been ripped off by the blast, one eyeball had been burnt out of the socket and his right arm had spun away like a boomerang that was never coming back. Word around the base was that it had taken two shots of morphine to stop the poor bastard screaming; but with massive trauma like that he was never going to make it. It took forty-five minutes for the casevac team to get there and by then he was already a statistic. *It is with sadness that the Ministry of Defence must confirm . . .*

And a few days before that, an American soldier had been captured by the Taliban. A politician's worst nightmare, and a soldier's too—but for different reasons. The Taliban were good fighters. Disciplined. Resourceful. And totally barbaric if they got their hands on you. Fuck only knew what sort of state that poor sod was in now.

Jack had to hand it to the Taliban. Sustained contact, day in day out, had made him familiar with an enemy as fearsome and cunning as any he had ever known. And these contacts weren't just a brief exchange of fire. They were the real deal, the sort of thing no amount of training on a wet moor in England could prepare you for—hours of sniper fire, RPGs and mortars. And although our troops knew they could call in fast air if the shit really hit the fan, everyone realised that a war like this was won or lost on the ground. It didn't matter what kind of air assets you had at your disposal, with the Taliban fighters dispersed among the civilian population it was always going to come down to men with guns. Jack had seen the Taliban walk

19

away from a battle laughing. Nothing fazed those fuckers. Of course, it was partly that they were on their own turf. It couldn't be more different for the Coalition forces. Six-month tours, then back home for another six and for all they knew they'd be on a Tristar back to the Stan for another six months after that. No wonder they looked fucked.

Jack's unit was standing in a little group in the open air well away from most of the regular activity, not far from a REME workshop and outside a small network of Portakabins that made up part of the Regiment's operations compound. Thick Hesco walls surrounded the compound itself; from the outside you could see nothing but the tall signalling masts and the top of ISO containers that contained anything and everything from small arms to Regiment quad bikes. Yellow light glowed from the windows of the Portakabins, and inside there were plenty of guys moving around. The Ruperts had been on edge for twenty-four hours and Jack knew why.

The previous day, a four-man SBS unit had been heading north by Jackal up the Sangin valley. They were good lads. Jack knew a couple of them well— as part of Boat Troop he'd been on ops with them. No waterborne insertion here in Helmand, of course, where it was drier than a nun's box, but with the general shortage of personnel most of the UK special forces found themselves out here no matter what their particular field of expertise. The SBS unit had come under attack and the boys had been forced to separate, leaving the Jackal in situ along with all the gear they were carrying. And that amounted to a hell of a lot of ordnance: a gimpy, with ten 200-round belts; a .50-cal and an

L96 sniper rifle. But that wasn't what the powers that be were cacking themselves about. Three Stinger missiles, complete with launchers, had also gone missing. These shoulder-launched, heat-seeking missiles could be used to bring down assets at altitudes between 200 metres and four klicks. They were particularly deadly against low-flying aircraft and definitely not the sort of thing you'd want to fall into the wrong hands.

But that was *just* where they'd fallen. One of the SBS boys had taken an enemy round in the head. RIP. The others managed to retreat to the nearest FOB, but their Taliban attackers had confiscated the gear before anyone could get down there to deny them. It was all meant to be hush-hush, but now that half the UK special forces in Helmand were out on the ground trying to locate the Stingers, news of the shakyboats' little boo-boo had spread like crabs around a brothel—ending up on the Prime Minister's daily briefing back in London. The MoD bods were shitting themselves that the Yanks would find out the missiles had gone walkabout, and their nervousness had been passed down the line. Heads were on the block, and for the men on the ground, that meant one thing: no fuck-ups acceptable.

As Jack joined the guys, one of his men turned to look at him.

'You're fucking late,' he said in a dour Scottish accent. 'What kept you? Getting your dick wet with that intelligence officer I saw you with last night?'

Jack winced. 'You got to be fucking joking. Just because I've been out here a while, Red, doesn't mean I've dropped my standards.'

The other man shrugged. 'No need to look at the mantelpiece when you're stoking the fire . . .'

'I wouldn't stoke her with yours, mucker.'

'You wouldn't get the fucking chance.'

Red Hamilton was just about the toughest guy Jack had ever known—and he'd known him since they'd passed selection and worked closely together during their continuation training more than twenty years ago. His real name was Tom, but everyone called him Red because of his thick shock of flame-orange hair. Red had decided that his nickname was better than any of the alternatives, and it would be a brave or stupid man that tried to use one of those. Now and then, back at Hereford, some pissed-up civvy would have a go, asking Red if the hair under his boxers was the same colour as that on his head. They usually regretted it.

Jack smiled at his friend, then turned his attention to the rest of his eight-man unit. 'All right, fellas,' he announced. 'Let's get loaded before the Ruperts can tell us how to do our jobs another fucking ten times over.'

Laughter from the guys. They knew what he meant. Some MoD goon had briefed the unit at 13.00 hrs the day before. Jack couldn't even remember his name, but he knew his type well enough. He was the kind that walked around Bastion like a dog with two dicks, loving that he was braving such a hostile environment—and ignoring the fact that the British base was probably the safest piece of sand this side of Blackpool. Put that tosser out on the ground, though, and there'd be an extra set of brown underwear for the laundry to deal with when he got back. *If* he got back.

22

The guy clearly got his kicks from standing up, with SAS top brass and a couple of his MoD colleagues behind him, handing out orders to Jack's unit.

It hadn't taken him long to rub them up the wrong way. His first sentence had done it.

'I'm absolutely certain there's no need to remind you,' he'd said with a smug smile and a plum in his voice, 'that everything you hear in this briefing is confidential and subject to the Official Secrets Act.'

He'd looked around the canvas tent in which the eight of them sat sweating in the blazing midday heat, and was met by an octet of stony faces. Clearly sensing that his patronising warning had been badly received, he'd tried to make up ground, to be all chummy. 'Like *you guys* don't know that . . .'

They'd carried on giving him the Madame Tussaud's treatment, so he quickly directed their attention to a map displayed on a board in front of them. It was a highly detailed satellite image of Helmand Province, the kind that any soldier out here—special forces or green army—was well used to studying. Most often, these images showed the built-up areas around the green zone—the fertile ground running along either side of the riverbeds, or wadis, that characterised the region. Most people in Helmand lived in or near these green zones, generally in the many high-walled compounds that surrounded the town centres. On military maps, these compounds were meticulously numbered. The maps would be updated frequently and the numbers changed in case any of them fell into enemy hands. This map, however, the one

23

they were all looking at, did not show compounds. It showed sand and rock. And in the middle, just where this asshole's well-manicured fingertip was pointing . . .

'A cave system,' the MoD man had announced.

'No shit, Sherlock,' Red muttered. 'And just remind me—which way is north? Up or down?'

The rest of the guys had laughed, and a hint of panic entered the MoD man's eyes—like a teacher who knew he'd just lost control of the classroom. It took a sharp look from Major Harry Palgrave, squadron OC, for the unit to fall silent again. The MoD man had squared his shoulders and continued the briefing.

'Your instructions are these. At 03.30 hrs, a Black Hawk will transport you to an LZ one klick from the mouth of the cave system.'

But Red had butted in again. 'What the fuck for? We're after the Stingers, right? If you're so goddamn sure they're in this cave system, why not call in fast air? Give them the Tora Bora treatment. There's no risk of civilian casua—'

'You're not after the Stingers,' the goon interrupted. 'We have information that there's an AQT poppy-processing centre located somewhere in there. Find it. Secure it. Any personnel you encounter are to be eliminated.'

He paused, as though he expected his last statement to cause a stir. It didn't.

'When we have confirmation from you that the location is secure, we'll be sending in a civilian observer by Chinook. You'll take further orders on the ground from them.'

The goon had looked around the tent to see if anyone had anything to add. Major Palgrave stood up. 'Operation call sign Delta Five One. You've got the rest of the day to familiarise yourself with the terrain. RV in the ops room in fifteen minutes. We'll brief you further in there. Any questions?'

Jack had put his hand up and looked towards the MoD goon. 'I didn't think it was an official secret that they grew poppies in Helmand,' he said.

The goon just gave him a smug glare. Jack shrugged. 'Just thought I'd—'

'All right, Harker, that's enough. Get on with it.' Palgrave had been brisk.

'Yes, boss.'

He'd spent the remainder of the afternoon with the ops officer, Matt Cooper, who was chewing, as always, on a stick of gum. Back in the day, Jack had spent a lot of time on ops with Cooper in Iraq, and as a young trooper in the latter days over the water in Northern Ireland, and he was never without a stick of gum. The tenser the situation, the faster he would chew.

They had spent hours together poring over maps and fine-tuning their strategy for the following morning. 'Who is this observer they're sending in?' Jack had asked.

'Some Whitehall type. Flying in from Kandahar tonight.'

'The Firm?'

'Could be. We haven't been told.' Cooper raised one eyebrow. 'Fuckers are playing it close to their chest. You know what they're like.'

Yeah. Jack knew. 'It's a lot of work to nail a few poppy dealers.'

Cooper didn't have an answer for that; he just chewed a bit faster. They both knew that poppy farmers were two a penny in Helmand. Coalition policy was pretty much to let them be—start taking away their only means of making a living and they'd be turning to the Taliban quicker than you could say fatwa.

And what was all the secrecy with this visitor? Jack had scowled. He didn't like the idea of playing host to stragglers, especially when he didn't know who they were. No point bitching about it, though. He just needed to make sure *he* was prepared, so he turned back to the maps.

When night fell, Jack and the guys had gone straight to the kitchen to get some scoff. And then he'd got his head down. The MoD goon had talked about the raid like it was a walk in the fucking park, but Jack knew damn well that he was leading his team into an area of Helmand where the Coalition couldn't hold the ground. It was common knowledge that Taliban activity was more concentrated in this part of Helmand than anywhere else. It was from this area that the commanders organised their troops; intelligence reports even suggested the existence of some kind of Taliban arsenal in the area. Other Regiment guys had been tasked to locate it, but up till now they'd been totally unsuccessful.

There were Taliban strongholds on both sides of the insertion zone, and if the fuckers got wind that an SAS unit was on ops in the area, they'd be all over them. The idea of being surrounded by heavily tooled-up militants wasn't exactly enthralling, but Jack slept well anyway. He never had trouble resting before an op, so now that it was time for the off, he felt clear-headed, prepared for whatever the Taliban decided to throw at him. He had given himself a few extra minutes to study the terrain where they were about to deploy. The unit was his responsibility, and he wanted everything straight in his head before he took them out on the ground.

And now it was T minus thirty. The lads had pushed a big flight case up against one of the thick Hesco walls. Jack approached the case. It contained all the tools of their trade. Jack already had his suppressed M16 with underslung 40 mm grenade launcher and Maglite torch attachment with IR filter strapped to his body, a full magazine loaded and plenty of extra rounds stashed in his ops waistcoat, along with his Sig 9 mm pistol, locked and loaded. His lightweight green Kevlar helmet, cut away round the ears, was fitted to his head, and a set of Gen 3 NV goggles was firmly attached to it.

'Everyone ready?'

He looked at each of the team in turn and they all nodded. Red, tooled up almost exactly like Jack, one kneepad over his right knee to protect the joint when he adopted the firing position; 'Fly' and Dunc Forsyth, cousins, both medics, both as good at hosing people down as they were at patching them up; Ray Duke—Dukey—a relative newcomer to the Regiment but no less respected for that; Al Heller, a Northern Irish Protestant—always tough bastards; 'Pixie' Tucker, a man with a squint so bad that if he cried his tears would roll down his back; and Frankie McBride, the squadron's favourite ladies' man. Piled around them was all the equipment they would be taking. Two Minimi light machine guns, sat phone, a laser target designator should they be forced to call in fast air, and an evil-looking black LASM—

complete with thermobaric rounds. All this in addition to their assault rifles, pistols and other bells and whistles.

Well prepared. Heavily armed. Grim-faced.

'Yeah,' they replied, almost with one voice. 'Ready.'

*    *    *

03.30 hrs. Ninety minutes until dawn.

The Black Hawk's blades were spinning, whipping up a cloud of dust around the Bastion LZ. Delta Five One ran towards it, heads bowed, loading their gear and climbing in. The two crew already had their NV goggles fixed—they'd be flying blind this morning—and within seconds the aircraft rose from the ground, quickly gaining height in order to put itself out of the range of most of the enemy's arsenal.

Estimated flying time to the insertion point, fifteen minutes. It was dark in the helicopter, the only light being the faint glow from the pilots' control panel and the reflection of the moon on the Helmand River far below. The unit made good use of their time, though, checking and rechecking their weapons.

'Five minutes out!' the loadie called.

'What do you reckon's going to happen to those shakyboats who lost the Stingers?' Fly asked above the noise of the chopper.

'OC's been given a one-way back to Poole,' Red answered. 'That's what I heard, at least.'

'Lucky fucker,' Fly shouted. 'Probably knocking the hole of his missus right now.' The guys laughed, but everyone knew they didn't really mean it. Poor sod had already lost one of his men, and now his career was down the pan for a fuck-up probably not of his own making. Anything to stop the suits taking the blame. But it had always been that way.

'One minute out!'

Jack felt the heli losing height. Take-off and landing in the field were always the most dangerous moments for the pilots, especially when they weren't making use of an established LZ, and especially at night. The downdraught from the blades kicked the dust up. As the dust hit the blades it had a tendency to spark, causing a glow that could illuminate their position for miles around. They wouldn't want to be on the ground for more than the couple of seconds it took for the men to exfiltrate. Once they'd dumped their load, they'd continue on the same flight path so it sounded to anyone that heard them as if they were just flying over. And to mask the unit's insertion even more, an F-16 would fly overhead just as they touched down—the boom of the fast air was hardly an infrequent noise over the Helmand desert and it would hide the sound of the Black Hawk.

The men took their positions, four of them on each side of the chopper, carrying all their weapons. Suddenly the view from the window took on a different quality of blackness as a cloud of desert sand surrounded them; and then the glow as dust hit the blades. The aircraft touched down.

They moved quickly. Two seconds, max, before they were out of the chopper and on to the sand. The F-16 appeared from nowhere overhead and as the boom resonated over the desert, the Black Hawk lifted off again and continued its flight path.

Thirty seconds later it was little more than a black shadow against the stars that glowed through the green haze of Jack's night-vision goggles, the hum of its engines like a distant insect.

And then it was gone.

Silence surrounded them.

'Only way to travel,' Dukey murmured into his mike. No one replied.

Jack took a moment to get his bearings, matching up the landscape to the maps he carried in his head. They were in a shallow valley. To the north, a line of hills, approximately one klick distant. The opening to the cave system was located at the foot of these hills. But to the west and the east, two wadis that formed a V-shape, meeting at its apex about three klicks to the south. Surrounding the wadis to the west and east, dense, lush areas of green zone, four klicks distant either way. The green zones were home to busy villages made up of maze-like patchworks of fields and square residential compounds. The villages were overrun by insurgents and the Coalition couldn't infiltrate them.

The ground ahead was undulating, which had its advantages and disadvantages. It meant they had a good chance of staying hidden; but it also meant that they'd be unable to observe any approaching enemy until the fuckers were practically on top of them. Fortunately, the Taliban had a useful habit of talking freely over their radios, and the guys in the ops room were a dab hand at listening in. If the enemy got wind of their presence, the unit would know about it soon enough.

And they'd need to. Geographical barriers to the north and south. Enemy villages to the west and east. The moon was bright and low and cast long shadows on the ground. Hardly ideal. In fact, in tactical terms, it was a fucking nightmare. Every man in the unit knew it, and there was an air of determination as they prepared to advance.

There was no need for Jack to issue instructions: every man knew what was expected of him.

Pixie and Al separated from the rest of the unit and took the Minimis to two raised areas of the undulating ground, 100 metres apart and facing the cave system up ahead. Pixie might have the kind of squint that made kids point at him in the street, but there wasn't a weapon in the Stan that he couldn't fire with pinpoint accuracy. From where they were stationed, they could now provide suppressing fire for the others should it all go noisy. The remaining six men formed a straight line, each ten metres from the other with Jack up front. In that extended-line formation they would be less easy to see for any shooters up ahead.

They advanced.

Jack didn't allow himself to think of the risk of IEDs. This was enemy territory, and if the Taliban were indeed using the cave system up ahead for whatever purpose, it was unlikely they'd have booby-trapped the approach. There was always the risk of legacy mines, of course, left over from the Soviet occupation when the Russkis had mined the whole country to hell and the Mujahideen had responded in kind, but that was a risk they had to take. They needed to approach the caves silently, and that meant on foot.

Three hundred metres to go.

Two hundred.

The hills started to tower above them; the moon

disappeared, and they found themselves in shadow at last. Jack raised one hand. Instantly the unit changed their positions to an arrowhead formation—easier to see, but now they were close to the cave it was important that each man had a line of fire if everything went Wild West.

A hundred metres.

Fifty.

And up ahead, an opening.

It was small—about three times as high as Jack and then twice as wide again. There was a large, craggy overhang and two man-size boulders obscuring the entrance. If you saw it in passing, you wouldn't give it a second look. And that, no doubt, was why the enemy had selected it. The sand was churned up with vehicle prints leading up to the cave. Stuff had been coming in and out of here—that much was clear. When they reached the boulders, Jack pointed at Fly and Dunc. They understood his instruction and took up position, crouching down on the outside edge of each boulder with their M16s pointing back out towards the desert. They melted into the darkness—you wouldn't know they were there until their rounds ripped through your skin.

The remaining four men silently slipped into the cave mouth.

It stank in here—the detritus of whatever animals or insects used this cave as a shelter. The cave stretched back to form a kind of natural corridor. And as they headed further in, Jack found that his NV goggles became less and less effective as the ambient light for them to magnify decreased. He flicked a switch on his Maglite. An infrared beam, invisible to the naked eye, shot straight ahead. The others did the same, and soon there were four beams, lighting the way ahead like moving spotlights. Jack stepped forward again, keeping close to the right-hand wall of the cave. He could sense the others: Red walking along the opposite wall a little behind him, Dukey and Frankie taking up the inside.

They moved with total stealth. Over the years Jack had learned to keep his footsteps light and he did that now; but every tiny crunch underfoot was like an alarm bell.

Something moved up ahead.

Jack stopped, dead alert. He put his left hand out with his thumb down. Everyone halted. They knew what the signal meant: enemy up ahead.

Jack cast around with his IR beam. Silence. Just the sound of his heartbeat thumping in his ears. And then, a scurrying sound. Jack caught the glint of two eyes just ahead, about half a metre from the ground. An animal of some kind, disturbed by its night-time visitors. Jack continued to move forward.

A minute passed. Then another noise ahead of them. He stopped and listened.

It was a humming sound. Electrical. And above it, maybe the sound of voices. Jack held up one hand and the others halted. He crossed the corridor to where Red was standing, and the others joined them. They were fifty metres from the mouth of the cave.

'Stay here,' Jack breathed at Dukey and Frankie. 'Me and Red to recce. Make sure we don't get any unwanted company from behind.'

'Roger that,' they murmured, and they quickly took up their positions.

Jack and Red raised their M16s up into the firing position and continued on into the darkness, following the wall of the corridor as it bent round to the right. The electrical hum grew louder. Jack found himself holding his breath. He forced himself to breathe normally as they continued to advance.

A light source up ahead.

As they grew closer, the ambient light grew too bright for their NV. Jack raised his goggles from his eyes. Red did the same. The light was perhaps thirty metres away. It was coming from an opening off to the left of the corridor, and what they were seeing was the glow escaping from the mouth of this cave within a cave.

They looked at each other. Jack nodded, and they moved forward.

There was no doubt now that the noise and light were coming from this side cave. Jack and Red reached the edge of the opening and, moving very slowly, peered round the corner. Jack's eyes narrowed.

A poppy-processing plant, the MoD man had said. Jack had never seen one, but he knew for sure that this wasn't what he was looking at.

The cave was too large and high for Jack to be able to see the back or the roof, but in the middle, approximately twenty metres from where they were now standing, were two floodlights, each one powered by a noisy generator. The floodlights illuminated three long, steel workbenches; and standing around the workbenches were a number of people. Jack counted them carefully. Twelve in all—ten men and two women—eight with dark Arab skin, four who looked more European. One

34

of the tables had several white all-in-one suits laid out on it, and each suit was accompanied by a black mask and breathing apparatus. The nearest bench carried a flight case, approximately a metre wide, half a metre deep and twenty centimetres high. Like a small suitcase, but Jack had the distinct impression it wasn't there to carry anyone's toothbrush.

Elsewhere around the cave were what looked like scientific instruments, a couple of laptop computers and other bulky items of electronics that Jack failed to recognise. He stepped back round the corner into the darkness and looked at Red.

'What the fuck?' he asked his friend, confident his voice was masked by the noise of the generators.

'Looks like our friend back at base was shitting us,' Red breathed in his dour Scottish accent. 'If they're processing heroin, I'm Howard fucking Marks.'

'Quiet!'

From inside the cave came a voice, louder than the others. 'All right everyone, protective gear on.' Someone else translated the instruction into Arabic.

Jack frowned. Whoever had just spoken was *British*. No doubt about it. But what were they doing here in this makeshift lab hidden away in the heart of Helmand Province? It didn't make any kind of sense at all.

'I don't fucking like it,' Red whispered, echoing Jack's own thoughts. 'I say we exfiltrate, get on the radio back to base.'

Jack thought for a moment. Maybe Red was

35

right. Report back, await further instructions. But then he looked at his watch. 04.12 hrs. Forty-five minutes until first light. They had the advantage of darkness and they weren't going to keep that for long.

They had their orders. Eliminate everyone.

'Get the others,' he said. 'Quickly.'

'Your call,' Red muttered, and he slipped away into the darkness. Jack peered round the corner once again. The occupants of the cave were starting to get into their protective gear. One of them even had their breathing apparatus on and was approaching the silver flight case. Jack felt his mouth going dry. Whatever was in there, he didn't want to get close to it protected only by standard-issue Regiment digital camouflage gear.

He heard the others approach. Their faces were expressionless, their eyes narrow. They all knew what they had to do next.

'Twelve targets,' Jack whispered. 'There's a table with a metal flight case on it. Fuck's sake don't hit it. Me and Red will take out the lights first, then we'll pick them off.'

Dukey and Frankie nodded, then engaged their night-vision goggles. Jack and Red took up position—Jack at the corner of the cave, Red against the far wall.

Jack held up five fingers.

Four.

Three.

Two.

One.

Their suppressed weapons hardly made a noise—just a low pop, like someone knocking on a door—but the floodlights shattered loudly as the

36

rounds hit them with unerring accuracy. Jack was momentarily blinded by the sudden darkness, but he could sense the others taking up position in the cave mouth. By the time Jack had engaged his own NV, four bursts had already been discharged, each of them nailing the nearest targets, and the smell of cordite had already overpowered the smell of the cave.

The darkness was cut by the four IR beams slicing through the air as the men cast around. Screams and shouts of panic echoed around the cave as Jack calmly got one of the green targets—a man looking blindly into the darkness—in his sights. He squeezed the trigger of his M16 and saw a burst of wetness: a perfect headshot that flung his victim a good two metres back. But Jack was already searching out another. His beam panned left and, as he expected, found one of the targets running to the edge of the cave.

He didn't run for long.

Jack's round caught him in the neck, causing the man to spin round, spraying blood around him like a Catherine wheel before he fell to the ground.

And then silence.

The guys stepped forward, their IR beams pointing exactly where their rounds would land so there was no need to use their viewfinders. Mangled corpses lay everywhere as they searched under tables and behind generators. But Jack could only count eleven bodies. Either he'd missed one, or there was a survivor.

It didn't take long to locate the twelfth target. It wasn't a him, though. It was a her. And it was the noise she made that gave her away. You can never tell how a person will react when they know they're about to die. Some shout; some beg; others whimper and become paralysed with fear. This was one of them. She was crouched against the side of the cave, her head in her hands and an uncontrollable sobbing sound escaping from her throat.

'Please,' she whispered. *'Please . . .'*

That was her last word. Jack nailed her from a distance of three metres with a short burst of fire. The bullets passed right through her hands and into the top of her skull. A brief fountain of blood sprayed through her clasped fingers, but it didn't last long, subsiding suddenly like a hose when the water's been switched off. She crumpled to the ground.

It had taken less than a minute to clear the cave.

'All right lads,' Jack instructed. 'Final check, then let's get the hell out of here and on the blower back to base.'

They knew what he meant. Each man removed the IR filter from his torch, filling the cave with white light once again, then delivered final headshots to each of the corpses. Nobody wanted any of the targets doing a Lazarus on them.

When the unit was satisfied that they were all dead, they didn't look back. They just returned swiftly to the mouth of the cave, where Fly and Dunc were waiting for them.

\*      \*      \*

'Zero Alpha, this is Delta Five One. Over.'

'Zero Alpha, send.'

Jack spoke clearly into the sat phone. 'Targets down, location secured.'

'Roger that. Nice work, Jack. The bird's leaving base now.'

Jack gave a quick double-click on the pressel to indicate that he'd understood, then looked at his watch. 04.24 hrs. First light in thirty-five minutes. It would take the Chinook fifteen minutes to get here, which only gave them twenty minutes until the sun peeped above the horizon and they'd be lit up for anyone with a pair of eyes. He just hoped that their guest—whoever it was—wouldn't want to stick around.

Each member of the unit had taken up a position around the mouth of the cave, pointing their weapons out into the darkness. The cover of night gave them a certain amount of protection, but it also obscured any enemy who might decide to attack.

Jack was on one knee, his weapon engaged as he scanned the desert in front of him. Nothing moved—at least nothing that he could see. He heard Red whisper to one side of him. 'Looks like the Taliban are still sleeping soundly. Perhaps they had a nice cup of Ovaltine before they hit the sack.'

Jack inclined his head. Sometimes silence could be more ominous than noise. After all, if *he* were trying to sneak up on someone, they wouldn't know he was there until they were dead.

'It's quiet for now,' he said. 'Another chopper landing on their turf might be a nice little alarm call for them, though.' His eyes continued to cast left to right, right to left, moving out in concentric circles as he scanned for anything that might indicate a threat: movement, shadow, silhouettes.

But all he saw was stillness. And all he heard was

silence. The kind of thick, impenetrable silence that arrives just before dawn. And then, very faintly at first, but getting gradually louder, the unmistakable buzz of a Chinook in the distance.

They didn't see it until it had practically landed, then they felt it as the force of the twin rotary blades billowed clouds of sand into the air, stinging their faces and catching in the back of their throats. Jack looked up into the sky through the lenses of his NV. Against the stars he saw the faint, flickering shadow of what he knew to be an Apache attack helicopter escorting the Chinook and threatening with its Hellfires anyone who wanted to take a potshot at that workhorse of a chopper. If the sight of a Chinook encouraged the enemy to grab their surface-to-air weaponry, the sight of an Apache encouraged them to run like hell.

Fly and Dunc ran towards the Chinook while the rest of the unit covered them from the cave mouth. The tailgate opened and through the dust storm Jack saw a figure emerge from inside. Fly and Dunc grabbed one arm each and hustled the newcomer towards the cave, just as the tailgate closed up again. By the time they had reached the cave mouth, the Chinook was already in the air again.

The figure spoke. 'Which one of you is Jack Harker?' It was a brusque voice, full of authority. It was also a female voice.

Jesus, Jack thought, thinking of the female he'd just nailed back in the cave. It's turning into the fucking Women's Institute out here.

The new arrival wore desert camo and full body armour. The standard-issue helmet didn't disguise

40

the fact that she was strikingly good-looking, even here. Pale skin, high cheekbones and little strands of auburn hair peeking from underneath her helmet.

'Me,' Jack said, stepping towards her.

'All right,' the newcomer replied with surprising confidence. 'Let's go. Show me what you've found.'

Jack looked over at Red. His friend had what could only be described as a smirk on his face; he didn't need to look at the others to realise that they'd be finding the way this chick talked to their unit leader funny. Jack ignored it. 'Red,' he commanded, 'come with me. The rest of you, keep watch.'

The men took up their positions again.

'Do you have a name?' Jack asked the woman. 'Or is that a secret as well?'

'No secret,' she replied crisply. 'Caroline Stenton.'

'All right then, Miss Stenton—'

'*Professor* Stenton . . .'

Jack and Red glanced at each other.

'All right then, *Professor* Stenton. Let's get the hell inside, shall we?'

The woman nodded and strode immediately into the cave mouth. Jack ran ahead of her then turned, blocking her way. 'Keep between me and Red,' he instructed, 'and do what I tell you.'

'My understanding,' Stenton said, still walking, 'is that you're to follow my orders while I'm on the ground.'

Another glance between the two Regiment men. Jack grabbed her by the arm. '*My* understanding,' he hissed, 'is that you'd like to fucking stay alive. *I*

41

go in front, *then* you, *then* Red.'

A pause.

'Do yourself a favour, missie,' Red murmured, 'and listen to the man.'

Stenton's eyes hardened, but she said nothing as Jack switched on the Maglite torch clamped to his weapon and, with the butt of his M16 pressed against his shoulder, stepped forward, lighting the way as he went.

With the way properly lit, they reached the side cave quickly. Jack stopped a few metres short of it and turned to Stenton. 'It's not pretty in there,' he said.

Stenton gave him a withering look. 'I'm not a child,' she said, before walking past him. 'Light the way.'

Jack gave a little shrug, walked to the entrance of the cave and illuminated the interior. Stenton looked in and for a moment her face was expressionless. After a few seconds, however, Jack watched as their guest twigged exactly what she was looking at.

It was carnage inside. Dead bodies littered the floor, their limbs contorted into whatever position they had fallen. Sides of faces had been blown away; skin was spattered in blood; thick grey brain matter lay in viscous pools around them. Caroline stared at the woman Jack had killed. Her long dark hair was matted and bloodied, her torso was mashed up, the exit wound from her skull had distorted her head and her expression was one of gruesome, unrestrained terror.

'How many times did you shoot that woman?' Stenton asked.

Jack sniffed. 'Nine or ten.'

Her face hardened. 'Why did you have to shoot her ten times?' she asked.

Jack gave her a direct look. 'I ran out of bullets,' he said.

Stenton took a short, sharp breath. She didn't reply, but instead just stepped inside, walking round the dead woman and up to the nearest workbench, where the metal flight case still sat with blood spattered over its surface. Stenton looked down at it, then around the cave in general.

'Any more containers like this?' she asked.

Jack shook his head. 'Didn't see any. But we had our mind on other things.'

'Search,' she replied. 'Now.'

It didn't take long. The cave was big, but the equipment was localised in a small area. Stenton helped with the search, and within a couple of minutes appeared satisfied that there was nothing there to warrant further attention from her. She turned to the two Regiment men. 'All right,' she said, pointing at the flight case. 'We're taking that with us. You might find it's heavy.' She eyed Jack up and down, and an arch smile crept on to her lips. 'Then again, maybe not.'

It took two of them to lift it, so Jack detached the Maglite from his M16 and handed it to the woman. 'Lead the way,' he said.

Stenton raised an eyebrow. 'Sure it's safe?' she asked.

'Not really,' Jack replied. 'But unless *you* want to carry the container—'

'Do us all a favour,' Stenton interrupted, 'and don't drop that thing, OK.'

'So I take it we're not transporting poppies.'

Stenton looked away. 'So you're not just a pretty

face after all, Captain Harker.'

She stepped into the corridor.

*　　　*　　　*

04.52 hrs.

'Eight minutes till sunrise,' Jack announced as they laid the container down on the sand next to one of the boulders. 'Fly, get on the radio. I want to be on that Chinook before the sun comes up. And you can tell our MoD friend there's no need for him to stick to his half-arsed, fucked-up horseshit about this being a poppy-processing plant.'

'Those exact words?' Fly asked with a half smile.

'No,' Jack replied. 'Don't be so polite.'

Fly nodded and immediately got on to the sat phone. 'This is Delta Five One. Do you copy?'

'How long before they arrive?' Caroline Stenton asked as Fly communicated with the ops centre back at Bastion.

Jack shrugged. 'Depends where they're turning and burning. With a bit of luck, no more than a couple of minutes.'

Fly approached them. 'New orders,' he said. 'We're to put the Professor on the Chinook with her goody bag. The rest of us are waiting behind to bring fast air on to target.'

Jack's eyes narrowed. 'Bullshit,' he hissed. 'They know our fucking location.' He grabbed the sat phone. 'This is Harker,' he stated. 'What are you fucking playing at? We're about to lose the darkness and we've got enemy strongholds on two sides. We don't have to be on the ground to direct the air strike. We're coming back on that

Chinook.'

A crackly pause. And then a voice on the other end, which Jack recognised as belonging to the MoD goon back at Bastion.

'Negative,' it said. 'We're monitoring Taliban Icom chatter. They are unaware of your movements. Repeat, they are unaware of your movements. Your instructions are to laser mark the cave entrance from a distance. We'll send a chopper in to pick you up once the caves are destroyed.'

Jack shoved the sat phone back at Fly. 'Idiots,' he hissed. He looked out into the desert—the black night was turning to the steely grey of dawn. They were going to be lit up like a fucking Christmas tree any minute now. He spoke into the radio again. 'We don't need eight men to lase the cave. I'm sending four back in the Chinook.'

A pause. And then . . .

'Affirmative.'

Jack scowled. He turned to Stenton. 'Looks like they want to make very sure your little cave system gets permanently put out of action.'

'It's not *my* cave system,' Stenton replied. At least she had the decency to look concerned about Jack's outburst. Not that Jack gave a shit. He knew he'd have to decide who was staying and who was going.

'Red, stay with me. We'll RV with Pixie and Al.' As he spoke he heard the sound of the Chinook approaching. 'The rest of you,' he shouted over the noise of the chopper, 'back to base. No questions. You're escorting the Prof back to Bastion. Get on with it.'

Shaking their heads, the unit started gathering

their gear. Jack nodded at Red and the two of them picked up the container once more.

'*Don't drop it!*' Stenton shouted over the noise of the aircraft touching down. Jack and Red ignored her and hurried with the flight case towards the back of the Chinook where the tailgate was already opening. They carried it up into the belly of the helicopter, then laid it carefully on the ground. Stenton was right by them. She held out one hand to Jack. 'Nice to meet you, Captain Harker,' she said, one eyebrow slightly raised.

Jack just gave her a flat, unfriendly stare, then turned and alighted from the aircraft along with Red just as Fly, Dunc, Dukey and Frankie got on.

The tailgate rose, then the chopper lifted into the air and flew off, its Apache chaperone hovering close above it, leaving the remaining members of the unit on the ground.

\*         \*         \*

05.13 hrs.

Jack and Red hadn't waited around. The sky was getting brighter by the minute. They'd immediately headed south again into the desert, moving silently and keeping to the low ground as they hurried the klick to where Pixie was on stag, signalled to Al to join them, then turned to look back at the hills where the cave system was located.

'I'll sort it,' said Pixie.

'Make sure you use your good eye,' said Red. 'I don't want you lasing my arsehole.'

Pixie grinned at him. He carried the laser target designator twenty metres away up a gentle slope so

46

that he had a direct line of sight back north towards the hills; then he clicked the khaki scope on to its small tripod before crouching down and peering through the viewfinder and focusing the apparatus on the cave mouth. There was a small whirring of machinery as Pixie charged up the LTD.

Jack got back on the sat phone while Red and Frankie took up positions on either side of him, pointing their weapons to the west and east.

'Zero Alpha, this is Delta Five One. We're in position. Over.'

A crackle. 'Roger that.' It was Matt Cooper, the ops officer. 'Fast air two minutes away. We'll have you out of there very soon, Jack.'

Jack didn't reply. They held their position and waited for the F-16 to arrive.

Silence on the radio.

'Come on,' Jack muttered. 'Come on, come on, come on . . .'

They waited.

A burst of activity from the radio.

*'Delta Five One! Delta Five One! You've got company!'*

Jack grabbed the handset. 'What the fuck do you mean?'

'Icom chatter. Jack, you've got Taliban approaching from the south, the west and the east. They think they know where you are. They're less than five hundred metres away.'

'How many?'

'Impossible to say, but they sound confident.'

*'Exfiltrate us now!'* Jack roared. *'Now, Matt!'*

'The chopper's on its way.'

'How long?'

47

A pause.

'*How fucking long, Matt?*'

'Three minutes. Coming in from the north.'

Three minutes. In situations like this, it was a lifetime. Jack addressed Red and Al. 'Did you get all that?'

'Yeah,' Al spat. 'We got it. How the fuck did they get so close without us seeing them?'

The same thought had been going through Jack's head. 'They must have clocked us the moment we landed.' He shouted up at Pixie. '*Have you lased the target?*'

Pixie looked over his shoulder and held up one thumb.

'*Get down!*' Jack shouted.

But too late.

The round came from the west, hitting Pixie square in his left shoulder. The SAS man fell to the ground, knocking the LTD on to its side. The remaining three members of the unit acted immediately. Red started firing slow, regular shots into the air towards where the round had come from; Al covered them to the east with one Minimi and Jack to the south with another while they moved, as quickly as they could, up towards where Pixie was lying.

He was still alive, but his shoulder was buggered. His arm was hanging limply and it was immediately obvious to Jack that he was going to lose it. His face was white and sweating and his breathing was short and irregular. Jack lowered his weapon and pulled out a morphine injection from his ops waistcoat, quickly breaking off the safety tab at the end of its plastic coffin and punching it down through Pixie's clothes and into the skin of his thigh. He didn't say anything—no words of comfort, no 'We're going to get you out of here,' because he knew Pixie didn't want any of that bullshit.

And besides, there wasn't time.

Jack could see the enemy now, advancing on three sides, their heads appearing and disappearing behind the undulating terrain. The ones coming from the west were the closest—about fifty metres away. Jack turned to Al, who had the LASM slung over his shoulder.

*'Let them have it!'*

Al didn't need telling twice. He lowered his rifle. Getting down on one knee he rested the back end of the LASM over his right shoulder, took a moment to correct his aim, and then fired.

A whizzing sound, then an immense bang as the thermobaric round found its target to the south. It had an immediate effect on the advancing enemy, who hit the ground and started shouting. Jack knew it wouldn't keep them back for long, though, and they still had Taliban advancing from two other sides, over the brow of the ridges to the west and east. They were seventy-five metres away and swarming.

A thumping sound.

*'RPG!'* Red shouted, and the three men standing hit the ground. Jack felt a sharp rush of air as the grenade whizzed over them, missing them by inches but starbursting twenty-five metres beyond them—sufficiently far away for its shrapnel to miss them, but only by a metre or so.

Pixie's whole body was shaking now. He needed attention, and fast, but they were pinned down, unable to move. *'We need that fucking chopper!'* Al bellowed.

And it was just as he spoke that the Black Hawk appeared over the brow of the hills to the north, a kilometre away. It sped towards them, skirting low above the desert—so low that it kicked up clouds of sand as it went. Seconds later it was hovering right above them, filling their ears with the noise of its engines.

It hung in the air for a moment, thirty metres high. And then its gunner started firing in bursts.

Thirty-cal rounds from the chopper's minigun ripped through the air, accompanied by the orange light of tracer rounds like molten metal and the mechanical chugging of the weapon. The gunner fired first towards the westernmost flank of the advancing enemy. Then the Black Hawk spun in the air, moving in a semicircle so its weaponry hit the enemy to the south and then to the east, before going back on itself to give them all a second helping. The guns fell silent and the aircraft lowered itself down on to the sand, no more than five metres from where Jack was standing.

Jack, Red and Al moved quickly. Jack handed Red his M16, then he and Al each grabbed one end of Pixie's body while Red, a rifle in each hand, fired quick single rounds towards the enemy. The side door of the chopper was already open—Jack recognised a couple of lads from the Parachute Regiment inside. They helped him and Al get Pixie on board.

Jack turned, just in time to see another RPG flying just forward from where Red was firing on the enemy still advancing from the west. Christ, these fuckers had been hit with thermobaric rounds from the LASM, thirty-cals from the Black

Hawk and now Red was raining M16 rounds on them, but they wouldn't lie down and die.

'*Get in the chopper!*' he shouted at his friend. '*Let's get the fuck out of here!*'

Red was happy to oblige. He and Jack launched themselves into the aircraft. As it rose into the air, Red continued to fire down on the enemy while the pilots spun the bird round, pointing it to the north—the only direction they could travel if they were going to get out of the range of the Taliban's rockets.

Jack turned his attention to Pixie. He was stretched out on the floor of the aircraft, his eyes were closed, but he was breathing—just. One of the Paras was fixing a tourniquet at the top of his shoulder just above where the round had entered. Another was inserting a saline drip into his good arm. His face was grim. 'He needs a hospital!' he yelled.

But the hospital at Bastion was fifteen minutes away.

Red had stopped firing and had his back pressed against the wall of the chopper, his face covered in sand and sweat, a picture of exhaustion. 'They knew where we were,' he gasped. 'It was a fucking ambush.'

Jack nodded. Red was right. He also knew that if they didn't get Pixie back to base quickly, he'd pay for it with his life.

He looked out of the side of the chopper. The sky was much lighter now, and he could see the desert below. As they flew over the brow of the hills, the ground grew much closer. And it was just then that Jack saw them.

Even from a height they were easy to distinguish.

They wore black and white keffiyehs and khaki camouflage jackets; on their shoulders each man carried a weapon. From this distance Jack couldn't make out the weapons precisely, but he had a pretty good idea what they were.

'We're going to take a hit!' he yelled at the pilots up front, but with their headsets and the noise of the engines they perhaps didn't hear him. *'We're going to take a hit!'*

Jack saw the rockets coming towards them. They didn't hit the chopper, but they starburst all around like some colourless, metallic firework display. It only took a second for pieces of that showering shrapnel to make contact with the heli, but that moment happened in horrible slow motion. Jack instinctively grabbed hold of the webbing on the side of the chopper, listening to a hailstone sound of metal on metal. He braced himself.

A massive explosion as more shrapnel hit the undercarriage of the aircraft.

A high-pitched warning alarm that started beeping inside the helicopter.

A thunder of fire as the side gunner started manically discharging his Minigun.

A sickening jolt.

A burst of heat that felt like it was scorching the skin from Jack's face.

They started to spin.

The chopper filled with smoke—thick, black smoke that it was impossible to see through. Jack heard himself choking as they continued to spin blindly towards the ground. Instinctively he grabbed harder on to the webbing, but then, through the smoke, he saw Pixie. The wounded man was rolling across the floor of the Black Hawk towards the opening at the side.

'*Get him!*' he shouted, but in the noise and confusion Jack didn't know if anyone had heard him. He moved almost without thinking, hurling himself at Pixie's body as it continued to tumble towards the side. He grabbed him by the ankle and tried to pull him, but the forces were too great and instead he found himself slipping towards the exit along with his comrade.

Suddenly Pixie's body was half out of the chopper, and he was bringing Jack with him. *Jesus, he could see the fucking sand.* Twenty metres and getting closer. He yanked at his mate's ankle in one final, desperate attempt to get him back into the chopper, but it was no good.

Pixie fell.

And then, in a moment of sudden terror and panic, Jack realised he was falling too . . .

A moment of freefall. A second? Five seconds? In Jack's confused mind he didn't know. Hell, he could barely tell which way was down. But the smoke cleared from his eyes just as Pixie hit the ground and Jack slammed immediately into him, feeling his friend's body mash and crunch beneath him. He ignored the pain that shrieked through him, rolled off Pixie's contorted limbs and crouched in a foetus position, protecting his head from what he knew was about to come.

The blast.

The noise came before the heat—a great, crashing explosion that didn't just shake Jack's body, but the very ground underneath him. When the heat came, though, it was like a wave of fire crashing over him. Jack screamed as he felt his clothes burn fiercely against his flesh.

After a couple of seconds, the first wave of heat subsided. Jack unfurled himself, not fully knowing what kind of damage he'd sustained from the fall. To his surprise his limbs, though painful, were in working order. He managed to push himself on to his feet and look around. His mind was dizzy and unfocused, almost as though it was refusing to take in what was going on.

The first thing he knew was that Pixie was a goner. Then, to his right, he saw figures. Keffiyehs and khaki. Maybe ten of them, maybe more. They carried guns and they were standing about twenty-five metres away. To his left was the chopper. What remained of it, at least. Jack could just make out the shape of the Black Hawk's shell, which burned ferociously, causing the sky and the sand beyond it to shimmer with the heat haze.

It was a nightmare vision. And it was about to get worse.

A figure burst out of the inferno. Jack recognised him not by his face—the skin had sizzled away to leave nothing but a charred, red mess—but by his enormous bulk. It was Red, and he was on fire. His clothes burned. His hair burned. His skin burned. He staggered from the wreckage of the blazing helicopter, still holding both his own M16 and Jack's, but his legs only carried him a couple of metres before he collapsed to his knees.

Jack's instinct was to run towards his friend, but the heat emanating from the fire might as well have been a steel barrier. Then, as Red hit the ground, two fragmentation grenades that he had stashed in his ops waistcoat exploded, one after the other, in quick succession.

Jack covered his eyes with his arms. By the time he lowered them, Red was just a smouldering mound.

Jack hauled himself to his feet and staggered back, turning to the group of figures now advancing towards him. In the absence of his assault rifle, he pulled his handgun from the holster strapped to his leg. He tried to remember how many rounds he had discharged back in the cave. Two? Maybe three? Whatever, he didn't have enough to deal with all these guys—but *they* didn't know that.

He pointed the handgun in their direction. Instantly, four or five of them raised their own weapons.

A moment of stand-off. Jack felt his head going thick with dizziness. The world around him seemed to spin, and he was aware of his arm wavering.

He fired, but the round discharged harmlessly into the air.

He started to fall.

By the time he hit the ground again, Jack had already blacked out.

*       *       *

The sun was high in the sky when he awoke. His head felt as though it was going to burst; his skin was raw and scorched; his mouth was dry. He was on his back and as he opened his eyes the sunlight was like knives in his brain. There was a sharp pain round his wrists, and he realised that someone had bound them with rope that dug into his skin.

Trying to sit up, he felt the same was true of his ankles. So he just let his head fall back on to the sand, and a ragged groan escaped from his lips.

A voice. Pashtun, maybe. Jack didn't understand what it said, but he understood its implication. Moments later, a shadow fell on his face as a figure stood over him, blocking out the sunlight. Jack squinted, trying to get a look at the guy's face, but it was just a silhouette.

The man spoke. A thin, reedy voice. A hiss almost. And when he had finished speaking, he booted Jack hard just underneath his ribcage. Jack coughed and choked as the man knelt down.

Now he saw his captor's expression. The guy had a black beard, flecked with grey; his eyes were brown, his brow was sweating and his lip was curled into an expression of undisguised hatred. He was holding a gun—an AK-47—his right hand firmly on the trigger, his left curled round the barrel. Jack looked at that left hand and saw only four fingers. The thumb was nothing but a rounded, weathered stump.

Jack closed his eyes. He fully expected his captor to shoot him.

But the shot didn't come.

It was just as he opened his eyes once more that the man with the missing thumb brought the end of his gun sharply down on to the side of Jack's head.

# 2

*Belfast. Northern Ireland.*
Grey rain spattered on the pavements. It ran in little rivers down the edges of the roads and into drains. In the centre of Belfast, shoppers huddled under awnings, trying to decide whether to stick it out or make a run for it now. Most decided to stay put.

On the northern edge of the city, in the poorest part of an impoverished and sprawling council estate, walked a thin man. He didn't care that his trainers—years old and with holes in the bottom— were soaked through. He didn't care that his clothes were saturated, or that water trickled down the back of his neck. He wanted to get home, sure enough, but that was nothing to do with the weather. It was everything to do with the small package he had stashed in the one good pocket of his hoody.

It had taken all day to get his hands on it. First he'd needed the money. Experience had told him that his best chance of success was to go for an easy target, so he'd followed an old lady back from the post office and relieved her of her pension at the door of her flat when there was nobody about to stop him. She'd been a feisty old bitch, and she'd forced him to hit her round the face. But it had been worth it—120 notes was a result, any day of the week. And it had meant he'd been able to spread the love a bit, and give his dealer rather more trade than he had been expecting.

Now the thin man kept his head bowed as he

approached the tower block, its cement covered with dark streaks from the rain. His trainers slapped against the floor as he walked into the deserted entrance hall. No point taking the lift—it hadn't worked for years—so he started the long climb up the stairs to the seventeenth floor.

It was as cold in the stairwell as it was outside, and it stank of piss. The man didn't even notice it, though. He was well used to this place and besides, he had his mind on other things. Five floors up he stopped to get his breath, and again on the eleventh. By the time he got to the seventeenth, he was exhausted, practically gasping as he stepped down the outdoor corridor and stopped at the third door. He took his key from his pocket, fumbled at the lock for a few moments, then stepped inside.

It stank in here, too, but a different smell. A musty, unwashed smell. The man walked down the narrow, dingy corridor, past a tiny kitchen filled with plates that were going furry, and into the main room at the end.

The TV—a big, boxy old thing that they'd picked up from a skip—was on, but the girl lying on the dirty carpet wasn't watching it. She was on her back, staring at the ceiling, a half-smoked cigarette in her hand and a crushed empty packet lying just next to her. She wore a pink tracksuit and a tight red top that accentuated the curve of her breasts even when she was lying down. The man stood in the doorway for a minute, rain still dripping from his clothes, and looked at her. He felt a strange mixture of arousal and contempt; he knew that she only felt one of these emotions towards him, and it wasn't arousal. This was a relationship of convenience. Of necessity.

She opened her eyes.

'You score?' she asked in a throaty voice.

He didn't reply immediately. He walked inside, kicked off his shoes and sat on one of the upturned milk crates that were the nearest thing they had to furniture in this place. Only then did he pull out the little sealed polythene bag from his pocket and dangle it in front of her.

That made her sit up. She took a last, heavy drag on her cigarette, stubbed it out on the empty fag packet and made to grab the bag. He pulled it away at the last minute.

'Uh-uh,' he said with a smug little shake of his head. 'You earn your keep, *then* you get your treat.'

He smiled at her. Two of his upper teeth were missing, and he had a habit of flicking his tongue from the roof of his mouth into one of the gaps. He did that now, spraying her with a tiny shower of saliva.

She curled her lip at him. 'Cocksucker,' she murmured.

His smile grew even broader. 'No,' he replied. 'That's *your* job.'

And it was. The man's habit meant sex itself was beyond his capabilities. But there were still certain things she could do for him.

He put the stash back in his pocket and waited for her to get to work.

*       *       *

She spat into the bathroom sink.

Her whole body ached for a hit; *screamed* for a

59

hit; she'd do anything for it. But even so, she managed to feel disgusted with herself as she coughed and retched into the filthy basin. She caught a glimpse of herself in the mirror. She was an attractive girl—she knew that. But she didn't look it now. Her honey-coloured hair was greasy and matted; her blue eyes were surrounded by deep, dark bags; her lips were cracked and the skin under her nose was red and sore, the rest of her face thin and pale. Only twenty years old.

She staggered back into the main room.

He was sitting cross-legged on the floor. He hadn't bothered to put his trousers back on, but was just wearing a pair of shapeless, stained underpants. Spread out on the carpet in front of him was the paraphernalia of their shared habit: lighters, spoons, a little bottle of vinegar, a couple of pipes and, of course, needles and syringes.

'Something special for you today,' he said without looking up.

She blinked at him.

'What?'

'Back to back,' he said.

She tried not to give him a reaction, but couldn't help licking her dry lips. 'Go on then,' she said, unable not to sound keen. 'Let us have it.'

He shook his head. 'We'll cook up first,' he told her. 'Don't want to have to do it when we're high.'

She let him perform the ritual by himself, watching as he sprinkled the brown powder into a spoon, poured a couple of drops of vinegar into it to dissolve the heroin, then lit a flame under the spoon to cook it well. A thick, acrid smell filled the room as the liquid bubbled and steamed. When he was satisfied that the H was cooked, he sucked it up into a hypodermic syringe, before laying it to one side and repeating the process for a second injection.

'Hurry up,' she told him, her nails pressed into the palms of her hands, but he ignored her.

When the two syringes were prepared, he turned his attention back to his polythene bag and pulled out a small wrap of paper. He carefully opened it up and pulled out what looked like two tiny milk-coloured pebbles. He held one of them up towards her between two fingers, like a jeweller displaying a fine diamond, and gave her another of his toothless grins.

She crouched down on the carpet next to him.

A back to back. A rock of crack followed by a veinful of H. It was a rare treat. God knows where he'd got the money for this kind of gear. She didn't care—it wasn't her part of the deal. She just gave him what he wanted in return for, well . . . this.

He was handing her a pipe and a lighter. She grabbed them hungrily, lit the rock inside and quickly sucked on the pipe, not wanting to waste any of the precious vapours.

She closed her eyes and waited.

It took about fifteen seconds for the high to hit, a rush of pleasure running through her veins. She toked on the pipe again, and again. It didn't take long for her to use up the whole rock.

By that time, he had already finished his own rock and was rolling up his sleeve, a dreamy look on his face. He pulled an old leather belt from the trousers that were dumped by his side, strapped it round the top of his arm and pulled tight. He waited for a vein to appear, then gently pierced the surface of his skin with the needle. As he squeezed the syringe with a trembling hand, ecstasy passed over him.

He closed his eyes, then fell backwards. His head caught on the corner of the milk crate but that didn't seem to worry him as he lay on the floor.

She looked at him, her mind filled with hate. Was it him she hated most, or herself? She didn't even know any more, but her loathing for that bastard was almost limitless. If only she could walk away.

But she couldn't. How many times had she almost walked out of the door of this miserable flat in this miserable tower block, only to find herself pulled back in by the certain knowledge that she couldn't survive more than a day without the hits that her so-called boyfriend provided her with.

She snorted. *Boy*friend. He was twenty years older than her. Scumbag.

She reached out with trembling fingers for the remaining syringe. There was no way she could resist it. Crawling over to where the man lay, she unstrapped his leather belt and wrapped it round her own arm. She spat in his face—her one, pointless act of rebellion.

The inside of her arm was bruised, the veins collapsed—it took a minute or two for her to coax a bulge out of them. But as soon as she did, she slid the needle into her flesh and squeezed the syringe.

Within seconds, she felt all her anxieties melt away, like snow in the sunshine. A smile spread across her face as she too lay back on the floor.

It was only in a tiny corner of her mind that she realised something was different. That there was a sensation she neither recognised nor wanted. A nausea that seemed to paralyse her limbs and numb her brain.

And even through the calming effect of the opiate she knew that something was very, very wrong just before she passed out.

*　　　*　　　*

They lay on the floor. To look at them, you'd think they were dead. Maybe they were. Certainly they didn't hear the television that still chattered in the corner of the room and filled it with its glow now that the light outside was failing.

Politicians were arguing on the screen, their suits smartly pressed and their faces fat and ruddy. 'Men are dying,' one of them announced. 'They're not just statistics. They are people's sons, husbands and brothers. The terrorism threat level in the UK remains critical. Our streets are being flooded with heroin that comes directly from Helmand Province. And yet the government refuses to acknowledge that its strategy in Afghanistan is failing miserably . . .'

The junkies lay there, perfectly still.

A knock on the door.

Another knock. And then a crash. The door burst inwards as a hydraulic battering ram whacked against it. Police entered, carefully at first. Gingerly. But when they saw the two figures lying motionless on the floor, they moved with a new urgency.

One of the officers knelt down by the man and pressed his fingers to the junkie's neck.

'No pulse,' he said, his voice terse, just as one of his colleagues checked the pulse of the girl.

'Nothing,' the second police officer said.

The others lowered their heads slightly.

'Wait. I've got something.' A faint pulse. *'Get an ambulance here, now!'*

The police officer moved the debris of the drug binge away from the girl's body, then stuck two fingers down her throat to check for obstructions. Nothing. 'She needs CPR!' he shouted. 'Help me!'

A third officer bent down, held the girl's nose and performed two rescue breaths in quick succession. His colleague put his hands, one on top of the other, on her ribcage and pushed down thirty times.

'Go again,' he said, and the two of them carried out the CPR routine another time.

It didn't really look like it was doing much good. The girl's face remained deathly white; she didn't regain consciousness; she didn't move. When the paramedics arrived, they covered her face with an oxygen mask, transferred her to a stretcher and carefully manoeuvred her back down the seventeen flights of stairs and into the back of a waiting ambulance. Her face looked even more deathlike bathed in the glow of the flashing blue lights, as a small crowd looked on in the rain.

Back up in the flat, a forensics officer took photographs and made notes. 'What a shithole,' he observed to no one in particular.

'Yeah,' one of the cops replied. 'They didn't spend their spare cash in Ikea, to be sure.'

When the forensics officer gave the word, the dead junkie was zipped up into a body bag and taken away to be opened up and examined by the coroner. But with a crack pipe and a hypodermic syringe by his corpse, no one doubted for a minute what cause of death the coroner would record.

Back to back. A lethal cocktail, if you fuck it up. And as drug fuck-ups go, this was sterling silver. The girl was lucky to be alive, the cops said as they left the scene.

None of them really thought she'd make it through the night.

# 3

*Another part of Belfast. The same evening.*
If Siobhan Byrne was very honest with herself, she had been looking forward to this moment. They were standing in the kitchen of an unassuming two-up two-down in the southern part of the city. She kept her old leather jacket zipped up, not just because it was cold in here, but because it concealed her standard-issue Glock 9 mm. Siobhan, though, wasn't a standard-issue kind of girl, which was why she also had a PPK strapped to her ankle.

'Now don't take this the wrong way,' her companion was saying in his broad Belfast accent, eyeing her up and down like a john checking out a hooker. 'You're a fine-looking woman and I'm a sucker for a nice tight pair of jeans.' He walked up to her and lightly touched Siobhan's shoulder-length blonde hair; she caught the whiff of cigarettes from his nicotine-stained fingers. 'They say, don't they, that gentlemen prefer blondes. Personally, I'm more of a brunette man, but I'd be willing to make an exception in your case. If it weren't for the fact, of course, that you're a pig and I don't know what kind of diseases I'd catch.'

His smile became a sneer as he let his fingers fall, turned and looked around the room. 'What is this fucking place you've brought me to anyway?'

'It's just what I said it was,' Siobhan replied in an accent that was almost, but not quite, as broad as his. 'A little place out of the way where we can talk. You know what we pigs are like—always wanting to know the craic.'

No one lived in this house. It had a history. In the corner of this room there was a white door with peeling paint. Open that door and you'd find a flight of steps that led down to a basement. During the Troubles, if you were one of the PIRA boys—or, on occasion, one of the girls—the last thing you wanted was to find yourself being walked down those steps. All you'd see was a table, a chair and a directional lamp. Special Branch never admitted it was there, naturally; but they were always very happy with the intelligence that the JSIW guys coerced out of known Republican terrorists down in that basement. The room was soundproofed and lined in concrete, with a sloping floor down to a drain in the corner. It made cleaning up after the interrogation sessions a bit easier, but Siobhan was pretty sure that if you looked hard enough, you'd still find traces of blood down there.

Those days were gone, but the house remained. It was unknown by most of Siobhan's colleagues in the police, though she supposed it still showed up on a list of government assets somewhere in Stormont. And while it was there, and empty, she was more than happy to make use of it. Not that she needed the underground facilities. The photographs she had in a brown A4 envelope would do the job just as well. At least she hoped they would. She opened up the envelope and started laying them out on the table.

The man didn't look at them at first. He just eyed Siobhan warily. 'What are these?' he demanded. 'Holiday snaps? No, don't tell me. Porno shots. You and your boyfriend. Look, darling, I mean what I say. No means no. You're just not my type.'

Siobhan ignored him and continued to lay out the photographs. When she had finished, she took a step back. 'Take your time, Kieran,' she said, her voice quiet and calm. 'Have a good look. Tell me when you're ready to talk.'

She smiled at him, and waited.

Kieran O'Callaghan. She knew more about this slimeball than she'd ever wanted to. Forty-two years of age, though despite his alcohol-reddened nose he looked a good ten years younger, his thick black hair not showing even the slightest sign of grey. His blue eyes, normally full of arrogance, were suspicious now. Despite all his bluster, there was something almost fragile about him. He was thin, quite slight, and you wouldn't have thought he'd served five years in the Maze, or that he'd still be inside if it hadn't been for the Good Friday Agreement that let lowlifes like this back out on the street. And they didn't get much lower than Kieran O'Callaghan. The man had form. Back during the Troubles, you could pretty well divide the PIRA boys into two groups—those who were politically committed to the Republican cause, and those who just used it as a front for their illegal activities. Kieran fell firmly into the latter camp.

The O'Callaghan family would pay lip service to the cause, they'd go on the marches and they'd pay their dues, but only because you couldn't operate as a criminal in Belfast without doing so. When Kieran bought himself a stint in the Maze by putting a bullet into the skull of an RUC officer, it wasn't because the poor bastard was on the wrong side of the political fence; it was because he'd stumbled across an O'Callaghan arms cache.

Kieran had been a free man for ten years now, but under the terms of the Agreement he only had to put one foot wrong and he'd be back behind bars before he could so much as whimper. And Siobhan was gambling that beneath the bluster lay the heart of a coward.

Kieran stood at the table, glancing almost nonchalantly down at the photographs, as if they were of only passing interest. But behind those bright blue eyes, you could see his mind working. Hell, you could practically hear the cogs whirring.

He said nothing.

'I was reading the papers the other day,' Siobhan said, keeping her voice as conversational as she could. 'Some psychologist. He was saying that when kids reach the age of three and a half, their memories get, you know, hard-wired. So stuff that happens to them after that age, they remember it in later life.' She gave him a piercing look. 'Your boy—little Jackie, isn't it? How old would he be, now?'

Siobhan knew the answer, of course, and Kieran knew she knew. He narrowed his eyes at her and didn't reply.

'Four years of age,' she continued. 'And to see his father put away for, what, another fifteen years?

And with your previous, Kieran, I think you can kiss goodbye to any chance of parole. That would sure be a terrible thing for a young boy to have to endure, wouldn't it now?'

Try and wriggle your way out of this one, you murderous bastard, she thought to herself.

'Still,' she persevered, 'there's always his mother. Janice, isn't it? Janice and Jackie, together against the world. I suppose your uncle will throw them a bone every now and then, make sure they're not out on the streets. But you're looking at a long stretch here, Kieran. Janice has other needs, you know—I can't help thinking that she'll find the bed a little too big without you—'

'*Shut up!*' Kieran hissed. It was the first time he'd spoken since she had laid the photographs out in front of him.

It had taken Siobhan a long time and a long lens to get them. Even when she had been snapping—a week ago, hiding out on a clifftop on the southern coast of the Republic—she had doubted that she was going to get anything worth having. And her colleagues, no doubt, wouldn't have given them a second look. Truth was, any brief worth their salt would get these pictures laughed out of court in two seconds flat—if they ever even got as far as court. Siobhan knew that, but she reckoned that Kieran didn't. As soon as she'd brought the images up on her computer screen, she had known that she could work with them. He wouldn't see a mess of legal technicalities. He'd just see the fifteen years in glorious Technicolor before him.

A moment of silence, then Siobhan tapped her finger on the middle photo of five. '*That's* the one that's going to nail you, Kieran. That's the smoking gun.'

It showed him by a boat on the beach. He had jemmied open a wooden crate to reveal—you could see it quite clearly—a neatly packaged stash of golden brown powder.

'What would you say the street value of that would be now, Kieran?' she mused. 'A few hundred thousand? Half a mill? Enough to keep your uncle very comfortable for a while, anyway. Worth a bit less once he's laundered it, of course, but still . . . I wonder how much of that you'll be taking home, Kieran. Doesn't seem quite right, does it? You take all the risk, and he takes all the profit.'

She smiled at him.

'We're very close to nailing him, Kieran. But when we do . . .' She held up her hands in a gesture almost of apology. 'When we do, it will be difficult to keep your name out of it. So the way I see it, Kieran, you've got two options. Prison, or not prison.' She put one hand to her head. 'You know what, there's something I forgot. I took the liberty of transferring a grand into your bank account. It won't take much for me to make sure the details of that little transaction end up in your uncle's hand. I'll wait till you're banged up, of course, but I suppose that if Cormac thinks you've been doing a bit of work on the side, your sentence might be shorter than everyone thinks.'

She didn't take her eyes from him.

'Of course, if you go for the prison option, well that's fine by me. But if you go for the *not* prison option, I'll need a little something in return.'

He looked as if he might hit her.

'I'm not a grass,' he whispered.

A pause.

70

'I'm sure you're not,' Siobhan replied. 'People like you never are. At least, not at first.'

*'I said, I'm not a grass.'*

He sounded like he meant it. She felt her stomach sink, but did everything she could not to show it. Instead she just shrugged. 'Well then,' she said, starting to gather up the photographs. 'I guess that's that.' She turned round and made for the door. 'You can show yourself out, can you?'

Siobhan was glad that her back was turned. This was it—the moment when he would make his decision—and she didn't know whether she'd be able to keep the nerves from her face.

'Wait,' he said.

She turned.

He looked like he was deliberating.

'It won't be like the Maze, you know, Kieran,' she purred. 'You won't be with your own. You'll be with rapists and kiddie fiddlers. It's a long time to spend with—'

'You know what my uncle will do if he finds out?' Kieran interrupted. 'You know what will happen to me?'

Siobhan shrugged. 'It's your choice. But you need to make it now. The offer won't be on the table in ten minutes' time.'

He turned and walked to the ancient kitchen units that lined the back wall, clutching on to the edge of the sink. His head was bowed, his shoulders hunched. For a brief, irrational moment, Siobhan wondered if he was going to cry.

'What do you want me to do?' he whispered.

Siobhan felt a small surge inside. 'Well now,' she said. 'Why don't we just sit down and talk about it?'

Kieran turned. 'I don't want to sit down. Just tell me what you want, woman, and be done with it.'

Siobhan inclined her head. 'Information, Kieran. Good information. Gossip is no good to me. I need information that will put your uncle behind bars. You deliver the good stuff and maybe— *maybe*—I can keep you out of jail. Do we have a deal?'

Kieran O'Callaghan looked at her with hatred. 'Yes,' he murmured. 'We have a deal.' He finally took a seat at the table, looking totally dejected.

'OK, Kieran,' Siobhan said. 'I'm going to tell you what I know. It's all about heroin. The price on the street is down and there's more high-grade product than we've seen for years. Your uncle is at the centre of all this.'

She paused and surveyed his face for any sign of acknowledgement. There was none, so she continued.

'I'll give him this, Kieran. Cormac is smart. I know about his building business. I know about his restaurants. They're all clean, all legit, but he's using them to launder his drug money so it comes out squeaky clean. What *you* need to give me, Kieran, is something to get at him with.'

'You'll never do it,' Kieran said, his voice curt.

'You'd better hope I do, Kieran,' Siobhan replied.

'Cormac's too fucking switched on for that, lady. Everything's at arm's length. You think you'll get a picture of *him* unloading crates from a boat? Jesus, I don't think he's ever even *seen* a wrap of H, let alone moved a stash. Shit doesn't stick to Cormac. Sometimes I wonder why he bothers buying bog roll.'

Siobhan nodded slowly. 'So I'm right,' she said. 'It's all heroin now.'

Kieran looked down at his palms. 'It never used to be,' he murmured. 'Before, it was all coke, in from Colombia. But then, about a year ago . . .'

He looked up at her again, doubt suddenly shadowing his face.

'Go on,' Siobhan told him.

Kieran squeezed the bridge of his nose between two fingers before continuing. 'About a year ago, it all changed. The product changed, the importation routes changed, and the money certainly changed. Cormac's got more cash than he can damn well spend. Not that you'd know it.'

'What do you mean?'

'You'd think someone with all that money would buy himself a few luxuries once in a while. The way my uncle runs the business, you'd think he was damn well broke. He sits in the back room of that pub, giving out his instructions like he was—'

'So the heroin,' Siobhan steered him back. 'Did your uncle tell you where it's coming from? Who his supplier is?'

Kieran seemed to find that genuinely funny. '*Tell* me? You must be shitting me, woman. Cormac doesn't tell anybody anything. What's that they say, about the left hand not knowing what the right hand's doing? That's what it's like with him. Nobody who works for the family knows anything more than they need to.'

He gave Siobhan a combative look, but she was a match for it.

'Sorry, Kieran. You'll have to do better than that.'

'I'm telling you, woman. He plays his cards close

to his chest.'

'Then you're going to have to sneak a look at his hand, aren't you.'

Silence.

Kieran put his hand in his pocket and Siobhan's fingers automatically started feeling for her handgun. All he brought out, though, was a pouch of baccy and some skins. Siobhan could tell that the cogs had started whirring again as her new tout worked out the pros and cons. Finally he seemed to decide on something. 'You're not the only one with a set of eyes on the inside,' he said in a low voice as he rolled a ciggy.

Siobhan stayed very calm. 'What do you mean?'

'Just what I say. Cormac's got a pig on the payroll. Don't ask me who. Drugs Squad, that's all I know.' Siobhan could tell what he was thinking: what if this bitch is Cormac's bent copper? 'How do I know it's not you?' he asked.

Siobhan shrugged. 'If you wake up dead tomorrow morning, it *is* me.' She didn't feel at all inclined to put his mind at rest. The more this little shit was made to squirm, the better as far as she was concerned. In any case, she was suddenly distracted by this new piece of intelligence. It didn't really surprise her that one of her colleagues was playing for the other side—she knew that anyone could be bought for the right price.

'Find out,' she told him.

'I can't.'

'Well then maybe I can give you a helping hand. You'll find I'm very generous like that, you know.'

Siobhan removed an item from her pocket. It looked like a simple black box, about the same size and shape as a matchbox, but several times heavier. She held it up between a thumb and two fingers. 'Present for you,' she said.

'The fuck's that?'

'That, Kieran, could be your ticket out of the clink.' She winked at him. 'It's a listening device. You hide this somewhere your dear uncle spends a lot of time and I'll be able to listen in on him. I'm thinking somewhere in the Horse and Three Feathers. I'd do it myself, but I don't think someone like me would be all that welcome there. Do you think you could manage that now, Kieran?'

The tout took the box and weighed it in his hand. 'How does it work?' he asked.

'There's a magnetic backing which means it'll stick to anything made of metal. Down the back of a radiator is good. Just avoid anything electrical that could interfere with the signal. And I suppose I don't need to tell you to keep it well out of sight.'

Kieran examined the box, turning it round in his fingers and holding it up to the light like it was a glass of wine. Then, with another aggrieved look at his handler, he shook his head. 'Too dangerous,' he said. 'I'd be busted in minutes.'

Siobhan bent down so that their eyes were only a few inches away from each other. 'Listen to me, you little piece of shit. I want to see Cormac O'Callaghan in prison for the rest of his life, but believe me, putting you away will come a very close second, so you'd better start playing ball. We're going to meet every two days, here, at midday.' She pulled a bit of paper from a pocket in her leather jacket. It had an email address scribbled on it. 'You can't make it, you leave a message at this email address and turn up at midday the following day. Stand me up more than twice, I pull you in.

And let me tell you, Kieran: you'll be working a damn sight harder for me than you ever did for your uncle—unless you want to spend the next fifteen years sharing a room with the sort of fella little Jackie's not supposed to accept sweeties from. Have I made myself absolutely clear?'

The two of them stared at each other—a look of mutual contempt.

'Yeah,' Kieran O'Callaghan said finally.

'Good. Then get out of my sight. I don't want to spend any more time with you than I have to.'

Kieran stood up and walked to the door, then turned. He looked as though he was about to say something, but then thought better of it and slipped out of the house, closing the door quietly behind him.

# 26 JUNE

# 4

*Somewhere in the back of his mind he knew it was a dream. But that didn't make it any less real. He saw a child. His child. She was small—six years old—with mousy, curly hair that tumbled over her forehead. She was looking at him.*

*'Daddy?' she asked.*

*He tried to answer, but couldn't.*

*She looked at him sadly. Accusingly, almost. And then she started to fade away. He tried to reach out for her, to stop her from disappearing. But he couldn't. She melted away, leaving nothing but an agonising emptiness . . .*

Jack woke up.

He didn't know where he was. Ropes still bound his wrists and legs, and he felt like he was spinning—a mixture of pain, hunger, acute dehydration and the uncomfortable remnants of his dream. It was a relief that he was lying on the floor; if he had been standing up, he'd have just fallen over anyway.

He wanted to vomit, but there was nothing to retch up, so he lay there, shivering for a while despite the heat. He didn't want to fall asleep again but he couldn't fight it. It was only a matter of minutes before he passed out again.

This time, he dreamed of fire—Red's burning body staggering from the blaze of the Black Hawk—and of water. Cool and thirst-quenching.

It was water that woke him. Not icy cold, but cold enough for it to be a shock as someone threw a bucketful over his body. And it wasn't just the water that hit him, but the bucket too. Jack breathed in sharply and looked up. There was light in the room, streaming in from the open door. Two figures advanced.

A dull thump as one of them threw something on the floor.

Jack's vision was blurred, but he could see they wore grey dishdashas and full beards and had dark, ugly looks on their thickset faces. They were not muscular, but naturally big. One of them carried a gun, which he pointed at Jack's head while the other pulled a long, wicked-looking knife.

The blade twinkled in the light coming from the doorway as its owner bent down and held it towards Jack's body. He grinned horribly, circling the point of the blade in the region of Jack's face.

Jack did what he could to prepare himself for the sensation of the blade slicing skin.

Instead, his tormentor shuffled down to Jack's wrists. With a single swipe, the sharp blade cut through the ropes binding them. The knife man stood up quickly, leaving Jack's legs bound tight. He and his colleague walked backwards out of the door, closing it in front of them and locking it from the outside.

Enough light seeped in from around the door and from a small opening high in the opposite wall for Jack to be able to see. He sat up painfully, rubbing his sore wrists. The bucket they had thrown at him was about a metre from where he was sitting. It was rusty, and touching his face where it had hit him, Jack felt a small stream of blood. He pressed hard on its source to stem the bleeding while looking around the rest of the room.

80

It was a square space, about five metres on each side. Although it was largely empty, Jack had the impression that it was used as a storeroom. The walls were made of hard-baked mud—the sort of material the inhabitants of Helmand had used for centuries to build the square, high-walled compounds in which they lived. These walls were thick and unbelievably sturdy, often able to withstand the impact of artillery fire. There was a stale smell of animal shit in the air, and along one of the walls was some kind of dried crop and a small pile of firewood. Jack was sitting almost up against the back wall. Between him and the door he saw whatever his two visitors had dumped on the ground when they arrived. Shuffling up towards it, he realised what it was. Food—a large piece of flatbread—and a plastic bottle of what he hoped was water. His mouth was drier than the dust on the ground.

He ate the bread in big, ravenous mouthfuls, ignoring the bits of grit that clung to its underside. The water was warm and stale, but as he gulped it down, Jack felt his body absorbing it like a sponge. When he had finished, he looked around a little desperately to see if they had left him anything else to eat or drink. In the bottom of the rusty bucket there was still a bit of water, so he carefully decanted this into his bottle, then screwed the top back on. He'd leave that for an emergency.

Fuck, he told himself. Like it isn't an emergency already.

Jack felt a surge of fear. He knew he had to master it. His priority was survival, and fear was his worst enemy. If he let it, it would affect his ability to think, to make intelligent decisions.

He needed to keep a cool head. Not easy. Not very fucking easy at all.

He took a deep breath and tried to work out what the hell was going on.

The first thing was this: he was alive. There had to be a reason for that, because his captors could have killed him at any moment. What was more, they had just given him food and water, which meant they had plans for him. And Jack could guess what those plans were. He was an enemy combatant, and you didn't have to be a military fucking genius to work out he was SF—they'd already have examined his digital camouflage and his SF helmet cut away round the ears. That meant he was a good prize, and potentially a good source of intelligence. Jack looked down at the bottle of water. He'd conducted enough field interrogations of his own to realise that you didn't want your subject to be halfway to Hades before you started on him. You wanted him conscious and alert. *No point torturing a comatose man.*

He got up on tiptoes and looked through the opening. The sun was high. It was past noon. The first three hours after capture were critical—that was the time frame in which you were most likely to be rescued. But that three-hour limit was long gone. To make matters worse, he estimated that there were still another four or five hours until sundown. If he escaped now, that was four or five hours when he would be running in daylight . . .

He held on to the last glimmers of hope. Maybe a backup squadron was out trying to find him. Even that thought had its worries: if the Taliban heard the noise of vehicles approaching, chances were they'd come in and execute him immediately, just to be rid of him. And he'd seen enough video clips on the Internet of Taliban executions to know how brutal that would be.

Fear again. He did what he could to control it. He didn't know how long it would be before they got to work on him. Maybe their strategy was to make him sweat it out. Once they started, it would only be a matter of time before he cracked. He knew any information he had now would be useless. The guys back at base would have recovered the bodies from the wreckage of the bird. They would know Jack was missing. They'd have changed any operational details he was privy to.

During training they always told you that if you were captured, you had to last twenty-four hours. Easy for some instructor in the safety of Hereford to say but once your balls were in that vice all fucking bets were off. Might take an hour, might take a day, might take a week. But sooner or later he'd be singing like a canary on speed.

That meant Jack's only loyalty was to himself. His only focus: to get out of there. If that meant pretending to be compliant, if it meant making them think he was a soft touch, so be it. Jack would tell these bastards whatever they wanted to hear. Humanise himself. Appease them. If it bought him a little time to cook something up, anything was acceptable.

And then, when he got the chance—*if* he got the chance—he'd kill as many of them as he could.

\*       \*       \*

Time passed. Two hours, he estimated. The sun

83

was lower now and shooting a beam through the tiny opening.

Jack sat in the corner of the room, sweating in the afternoon heat, having untied the ropes round his ankles. He was sitting still, conserving his energy. At one point he pulled down his trousers, crouched on the bucket and took a shit. The smell that leached into the air of his prison was foul, but he knew from experience that during a 'tactical questioning', the bowels were often the first to go. Better to evacuate himself at a moment of his own choosing.

He made a mental list of everything he had at his disposal, and it wasn't a long one. They'd confiscated all his weapons, of course, along with the spare ammo and fragmentation grenades that he'd stashed in his ops waistcoat with his now missing escape and evasion kit. The shoelaces had been removed from his boots to make walking more difficult. In fact, the only thing they'd left him with was his Silva compass, because that was no good to anyone. The body of the compass had cracked and the needle had detached itself from its spindle. His compass wouldn't get him out of this room, let alone back to base. And apart from that, they'd left him with nothing other than the clothes on his back. Even his belt had gone . . . But his captors had missed the pliable saw blade that all the guys wore sewn into the elasticated cord round the top of their trousers. He loosened the blade, ready to pull it out when he needed it.

The door opened. Jack looked up slowly from his sitting position. Four men walked in. They all had assault rifles, but only two of them had their weapons pointing at Jack. A third clutched a small video camera, and the fourth had the swagger of a leader. He was the only one that still wore combat camo. Bin Laden chic. Jack thought he recognised his face, and his eyes flickered towards the man's left hand.

Four fingers. It was the same guy he'd seen out on the ground earlier.

The armed men stood by the door while their leader approached Jack, who remained still in the corner. He was tall—almost as tall as Jack—and he towered above him, looking down impassively at his prisoner. He stank of sweat.

And then he spoke. His voice was heavily accented, but his English was surprisingly good. 'You will speak into the camera,' he said. 'You will give your name and tell the world that you are being well treated, for now, but that you will die a painful death unless the President of the United States announces the immediate withdrawal of his troops from Afghanistan. If you attempt to say anything different, you will be dead before you finish the sentence.'

Jack took a deep, slow breath.

*Control your fear. Keep your mind calm.*

He had to do what they said for now—try anything macho and they'd be forced to assert their authority. And if Jack wanted to have any chance of escaping, he needed his body to be in as good a shape as possible. He nodded at the man, doing what he could to look as unprovocative as possible, then waited while the cameraman took up his position in front of him. A little red light shone at the front of the camera.

'Speak now,' said the leader.

'My name is Jack Harker,' he said. 'Royal

85

Regiment of Fusiliers.' Then he licked his lips, kept his eyes on the camera and repeated the message his captor had given him.

The cameraman lowered the machine. He stepped back while the leader approached Jack once more. He crouched down so that their faces were at the same level. Jack could see the pores on his dark skin, and the sweat on his brow.

'Jack Harker,' he rasped, fixing Jack with a passionless stare. Then, quite unexpectedly, his lips moulded into a smile. 'You are lying, of course.'

Jack shook his head. His captor's smile grew broader.

'You will deny it now. But given time, you will tell us everything we want to know. You will be *begging* to tell me things, because you will understand that I will only let you die once I am satisfied. And believe me, infidel, you will want to die very soon.'

'Please,' Jack insisted, his voice croaking as he did his best to sound deceptively weak. 'I'll do what you ask. I'll tell you anything you want to know. My name is Jack Harker. Royal Regiment of—'

'*Quiet!*'

His four-fingered captor raised his good hand. Immediately the cameraman handed over the camera.

'You are not the first soldier we have captured in recent days,' the Talib continued. 'We caught a younger man than you. An American. I will show you what happened to him.'

He opened up the viewing screen of the camera, fiddled with the controls for a few seconds, then turned it round for Jack to see. The screen glowed bright in the dimness of the room, and the sound from the camera, even though it was quiet, seemed to echo off the walls.

It was a scream. It sounded like an animal being slaughtered, but Jack knew it was a human. The image was blurred and shaky, and it wasn't until the camera panned out a little that he realised what he was seeing.

The kid was being filmed from behind. His body had been bound, using rope, to a cross, which his tormentors had leaned at an angle against one wall. He was fully clothed. At least, Jack *thought* he was. His arms were covered, and so was the bottom half of his body; but his back was such a bloodied pulp of devastated flesh that it wasn't fully clear whether it was clad or not. The victim was struck from behind by some kind of lash; liquid spattered from his mashed-up back and he screamed again . . .

Jack's captor closed the camera. 'That was the first day,' he said. 'The infidel did not die until the third day. We are looking forward to sending the tapes to his family, so they can see how their son died, squealing like a goat. Do you have a family, Jack Harker?'

Jack nodded, and he could feel the skin round his eyes tightening.

'We will find out soon enough,' the man continued, his voice calm. He scratched his beard with his four-fingered hand. 'You Westerners, you are so stupid. Your white-faced British soldiers crawl around this land like ants, and you cannot defeat us. With all your weapons you still cannot hold the ground.' He took a few steps closer to

Jack and his lip curled. 'You are more stupid even than your grandfathers. They at least could not look to history when they came here only to be slaughtered by the thousand. *You* should know better, but you don't.'

He was warming to his theme now. Jack hung his head and let him say his piece. 'Your women are worse than you,' the man continued. 'Not only stupid, but loose. They prostitute themselves for so little and you do not have the brains to see it. You should use your violence on them, not on us.'

He leaned in closer.

'When I was very small, my grandfather told me something. I have never forgotten it.' His voice grew quiet. 'It is with your weapons that you win the battle, but with your mind that you win the war. And that is why this war, for you, is already lost.'

The man's eyes shone in the gloom as he tapped on his own head with two fingers.

'You do not believe us, perhaps. But our ambush easily destroyed your helicopter in the desert. Oh, we filmed that too, and soon the world will see that your instruments of war are no match for our cleverness.'

Jack felt his nostrils flaring, but he remained quiet. *Let him say his piece. Don't get him angry. Buy yourself some time . . .*

The man stood up. 'I will leave you to think about what happened to the last soldier we interrogated. Expect the same treatment when the sun goes down.'

And without another word, he turned and left the room along with the other three. Jack heard the door being locked firmly behind them.

Jack felt heavy with tiredness. He did what he could to fight it. Tiredness led to lethargy, and lethargy would be fatal. He had to fight to survive. And to do that he needed to be obstinate. Stubborn. He knew in his heart that by now the guys back at base would most likely have him down as dead. Even if they didn't, there was no way he could expect a rescue operation. Nobody knew where he was. No one was going to provide help, except himself.

*Think positive. Think what you have. Value your own life. Fight for it.*

He put his ear to the door and listened for voices. Nothing. Just a goat bleating. He couldn't draw any conclusions from that, though. Just because nobody was speaking, it didn't mean they weren't there.

He drew strength from the certain knowledge that his captors had already made their first mistake. Rule number one of field interrogation: let the bastards know you're serious. Had he been in the Taliban's position, he'd have started as he meant to go on. Cut off a digit, break a limb— make them think about what was for the main course, if that was just the starter. His captors had obviously thought that showing him footage of that fucked-up squaddie would mess with his mind. He could deal with psychological stress; a broken leg, however, and he'd be out of the game.

He pushed himself to his feet and walked over to the bales that were piled up against one of the walls. It was only as he pulled out one of the straws that he realised what they were: dried-out poppy stalks. The milky sap had already been extracted from the heads, leaving dark tear stains where it had wept out; what remained would be used during the harsh winter as kindling for fires.

And that gave Jack an idea.

The beam of light let in by the tiny window had moved across the floor. He winced slightly as he looked at it, and that was good: it meant the light was strong enough. From his ops waistcoat he took his fucked-up compass, walked to the wall and smashed it a couple of times against the stone. The compass itself broke away from the housing and with another couple of smashes he managed to get the plastic disc away from the front. He saw, as he had hoped, that it was slightly convex. It would work as a lens.

Jack turned his attention to his clothes. Under his camo he had a thin T-shirt, which he always wore out here to wick the moisture away from his skin. He took off his jacket, removed the T-shirt and got dressed again. The T-shirt itself he tore into three strips. He tied two of them round his ankles to bind his boots to his feet, because he knew he wouldn't get far in bare feet. The third strip had a different purpose. It was slightly damp from his sweat, but he knew that in this heat it would only take a minute or two to dry out. He made use of that time by moving over to where the poppy stalks and firewood were stashed. Then he rummaged through the wood until he found a suitable piece—about the length of his forearm, fairly flat and thinner at one end than the other, like a wedge. He lay this piece of wood half a metre from the door with the thin end pointing towards it. Then he returned to the poppy stalks. Grabbing a couple of handfuls, he dropped them into the shit-filled bucket, then prepared several more bundles, which he laid by the door.

The strip of cloth was dry now. He placed it in the small patch of light thrown by the window, then grabbed the disc from the compass and held it into the beam of light. It took a few moments for him to find the right position to concentrate the light through the lens on to a point at the edge of the material, but once he had, it took about five minutes for the cotton to start crisping and turning brown. Two or three minutes later a thin tendril of smoke began to rise from his tinder.

Jack picked up the tinder, then let it flame for a moment before dropping it into the bucket.

He held his breath while he waited for the kindling to catch.

It took a few seconds, that was all. The poppy stalks were bone dry, and soon the bucket was filled with fire. Smoke billowed out, and with it a thick, pungent smell.

Jack needed to keep the fire burning, so he carefully placed more kindling into the bucket. Gradually, his prison became cloudy—so much so that he had to put the remains of his T-shirt over his nose in order to breathe. When he was satisfied there was enough smoke to hide his captors' vision, he grabbed yet another fistful of poppy stalks and carefully set fire to one end of them. Gently, so as not to extinguish the flames, he tucked them into the small gap underneath the door. He lit a second fistful of stalks, shoved them into the gap too, then worked the flexible saw loose from his waist and stood by the door.

It took about a minute for someone on the other side to notice the flames. There was a good deal of shouting, and then the sound of multiple footsteps running up to Jack's prison.

A key in the lock, and someone pushed the door open. It hit the wedge and got stuck. If anyone wanted to come in, it would have to be in single file.

The first guard had a gun, of course, and there was a second man behind him. But Jack had the element of surprise. He wrapped his arms round the leader's throat. One swipe, and the saw blade cut deeply into him. The guy didn't even have a chance to scream. He lifted both his hands to his pumping throat and dropped his AK-47.

Jack still had the man by the throat and now he pushed him hard through the gap in the door so that he knocked the second guard backwards. Jack quickly bent down and grabbed the fallen AK. With one swift movement he switched the safety to semi-auto and fired a single shot into the head of the second guard who collapsed dead under the weight of his companion. The moment he fired, however, there were shouts.

It took a split second to assess the threat. He was in a compound, no different to any of the hundreds that made up the villages and towns of Helmand. It was big—probably thirty metres by thirty—with walls twice as high as a man and a corrugated iron entrance gate in the far wall directly opposite him. That was his most obvious escape route, but it was closed, with two armed guards at either side. Covering the length of the wall to his right there was a long, low building; and on the high walls of the compound he could see four Taliban snipers, two looking in, two looking out. On the ground, in the middle of the sandy yard, was a well. Between Jack and the well, fifteen metres away, were two low mulberry trees with thick, gnarled trunks and blood-red fruit. The noise of his gun and his sudden appearance had caused screams from the far left corner of the compound. Two women in burkas were disappearing into a door that they slammed shut behind them. Goats started to scurry around in the dust, gathering in a frightened huddle by the left-hand wall. The snipers on the roof turned inwards and started to shout; five seconds later the air was full of the cracking of guns.

The dust on the compound floor exploded in little bursts as the rounds hit it. A couple of bullets slammed into the wall behind Jack, who threw himself to the ground, then crawled as fast as he could towards the scant cover of the mulberry trunks. He saw one of the guards from the gate running at him.

One shot from the AK-47, and the fucker was down.

More shouting. More gunfire. From nowhere, three more guards had appeared at the front gate, and the wall-top snipers were firing at random in Jack's general direction. He knew that if he stayed where he was, he'd be dead in seconds.

There were only two other places he could get cover: the room he'd just left, and the long building fifteen metres to his right that extended the whole length of the compound. There was no advantage to going backwards, so he pushed himself to his feet and ran to the door of the building, firing above him and around him in short, random bursts, then charging into the wooden door of the building at full speed.

The door splintered open and Jack rolled to the ground, coming to a halt with his gun facing the entrance.

Silence from outside, but he wasn't fooled by that. Everyone in the area would have heard the gunfire. Any militants would be grabbing their weapons and rushing to help nail him. The Taliban knew he was armed. They knew what would happen to the first man who walked through the door. But that didn't alter the fact that Jack had manoeuvred himself into a corner. He felt a sickness twist inside him. He'd had his chance to get out of here, and he'd fucked it up.

Or had he?

It had been bright outside, and now that he was in the building it seemed very dark. It took about twenty tense seconds for his vision to rectify itself, and he saw that he was in one long room. The walls were lined with lengths of rickety wooden shelving; and on these shelves, neatly arranged, was the biggest weapons cache Jack had ever seen. AKs precisely lined up, stacks and stacks of dark brown wooden ammo boxes with rope handles and Chinese writing on the side, mortar rounds, fragmentation grenades, RPGs, landmines—even what looked like a couple of heavy DShK machine guns stashed in one corner. Anything the Taliban used to battle against the Coalition forces was here. If his bosses back at Bastion knew what he'd found, they'd be cock-a-fucking-hoop, but Jack wasn't thinking about them; he was thinking about how he was going to get the hell out of here.

He pushed himself up to his feet, then fired

several rounds out of the door, just so his captors knew he was up and running and fully prepared to slaughter anyone who ventured inside. Then he ran up to the cache and started cramming fragmentation grenades into his ops waistcoat. When he had as many as he could carry, he returned to the door, pulled the pin on a couple and hurled them just outside. They exploded and someone screamed.

Jack quickly returned to the shelves. It was only then that he noticed them. Three long, green boxes, about a metre and a half each. Coalition serial numbers and ID codes printed in white military lettering on the side. Jack recognised them immediately, of course. He didn't need to open the carrying cases to know what was inside.

'*Fucking Stingers* . . .' he breathed.

He looked around to see three launchers propped almost carelessly in one corner, their serial numbers and ID codes printed on the side in white.

Shouting outside. The enemy were regrouping.

He had to move fast. Choose his weapon carefully but quickly.

More shouting. Urgent. Angry. Nearer.

Jack turned away from the Stingers and helped himself to an RPG launcher. The Taliban's favourite weapon: it felt good that he was about to use it against them. He grabbed a warhead, loaded the weapon, then turned to face the far end of the room. From where he was standing, it was about thirty metres.

Close enough, he thought to himself. But not too close.

Voices outside the door. Barked instructions. He

95

couldn't hesitate. He pointed the RPG towards the end of the room and checked behind him. Three metres. Not a lot, but just enough for the back blast. He steeled himself, closed his eyes, then fired. Jack felt the weapon flaring behind him, and a burning sensation as the heat scorched his clothes. He threw himself into the corner and covered his head with his arms.

And then, a split second later, impact.

In that confined space, when the explosion came it was immense. A huge blast, then a hailstorm of rubble and shrapnel that only just fell short of where Jack was crouching.

The room filled with smoke, but through it all Jack could just see a glimmer of daylight at the other end. He ran towards it, turning sideways as he passed the door and spraying AK-47 rounds out into the main compound.

The RPG had totally demolished the end wall; part of the ceiling had collapsed too. Jack's eyes were smarting from the thick clouds of dust, the back of his throat burning, but he knew he couldn't let that slow him down. At the opening he stopped and threw two grenades, one to each side, then waited for them to explode. They did so just in time—there were voices behind him, and he needed to get out quickly. He climbed over the rubble and out of the compound.

He was in a kind of alleyway, about three metres wide. Directly in front of him was the high wall of another compound. He looked to his left. At the end of the alley, about twenty metres away, were two kids in shabby robes. They pointed to him and started shouting.

Jack sprinted off in the opposite direction.

The compound wall on his left stopped after fifteen metres. He turned left, ran, then took a right. He made a choking sound as he tried to clear the dust from his throat, then saw a villager—an old man, his face gnarled and lined, gazing at him with intense eyes. He quickly turned and took another route before the old guy could shout and give away his position, and before long he was lost in a maze of alleyways.

He ran blindly, then stopped.

The end of the alleyway he was in was half obscured by an old truck that had parked in front of the opening. It led on to a main street, full of activity. Opposite him, on the other side, was a fruit and vegetable stall, its colourful wares neatly laid out; next to that was some kind of motorcycle shop, with nine or ten greasy-looking bikes on display. Scraggly hens pecked around in the dust; one stall had a ragged awning and beneath it, upturned and hanging from a hook, a beheaded and eviscerated sheep with flies buzzing all around.

And there were people. Villagers. Hundreds of them, in their traditional dishdashas and headdresses. Some were armed, others weren't; but Jack knew that if he stepped out into that dusty, busy street in his army gear, he'd stick out like a turd in a punch-bowl.

He pressed his back against the alley wall, sweating and out of breath. He needed to blend in, and he needed to do it fast. But as his brain ticked over, he heard shouting. In the main street, a swathe of armed militia in military camo and keffiyehs had appeared. They were barking instructions, and although Jack couldn't understand them the villagers clearly could. They began to scatter, making themselves scarce, muttering to themselves and casting worried glances all around. Stallholders started packing up their wares and more armed men arrived.

Jack cursed under his breath. They were closing down the fucking town. He looked back over his shoulder. There was no one there, but that wouldn't last for long. He retreated from the main street and returned to the maze of alleyways created by the compounds.

He moved more slowly now. With greater care, checking before he turned that he wasn't heading into trouble. He could hear shouting, but couldn't tell where the voices were coming from; although he still had his AK, he didn't want to fire any rounds because that would give away his position. He continued like this for five minutes, keeping a lookout for places to hide, but the alleyways outside the compounds were barren.

He turned a corner and the terrain changed. He had reached the outskirts of the inhabited part of the village and could see the wadi up ahead and to the left, with a line of trees running along it. In front of him there was a cornfield—two metres high and the size of a football pitch. The wadi was his route out. Once the stars were out he could use it to get his bearings, but he needed the cover of the cornfield until then. To get there, Jack needed to cross twenty metres of open ground. He checked the surroundings and couldn't see anyone. Perhaps the Taliban chasing everyone indoors was working to his advantage.

He sprinted, covering the open ground in only a few seconds before plunging into the cornfield. He ran about ten metres in, then hit the ground and lay still, gasping for breath, sweat pouring from his body. He just prayed nobody had seen him take cover here. If they had, he was history. If they hadn't, all he could do was mark time and wait for nightfall.

He felt dizzy through lack of water. His mouth was like sand, he was knackered, his muscles burned with exhaustion and his skin was still raw from the proximity of the burning Black Hawk. He was a fucking mess.

But as he lay there in the cover of the cornfield, Jack knew he had to forget all that if he had any chance of survival.

\*     \*     \*

It seemed to take an age for the light to fail and for darkness to come. Every few minutes he heard voices and felt his muscles tensing up. The voices always disappeared, but the tension didn't.

He had to fight the urge to move as soon as it was dark. They'd be expecting that. Better to wait a couple of hours before he crawled out of the cornfield. Jack estimated that it was about 22.00 hrs when he decided to move. He crawled slowly, stopping every three or four metres to listen.

No sound.

It took him five painfully long minutes to reach the edge of the cornfield. He lay there, preparing himself to make a run for the wadi, which was thirty metres away over open ground, just beyond a line of trees. Sounds reached him over the night air—the howling of a dog, the purr of a distant motorbike. But no voices, so he prepped his weapon, pushed himself up and ran.

Twenty metres.

Ten metres.

Five.

He reached the trees and then rolled into the protection of the dried-up wadi.

The moon was up and the wadi was about 100 metres wide, dotted with bushes and veined with deep crevices that he could use as cover. He moved from hiding place to hiding place, keeping low and staying in the shadows, across the dried-up riverbed and up out of the other side.

Jack lay on the ground and looked up. The stars were dazzlingly bright, and he studied them carefully to get his bearings. Ursa Minor wasn't visible, but overhead he could make out the saucepan shape of Ursa Major and the W-shape of Cassiopeia. Halfway between the two constellations he located Polaris, the North Star. Once he had his bearings, he realised that the wadi was heading north-west to south-east. That meant, according to the map of the area he had studied that morning, that it was the westernmost riverbed. If he headed west from here, approximately five miles from the village there was a Coalition forward operating base.

Which meant safety.

As if to confirm Jack's deductions, the sky to the west suddenly lit up, illuminating the ground all around. He pinned himself to the floor, waiting for the light to fade. He knew what it was, of course— a lume, sent up from the FOB so that the guys on stag could light up any militants out on the ground trying to dig in IEDs. If they caught anyone, these enterprising Taliban could expect a barrage of artillery shells to be dropped on them with pinpoint accuracy. All Jack could do was hope, as he set off across the sand, that he wasn't mistaken for the enemy. To have got this far and then be mashed in a blue on blue would take the fucking cake.

But he let the lume fade away, pushed himself up on to his feet and started to trek across the desert.

## 5

*The Republic of Somalia. About two miles outside the capital, Mogadishu.*

The road on which the open-topped Toyota truck drove was little more than a dirt track. As the harsh midday sun beat down, the wheels of the truck kicked up clouds of dust, which mixed with the diesel fumes to create a thick, choking miasma.

It didn't seem to bother any of the men on the vehicle.

There were seven of them—two in the front seats and five outside on the back, one of whom was minding a .50-calibre machine gun mounted on a platform so that he could fire it over the cab of the truck. They were young—all of them between the ages of sixteen and twenty-two. The top-gunner had a bony face wrapped round with a red and white keffiyeh. His skin was dark, his sharp eyes bright and wary. He firmly held on to the .50-cal as the vehicle bumped and trundled down the road.

The four men surrounding him looked similar. They all wore keffiyehs to protect their heads from the punishing heat of the day. Their dirty jeans and T-shirts didn't disguise their lean, weathered bodies. Unlike the top-gunner, they were armed with assault rifles, and they each had a bandolier of ammo strapped round themselves. They wore casual expressions, and smiles.

None of them spoke, and only occasionally did any of them look down. At their feet there was a silver flight case, firmly locked and strapped to the bottom of the truck to stop it from slipping around. It was no bigger than a small suitcase.

The Toyota hadn't been going very fast, but now it slowed down.

It ground to a halt.

All the men stood up, guns trained forwards. The top-gunner narrowed his eyes.

A roadblock up ahead. About fifty metres.

It wasn't an official roadblock, of course, because nothing was official in this country. Just a few shacks by the side of the track, and a couple of ragged-looking men with AKs blocking the road and pointing their weapons directly at the Toyota.

The vehicle's engine turned over noisily as the top-gunner waited for the man in the passenger seat to give his instructions.

\*　　　\*　　　\*

In one of the roadside shacks, a baby girl wailed. She was hungry, but that was something the kid was going to have to get used to. Her mother was hungry too, and her large, dark breasts had no more milk for the infant. They had named the child Khadra, which meant 'lucky', but there wasn't much luck to go around in their world, and what luck there was seldom found its way into this poor, one-roomed home. All Khadra's mother could do was hold the little girl in the crook of her arm and comfort her.

The child's father scowled at the crying baby. 'Can't you do something to shut her up?' he demanded of the woman, speaking the Somali language in a thin voice. The woman didn't reply or even look at him. She just continued to rock the child gently.

The man was less hungry than his wife and child, but that was only because of the khat he was chewing. He'd spent his remaining money on a bunch of the leaves two days ago, and the mouthful that he rolled round between his tongue and his cheek was the last of it. He made a sucking, slurping sound as he milked the leaves of their precious stimulant juices.

A shout from outside. The father grabbed the rifle that was leaning up against the wall of their shack and ran out into the road, ignoring the woman's shout of 'Dalmar, no!'

Dalmar's friend Korfa was there, if friend was not too loose a word for the bandit who stood pointing his own rifle towards the truck that was arriving from the distance. Dalmar knew that Korfa would put a bullet in him any time it suited him, but that would leave just one of them to man this roadblock where they stopped any passing vehicles and extorted cash from the occupants at gunpoint. How else were they going to earn any money around here? Extortion was the local industry. The police couldn't stop them because there *were* no police. No, out here, you earned a living however you could, if you didn't want to

103

starve.

'Clients,' Korfa said. Dalmar stood by him and raised his rifle as well.

The truck stopped.

Sweat dripped down Dalmar's face.

They waited.

\*       \*       \*

The driver of the Toyota turned off the engine.

His passenger opened his door. He bent over and leant out, using the metal of the door as a shield against the gunmen up ahead, then addressed the top-gunner. 'Fire above their heads,' he instructed.

The top-gunner didn't need telling twice.

Dalmar, who stood fifty metres away, had heard the sound of many weapons in his life. In his country, firearms were more common than toothbrushes. But he had never been fired at by a .50-cal machine gun before, so he was unprepared for the noise.

The thundering of the rounds sent a shock all the way through him, and for a moment he thought he had been shot. But they landed harmlessly about twenty metres behind him, kicking up bursts of dust. Dalmar stood his ground.

The same couldn't be said of Korfa. The moment the gunner had opened fire, Dalmar's accomplice had hit the dirt, and was even now crawling to the side of the road. Dalmar watched him from the corner of his eye. If Korfa wanted to be a coward, that was his decision; but if Dalmar got any money from this lot, there was no way he was going to share it. He sucked a little bit more enthusiastically on his khat.

'*Dalmar!*'

His wife's voice from the door of the shack. Dalmar looked over his shoulder. She still had the baby in her arm.

'Don't be so stupid!' the woman told him. 'Get back inside!'

Dalmar stared at her, his eyes a little wild. 'This is *my* roadblock,' he hissed. 'If they want to pass, they must pay.' He was vaguely aware of Korfa, who had reached the side of the road and was now up and running away.

'Don't be an idiot!' his wife screamed. 'They will kill you. And who will look after your child then?'

'What is the point of having a roadblock, if I don't use it to get money?' Dalmar countered. 'We have nothing for food.'

His wife narrowed her eyes. 'If you hadn't spent it all on khat—' she started to say, but she fell quiet at a harsh look from her husband.

Suddenly, the .50-cal thundered over his head again. The child woke up and started to scream. Dalmar sucked harder at the leaves in his mouth as he turned back to the vehicle. '*You* get inside,' he instructed. And then, as an idea hit him: '*No! Wait!*'

He turned to the woman and child again. 'Come here,' he said.

The woman looked at him suspiciously, then started backing away into the shack.

'*Come here!*' He strode towards his wife, grabbed her by the hair, then pulled her and the screaming child out into the road. Dalmar faced the stationary vehicle, then raised his AK-47 in the air and fired it in a gesture of defiance.

'Please, Dalmar,' the wife whimpered. 'Think of the child.'

He stood behind his wife and child and grinned. They thought they were men, with their expensive truck and big gun. But his khat-addled brain persuaded him that they wouldn't fire upon an innocent woman and her child. They were the perfect shield, and Dalmar felt pleased with himself.

He would charge these people double, he decided. And none of it would go to that coward Korfa.

\*       \*       \*

In the Toyota, nobody spoke.

The man in the passenger seat watched as the idiot ahead fired his rifle in the air, then stood in the road with the woman and her child. He looked at the driver sitting next to him.

'We could just pay him,' the driver said.

The passenger shook his head. 'And let him try to rob us? With what we are carrying in the back?' He looked towards the gunman again. 'You think the boss would let us live if we mess this up?'

The driver's knuckles whitened as he gripped the steering wheel a bit more firmly. 'We have more men than him,' he countered. 'More weapons. We could overpower him easily. Do you really want to kill a woman and her child?'

The passenger thought for a moment, then spat out of the open door. 'Look at them,' he said in his raspy voice. 'Look at where they live. You think that child will live long enough to be a man to

106

fight?' He raised one eyebrow. 'Or a woman to fuck.'

And he was right, of course. These people were at the bottom of the food chain. And those at the bottom of the food chain got eaten.

He leaned out of the door again and called up to the top-gunner.

'Kill them,' he said.

The first round to be fired from the .50-cal killed the woman immediately, blowing away half her head but miraculously missing Dalmar, who was still standing behind her.

As her body slumped, the screaming baby fell to the ground. Dalmar did nothing to help his daughter. He just turned and ran. But he didn't get far. The second burst of fire followed him up the road, before slamming three rounds in a neat line up his spine. A fourth round just missed his head, but by that time he was dead.

The gunner wasn't taking any chances, though. He aimed his weapon at Dalmar's body again, discharging another short burst straight at it. The corpse shuddered from the impact of the rounds, and blood sprayed on to the road around him. When the gun fell silent, there was only one sound to be heard. The noise of a small child crying as it lay helpless on the floor.

The gunner readjusted his sights and aimed at the prostrate figure of the woman. Then he sprayed another burst of fire in her general vicinity.

And when the gun fell silent this time, there was no crying.

There was no sound at all.

The passenger pulled his door shut and the

driver started the engine. The smell of cordite permeated the air, overpowering even the diesel fumes. In the back of the van, the armed men sat down again, but this time they had their guns pointed over the edge of the truck in case the shack by the side of the road contained any unseen surprises. They didn't look overly disturbed by what had happened—gun battles were an everyday occurrence for them, after all. They did, however, glance at the silver flight case perhaps a little more frequently.

As the Toyota reached the corpses, it swerved round them.

None of the occupants looked down, so they didn't see the remains of the woman and her child, turned into mincemeat by the vicious rounds of the .50-cal. Certainly they didn't think of stopping to move them off the road. The wild animals could take care of that. They had other things to attend to, such as the safe delivery of their small cargo.

The truck swerved a second time to avoid the body of the man. Then it kicked up a bigger cloud of dust and accelerated so that soon it was just a trembling, shining mirage in the sun-ravaged distance.

# 6

*The residence of the American Ambassador, Regent's Park, London.*

Nathaniel D. Gresham looked out from one of the elegant white windows on the first floor of Winfield House on to the acres of parkland below, golden-green in the early evening sun. He'd been in the job a couple of years now, but it never failed to impress him that such a large, peaceful space should exist here in the heart of London. His days, whether at the embassy or here at the residence, were busy. To be able to take a few moments between meetings to gaze at the grass below was, for him, like taking a lungful of fresh air.

A knock on the door. With a slight pang of regret, Gresham turned back to look into the room. It was richly appointed, with a Gainsborough on the wall and finely upholstered furniture. Not quite to Gresham's taste, nor to his wife's—they thought of themselves as more modern than that. But hell, as he'd said to her more than once, you don't look a gift horse in the mouth, and as far as gift horses went, the residence was a goddamn thoroughbred.

'Come on in,' he called.

The door opened and Elsa, a young intern, appeared. She was a fine-looking thing, with a short brown bob, a little upturned nose and what Gresham thought of as a 'fuck me' face. He had to remind himself that he was fifty and she was twenty. Not that it had worried that old dog Clinton, of course, but Gresham had known Bill since his Arkansas days and was man enough to admit that the former president had been more of a pussy magnet even without the aphrodisiac of supreme power; whereas Gresham had to admit ruefully that his best days were behind him. Hell, his own breasts were only slightly smaller than Elsa's.

So he did his best not to be lecherous as he talked to the girl. 'Yes, Elsa?'

109

'Your five-thirty appointment is here, Mr Ambassador.' She looked at her clipboard. 'Mr Khan, from the Islamic Council for Peace.'

He gave her what he hoped was a fatherly smile. 'Show him in, would you?'

A minute later, Elsa opened the door again and a man entered. He was a slight-looking guy, with a short black beard, round glasses and a thin face. Kind of like a Middle Eastern Gandhi, Gresham thought to himself as he stepped forward to shake the man's hand. Come to think of it, the resemblance didn't stop at his physical features. Habib Khan had twice been nominated for the Nobel Peace Prize. People who talked about such things—and Gresham was one of them—had two theories as to why he had never been awarded the prize itself. Firstly, he wasn't a big enough celebrity. And secondly he was, by all accounts, thoroughly unpredictable. There was always a chance that he would reject the award for some high-minded reason of his own, and that would be an embarrassment the Nobel Committee couldn't countenance.

Still, no one could deny that Habib Khan had done his bit to keep the British Muslim community on the right track, and Gresham was curious to meet him. 'Mr Khan,' he announced, affecting that jolly, booming voice he always used for official meetings. 'It's a real pleasure to welcome you to Winfield House. I know you must be a busy man, and I sure appreciate you taking time out of your schedule to come see me.'

Khan bowed his head. He looked a little bit awkward, as though he thought he didn't quite deserve to be here. 'The pleasure is mine,' he said,

110

his voice quiet and his language precise. 'This is a most magnificent building, Mr Ambassador.'

'Please, call me Nat. Isn't it though?' He put one hand conspiratorially on Khan's shoulder. 'Let me tell you something—I gotta keep hoping my wife doesn't get too used to it. In my job, you never know where you'll end up next. Word is that the embassy in Kabul's a bunch of crap.' He laughed at his own joke, then winced inwardly when he realised Khan was uncomfortable with that kind of language. 'What can I get you, Mr Khan? Tea? I'm more of a coffee man myself, but please—whatever you like.'

Khan held up one hand. 'Nothing, really,' he said.

Gresham looked over at the intern. 'Thank you, Elsa,' he said, and she quietly left the room.

'Have a seat, Mr Khan.' The ambassador led his guest to one of the sofas surrounding a glass coffee table, and they sat down together. 'You're probably wondering,' he said, 'why I've invited you here.'

Khan smiled. 'The thought had crossed my mind,' he said.

'Sure, sure.' He moulded his face into a more serious expression. 'Mr Khan,' he continued. 'For reasons of security, I'd appreciate it if this conversation went no further than ourselves for the time being.'

'Of course, Mr— Of course, *Nat*.'

They smiled at each other.

'The President will be making a visit to London this year on July seventh. He'll be dining at the Houses of Parliament, then giving a speech to reinforce the special relationship that exists

111

between Great Britain and the United States. He feels that to do this on the anniversary of the London bombings will be an effective way of reminding the world why the Coalition remains in Afghanistan, and what our aims are. There will be all the usual . . .' He rolled his hand in the air as he searched for a word. 'All the usual flummery—an audience with the Queen, the usual meet-and-greets. I'll be straight with you, Mr Khan—most of that stuff is window dressing, nothing more, but the President is keen to do some real work while he's here. He's aware of your efforts, and those of your organisation, to promote the peaceful observance of Islam, and he's very keen for me to arrange a meeting. To show the world that our fight is not with Islam itself, but with extremism.' Gresham interlinked his fingers and laid his hands on his ample stomach. 'Is that something that might appeal?' He didn't wait for an answer, but continued to gabble. 'The President arrives at RAF Northolt at about five-thirty p.m. on the seventh. From there he goes straight to Parliament, so really the rest of that day is out. But he'll be staying here overnight and has a lunchtime audience with Her Majesty before returning to Washington, so perhaps breakfast here on the eighth? We could arrange a photo call for ten a.m. ?'

Gresham leaned back. If he was honest, this was one of the most enjoyable parts of the job. Offering an audience with the world's most powerful man made him feel powerful himself.

Khan removed his spectacles, cleaned them on his rather unfashionable tie, then returned them to his nose. 'Nat,' he said, 'that is a most thoughtful offer. I regret immensely that I must decline.'

Gresham blinked. Decline? *Nobody* declined. If the President of the United States wanted a meeting with this guy, he *got* a meeting with this guy. Washington would go nuts if he reported back that he'd said no.

'Ah, Mr Khan,' he said delicately. 'Please don't feel obliged to give me your answer now. Perhaps you could think about it overnight.'

Khan gave him a gentle smile. 'Mr Ambassador,' he said, 'that is very kind of you. But I do not need to give the matter any more consideration.'

Gresham frowned. This was beginning to be tiresome. 'May I ask why?'

'Of course,' Khan replied. He stood up and walked over to the window. 'Your President,' he said, 'is a good man. In the struggle for peace between Islam and the West—and I truly believe, Nat, that this is the principal struggle of our times—he is a tireless fighter. You and I know that, because we see things how they are.' He turned to look back at the ambassador. 'But there are many people who do *not* see things as they are, Nat. Their view of the world is filtered through a film of hatred and misunderstanding. It is these people—these extremists and terrorists in waiting—that I must reach out to. If they have the impression that I am too close to your President, a man who—forgive me—they despise with all their heart, any good I can achieve will be immediately undone.'

Gresham stared at him. In his world, the world of politics and public relations, anyone would give their eye teeth for a photo op with the President. It wouldn't be anything to do with their cause,

113

whatever that happened to be, and everything to do with their own vanity.

But not this guy, it seemed. Habib Khan, with his owl-like features and understated presence, didn't *have* any vanity—at least none that Gresham could detect.

Khan clearly noticed that the ambassador was at a loss for words, and so he filled the awkward silence. 'Your President and I,' he said, 'want the same thing. We want peace. But we must go about it in different ways. I hope he will understand that.'

He offered his hand and Gresham shook it, not knowing quite what to say.

'Thank you for your time, Nat. I have enjoyed our meeting.'

'Me too,' Gresham murmured, 'me too.' And then, as Khan headed towards the door to leave, he spoke up. 'Mr Khan!'

'Yes, Nat?'

'We keep the details of the President's foreign engagements under wraps for obvious security reasons. The announcement of his visit won't be made until the day before. I can rely on you to respect that, of course.'

'Of course.'

Khan smiled, nodded and quietly left the room, leaving Gresham to stare once more out of the window at the parkland beyond.

\*     \*     \*

The Horse and Three Feathers, a stone's throw from the Falls Road, had a colourful past. During the Troubles it had been a well-known Republican hang-out. Stories abounded about what would

114

happen if a Loyalist stuck his nose past the front door, but stories were all they were because no one ever did. This was PIRA turf, pure and simple.

Times had changed, but the Horse and Three Feathers hadn't. Not really. If any stray tourists happened to venture in here, they'd have to be pretty thick-skinned not to realise how unwelcome they were. The management of this pub wasn't fussed about customers, after all.

Kieran O'Callaghan stepped into the main lounge bar. It was dim in here, dingy enough to hide the fact that the red fabric on the seats was almost uniformly worn through, and The Corrs played blandly in the background. Behind the bar, a fat woman with a bored expression and huge arse sat smoking a cigarette and reading a newspaper. It sometimes seemed to Kieran that Fat Betty had been in that exact same position for twenty years. She was as much a part of the furniture as the defunct cigarette machine hanging on the wall, or the sticky, shamrock-green carpet. Betty was like a gatekeeper. No one got in to see Cormac O'Callaghan without getting past her.

She looked up at Kieran, then nodded at him. 'He's waiting for you,' she said.

Kieran sniffed, looked around the empty room, then walked towards her. At the end of the bar was a section that could be raised to allow access to the serving area. He did so, then squeezed past the fat woman, along a row of optics that hadn't been changed for months, through a door that led into a thin corridor, and from there into a back room.

It was dark in here, too, lit by a single low-wattage bulb hanging by a cord from the ceiling. This had once been the games room of the pub, and there was still a pool table and a football table in the middle. They were seldom used, however. No one came here to play games. No one came here for any reason other than to have an audience with Cormac. Why would they? It was a dump. Kieran could never understand it. His uncle must have been one of the richest men in Belfast, but he still lived as if he were some shitkicker from the estates. Sometimes he wondered if money meant anything to Cormac, other than just a way of keeping the score.

'You're late.'

Cormac's voice was as rough as his surroundings. Kieran licked his lips. They were dry. Just looking at his uncle, knowing what he was about to do, made his skin cold and sweat drip down the nape of his neck.

'Sorry about that, Cormac,' he said. 'Trouble at home with little Jackie. The missus is—'

'I've got a little job for you. The usual. Sit down.'

Kieran hesitated. His right hand was in his pocket and he was absent-mindedly fiddling with the listening device the pig bitch had given him.

'I said, sit down.'

Kieran did as he was told, taking a seat on the other side of the small, round pub table at which Cormac was himself sitting. Kieran's uncle's face was thin and lined, his eyebrows as grey and bushy as his hair. His skin was inexplicably tanned for someone who spent almost all his time in this dimly lit room, and on one side of his mouth there was a scar that followed the line a clown would paint to give himself a big smile. The scar didn't make Cormac O'Callaghan look happy, though. Not even half happy.

Far from it.

He was a thin man, and he wore—as he always did, no matter what the weather—a heavy overcoat. Some people said he favoured this garment because he could easily hide weapons underneath it; others said that it was because he wanted to look more impressively built than he actually was. Kieran didn't believe either suggestion. Cormac was too smart to carry firearms; and he had no need to appear more threatening than he actually was. Tales of his ruthlessness and brutality were almost part of the fabric of Belfast.

If you weren't scared of Cormac O'Callaghan, it was because you hadn't heard those tales.

'When you say the usual, Cormac . . .'

'Young Michael Elliott is giving me grave cause for concern, Kieran. I think we need to make sure that we can rely on his continued support, do you not?'

Kieran felt a twist in his stomach. 'If you say so, Cormac,' he said, his voice several notches quieter.

'I *do* say so. You know the drill.'

Kieran nodded. He knew. His uncle ran his drug distribution network by fear. Every so often—at irregular intervals and without warning—he would decide to make an example of one of his employees, then spread the word that the unfortunate victim had been tempted by disloyalty. It didn't matter that it wasn't true—nobody was going to go to the police, after all—but it was certainly effective at keeping the workforce on their toes.

But Mikey Elliott. No one could be more loyal than him; and no one had more to lose.

Kieran stood up and wandered over to the football table, standing on the side furthest from Cormac. He spun one of the rows of men round. Mickey had a family, two kids not much older than Kieran's own little Jackie.

'Are you sure, Cormac? I mean, Michael Elliott, with the young 'uns and all . . .'

His speech faded away under the withering heat of his uncle's gaze.

'I'd hate to think,' the older man said in little more than a whisper, 'that it was *you*, Kieran, whose loyalty was in doubt. My own flesh and blood.'

It was all Kieran could do to look his uncle in the eye. 'Course not,' he said. But what he really thought was, *If you'd do this to Mikey, what's to say you wouldn't do it to me? And where would that leave little Jackie then? And where does it leave me? Should I play for your side, or the police's side?*

*Or maybe,* he thought to himself, *maybe I can play for both.*

He casually felt the underside of the football table. Cold metal, so he pulled the listening device from his pocket and held it underneath the table. Immediately he felt it being sucked firmly up.

'Course not,' he repeated, deeply aware that his voice was quavering slightly.

Cormac didn't notice the quaver—or if he did he gave no indication. 'Then do it,' he said. Across the table he pushed a small piece of paper. Kieran walked back towards him and picked it up. An address scrawled in spidery writing. 'There's tools for the job stashed here, along with one or two other bits and pieces. Take what you need and be sure to replace them when you're done. I want it

118

done quickly, Kieran. Tonight. Don't let me down.'

Kieran nodded and put the scrap of paper in the pocket recently vacated by the listening device.

'I won't let you down, Cormac,' he said. 'You know you don't need to worry about that.'

Kieran couldn't get out of there fast enough. He nodded, then turned and left, squeezing past Fat Betty and out into the relatively fresh air of the Belfast dusk.

\*          \*          \*

Mikey Elliott lived in a good part of Belfast, near Osbourne Drive just off Lisburn Road. Whereas most of the men who earned their living working for Cormac's drug empire squandered their cash-in-hand earnings, Mikey put his own income to good use. The semi-detached house outside which Kieran now stood was trim, almost middle-class. The hedge had been recently cut, and a child's bike lay in the driveway.

Kieran took a moment to steady himself. The handgun that he'd acquired from Cormac's lock-up weighed heavily on the inside of his jacket; the job weighed heavily on his mind. Mikey was a good man. A friend—or as near to a friend as Kieran had. His blood tie to Cormac meant that people always trod lightly around him.

He stepped round the child's bike as he approached the house, then knocked on the door. Mikey's wife answered. Maddy was a good-looking woman, but as fiery as her flame-red hair. Her piercing green eyes now looked at him with suspicion.

'What is it, Kieran? We're about to go to bed.'

She didn't like him and she never had.

'I just wondered if I might have a quick word with Mikey.' He gave her what he hoped was a reassuring smile. 'Business, you know. Won't take a minute.'

Maddy didn't move from the doorway. Instead she looked over her shoulder and called to her husband. When Mikey appeared he had a beer in his hand and a slightly vague look on his face. He'd been drinking. Might make it easier, might make it harder. Could go either way.

'Let the man in, Maddy,' he said.

Maddy stepped aside, but she didn't look any less unwelcoming as Kieran stepped past her. 'Is there somewhere we can talk?' he asked Mikey.

Mikey looked at his wife. 'Why don't you go upstairs and check on the boys, my love?' he said. 'Kieran and I won't be long.'

Maddy gave them both a cool look. But she knew her place. She shut the door and wordlessly climbed the stairs.

The men walked through the ground floor of the house until they reached a living room at the back. The decor was chintzy, but it was comfortable enough, with a large sofa and smoked-glass coffee table. Mikey was a music lover, and he had a large selection of classical music CDs that took up most of one wall. Kieran's host pulled a bottle of Jameson's and a couple of glasses from a cabinet at one end of the room, before pouring out two shots and handing one to Kieran.

'That's quite a collection,' Kieran said, nodding at the CDs.

'More than a thousand,' Mikey replied. 'More Beethoven there than you get at the Waterfront

Hall. So what's the craic? Business good, as far as I can see.'

'Put one of those CDs on, why don't you?'

Mikey shook his head and pointed at the ceiling. 'The kids,' he said. 'Wouldn't want to wake them.'

'Put one on, Mikey.' Kieran took a sip from his glass.

Mikey's eyes narrowed, but he did as he was told. Classical music seeped through the speakers of his stereo system. Kieran's eyes caught the CD box. Wagner. It meant nothing to him. That shit all sounded the same to his ears. But as the orchestral strings swelled, he pulled his handgun from his pocket.

'Sit down, Mikey,' he said as he nudged the gun in the direction of the sofa.

Mikey didn't seem to know, as he stepped backwards, whether to look at the gun or at Kieran's face. He'd gone white, though. He flopped backwards on to the sofa as the music grew louder.

Kieran placed the whiskey bottle on the table. 'Go ahead,' he told his friend. 'Pour yourself another.'

Mikey did—half a tumbler, which he necked in a single gulp.

'Nice music,' Kieran said, as if he was just making idle conversation.

'Jesus, Kieran. What the fu—'

'I've got a message from Cormac. He's worried, Mikey. Worried that he can't trust you. Worried that he might have a rat on his hands.'

Mikey shook his head. 'For God's sake, Kieran. I'm not a rat . . .'

And Kieran knew it was true. He also knew that

121

if he'd tried harder, perhaps he'd have been able to talk Cormac out of making an example of the terrified man in front of him. As he stood over his friend, though, the image of the female cop rose in his mind. She had him by the bollocks, and his only option was to carry out Cormac's instructions to the letter if his uncle wasn't going to start getting suspicious.

'That's not what Cormac thinks, Mikey.' He raised the gun, pointing it at his victim's head.

A trumpet fanfare over the speakers. And, almost as if someone had orchestrated it, Kieran saw a wet patch spread across Mikey's crotch; moments later, liquid started dripping from the hem of his trousers.

'*Will you not turn that music down, Mikey?*' Maddy yelled from upstairs.

'Mind your own business, woman,' Mikey shouted back. Then he closed his eyes and spoke more quietly. 'I've got kids, Kieran . . .' he whispered. 'You can't leave them without a pa—'

'Turn round, Mikey. Hands on your head.'

Mikey was shivering with fear. He'd performed enough punishments like this himself, so he knew what was coming. It looked like a huge effort to twist his body round so that he was face down on the seat of the sofa, his legs kneeling on the floor, his hands on the back of his head.

The music was loud now. Just loud enough. Mikey's head was pressed into the cushions so he didn't see Kieran lower the weapon so that it was pointing not at his head, but at his bent left knee.

Kieran sniffed.

Then fired.

Kieran liked to think of himself as something of

a kneecapping expert, thanks to his days in the nutting squads. A shot through the front of the knee was commonplace for minor offences; going through the back like this was a more serious punishment because it would fuck up all the soft tissue and blow the kneecap away from the body— a much more difficult wound to repair. But the surgeons had begun to get adept at both, so the nutting squads started targeting the ankle. You'd need Christ Almighty himself to lay hands on you if you wanted to be healed from a wound like that.

During the Troubles, punishments like this were two a penny. Nowadays a kneecapping was rarer, but just because the IRA had gone the way of the dodo, it didn't mean their techniques had. It was a messy business. As the round slammed into Mikey, his whole body shook like he'd been given an electric shock, and blood sprayed over the carpet, some even landing on Kieran's shoes.

And then the scream. There weren't many more painful places to shoot a man. Mikey's short, sharp scream only stopped because he bit on the fabric of the sofa. By that time, though, Kieran was already walking out of the room. He strode to the front of the house and quietly let himself out.

Outside, he could still just hear the Wagner playing. Tucking his gun back into his coat, he bent down and picked up the child's bicycle. As he propped it neatly against the wall, he knocked a button on a brightly coloured electronic bell. It started playing the theme tune from a children's programme that Kieran vaguely recognised from when little Jackie watched TV at home.

He stood in the darkness and listened to it for a few seconds, but that was all. The gun needed returning, and he didn't want to be in the vicinity when the ambulance arrived.

# 27 JUNE

# 7

In the Strandtown Police Station in East Belfast, two officers sat in the corner of a large, busy room. Photocopiers chuntered under the strip lighting; colleagues examined wall-mounted maps of the city; secretaries typed up SOCO reports. One of the officers—an older man with a balding head, a tubby stomach and tufts of chest hair escaping from the top of his open-neck shirt—had his feet up on his table and a half-drunk plastic cup of coffee in his hands. If he worried that his boss—a DCI sitting alone in the glass-walled office in the far corner of the room—might disapprove of his inactivity, he didn't show it.

The other man was much younger and new to the Drugs Squad. You could tell at a glance. He sat up straight and wore a jacket and tie. Both men had their gaze firmly fixed on one of their female colleagues—shoulder-length blonde hair, large eyes, figure-hugging jeans and a leather jacket. Their eyes followed her as she headed towards the door, like spectators at a tennis match watching the ball.

As she walked out of the room, the rookie looked at his colleague. 'I wouldn't throw her out of bed for farting.' He grinned.

'With an arse like that, I wouldn't throw her out of bed for shitting on the pillow.' The older cop's voice sounded like a thousand cigarettes. 'But take some advice and forget about it, Danny boy. You might as well stick your johnson in a cigar trimmer as start chasing that bit of tail.'

Danny gave him a casual look. 'What's the matter, Frank? Wanting to keep her for yourself? Face it, man, you're an old-timer. You should just step back and let the young 'uns take a crack . . .'

Frank Maloney sighed, hauled his feet off the table and turned to look at his partner. 'Listen and learn, Danny boy,' he said. 'That piece of eye candy getting you all chubbed up is Siobhan Byrne. Currently officer in Her Majesty's Drugs Squad, formerly of the Det. Mean anything to you?'

Danny shook his head.

'Hmm . . .' Frank breathed. *The Det,*' he said clearly, like he was talking to a child, '*14 Company*. Jesus, where've you been for the last twenty years? Oh, I forgot—having your little botty wiped by your mam.'

'Go fuck yourself, Frank.'

'Happy to, Danny boy.' He brushed some imaginary crumbs from his paunch-filled shirt. 'Closest I get to a half-decent shag these days, anyhow. But allow me to enlighten you with my great and superior experience. The Det: the best surveillance operatives in the world, trained up in Hereford by the SAS to work in the Province—you know who the SAS are, do you?'

'Very funny, Frank.'

'Aren't I though? You're too young to remember how much the Provos hated the Det, Danny boy. That's why agents like your girlfriend there had to be ready for the worst. Those Regiment lads used to administer beatings to the Det in training far worse than anything they had to deal with themselves, and with good reason. Ever heard of Operation Congo, lad?'

Danny shook his head.

'It's what they put in place if a Det officer ever went missing in the Province. Every operation stopped, every military and police asset was directed to recover them, because they knew it'd be curtains for the poor bastard the minute the Provos got their clutches on them. Don't you worry about it, lad—that girl's harder than a gravedigger's heart. I'll bet you a pint of plain that she's pulled more pieces on our Republican brothers than you've had hot dinners, but she wouldn't need a PPK to put *you* in the Royal if you got fresh with her. Unarmed combat being one of their specialities and all.'

Danny smiled. 'Ah, c'mon, Frank.'

Frank shrugged. 'What more can I say, Danny boy? Go ahead and give it a crack.' He put his feet back on the desk. 'They're your bollocks.'

'So if she's such a fucking wonder woman, what's she doing chasing drugs with the rest of us?'

Frank took a sip from his coffee, then made a sour face. He shrugged and downed the rest of it anyway. 'Word is,' he continued, 'she had a kid. Off the rails. Junkie. Usual story. Went missing three years ago. She transferred to our unit and since then she's been like a dog with a fucking bone. No personal life, no nothing. On the job 24/7.' He smiled. 'Which wouldn't leave a lot of time for you, Danny boy, now would it?'

Danny sniffed. 'Ah well,' he said, 'you know what they say. Don't dip your pen in the company inkwell.'

'You're a fast learner,' said Frank. He looked at his colleague's desk. 'You finished that report yet, lad?'

Danny shook his head, then turned back to his

129

computer and continued his slow, two-fingered typing.

Kids, Frank Maloney thought to himself. Fucking useless, the lot of them. No wonder the country's gone to the dogs.

\*       \*       \*

Siobhan Byrne had important things on her mind.

Like meeting with Kieran.

Her tout looked bad. Really bad. He stood across the street from the safe house, leaning against a tree and chain-smoking the thin roll-ups that lasted a couple of minutes before he had to roll another. Siobhan didn't acknowledge him as she entered the house. She knew he'd walk through the door in his own time—when he could be sure there was no one watching.

And he did. The smell of his cigarettes entered with him as he gave Siobhan a surly look.

'C'mon now, Kieran,' she said with a mocking little lilt to her voice. 'Can we not just be friends?' And then, when he didn't reply: 'You look like shit.'

'Didn't sleep well.'

'Little Jackie keeping you up?'

Kieran shook his head. 'Let's just say I had a bit of knees-up with an old friend.' He put his hand in his back pocket and fished out a scrap of paper, which he handed to Siobhan without looking her in the eye. Siobhan examined it. An address in the west of the city.

'What's this?'

Her tout started to roll another ciggy. Siobhan waited while he licked the skin, removed a packet of Swan Vestas from his pocket and lit up. 'A lock-up,' he said once he had taken a deep drag. 'One of my uncle's. A new one. You'll find stuff there.'

'What sort of stuff, Kieran?'

Kieran shrugged. 'You know. Guns, money, a bit of product . . .'

Siobhan nodded. 'There,' she said. 'Now that wasn't really so difficult, was it?'

The tout finished his cigarette. 'So,' he said, avoiding Siobhan's eye, 'are we good now?'

Siobhan blinked. 'Are we *what*?'

'I've given you good stuff on Cormac. Debt paid.'

She started to laugh.

'What's so fucking funny? Will you not stop laughing, woman?'

'I'm sorry, Kieran. It's just . . . Did you *really* think that would be enough to get me out of your hair? You and me are going to be having these little get-togethers until your uncle is behind bars. You start relaxing, Kieran, and you'll be joining him.' She waved the piece of paper in his face. 'This is all right, Kieran, but it's just a start. You'd better keep these tidbits coming.'

'Jesus, woman. It's not as easy as that, you know.'

He started rolling another ciggy and Siobhan noticed that his hands were shaking.

'I didn't promise you easy, Kieran. Easy doesn't come into it.'

Kieran looked up, suddenly murderous. Siobhan found her fingers edging towards her concealed firearm. 'Careful now, Kieran. I've floored tougher bastards than you. Don't go doing anything stupid.'

In the end her tout just spat copiously on the floor.

'Did you plant the listening device?'

131

He nodded. 'Under the football table.'

'Anything more to tell me?'

'Yeah. If you didn't have my balls in a G-clamp, I'd fuck you over so bad you'd be begging me to put you out of your misery.'

'You're a charmer, Kieran, I don't care what anyone says. But actually I was thinking more along the lines of Cormac's bent police officer. You have any more information on that?'

'If I did, I'd tell you, wouldn't I?'

'Sure, I hope so, Kieran,' Siobhan told him with an exaggerated sigh. 'For your own sake, I really hope so.'

*       *       *

It looked like it was going to be a long shift for Dr Sandra Philips at the Royal Victoria Hospital in Belfast, but that was nothing new. Every shift was twelve hours long in the intensive care unit. The beds were full and they were turning people away, diverting them to nearby ICUs. In the last hour, they'd had to make the call to divert two road-crash victims to City because they just didn't have room for them here.

It was always difficult to turn patients away, but doubly so tonight. They'd given the last bed to a comatose junkie from some estate in the north of the city. Didn't seem quite right that she should get the care when the others couldn't, but there was nothing Sandra could do about that. Her job wasn't to judge her patients; it was to make them better, and she'd have her work cut out with this girl. She checked her vital signs. Weak but stable— just. The kid looked like something from a science

132

fiction movie, though, with all the tubes and needles and drips that covered her body.

'She looks bad.' Dr Philips looked at the young uniformed scene-of-crime officer who stood at a respectful distance from the bed. 'I mean,' the officer continued, 'face as white as a—'

'This is the ICU, officer,' Dr Philips interrupted him. 'You'll find that most people here tend not to look like they've come back from two weeks on the Costa del Sol. You can do it now, but be quick please.'

The officer nodded and Philips watched as he opened a small plastic box containing his fingerprint kit. She didn't offer to help as he awkwardly raised one of the patient's limp hands to take her prints. She was firmly of the opinion that this sort of thing should wait until the patients were out of the ICU. She had to admit, though, that could be a long time for this one. Still, she stood by thin-lipped as the young officer completed his work.

'Her personal effects?' the officer asked.

Dr Philips handed him a plastic tray. It contained a single Yale key, a condom, a crushed packet of cigarettes and a photograph. 'I'll need to take these,' he said, producing a see-through evidence bag and dropping them inside. 'I can return them once they're properly logged.'

'Whatever,' Dr Philips said. 'I'd like you to leave me alone with my patient now.'

The officer left without saying another word.

\*       \*       \*

Siobhan wouldn't be walking straight into the lock-

133

up. That would be stupid. Kieran was a tout, and touts were by their very nature untrustworthy little shits. She wanted to be very sure this wasn't a set-up.

She parked her car—a dented brown Volvo—a good half-mile from the location. She wanted to stake the place out, but a car would be no good for that. Someone sitting in a vehicle by herself for a few hours would stick out. She needed to blend in, and for that reason she had placed a child's car seat in the back of the car, with a doll wrapped in blankets strapped into it. Siobhan opened up the boot and set up a buggy she had stashed inside. She gently removed the doll from the car seat and strapped it carefully into the buggy. Then she took a bag from the back seat. It was bright pink and padded, the size of a large handbag, the sort of thing every mum carries when she's out with her baby. But this bag sure as hell didn't contain any nappies. She shoved it under the buggy, then started to walk. Just another mother, out for a stroll with her kid.

The lock-up was an old garage that belonged to an apartment in a low-rise block on the northern edge of Belfast.

Siobhan entered the block with her buggy and took the lift, which stank of shit, to the top floor. She passed no one. Siobhan knew these buildings from the past, and she knew what she was looking for. She found it soon enough: a fire door. A sign on the door warned that it was alarmed, but she'd have bet her own apartment that the alarm mechanism hadn't worked for years. She was right. Nothing happened as she pushed it open, checked nobody was there, then carried her buggy up a thin metal staircase on to the roof of the building.

The roof was littered with rubbish—beer cans, plastic bags, a used condom draped over the end of a television aerial like a flag. Siobhan ignored all that while she got her bearings before settling down by the low perimeter wall overlooking the lock-up. She turned off her mobile phone. The ringtone would act like a beacon, and anyway, she didn't want to be disturbed. Concentration was everything.

It was cold up here. The afternoon sky was overcast and the wind was stronger than it was down on the ground. Siobhan pulled her jacket more tightly round her body and prepared to shiver. She'd give it till nightfall. Any suspicious activity before then, anything to suggest that she was walking into something, and she'd abort. Till then, the only thing to do was watch.

And wait.

\*　　　\*　　　\*

It had taken the SOCO ten minutes to get back to the station and ten minutes to scan the prints. Routine stuff. He'd done this enough times to know what he was likely to bring up. The junkie would no doubt have a string of small offences on file. Petty theft, mostly; shoplifting; a bit of soliciting if she'd been desperate. And sure enough, as the computer screen in front of him brought up a match, he saw pretty much what he'd expected. The name was Alice Stevens. He scanned down the criminal record: three counts of shoplifting, two warnings for possession of a prohibited substance. He shrugged, then emptied the contents of the evidence bag on to the table and started typing the details into the computer.

A door opened and another officer walked in. Yvonne Evans was an old-timer. But unlike most of them, she hadn't been tempted to climb the greasy pole to a cushy office job. She liked to work cases and that made her popular with the younger ones.

The officer nodded at her; he didn't even complain when she started looking over his shoulder at what he was doing. But he was surprised when she bent over and picked up the photo.

'Where the hell did you get this?' she asked.

'Personal effects of a junkie that just landed in the Royal. Boyfriend OD'd.' He looked up at her. 'You OK?'

She didn't look OK. Her face had gone white.

'Mind if I keep this?' she asked.

He frowned. 'It's evidence, Yvonne . . .'

'Favour to me?'

He exhaled heavily. 'We never had this conversation, right?'

'Course not.' She walked promptly out, taking the photo with her.

\*    \*    \*

Siobhan waited and watched.

At about 15.00 hrs a group of kids turned up and started playing football against the line of garages. They gave up pretty soon when it started to spit with rain; Siobhan just stayed where she was. Immobile. Ever watchful. She'd been on enough stake-outs to know that they were made up of long periods of boredom punctuated, if you were lucky, by a few seconds of activity. You couldn't let your attention wander. You had to stay on it.

A car arrived. The owner climbed out, then opened up the garage three along from Siobhan's before parking the car inside, locking it up again and disappearing. Siobhan looked at her watch. 16.38 hrs. More drizzle. Her skin was damp. Clammy. She didn't move. She kept watching.

It was as the sky was getting dark that the rain became heavier. Siobhan grabbed her chance. Rain was a good time to do anything under the radar. It kept people off the streets, meant she could go about her business unobserved. She hurried away from the roof and back down the lift with her buggy, checking that her handgun was safely strapped to her body and slinging the nappy bag over her shoulder.

Back on the ground, she scoped the area around the lock-up once more before approaching it. Nothing. And no street lamp to illuminate her. Just large droplets exploding on the tarmac.

She walked swiftly to the lock-up.

It was sealed with a heavy padlock, but that wouldn't be a problem. In her nappy bag, Siobhan had a set of picks and a tension wrench that she could have used blindfolded. Less than a minute at the entrance to the garage and the lock clicked. She opened the door and slipped inside with the buggy before closing the door behind her.

It was dark. Siobhan stepped to one side, feeling her way to the right-hand corner. She loosened her handgun from its holster then held it out towards the entrance. She'd give it five minutes. If anyone was following her in, she'd have the advantage.

It took about twenty seconds for her vision to adjust to the darkness, but the only sound was of her own breathing.

The minutes passed. No one came.

From the nappy bag she drew a thin torch. She had covered the lens with a red filter—white light would affect her night vision, whereas red light wouldn't—and blocked out the edges of the filter with some thick black gaffer tape so that she had a small, highly directional beam. Siobhan loosened her handgun from its holster and then, with the weapon in one hand and the torch resting on top of it in the other, she stepped further into the lock-up, illuminating everything ahead of her with a red glow.

It was a biggish garage, maybe six metres by four, but largely empty. The faint smell of oil in the air suggested it had once housed a car, but if this really was an O'Callaghan lock-up, Siobhan knew they wouldn't be so stupid as to keep a vehicle here any more. They were too easy to track back to the owner. No, she felt sure that there would be nothing here to link the place with Cormac. He was too cute for that.

There was shelving along the left wall, filled with half-empty pots of paint, a few brushes and a bottle of white spirit. An old bicycle lay on the floor, one wheel detached. And along the back wall, three metal cabinets with dented doors. Siobhan approached them. They were locked, of course, but these cabinets were even easier to pick than the main padlock had been. In next to no time, they were open.

The first cabinet contained money, wads of tens, used. Twenty grand, minimum, Siobhan reckoned.

138

An easy stash to get hold of should anyone need to disappear in a hurry. The second cabinet held weapons and ammo. Two shotguns, expertly sawn off, and a 9 mm Beretta. It was the third cabinet, though, that interested her. Tupperware boxes. Four of them. Filled to the brim with a pure white powder.

Siobhan didn't need to taste it to know what it was, and she had to fight an urge to take the boxes of heroin and empty them down a drain. But she was in this for the long game, and needed to leave everything untouched. From her bag she removed a small camera that she had modified specially to take pictures using an infrared flash. She quickly snapped the stash, the guns and the money, then relocked the cabinets with her picks. Back home she would carefully write up her notes, detailing where, when and why the pictures were taken. It wouldn't be enough to bring a charge against anyone, but as corroborating evidence further down the line, it might be worth something...

She headed back to the door. One ear against the thin metal told her it was still raining heavily outside. That was good. She secreted her torch and camera in her nappy bag, reholstered the gun and slipped out of the garage. Moments later the padlock was fastened and Siobhan Byrne was pushing her baby back to her car. Not too fast, not too slow.

Doing nothing to draw attention to herself...

Back in the car, she strapped the baby into its seat, stashed the buggy, then got the heating going. She was soaked through and shivering and could think of nothing but getting home and getting warm. As she kicked the engine into life and pulled out into the road, she eased her mobile out of her pocket, switched it on and put it to her ear to listen to her messages.

Just one. A woman's voice, slightly uncertain of itself.

'Siobhan, this is Yvonne. You need to call me back as soon as you get this. It's important.'

She sighed. Yvonne and she went way back. She was a nice girl, but neurotic. Siobhan was cold, wet and not in the mood, but she'd be even less in the mood when she got home, so she dialled her number.

The phone was answered immediately.

'Yvonne, it's me.'

'Siobhan.' She sounded relieved.

'What's wrong?'

'Where are you? Are you with anyone?'

'No, I'm in the car. Look Yvonne, I'm very—'

'I've just been speaking to a scene-of-crime officer. He's dealing with a young girl, drug addict. She's in the Royal now.'

'And?'

'He was going through her personal effects.'

'Yvonne, I've had a long day—'

'*Listen* to me, Siobhan. She had a photograph on her. Just an old Polaroid. I don't know how old it is.'

'Uh-huh . . .'

'I recognise the girl in the photo, Siobhan. I'd know her anywhere.'

'Who was it?'

A pause.

And then, with a catch in her voice, Yvonne spoke. 'It's Lily,' she said. 'It's your daughter.'

Everything was a blur. The lights of Belfast, the traffic, everything. As Siobhan floored it to Yvonne's house, her friend's voice rang in her head. *It's Lily. It's your daughter . . .* She felt sick with apprehension. A small part of her mind hoped Yvonne was mistaken, that the picture she had found wasn't Lily at all. Ever since her daughter had disappeared she had dreaded receiving any information about her because she knew, in all likelihood, the news would be bad. The worst . . .

But Yvonne wasn't mistaken. She stood on the doorstep of her two-up two-down, her eyes wide with sympathy as Siobhan stared numbly at the Polaroid.

'Where's the girl who had this?' she demanded.

'Siobhan,' Yvonne said, 'you should go through the proper—'

'*Where is she?*'

Yvonne sighed, and told her.

'The boyfriend. What do we know about him?'

'One of O'Callaghan's crew. At least he used to be. Started dabbling with his own product. No good to anyone after that.'

O'Callaghan. Everywhere she turned, his name cropped up.

Thirty minutes later she was glancing through the window of the door leading into the ICU of the Royal, the dog-eared Polaroid in her hand.

The place was silent—a row of beds, their occupants cabled up to complicated machines and life-support systems. There was one doctor on duty, who stood at the end of one of the beds with

141

a clipboard in her hand. Siobhan steeled herself, and walked in.

The doctor looked at her in shock. 'Excuse me, this is the ICU. Members of the public—'

Siobhan held out her police ID. 'Detective Inspector Byrne. I need to speak to Alice Stevens, Dr . . .'

'Dr Philips. And Miss Stevens is in no state to speak to anyone.'

Siobhan gave her a hard glare. 'We've got two options,' she said. 'Either you let me speak to the girl, or I arrest you now for obstructing a police investigation.' She kept the glare up, hoping that this doctor wouldn't realise how many regulations Siobhan was breaking.

A silence. And then . . .

'Five minutes, not a second more. Third bed along.' And with an unfriendly look she walked to the other end of the unit.

Siobhan approached the girl's bed. She looked a mess. Desperately thin, her chest rose only fractionally. A clear oxygen mask covered her mouth and nose, a saline drip sprouted from her right hand and she looked like she was barely hanging on.

But she was awake.

Siobhan sat by her side. 'Alice,' she whispered. 'I need to talk to you.'

Alice's head stayed still, but her eyes moved to the right. 'Who are you?' she breathed. Her voice was muffled because of the oxygen mask, which clouded over with water vapour as she spoke.

Siobhan didn't answer that question. She just held up the photograph. 'I need to know where this girl is. I think you can help me.'

The patient glanced at the photo, then her eyes fell shut. She didn't say anything.

'Alice? *Alice?*' Siobhan put one hand on the patient's arm and shook her gently. Her eyes opened. 'Where is she, Alice? I have to know.'

'You the filth?' Alice asked. And when Siobhan didn't answer: 'You *are* the fucking filth. Piss off.'

'I'm not the police, Alice,' Siobhan lied.

'Then why're you so interested in Lily?'

'She's my daughter. If she's in trouble, you've got to let me help her.'

'She doesn't want your help.'

'Then let her tell me that to my face.'

Alice looked like she was thinking about it. 'I don't believe you're not the police,' she said. 'I'm not telling you anything.'

Siobhan glanced over her shoulder. Dr Philips was at the other end of the ICU, clipboard in hand, recording the vital signs of another patient. The police officer turned back to Alice and began to examine the tubes emerging from her body. The saline drip would be no good. Remove that and it would take an hour or so for it to have any effect on the girl. But the oxygen mask was a different matter. It had two small ventilation holes on either side, and a clear pipe that snaked from the bottom of the mask, across her chest and towards a dull green oxygen canister on the opposite side of the bed. Without hesitation, Siobhan used two fingers on her left hand to cover up the ventilation holes on the mask; with her right hand she gently lifted the pipe and held it up so the girl could see what she was doing. Then she bent it, creating a kink in the pipe and stopping the patient's precious oxygen flow.

143

It took about five seconds for Alice to realise what was happening. She opened her mouth to cry out, but she was too weak and in any case the lack of oxygen had an immediate effect. She gasped and Siobhan felt the suction pulling the mask against her skin. The patient's eyes widened and her feeble body shook. Siobhan gave it ten seconds, then released her grip on the oxygen tube and removed her fingers from the mask.

Alice's breath came in short gasps and it took a minute for her to breathe normally again. 'Listen to me, Alice,' Siobhan whispered. 'I'm not messing around. Next time, they'll be sending a hospital porter in to take you down to the morgue. Understand?'

Alice just looked at her like she was looking at a monster.

'Where's Lily?'

'I don't know,' she whispered.

'Is she a friend of yours?'

Alice nodded. 'She was. I haven't seen her for months.'

'How many months?'

'I don't fucking know. I've been high. So has she, knowing Lily.' Alice said this aggressively.

Siobhan felt her body chill, but she didn't let it show. 'You'd better give me something else to go on, Alice.' She held up the oxygen pipe again.

'There was a guy,' Alice said quickly. 'Lots of guys. They kept us in this house . . .'

'Who were they?'

'Who cares?' Alice whispered. 'They all want the same fucking thing, don't they? Lily gave them anything they wanted, long as they gave her enough gear to chase the fucking dragon every night. There was one guy, though. Important guy. Paki or something, like the rest of them. Took a shine to her. She was well fucking gone by then. Doing anything. Anal, you name it, just to get a hit.'

Alice's eyes started to fill with tears at the thought of it, and Siobhan stared in shock at this messed-up girl who was weeping for her daughter.

'Who was this guy, Alice?' Her voice was a bit more gentle now.

'I don't know his name. He took her away and I managed to get the hell out of the house. I haven't seen either of them since she left.' Alice closed her eyes. 'You'll never find her,' she said.

'Why not?'

'There's rumours. About what happens to girls when they disappear like that, when the guys have finished with them.'

'What kind of rumours?' She glanced over her shoulder to see the doctor looking at them. *'What kind of rumours?'*

'They ship them out. Africa, they say. Places where white girls fetch a price . . .'

Siobhan closed her eyes and looked away. *'Jesus . . .'* she whispered. She felt sick. She took a few deep breaths to get a hold of herself, to steel herself to ask more questions.

But the questions would have to wait.

All of a sudden, Alice's eyes were rolling, her body twitching. One of the machines by Alice's bedside started to beep. Dr Philips was there instantly. 'Officer, you have to go.'

'I just need to—'

But the doctor wasn't even listening to her. *'Get out!'* she hissed. 'She needs treatment, *now.'*

145

One look showed that the doctor was right. Siobhan nodded, then hurriedly left the ICU just as a team of three doctors rushed in. From her vantage point at the other side of the door she watched them get to work on the patient. One of them performed CPR; another slid an injection into her right arm; they worked on her for three minutes, maybe four.

But whatever they did, it wasn't enough. Siobhan could easily read the body language: the way the four doctors stepped back away from the bed; the way Dr Philips hung her head; the way Alice's arm hung limply from her side. Siobhan turned. She didn't need to watch them pulling the bedclothes over the girl's head to realise that she was dead.

\*          \*          \*

Back in the car, Siobhan stared through the windscreen for a full ten minutes. She felt numb. Cold. Then she put her head against the steering wheel and wept. Her whole body shook and it felt as though the tears came from deep in her veins. She didn't even know why she was crying. Was it horror at what she'd heard? Panic? Revulsion? Or was it relief that her daughter might—*might*—be alive? Great, racking sobs coursed through her as the guilt that she lived with every day became more raw. Guilt that she'd not been able to do anything to stop Lily going off the rails back then, and she seemed just as impotent now. Guilt at her inability to be a good mother. God knows it hadn't been easy, bringing Lily up by herself while she tried to hold down a job that wasn't exactly family friendly; but she blamed herself for Lily's situation,

146

even though she knew she was hardly cut out to be a cookies-and-milk kind of mum.

Sitting in the darkness outside the hospital she cried all the tears she had in her.

When she could cry no more, she took deep breaths. Tried to get control of her body and her mind.

She looked at the Polaroid and Lily stared back at her, as though begging her for help.

She was *going* to find her daughter.

She didn't know how and she didn't know where, but come hell or high water, she was *going* to find her. She'd let Lily down once before and she wasn't going to do it again.

There was something else she had to do. Someone she had to tell. Lily's father deserved to know what was happening. He hadn't exactly been the best dad in the world; they might not have even spoken for, what was it? A year? But although he'd been an intermittent figure in their lives, that didn't mean she shouldn't tell him the horrific news about their daughter.

And it didn't mean she shouldn't ask him for help.

Siobhan's mind was a mess but one thing was perfectly clear to her: if she was going to find Lily, he was one of the few people she'd trust to be on board.

She took another deep breath, then pulled her phone from her leather jacket. She scrolled through the address book and a name appeared on the screen.

Harker, Jack.

She imagined the phone ringing in the little flat in Hereford. An answer machine, naturally. No name, of course. No indication of where he was. Just an electronic voice asking her to leave a message. And so she did.

'Jack,' she said, unable to stop her voice wavering. 'It's Siobhan. I don't know where you are but . . . I just have to speak to you, all right? Just call me . . .'

Siobhan hung up. She knew she should really have called the Regiment offices, gone through the official channels. But that wasn't her way, and it wasn't Jack's either. He'd call her when he was ready.

But God only knew where he was now . . .

# 28 JUNE

# 8

*Camp Bastion Field Hospital.*
12.00 hrs.
'Jesus, doctor. Not my legs . . . *Don't take my fucking legs . . .*'

The voice was slurred but frightened. Its owner screamed. Then sobbed. It was this noise that woke Jack.

He opened his eyes and tried to look around, but his movement was obstructed by the oxygen mask on his face. He ripped it off and sat up, then winced as every muscle in his body seemed to shriek at him.

He was in a hospital bed, one of many, all of them filled with casualties. The screaming faded away as the injured man was hurriedly wheeled into surgery.

It was a big ward—perhaps twenty beds—with bright strip lighting shining overhead and all the paraphernalia of an up-to-date field hospital. A drip stand with a saline bag stood next to Jack's bed, and a machine monitoring his pulse and blood pressure. He flopped back down on the bed and tried to remember how he'd got there.

There were just flashes in his memory. Trekking across the desert towards the FOB and pressing himself into the sand every time a lume lit up the sky. Forcing himself to move on, despite his body shouting out for water and rest. The constant worry of IEDs. And on arrival at the FOB, which he'd approached with arms in the air shouting, '*British soldier! British soldier!*', being casevaced back to Bastion by Chinook. That was the last thing he remembered, and he didn't know how long ago it was. Could have been an hour, could have been a day, could have been a week . . .

And then he remembered the helicopter crash.

Pixie, Al and Red. Jesus, Red.

Jack could hardly believe he was alive.

'What's happened to your oxygen mask?' A nurse was standing over him, a frown on her plain face.

'How long have I been here?' Jack demanded.

'Not nearly long enough. You've been out cold for more than twenty-four hours and you need your oxygen mask on. Your blood count—'

'Look, love,' Jack interrupted her. 'Do me a favour and treat the guys without legs.' He pushed himself up on to his elbows again and tried to ignore the wave of dizzy nausea that crashed over him. 'I need to see my OC. Will you get a message to him?'

The nurse's lips thinned, but she nodded. Then she looked over to the other side of the ward. 'Looks like you've got a visitor,' she said.

Jack followed her gaze. Walking across the ward towards him was a woman. For a moment, he failed to recognise her: auburn hair, blue-grey eyes and the kind of pale skin that suggested she hadn't been in the Stan for long. Only when she was a couple of metres from the bed did he realise who it was.

'Morning, Professor.' He looked around. 'Or maybe it's afternoon.'

'About midday,' Caroline Stenton said, her face expressionless. 'It's good to see you, Captain Harker. They told me you were dead.'

152

'They exaggerated.'

A silence.

'I'm sorry about your friends,' Caroline said.

Jack looked away. Images of the burning helicopter branded themselves on his mind yet again. He only looked back when he realised that the woman had laid one hand on his arm. Her lips were glossy and slightly parted, and in the back of his mind he wondered what the hell kind of a person brought lipstick out to Camp Bastion.

'I feel responsible, Jack,' she said, and there was a catch in her voice. 'Can I call you Jack?'

He nodded.

'They told me it would be dangerous,' she continued, 'but I never thought . . .'

Her curly auburn hair was pinned up at the back to reveal the nape of her neck, but now a tendril fell over her face and she brushed it gently away with her free hand. She brushed the other hand gently up his arm.

Jack felt something stirring inside, but he ignored it. Nothing like that was going to happen out here.

'You want to make it up to me,' he replied in a gruff voice, 'how about telling me what the hell was in that suitcase I nearly died trying to recover.'

For a moment she didn't reply. She just stared at him, as though sizing him up. Eventually she lifted her hand from his arm. 'I can't tell you that, Jack. I'm sorry.' She looked across the room. 'Looks like you're a popular man. I don't want to monopolise you. I fly back to London today.'

'Lucky you.'

'Lucky me.' She pulled a card from her pocket and laid it gently at Jack's bedside. 'Any time you

153

need a shoulder to cry on . . .' She allowed her eyes to linger on his bare chest.

And with that, she walked away from the bed and out of the ward. Jack watched her hips as she went.

Her place was taken by Harry Palgrave. The squadron OC was a stern man at the best of times, but he wore a particularly serious expression now. 'Hope I didn't interrupt,' he said in a voice that made it plain he didn't give a shit.

Jack watched Caroline disappear with a hint of regret. Then he turned back to Palgrave. 'No, boss,' he said.

'Fuck me, Jack,' the OC continued quietly. 'We were all ready to carve your name on the memorial along with the others.'

'What can I say, boss? I lucked out.'

Palgrave shrugged. 'There's two kinds of luck, Jack—the luck you get, and the luck you make yourself. You don't survive an attack like that without a bit of the second kind. How you feeling?'

'Like shit.'

'You look like it too. We're going to let them patch you up a bit in here, then we need to do a solid debrief. You good with that?'

Jack looked around. The ward stank of disinfectant and illness; injured soldiers lay perfectly still in every bed. Not his kind of place at all. In a sudden movement he swung his legs over the edge of the bed, then carefully extracted the drip needle from his arm. He felt momentarily dizzy, but mastered it.

'Boss,' he said, 'I know where the Stingers are.'

Palgrave narrowed his eyes. 'What do you mean?'

'There's a weapons arsenal where they held me.'

The two men looked at each other. 'I need to get you talking,' Palgrave said, his face grim. 'You up to it?'

Jack nodded. 'How does now suit you?' he asked.

'Ops centre in fifteen?'

'Make it ten,' Jack said, and he started to get dressed.

\*       \*       \*

There were three of them in the ops centre: Jack, Palgrave and ops officer Matt Cooper. Palgrave smelt of ciggies, Cooper smelt of chewing gum. They both looked like they'd had a hell of time of it back at base. The air conditioning was on, but it just brought the heat down from fifty degrees to forty-five. They were sweating like pigs as they settled down to talk.

The door opened, and a figure walked in. Jack recognised him at once—the MoD goon who had briefed them before the op, and whose instruction it had been to stay behind and lase the cave. His short, tightly curled hair was greased straight back, and he had a moustache that looked like someone had shat on his lip. He saw Jack and smiled. 'Captain Harker!' he announced, his voice all Eton and Cambridge. 'Nigel Willoughby. You'll remember me, of course. It's good to see you alive, sir!'

Jack was already on his feet. His chair fell to the floor behind him as he strode over to the goon, grabbed him by the neck and pressed him up against the wall. 'Yeah,' he growled, 'I remember you. You're the asshole who kept me and my men

155

on the ground long after we should have extracted.'

A sharp voice from behind. Palgrave. 'Put him down, Jack!'

'With pleasure.' He flung the goon to the ground like he was a rag doll. Willoughby scrambled to his feet, shot Jack a poisonous look, then quickly dusted himself down and picked up a folder full of documents that had tumbled to the floor with him. He straightened his hair, then spoke like a thin-lipped schoolmaster. 'I shall put your behaviour, Captain Harker, down to the stress of the last forty-eight hours and not report it to the appropriate authorities. But let me assure you, if there is any repeat—'

'Leave it, Willoughby,' Palgrave interrupted in a menacing voice. 'Just sit down and we'll get on with the debrief.'

Willoughby sniffed, passed his palm over his greased hair for a second time and took a seat.

'All right, Jack,' Palgrave continued. 'Let's have it.'

The three of them listened carefully as Jack described what had happened since the cave raid.

You think you'd recognise this fucker again?' Palgrave asked.

Jack nodded. 'I'll just the fingers.'

'Actually, gentlemen,' Willoughby interrupted, 'that won't be necessary.' He sounded a bit less sure of himself than when he'd first entered.

Jack gave him a sour look. 'What are you talking about?'

The goon opened up a file that he had on the table in front of him, rummaged through some papers and pulled out a photograph. 'Is this your man, Captain Harker?'

It was a grainy photograph, taken from distance, of a man with an assault rifle strapped to his body standing next to an armoured vehicle. Behind him, Jack could see snowy mountain peaks—this had obviously been taken during the winter—but there was no mistaking the face: the black beard, flecked with grey; the brown eyes; the look.

Jack laid the photo back down on the table. 'Yeah,' he said. 'That's him. Friend of yours?'

'We're well aware of him,' said the goon. 'Let's just say he's high up on our wish list.'

'Let's just say he's pretty high up on my wish list, too.' He remembered the video footage of the American soldier screaming as he was being flayed. 'What's the bastard's name?'

Willoughby seemed to regain his arrogance. Being the man in the know suited him down to the ground. 'Gentlemen, allow me to introduce you to Farzad Haq. Iranian national, orphaned at a young age. He and his younger brother . . .' The MoD man checked his notes. '. . . Adel were brought up by his grandparents, but they go off our intelligence radar when Haq was about nine years old—we don't know how or why, and we don't know how the boys managed without anyone *in loco parentis*. What we do know is this: when the Iraqis invaded Iran later that year, Haq's younger brother was killed by Saddam's forces. Scud missile attack on the border, I believe. There were a great many fatalities. This was in the days when we and the Americans supported Saddam's regime.' He smiled at Palgrave and Cooper. 'Funny how things change, isn't it?'

If the others thought it *was* funny, they didn't

show it.

The goon continued. 'Haq next pops up on our radar about ten years later as part of an Al Qaeda cell. When the Taliban came to power in Afghanistan in ninety-six, they gave him sanctuary, and he was able to establish a number of terrorist training camps in the north of the country. We have pretty good intelligence that he was involved in some way with the World Trade Center bombings *and* 9/11, so we can assume he's had some sort of direct contact with Bin Laden.'

'Sounds like a textbook fundamentalist fuck,' Matt Cooper said.

The goon shrugged. 'Yes and no,' he said. 'He's certainly a major AQT player, and there's no doubting that he's ideologically driven. But he's obsessed with our American cousins. Blames them for supporting the Iraqi regime that killed his brother. There's a videotape somewhere in the archives of him promising to eliminate any American he comes across, just like they killed Adel. Makes for charming viewing.' He turned to Jack. 'You had a lucky break, old boy. If you'd have been an American soldier, Haq would have killed you immediately.'

Jack gave him a cool look. 'Your idea of a lucky break, old boy, is a bit different from mine,' he said.

Palgrave cut through the tension. 'Jack, I'm going to send this intel upwards. If we get the shout, do you reckon you could lead a unit back there to destroy the cache? Immediate action.'

The goon interrupted, giving Jack a weak smile. 'I'm sure the MoD's stance will be that Captain Harker's taken enough punishment for little while.

Wouldn't you agree?'

But nobody in the room paid any attention to him. Jack thought about his fallen mates, consigned to a fiery death by the weapons his captors had wielded; he thought of the things that the bastards had no doubt been preparing to do to him. Jack Harker wasn't the sort of man to let things like that pass, no matter how much 'punishment' the moron across the table thought he had received.

'Just say the fucking word,' he told his boss.


## 9


13.45 hrs.

The Regiment base was alive, like a bolt of electricity had crackled through it.

Palgrave had put the call through to Kandahar, and four Chinooks, two Apaches and two American Black Hawks were in transit from the main US base to Bastion. This time they were going in mob-handed. Outside the SAS compound, the green army guys knew something was going down—word spread quicker than shit on a blanket in this place—but nobody involved in the upcoming op could worry about that. Matt Cooper, chewing furiously on his gum, was liaising with the OC of 1 Para who were in-country to support the Regiment. The fifty boys from the Parachute Regiment already knew they were required for immediate action, and were preparing themselves and their weapons for insertion into the combat zone.

While that was happening, Jack carefully scanned the most recent satellite images of the town from which he'd only recently escaped. They were incredibly detailed, and it didn't take long for him to pinpoint the compound where he'd been held—he recognised the well in the centre, the trees between the well, the room where they'd imprisoned him, and of course the long, low building that was home to the weapons cache and the Stingers. The only difference was that at the time this image was taken, the outside wall of the compound had still been intact.

Palgrave entered the Portakabin. 'They're ready for you,' he said.

Jack nodded. 'Boss,' he said. 'Do me a favour and keep that MoD numpty out of my face.'

'Roger that,' Palgrave said in a low voice that made it clear he shared Jack's views. 'Willoughby's gone to ground anyway. We've had to fess up to the Yanks about the Stingers and they're ripping the arse off him right now.'

The troops were seated and waiting for them in a tented area. There was a tense buzz of conversation among the fifty Paras and the twenty-odd men of D Squadron, but that fell to silence as Jack, Cooper and Palgrave strode in.

Palgrave addressed them. No greetings. No niceties. There wasn't time for any of that. 'Listen up. Your target is a Taliban weapons cache here in Compound 32.' He turned to a map of the village and indicated the compound where the Taliban had held Jack. 'Our intel is that three missing Stinger missiles are stashed there. I don't need to tell you what sort of damage they can do in the wrong hands. D Squadron, your objective is to retake the Stingers and destroy the weapons cache. Compound 32 is in enemy territory, and we expect there to be a Taliban commander, name of Farzad Haq, in the vicinity.' Haq's face appeared on an OHP behind Palgrave. 'If Haq's there, you shoot on sight. Captain Harker's leading the op and he'll brief you in a minute.

'Parachute Regiment, your objective is to cause a distraction to the north. The Taliban can't resist a fight, so our expectation is that as soon as they realise you're attacking they'll be drawn away from the location where D Squadron are going in. You'll be inserted by Chinook on the northern boundaries of the village, approximately one klick from Compound 32. There's a demolished compound here that offers a firing line on to what we suspect is the Taliban's main northern defensive position. The moment you're on the ground, 1 and 2 Platoon advance to contact. We expect the Taliban to engage you, then use their SOPs to outflank you to the west and the east. We'll be monitoring their Icom chatter, so we should have a good fix on them. Fire support split into two groups: 3 Alpha and 3 Bravo. Lie in wait and hit them when they come at you. Gentlemen, we *want* this to go noisy. Remember: *you are a distraction*. We need every last enemy combatant to think it's a concerted attack on their defensive positions so their numbers are reduced when the assault team goes in. Draw them out then suppress their fire. There's a high density of civilians in the area and you can expect the Taliban to make use of them. So keep civilian deaths to a minimum, but collateral damage is—repeat *is*—acceptable. Any questions?'

161

Nothing. Just serious faces, full of sweat and concentration.

Palgrave continued. 'D Squadron. Fast rope into Compound 32 in two units. First unit to secure the compound and locate the Stingers; second unit to lay the charges and prepare the ground for exfiltration. Any questions?'

A guy at the back put his hand up. It was Frankie McBride, whom Jack had sent back to Bastion with Professor Stenton. There was a menacing glint in his eye. Palgrave nodded at him. 'Are we hitting the fuckers that brought our lads down?' he asked.

Palgrave looked tempted to answer him, but he was too professional for that. He just turned to Jack. 'Captain Harker will give you the low-down now.'

It didn't take Jack long to explain the layout of the compound and to walk D Squadron through what was required of them. Even as he spoke, the sound of the fleet of American choppers hit their ears and he could sense everyone start to get twitchy. When he'd said his piece, Palgrave took the floor again. 'All right, gentlemen. You have your instructions. Let's put those bastards in the hurt locker. Go.'

It took ten minutes for 1 Para and D Squadron to get their kit to the LZ and load up. The mid-afternoon sun was crushingly hot, like a furnace, but hitting the village at this time had its advantages. In Helmand there was always an afternoon lull in hostilities while both sides sheltered from the sun. Hit them now and you'd be going at them when they didn't expect it.

At least that was the theory.

162

Jack piled into the Black Hawk that was transporting him back into the desert with nine other guys, plus the SF flight crew. The pilot was practically enshrouded in Kevlar to protect him from small-arms fire, and the loadie—who doubled as a side-gunner—was at his Minigun station.

'So what's the craic, Jack?' one of the boys from D Squadron demanded. '*Are* we going after the fuckers that downed Red and the others?'

Jack looked at him and nodded. 'And they properly mashed up that missing Yank a few days ago. Crucified him. Took him three days to die.'

No word of response.

Theirs wasn't the first chopper to leave. That pleasure was left to the Chinooks carrying the Paras, along with one SAS sergeant who would act as a liaison between the men on the ground and the assault team hitting Compound 32. But within five minutes Jack's team was in the air.

Flight time fifteen minutes, but as they approached the village, the pilot peeled the chopper off to the left. D Squadron would be circling nearby while the Paras started their attack. For the distraction plan to be effective, the assault team needed to wait out of sight while the Paras did their bit.

The Black Hawk circled over the west side of the Helmand River. Through the side door of the chopper, Jack saw the other Regiment chopper doing the same. And they would keep on circling, he knew, until the word came through to attack.

\*　　　\*　　　\*

163

On the northernmost edge of the village, where the Paras were to make their distraction, three Chinooks descended with their Apache chaperones hovering above. 1 and 2 Platoon and the Fire Support Group spilled out. As well as their personal weapons, two men carried a ground-mounted .50-cal, while another two lugged its tripod and ammo boxes. Three men moved a Javelin anti-tank missile launcher; and there was a selection of 66s, Minimis, HK40s and gimpies. The company of Paras moved swiftly to set up their positions behind the rubblised walls that gave them both cover and a firing point. The guys carrying the .50-cal set it up on a well-protected section of wall. The Chinooks rose up from their impromptu landing zones, sharp and fast so as not to give any of the militants time to take a potshot. In seconds they were high up, immediately clearing out of the airspace above the village.

The Fire Support Group quickly moved from the firing position: 3 Alpha 100 metres to the west, 3 Bravo 100 metres to the east, ready for the Taliban counter-attack, which they knew was bound to come. When it did, the FSG would fuck them up; until then, 1 and 2 Platoons could expect fierce contact. The bosses were shoving a stick into a hornets' nest. The Taliban were the hornets; 1 Para were the stick.

Activity all around as they set up the remaining weaponry. Within ten minutes the Taliban village would have enough firepower aimed at it to put the shits up any normal person. But they knew that the enemy they were fighting in Helmand was far from normal. Most people, when you showered them with .50-calibre rounds, would run or cower.

Not the Taliban. For them it was a call to arms.

A shout from twenty metres behind. The Regiment liaison guy, crouched down at his TACSAT. *'3 Alpha and 3 Bravo in position. Assault team ready. 1 and 2 Platoon advance to contact! Advance to contact!'*

The .50-cal gunner had already fed a 200-round belt into the weapon. It was primed and ready to go. They fired towards a copse of low trees that surrounded a compound about 200 metres away. There was a short burst of deafening fire that sucked in a quarter of the ammo belt, the spent cases dropping into the dirt below the weapon. In truth the gunner wasn't really aiming at anything or anyone. It was a statement of intent.

Protected by the rubble, those who weren't operating heavy weaponry were crouched behind defensive positions with their assault rifles ready. A burst of fire from the gimpy, then a second burst from the .50-cal.

No doubt about it. If the Taliban were enjoying an afternoon snooze, they'd have woken up now. And everyone knew they'd return fire.

They just didn't know when.

\*     \*     \*

In Compound 32, all was quiet.

One Taliban fighter—a thickset young man in a dirty smock—stood guard at the main entrance; two more watched over the hole in the wall that the accursed British soldier had blasted two days previously. They did not dare stray from their positions. But the sun was particularly hot, and the village was silent. They were not, truth to tell, as observant as they might be, although they were a good deal more observant than the eight others inside the compound, who were sleeping in the shade of the mulberry trees.

Their commander was also in the shade of the trees. But he was not sleeping. Farzad Haq had trained himself to survive on very little sleep, to keep his mind focused and alert. He sat with his back to one of the trees and by his side there was a flexible metal saw blade, still stained with dried blood. Haq had removed it from the throat of the man killed by the infidel who had called himself Jack Harker. The memory of it angered Farzad Haq. Angered him deeply. He was not a man who liked to be outmanoeuvred, and he kept the saw with him as a reminder to himself not to let his guard drop. In his four-fingered hand he held a large flat stone; and in the good one, a long knife. With great precision he slid the blade slowly along the length of the stone. It made a hissing sound, regular and monotonous, which only stopped when Haq held the knife up to test its exquisite sharpness.

It was as he tested the blade for the third time that the thunder of gunfire hit his ears.

By the time the second burst of fire filled the air, the Taliban under the tree were on their feet. They started shouting at each other and collecting their weapons. Two of them entered the arsenal and came back out with a rocket launcher and an armful of warheads. They continued to bark at each other as they headed towards the exit.

Haq did not move quickly. He sheathed his knife, then slowly rose to his feet, his mind ticking quickly.

166

'Wait!' he commanded.

The others stopped and looked at him as if he were mad. They could hear shouting now from other compounds as their fellow militants got themselves together and started rushing towards the northern edge of the village where the gunfire was coming from. Haq selected four men at random. 'You and you,' he said to two of them, 'come with me. You two stay here and guard the compound. The rest of you, go and fight.'

Fight and die, he said to himself. Because that is what will happen.

One of the men he had ordered to stay started to complain. 'But the enemy are not *here*. There is no point—'

One dangerous look from Haq caused him to fall silent. The commander didn't feel inclined to explain his thinking to these subordinates, but he was enough of a tactician to recognise a diversion when he heard it. He nodded at the two who had received instructions to follow him, and led them into the long low room containing the weapons cache. The two men started to help themselves to another rocket launcher, but Haq turned to them. 'Leave them,' he instructed, before pointing at three long, green carrying cases stashed at the far end of the room. 'Those,' he said. 'One each.' He grabbed one of the cases himself.

A slow grin spread over the face of the man nearest him. 'We will use these weapons against the Americans?' And then, his expression slightly puzzled: 'What *are* they?'

'*Idiot*,' Haq muttered under his breath. '*They* are not Americans. But these weapons we will use to catch bigger fish. Take them and follow me.'

The men did as he said. Once they had removed the weapons from the shelves, Haq ran back outside to where the flexible saw was still lying in the dust, picked it up, then returned to the cache and placed it in the spot that had just been vacated.

He smiled. A message for Captain Harker and his idiot companions.

Haq barked another instruction at the two men and they hauled the carrying cases, not back into the compound, but through the hole in the wall at the end of the room. Once outside they turned right. There was no getting out of the village. Not yet. But the enemy would not be here forever, and in the meantime . . .

The sound of heavy weaponry on the outskirts of the village was relentless now. The Taliban had clearly started engaging the enemy. Haq and his men burst into a nearby compound almost at random. A man stood by the door, shaking his head, his face full of panic. 'No,' he said, unable to hide the fear he felt at standing up to a man of Haq's reputation. 'If you come in here, the enemy will follow. My family—'

Haq didn't hesitate. He carefully laid his carrying case on the ground, unsheathed his knife and thrust it into the man's belly. His victim's eyes widened as he pulled the blade outwards and upwards, feeling it slide along the meeting point of his ribs. The man fell to the floor and a woman's voice shrieked—Haq hadn't even noticed her before—followed by the wailing of children. Haq located the woman.

'If your children are not immediately quiet, they will be the next to die.' He brandished his bloodied

168

knife in her direction to emphasise his point.

The woman quickly gathered up the children and hustled them into a room. Haq and his men entered another room on the opposite side of the compound. It was deserted, small, dark and relatively cool. The dusty floor was covered by a shabby old carpet and someone had propped a scythe and a hoe up against the wall. This was clearly the home of farmers. There were two low cots covered with thin mattresses and a couple of soiled dishdashas draped over the end of each of them. Haq slid his carrying case under one of the cots and instructed his men to do the same.

And then they took up positions, pointing their assault rifles out of the door. Farzad Haq did not expect anyone to find him here. But if they did, he would be ready.

\*       \*       \*

At the northern edge of the village, the firefight was blazing. The Paras' ears were ringing, their bodies covered in sweat. Tracer rounds hissed around them; the .50-cal and gimpy thundered at the enemy position and the air was thick with the stench of cordite. RPGs blasted towards them from the enemy position, but although the noise they made when they exploded was loud enough to send a shock through the soldiers, the enemy's aim was off and so far, without exception, the warheads had fallen no less than thirty metres short of their positions. They were getting closer, though, as the enemy got their eye in. It wouldn't be long before they took a direct hit.

A shout from behind. The Regiment liaison guy.

'Three Alpha have eyes on. Icom chatter confirms enemy advancing from the side. I'm calling the assault team in.'

And in an instant the firefight that had only been blazing to the north had surrounded them as 3 Alpha and 3 Bravo rained their fire down on the enemy trying to outflank 1 and 2 Platoons. There would be a lot of dead Taliban to plant before sundown.

Their manoeuvre was working. They'd drawn the enemy out.

Any moment now, the assault team would be ready to insert.

*     *     *

Jack felt a sudden lurch as the Black Hawk straightened up from its holding pattern. Instructions from the ground through the comms: enemy engaged, bring in the birds.

One of the loadies shouted over the noise of the engine. *'One minute to insertion! One minute to insertion!'* He turned his attention back to the Minigun as the rest of the team prepared themselves. The ten men divided themselves into two groups, five on either side of the aircraft. Two thick, sturdy ropes were clipped to the interior of the chopper, one by each side door, and they lay curled up like sleeping snakes as the aircraft flew low over the southernmost edge of the village. From the open doors, Jack could see the compounds whizzing by just metres below. No civilians, of course—they were hiding from the brutal noise of the Paras' distraction. They'd lived in a war zone for long enough to realise that this

170

wasn't a courtesy call.

And then the helicopter was just hovering—height, about twenty metres—and Jack recognised the compound. The dust below them kicked up in swirling clouds of confusion. The loadies, leaning out of each side of the chopper, fired their Miniguns into the compound, spraying rounds in short bursts and taking out any targets they could get their eyes on. Jack saw two guards by the main entrance go down. Then the guns fell silent and the order came. *'Go, go, go!'*

Two of the team kicked the ropes out of the side doors and, in a manoeuvre they'd all executed more times than they could count, the ten men slid down. It took two seconds for them to hit the ground between the two mulberry bushes and the well, then peel off into their positions. The moment they were all down, the two ropes tumbled to the ground with a flat thump—it would be too dangerous to leave them hanging in case they got caught on anything as the chopper moved away, which it did immediately.

In that instant, Jack took in his surroundings. By the entrance, the bodies of the dead guards were bloodied and contorted. Apart from that, no one in sight. Of course, that didn't mean the place was empty, and the unit proceeded to conduct a swift compound clearance as the second Black Hawk containing the remaining ten men appeared above them. They fast-roped in just as quickly and efficiently, and the chopper disappeared.

*'Compound clear! No targets!'* Jack heard Fly's voice from the other side of the compound. Was it Jack, or did Fly sound a bit disappointed?

He ran into the weapons cache. Four guys were

already in there, laying explosives among the weaponry and rolling out lengths of fuse, a metre for each four seconds. Jack let them get on with their work. His eyes were looking out for just one thing: three long green carrying cases with white military writing on the side.

But they weren't there. Instead there was a bloodied flexible saw blade. *His* saw blade. Jack understood the message. That bastard Haq had removed the Stingers. The Paras' diversion had started thirty minutes ago. The fucker could be anywhere.

He felt a hot surge of frustration. Part of him wanted to go after Haq, right now. Find the fucker. But he knew that wasn't an option. This was an in-and-out job. Go out on a limb and he'd be putting everyone's life in danger, not just his own. The guys were rolling the fuse out of the door now, and from the centre of the compound came two loud explosions in quick succession. Jack knew what that meant: some of D Squadron had wrapped det cord round the base of the mulberry trees and exploded it to bring the trees down and make a safe landing zone for the Black Hawks to set down and exfiltrate them.

Out in the sunlight he saw the trees on their sides. He ran up to Dukey, who was i/c the sat phone.

'Call them in,' he said curtly.

Dukey raised an eyebrow. 'What about the Stingers?'

'Fucking gone,' Jack spat. 'Call them in.'

Dukey's face hardened, but he followed Jack's instructions. Moments later the air was filled with the deafening sound of rotary blades and the dry,

172

heavy dust on the ground of the compound kicked up into thick, impenetrable clouds as one of the Black Hawks touched down.

The first ten men loaded themselves in as quickly as they'd fast-roped out. Jack gave the pilot a thumbs-up and the aircraft instantly lifted into the air and flew away. The dust barely had time to settle before the second chopper descended. The remaining men sprinted to the two open side doors. All of them except Jack and Fly, who was attaching a detonator to the end of the fuse leading into the cache.

'I'll do it,' Jack said curtly.

Fly looked as though he was about to protest, but one stern glance from Jack and he gave a nod of understanding. He handed Jack the detonator and bundled back into the Black Hawk, leaving Jack alone in the compound, the dust kicking up all around him and his camo rippling in the swirling air.

Jack hesitated for a moment only—a moment in which he saw Farzad Haq's face and heard his voice. *Your instruments of war are no match for our cleverness . . .*

Jack frowned as he dealt with the fact that Haq had, indeed, outwitted them. Then he clicked the detonator and hurled himself into the chopper.

The loadie's voice—'*Go!*'—and the aircraft rose into the air. It peeled away from the compound, but Jack just managed to catch a view out of the side door as the explosives detonated.

One bang followed another, then a huge barrage of quickly repeated cracks as the ammo within the cache exploded. A massive cloud of dust and shrapnel mushroomed up from what had once

173

been Compound 32, the shock waves jolting the chopper even as it sped away. Jack gripped the webbing inside the chopper as the ground below changed quickly from compound to green zone to open desert. It was all he could do not to yell with rage.

They were on their way back to Bastion. The cache was destroyed. The whole compound was destroyed. No doubt the Paras had managed to nail a good load of Taliban. But that wasn't enough for Jack.

Haq was still on the loose. And what was worse—much worse—was that he had the Stingers with him . . .

*  *  *

17.30 hrs.
Jack was tired. More tired than he'd ever been. His body hurt and his mind was blurred and blunt. He felt brutalised by the events of the past few days. Hammered by them. But even though half of him wanted to collapse in his bunk and sleep for a week, he stood outside in the overpowering heat, counting the Chinooks back into Bastion and watching the Paras spill out on to the landing zone. Their faces were streaked with dirt and sweat and they lugged their heavy weaponry with them, but they'd extracted safely and there were the same number of men returning to Bastion as had left it earlier that afternoon. A cause for relief, if not celebration. But word that the Stingers hadn't been in the weapons cache had travelled around the Regiment. Everyone knew that the missing weapons would have the bosses shitting bricks.

And when the bosses shat bricks, they did it from a great height.

Jack was still staring at the Chinooks, hazy in the sun, when Palgrave approached him. 'Jack, debrief.' His eyes said it all.

Willoughby was waiting for them in the ops centre. His well-greased curls were dishevelled, as though he had been clutching his hair and it had stayed in that position. There were beads of sweat on his upper lip and the lines on his forehead were more pronounced than before. He gave Palgrave and Jack a nod as they entered, and indicated that they should take a chair. Neither man did. Jack perched on the edge of a table; Palgrave remained standing.

A tense silence.

'I suppose I don't need to tell you, gentlemen, that the loss of these Stingers is an acute embarrassment to the Regiment.'

Jack and Palgrave glanced at each other. 'The Regiment didn't lose them, Willoughby—'

'Major Palgrave,' Willoughby snapped. 'Your man,' he waved one hand dismissively at Jack, 'your man claims to have been in the same room with these blasted weapons and yet *somehow*, and I confess myself startled as to how this might have occurred, *somehow* they remain in enemy hands. I hardly need to remind you that the SAS is highly regarded around the world. This kind of . . . this kind of *balls*-up is likely to reduce our standing—'

Jack didn't know what came over him. For days now, he'd been working at the limit of his ability. Now there was nothing left in him.

'Why don't you shut the fuck up, Willoughby?'

The goon narrowed his eyes. 'Careful, Jack,'

Palgrave murmured.

'Kindly remember, Captain Harker,' Willoughby hissed, 'that in my job I hold the equivalent rank of colonel. You do realise that insubordination of this kind—'

He didn't finish his sentence, because the next sound to come from his face was the cracking of his jaw.

'*Jack!*' Palgrave shouted as blood from the MoD man's face spattered against the back wall of the Portakabin. He felt his OC restraining him from behind, but shook him off with ease and bore down on Willoughby, who had his hands pressed over his bleeding mouth and nose as he stepped backwards and cowered in a corner. From behind him, he was vaguely aware of Palgrave opening the door. '*Get in here!*' the OC roared outside. '*Now!*'

'Listen to me, you little piece of shit,' Jack said. 'In *my* job you hold the equivalent rank of a turd I did in a bucket when I was captured. Men *died* because of you. Burned to death. Ever wondered what that feels like, Willoughby? Burning to death?'

Willoughby didn't reply.

'No,' Jack pressed. 'I guess not. Because you just stay here safe and snug while the rest of us are risking our arses on the ground. Well if you think you're going to get us to take the rap just because *you're* getting heat from the pen-pushers who tell you what to do . . .'

He raised his hand again, one vein on the side of his neck pulsating with anger. But Willoughby cowered so pathetically that Jack just let his fist fall and stared at him with total contempt.

Jack looked over his shoulder. Palgrave was

176

there, and so were Fly and Dunc Forsyth. The OC's face was stern, but the other two looked confused.

'All right, Jack,' Palgrave said, his voice full of authority. 'Step back . . .'

'Take it easy,' Jack spat. 'I've finished with him.'

Nobody in the room moved.

'You two,' Palgrave addressed Jack's mates. 'Take him to his bunk.' He looked over at Willoughby. 'I'll smooth this out.'

But Willoughby had straightened up now. He moved his hand from his bloodied face and shot Jack a look of pure poison. 'There's nothing to smooth out,' he stated. 'Captain Harker will be on the next flight back to the UK. I hope you've enjoyed your time with the Regiment, old boy, because it's at an end. Bodyguarding celebrities for you from now on.'

He put his hand back up to his bleeding nose, pushed past the soldiers and left the room, dripping small spots of blood on to the floor as he went.

\*     \*     \*

The burial of the Taliban dead near the poppy fields on the edge of the village was a swift, unsentimental affair. They had been called to the next world, that was all. Farzad Haq had no time to mourn foot soldiers or mercenaries. He had more important things to attend to.

It was after dark that he oversaw the loading into an old Toyota truck of the missiles from the compound he had commandeered during the assault. The drivers were men he could trust.

Loyal. Devout. He had contacted them two days ago and they had just arrived. If the British had waited until now for their assault, they might have troubled him. But they hadn't, and now his men would see to it that Haq's hard-won missiles successfully made the dangerous journey west out of Helmand, into Nimroz Province and across the border to Iran. From there, their transport would be easier. The missiles would reach their destination in just a few days. He watched the truck disappear into the Afghan night with pride.

He, in the meantime, had a different journey to make. South. Into the mountains of Pakistan where his people would be waiting for him. God willing, they had made the necessary arrangements.

Farzad Haq unconsciously stroked the stump of his thumb with his good hand. It was a habit of his. As he stood there under the cover of darkness, he thought back to a night thirty years previously. The image of himself, and Adel, and his grandfather, together for the final time, caused him pain as it always did.

But Haq smiled. Grandfather would be proud. He gathered his robes around him and started to make preparations to leave.

# 29 JUNE

# 10

In London the following morning, the sun was shining. Habib Khan stepped down from the bus that had brought him all the way from his small home in Muswell Hill to the shabby office in West Kensington where he spent his working day. His suit was old-fashioned—a pocket watch would not have looked out of place—and his beard was trim and neat. He looked a little smart for this part of town, but it didn't seem to worry him.

Situated just above a pub that Habib Khan wouldn't have considered stepping into even if he drank alcohol, the poky network of rooms that housed the office of the Islamic Council for Peace were far from glamorous. But that was OK. The organisation didn't exist to make its members comfortable. It had a higher purpose than that.

Khan punched in the code on the keypad of the office's front door, then headed up the dimly lit stairs. Walking into the main reception room, he greeted with a gentle smile the young woman who sat typing at her desk.

'They're all waiting for you, Mr Khan,' she said.

'Thank you, Mariam.'

Mariam was only eighteen years old, but the council couldn't operate without her cool efficiency. She had been granted asylum only a year ago after her family had been forced to flee Iran, and Khan had employed her soon after she arrived in London. How thin she had been back then, how black the rings under her eyes. Now, though, she looked like a different woman. Her lips were full and plump; her skin glowed. The freedom of the West suited her, but she remained a devout Muslim. Mariam worked with the enthusiasm of someone who was not only grateful for her job, but who truly believed in everything this organisation was trying to achieve.

'Perhaps I might ask you to join us, Mariam,' Khan suggested, peering at her through his little round glasses.

Mariam looked flustered. 'But Mr Khan, the phones—'

Khan held up one hand. 'It won't take long, my dear. What I have to say involves all of us. Please.' He indicated a door on the other side of the room.

Mariam put one hand to her short brown bob, clearly nervous at the thought of sitting with the members of the council—all of them men—whom she thought of as her superiors. But she stepped towards the door and allowed Khan to open it for her.

There were eight men in the next room, which had the faint smell of mildew. They were a selection of imams and businessmen who shared a common interest in promoting the peaceful observance of Islam. They all looked a good deal older than Khan, and although they all wore Western dress—it was the policy of the council not to don more traditional garb for fear of alienating people—there was an aura of quiet wisdom about them. Sitting quietly at a round table that was empty apart from a jug of tap water and a few glasses, they looked mildly surprised at Mariam's presence. She stood uncomfortably by the door. 'Have a seat, my dear.' Khan said this in the tones of an affectionate uncle, but she looked no more at

182

ease once she had sat down.

Khan remained standing. 'Gentlemen,' he murmured, then took a moment to gather his thoughts as he looked at each of them in turn. 'Gentlemen,' he repeated. 'Thank you for being here. We have congregated at short notice, and I appreciate you all making the time.'

The men around the table nodded.

'We are failing, gentlemen.'

A murmur of disagreement, but Khan spoke over it. 'I do not say,' he announced, 'that what we have set out to do is not worth doing. Far from it. Our struggle to encourage the Muslims of Britain to integrate peacefully into society, and for society to accept them and their beliefs for what they are, is the foremost struggle of our times. But we have not achieved enough. All over the country, young Muslims are being swayed, converted to a violent fundamentalism that has nothing to do with Islam and everything to do with hatred. We all know, in our hearts, that the situation is becoming worse, not better.'

An awkward silence around the room. But no dissent, because they all knew he was right.

'What, then, are we to do? Should we give up our struggle? Should we allow our peaceful religion to be hijacked by the forces of evil?'

One of the men—the oldest one there—spoke up. 'Of course not, Habib. But what more can we do? We are not a wealthy organisation. Perhaps if we had more funds—'

Khan raised one hand. 'Funds,' he said, 'will not be necessary. I have decided that we have a different weapon with which to fight.'

Looks of confusion around the table. 'What

weapon?' asked the older man.

Khan smiled. 'The truth,' he said.

The others blinked at him as he continued. 'Those Muslims in this country who are seduced by fundamentalism believe they are fighting in a holy war. But what if we were to show them that they are getting involved with people who are no more than common criminals? What if we were to show them how wrong they are?'

Khan stepped up to the table, poured himself a glass of water, then took a small sip. 'There are parts of the world where terrorists are allowed to operate without concern for the rule of law. We know where these places are—the western borders of Pakistan, Yemen, those parts of Afghanistan under Taliban control. And yet there are too many moderate Muslims in this country who remain unaware of these terrorist breeding grounds. If we can draw the attention of our communities to the fact that these overseas terrorist factions are having a direct influence on our impressionable youngsters, perhaps they will be further spurred on to do what is necessary to counter that influence.'

He looked around the room. All eyes were on him. 'There is one country,' he continued, 'that is worse than the others. Where Islamist rebel groups have aligned themselves with Al Qaeda. A safe haven for the most wanted terrorists in the world, where they are given sanctuary. A place where their operations are of only the slightest interest to what passes as authority. That country is the Republic of Somalia, and as leader of this council I have decided to make a trip there.'

He took another sip of water and watched the others over the brim of his glass. A hubbub of

184

conversation had suddenly started up; the men were staring at him and at each other in anxiety; Mariam looked as though she might cry.

The old man who had previously spoken stood up. 'Habib,' he said above the conversation. 'Nobody admires your dedication to our cause more than I. But to travel there—that is madness! You do not need *me* to tell you that they have no government and no laws. You do not need me to tell you that it is nothing but a—'

'A hideaway for terrorists, murderers and scoundrels. A safe location for Al Qaeda and any number of other fundamentalist networks from around the world.' Khan smiled again. 'No,' he said. 'I do not need you to tell me that. You do not need to tell me that it is ravaged by war, that it has no police force, nor that it is unsafe even to walk the streets. It is for these reasons that it has become a magnet for the very criminals who would divert our young people from the path of peace. I will walk into the terrorists' backyard. I will talk to them. I will tell them that they have no business with our peaceful Islamic communities, no business turning our youngsters towards the path of evil. It is not enough that Western politicians deplore the existence of these terrorist networks in troubled parts of the world. It takes one of *us* to put the spotlight upon them. To stand up to them publicly. To denounce them.'

'But Habib, if you go there to bring the world's attention to these people, you will be putting your life in great danger.'

Khan nodded. 'And it is for that reason that I will raise publicity for everything we are striving towards. We will let the news outlets know that I am travelling to Mogadishu, and we will let them know why. Though I doubt any of them will come with me, danger is always newsworthy. We will have more coverage than we have ever had before.'

'But Mr Khan.' It was Mariam who had spoken, and she looked embarrassed as all the men turned to look at her.

'Yes, Mariam?' Khan's voice was calm. Kind.

'What if . . . what if you *die*, Mr Khan?' Her voice was teetering on the edge of tears.

A silence. Khan took another sip of water before putting his glass back on the table.

'I sincerely hope I will *not* die, Mariam. But if I do, we will have made our point more eloquently than we could ever have hoped. Do not worry, my dear. I have prayed, and I know this is the right path. I intend to make my announcement this afternoon. When I do, I expect us all to be busy with interview requests and the like. We must remember that *I* am not the story. The story is that those who commit violence in the name of our faith seek refuge in the arms of criminals and gangsters. That they *are* criminals and gangsters and that we, members of the Islamic community, recognise that and condemn them.'

He removed his glasses and cleaned them, absent-mindedly, on his tie. 'I do not ask that anyone accompanies me,' he continued once they were back on his nose. 'I ask only that you support me in this endeavour. Do you?'

The members of the council looked at each other. Something unspoken seemed to pass between them, and the old man stood once more.

'Yes, Habib,' he said quietly. 'We support you.

And may God protect you every step of your way.'

*       *       *

Jonathan Daniels, Director General of MI5, dreaded trips to Number 10. He hated meeting with politicians, whose smiles were always broadest when they were shafting you the most. And audiences with the PM—he dreaded those most of all. It was his experience that the man in the top job was the most insecure of the lot. He hadn't met a prime minister yet who didn't appear to think, somewhere deep down, that MI5 was just a tool to be used in his political machine to help secure his precarious position. This one was no different. He looked across the table at the familiar face, the dapper suit and the blue tie. And as he always did when he was in the Prime Minister's presence, he reflected that the man looked like a boy, fattened around the jowls from too much chocolate. Of all the leaders Jonathan Daniels had met—and he'd met a few—this one was the least impressive.

'Good of you to make the time to see me, Jonathan,' the PM said, taking a sip from his cup of coffee.

'My pleasure, Prime Minister,' Daniels muttered.

'A week to go until the President's visit,' the PM noted. 'I thought it might be beneficial for you and me to have a little sit-down and discuss the arrangements. Make sure we've all got our ducks in a row, eh?'

'My people have been keeping the Joint Intelligence Committee up to speed . . .'

'Oh, of course,' the PM smiled. 'Of course, of

course. Wouldn't do any harm for us to have a little chat, though. Jolly important event for us, this. Sure I don't need to tell you that. The President's approval ratings are sky-high, and not just in the US. No harm in him scattering a little of his stardust. I'm, ah, just a *little* concerned about the terrorism-threat-level status, Jonathan. Critical, you know. Wondering if there's something we can do about that, eh?'

Daniels remained impassive. 'The terrorism-threat-level status, Prime Minister, reflects the threat of terrorism.'

A look of annoyance crossed the PM's face, but he quickly mastered it. 'Of course. Of course, of course. I'd just like your assurance that everything is being done to minimise the possibility of any . . .' He waved one hand in the air. 'Any unpleasantness.'

Daniels took a deep breath. 'Prime Minister,' he said. 'It's no secret that I'm unhappy with the timing of the President's visit. I consider it to be ill-judged and provocative. The anniversary of the July seventh attacks generates mayhem. Always does. We have every crank in the country tipping us off to bogus threats; and there isn't a single genuine terrorist cell that wouldn't love to pull off a spectacular a week from now.' He could see the skin around the PM's eyes tightening. This clearly wasn't what he wanted to hear. 'That said, I can assure you that the Security Service is working at full efficiency. I've cancelled all leave and we have our eyes firmly on the ball.'

The DG breathed deeply again. He'd gone a bit further than he'd intended, but perhaps that wasn't such a bad thing. The PM appeared momentarily lost for words, so Daniels continued. 'As you know, the President's visit is not yet public knowledge and we will not be announcing it until the sixth. We are in touch with the Secret Service regarding their requirements for the day. In addition, my people are liaising with our special forces to ensure that the security arrangements are as they should be. As regards the threat-level status, we raised it in response to a particular threat, and I expect to hear of some developments about that threat in the next twenty-four hours.'

He settled one hand on top of the other, and waited for the PM to speak.

It didn't take much for the semblance of civility to slip from the Prime Minister's manner. That made sense, Daniels thought. You didn't get to a position like that without a ruthless streak—he couldn't be quite the bumbling idiot he appeared to be.

'Director General,' the PM said quietly. 'A strong relationship with the United States is of course crucial to our ongoing security. The last conversation I had with the White House was distinctly frosty, thanks to a monumental cock-up in Helmand Province by our special forces. That's not something I intend to repeat, and it's my full intention, a week from now, on the anniversary of 7/7, to show the President that we are fully on top of the terrorism threat, and that we stand shoulder to shoulder with him in strength.'

He sounded for all the world like he was on the hustings.

'I'm sure I don't need to remind you that the role of Director General is quite within my gift,' he continued. 'I'll be most disheartened if I am

189

unable to tell the President that this threat you have identified has not been comprehensively dealt with. Am I clear?'

Daniels sniffed. 'Quite clear, Prime Minister,' he said. 'Will there be anything else?'

'Nothing else, thank you, Jonathan.' The smile returned to his face. 'Thanks once again for coming to see me. Now I'm sure you must be terribly busy, so be so good as to close the door on your way out, will you?'

Daniels stood. The button on his suit jacket had come undone as he was sitting, so he did it up, nodded at the PM, then turned and left.

\*         \*         \*

In Jack Harker's dream, his friend Red died a thousand times over. Like a phoenix, he came back from the grave only to burn another time in the furnace of Jack's mind. And each time he burned, Jack imagined a four-fingered man watching in satisfaction. Smiling as his friend screamed and Jack himself stood by, desperate to help, but unable to do a thing.

Jack woke suddenly. There was a banging noise. 'RPG,' he muttered to himself as he sat up quickly. But then he realised it was nothing of the sort. Just the coughing of a car engine outside. He blinked, confused as to where he was. Not the Stan, that was for sure. After he'd let fly at Willoughby they couldn't get him off the base quick enough. Fly and Dunc Forsyth, the two cousins from his unit, had been sent along to chaperone him and they had been pretty sheepish about it. The transit to Kandahar had taken forty-five minutes, and a

TriStar back to RAF Lyneham had been waiting on the runway, transporting green-army troops back to the UK for their two weeks R & R. Jack's own R & R, he knew, was going to be substantially longer. A seven-hour flight back to the UK, and a wordless MoD driver had been waiting to take them to Hereford in the small hours, dropping Jack back at the one-bedroom flat he called home. He was asleep almost before his head hit the pillow.

Now it was 3 p.m., and as he lay there quietly for a moment he thought he could still hear Red's screams. Talk about the sleep of the dead.

The phone rang. He grabbed the handset from his bedside table immediately. 'Yeah?' His voice sounded fucked.

'Jack, it's Bill Parker.'

Jack closed his eyes. Bill Parker was the adjutant's clerk at base—a well-liked, softly spoken man, but he obviously wasn't calling for a friendly chat.

'What is it, Bill?'

'Look, Jack. This is from the horse's mouth, not me, all right? You're to stay away from camp for the time being. The adjutant's in Washington for meetings but he'll be back in on the morning of the third and he wants to see you at 10.00 hrs.'

'Roger that,' Jack said without enthusiasm.

There was an awkward pause before the adjutant's clerk spoke again. 'Listen, Jack. I shouldn't be saying this so keep it to yourself. This has gone all the way to the top and the CO's feeling the heat. It's not looking good. They're after sacking you.'

Jack felt like throwing the phone across the

room. More than twenty years in the Regiment and now this. He kept his cool though. 'Thanks for the tip-off, Bill,' he said. 'I'll see you at 10.00 hrs on the third.' With that he hung up and hauled his arse out of bed.

Home, he thought to himself as he looked around. Hardly that. Just a place to keep his answer machine. He saw the little white box blinking at him. Three messages. Not exactly a whole lot, given that he'd been away for five months, but he couldn't face listening to them anyway. He padded into the tiny kitchen, made a brew, then plonked himself down on the sofa in front of the TV. For a while, there was something pleasurable about allowing the mindless babble of daytime TV wash over him. A hell of a sight less stressful than taking incoming. But after half an hour boredom set in. He flicked the channels from game show to cookery programme, before settling finally on a news bulletin. A dark-skinned man with a neat beard and round glasses spoke to the camera.

'. . . and it is for these reasons that I will be travelling alone to Mogadishu, to speak to the terrorists and to demonstrate to the Islamic community at large that it is only when we ourselves stand up to the rogue elements in our society that . . .'

'Fucking psycho,' Jack muttered to himself as he switched the TV off. Mogadishu was one of the few war zones he'd managed to avoid during his time in the Regiment and from everything he'd heard he would be perfectly happy to keep it that way. If some do-gooding civvy wanted to risk his life out there, he deserved everything that was coming to him.

Jack still couldn't shake the dream. It was like Red was haunting him. Back in Helmand everyone was shook up about the Stingers. But now that he was back home, Jack couldn't shake the feeling that the weapons were just a distraction.

Too many things didn't make sense.

Red's death, and the death of the others, had *not* been an accident. They'd been ambushed, plain and simple. If Jack hadn't made the call on the ground to send half the unit back to Bastion with Stenton and the flight case, the casualties would have been twice as bad. And you didn't have to be Napoleon to realise that you couldn't ambush someone unless you *knew where they were going to be*. So just *how*, exactly, did Haq and his Taliban cronies *know* that they were going to be right there, right then?

How, unless someone had told them?

He felt his stomach churning. What if the intention had been for them all to die once they'd completed the raid? It wouldn't be the first time the Regiment had been privy to secrets someone didn't want revealing. Wouldn't be the last, either. But if that was the case, it would mean someone had been feeding information to Farzad Haq.

Haq. Again he imagined the bastard's face, cruelly gloating, telling him how stupid he was.

'*Fuck you*,' Jack muttered. Back in his bedroom he rummaged around in his drawers for a pair of shorts and a T-shirt, before putting on running shoes and heading out the door to pound the streets of Hereford.

He ran further than he intended—the afternoon sun was bright, but without the heat of the Afghan day to sap his energy he felt as though he could

193

have gone on forever. It was good to clear his head and to push his body. To get his thoughts straight. When he did arrive back home, he was covered in sweat, and in a weird way that felt kind of normal.

Having showered and changed, he returned to his bedroom where the answer machine was still blinking at him. With a sigh he pressed play. The first message was nothing—just somebody hanging up once they realised they'd got an answer machine. Same for the second. But the third message made him turn sharply to the machine. He recognised the voice instantly, of course, even though he hadn't heard it for months.

'Jack. It's Siobhan. I don't know where you are but . . . I just have to speak to you, all right? Just call me . . .'

Her voice was on the edge. Jack closed his eyes. God knows what she wanted but it sure as hell didn't sound like she was calling for an affectionate little catch-up. She sounded stressed out, and a stressed-out Siobhan wasn't what you wanted when it felt like the world and his wife had just given you the mother of all bollockings.

No, Jack thought. To hell with that. She could wait. For now he had other things on his mind. He wanted to know why Red and the rest of his men had died. The longer he left it, the more difficult it would be to find out. He only had one lead, so he had to follow it.

The Bergan he'd carried all the way back from Bastion was propped in the corner of his room. He picked it up and a little shower of sand fell to the bedroom floor. Jack ignored that. He opened the bag and upturned the contents on to his bed. Dirty boots, old clothes, a couple of MREs that he'd cadged off some American troops but hadn't got round to eating. And, of course, more of the thick, dusty sand that got everywhere out there. He rummaged through his stuff until he found what he wanted. It wasn't much. Just a small card with a name on it—Professor Caroline Stenton—and a number. Moments later he was dialling it.

'Stenton.' Her voice was abrupt. Unfriendly almost.

'Afternoon, Professor.'

'Who is this?'

'A friend of yours from Helmand.'

A pause. When Caroline spoke again, her voice had softened.

'Jack?'

'Yeah.'

'Where are you?'

'Hereford,' he said flatly.

'Hereford? You're home rather sooner than I expected.' She was almost purring now, and Jack could tell it had been a good idea to call.

'When *did* you expect me home?' he asked.

Caroline ignored the question. 'If this is about what happened in Helmand, Jack, you have to know that I can't talk about it.'

'It's nothing to do with that.'

'Then I can't imagine why you're calling.'

'You can't?'

'Well . . .' He could imagine a faint smile on her face. 'Maybe.'

'Where are *you*?' Jack asked.

'At home,' she replied. 'London. Kensington.'

'Any plans for tonight?'

'Nothing I can't put off . . .'

It took ten minutes for Jack to shower, change

195

and jump into the BMW convertible on which he lavished a lot more care than he did the flat. He burned through the streets of Hereford, heading towards Gloucester where he could get on the dual carriageway to the M4.

At the back of his brain there was the nagging worry that the adjutant was going to give him his marching orders. He didn't let it worry him for long. *Fuck them all*, he said under his breath as the speedo tipped ninety. They might be preparing to shit on him but someone, somewhere wasn't telling him the truth. Who knew if he'd ever get to the bottom of it, but if they thought he was going to sit quiet and take it, they had another thing coming.

*       *       *

It was a little after 7 p.m. by the time he reached London and rang the doorbell of the address Caroline had given him. It was a large townhouse on the north side of Kensington High Street, divided into four flats, with Caroline occupying the penthouse. There was no reply over the intercom; just a buzz. Jack pushed the main door open and strode up to the top floor. The door to Caroline's apartment was ajar. He stepped inside.

It was a large flat, softly lit. Chopin tinkled inoffensively in the background—not Jack's kind of thing, but he wasn't here for the music—and the air was thick with the scent of incense. There were several doors off the square main hallway, but only one of them was open. Jack headed towards it. He found himself looking into a large, comfortable room, breathing in the faint aroma of menthol cigarettes. At the far end, floor-to-ceiling windows were covered by thick, embroidered curtains. Even though it was summer, a fire flickered in the grate and there were two long, comfortable-looking sofas strewn with pillows.

And on one of the sofas sat Caroline.

She looked a hell of a sight different to the last time Jack had seen her.

The professor wore a dress, though there wasn't much to it—a couple of flimsy shoulder straps and a whisper of thin material that stopped just above her knees and did little to disguise the curves of her body. Her feet were tucked underneath her, and she had a glass of champagne in her hand. The remainder of the bottle and a second glass were on a low table in front of her. Her eyes glowed with the reflection of the fire as she looked at Jack, and she took a slow sip of her drink before saying anything.

'A long way from Hereford, Captain Harker. But I thought you'd be here sooner.'

Jack shrugged. He stepped up to the low table and poured himself a drink which he swallowed down in two gulps. The booze—the first he'd had for months—oozed warmly through his body. It felt good.

'Didn't want to rush you,' he smiled as he topped up her glass and refilled his own.

'No,' Caroline replied. 'I'm not to be rushed. I like to take things slowly.' She smiled. 'So it's a good job we've got all night, isn't it?'

Jack sat down beside her, then stretched out his free hand and stroked his fingertips down her auburn hair. She smiled, put down her glass and shuffled closer to him. Their lips met, and Jack felt her hand slide inside his shirt, popping one of the buttons as it went. She ran her hand up and down his torso then suddenly, to his surprise, dug her long fingernails into his skin. He jumped, but she kept her lips pressed firmly against his.

Caroline pushed her body closer towards his. Jack let his champagne glass fall to the floor, then slowly slid the straps of her dress down the side of her soft shoulders. She was naked underneath the dress, which settled round her slim waist. Caroline pulled her lips away from his, and as she stood up, the dress slid further down her long legs, tumbling to a silent heap on the floor. She stepped out of it, raised one eyebrow meaningfully at Jack and walked slowly from the room.

Jack allowed himself to enjoy the sight before standing up himself and following her. By the time he was in her bedroom, she was already lying on the bed, with just the light of the moon through the window illuminating her body. Jack could hear her breathing—regular and heavy—and in the darkness of the room he smiled.

Caroline Stenton was a lead, nothing more. But that didn't mean he couldn't enjoy the process of following her up.

\*      \*      \*

Jack looked at his watch. 4 a.m. They had long since exhausted themselves. Now he lay there, listening to Caroline's slow, regular breathing. The moon had moved. Its light no longer filtered into the room. It was very dark.

He slowly slid the covers from his body and eased himself out of bed. As he stepped towards the door he used the edge of his vision—more sensitive to what light there was—to see his way. He didn't know what he was looking for, but if he was going to nose around Caroline's flat, now was the time to do it.

'Where are you going?'

Her voice was sharp. Not at all drowsy. He turned round to see the vague silhouette of her body sitting up.

'Bathroom,' he said.

When he returned, she was still awake. And as he lay down beside her, she turned to face him. She didn't say a word, but he could sense that his bed partner had one eye open. And that it wouldn't be closed till morning.

He allowed sleep to take him.

# 30 JUNE

# 11

When Jack woke up again, Caroline was no longer in the bed. She was fully dressed in an elegant trouser suit and was sitting at her dressing table, looking closely at the mirror as she applied her make-up. Jack looked at his watch. A quarter past six.

'Bit early, isn't it?' he asked.

'I've got a meeting,' she said. The abruptness had returned to her voice and all traces of the kittenish thing he'd spent the night with had disappeared. 'I've called you a cab.'

'I don't need a cab.'

'Then don't take it. But you'd better get dressed. I've got to be out of here in ten minutes.'

Jack shrugged. He got out of bed and pulled his jeans on while she finished her make-up and then turned to look at him. She looked as cute this morning as she had last night. He grabbed her hand and gave her a gentle pull towards the bed.

'Forget it, Jack. *I'm* late and *you've* got to go. I mean it.' She walked out of the room.

Jack finished getting dressed, then followed her. She was in the kitchen—a room he hadn't even seen yet—gulping down a glass of orange juice and eating a thin piece of toast. She didn't offer him anything; she just squeezed past him and out into the hallway, where she opened the front door.

'Bye bye, Jack,' she said.

'I'm beginning to think you don't love me any more.'

'Good*bye*, Jack.'

He shrugged. 'We must do it again sometime,' he murmured, before stepping out on to the landing and heading back down the stairs.

His car was still parked out on the street, and tucked behind the front windscreen wiper was a parking ticket. He looked around at the parking restrictions. No parking before 11 p.m. Fucking great. Jack pulled at the ticket and started to crumple it up to stuff in his pocket, but then he changed his mind. Flattening it out again, he replaced the ticket, then slipped to the end of the road where there was a bus shelter with three or four people queuing. He joined them, just another commuter. But while the others gazed in the direction from which they expected their bus to arrive, Jack kept his eyes firmly on the door of Caroline's building.

He didn't have to wait long for a vehicle to arrive. It double-parked just by Jack's own car, and a black-suited man got out and rang Caroline's doorbell before returning to the vehicle. Moments later, Caroline appeared. She carried a slim leather briefcase and climbed swiftly into the back of the car, which slipped instantly away.

Jack ran back towards his own BMW. In less than twenty seconds he had grabbed the ticket and was behind the wheel, pulling out into the road and following Caroline's car. They turned left on to Kensington High Street and headed along Hyde Park before turning right down towards the river and into Millbank. Jack drove patiently, keeping two cars between himself and Caroline's. But when her driver stopped outside Thames House, he drove straight past. Jack knew how not to be seen, and stopping at exactly the same place as the

204

person he was trailing was a sure way of drawing attention to himself.

And besides, the trail stopped here. He'd found out what he wanted to know, and there was no way he'd be able to follow Caroline into the building. As he drove away, he glanced in his rear-view mirror and could just see the slim, efficient figure of Professor Caroline Stenton striding directly into the offices of MI5.

'Fucking Five,' he muttered as he drove away.

He tried to tie the strands together in his head. Caroline was clearly working for military intelligence in some capacity. What that capacity was, he didn't know. What he *did* know was that someone in Helmand had known where they were, and as a result his men were dead. If Jack's luck had been different, he'd have joined them.

But would someone in the echelons of MI5 *really* want to dispense with eight Regiment men, plus flight crew? Would they *really* pass on intelligence about their location to a scumbag like Farzad Haq? Jack shook his head. It didn't add up. At least not with any kind of maths that Jack knew.

Maybe he'd got it all wrong. Maybe the ambush had just been a lucky break for the enemy. Maybe he was just seeing shadows.

Jack Harker shook his head and performed a quick U-turn. A black cab skidded to an abrupt halt and the air was filled with the angry sound of blaring horns. Jack ignored them all as he directed his vehicle back out of town. It was time to go home.

\*　　　\*　　　\*

The members of the Joint Terrorism Analysis Centre were waiting for Caroline. This morning's meeting had been called for 7 a.m. and it was now three minutes past. Of the twenty or so members of the JTAC, a couple of them were looking impatiently at their watches while the others helped themselves to coffee and pastries. At the head of their large table sat the Director General of the Security Service. The JTAC wasn't part of MI5, but it was answerable to him, so Jonathan Daniels was present for its more important meetings.

Like this one.

Caroline took the one remaining seat at the table, next to Colonel Bruce Sterne, a representative from the MoD—one of those grandfatherly types who had a knack of getting on with anyone. Sterne stood up, cleared his throat and the murmur of conversation in the room fell to silence.

'Ladies and gentleman,' he announced. 'Now that we're all here, I suggest we begin.' He gave Caroline a benevolent smile. 'Most of you already know Professor Stenton,' he continued. 'Her advice has, of course, been invaluable to us over the past couple of years. For those of you who haven't yet had the pleasure, Professor Stenton is a fellow of University College London, and she specialises in the field of radiological warfare. As you are no doubt aware, there have been intelligence reports over the last few weeks of a potential terrorist threat to the UK, which is why the terrorism-threat-level status has recently been increased to critical. The source of this is understood to have been in Helmand Province, but

I'm happy to announce that . . .' He turned to look at Caroline again. 'Well, perhaps Professor Stenton would like to take the floor.'

Caroline stood up. 'Thank you, Bruce,' she said. 'Ladies and gentlemen, I've recently returned from Helmand Province. While I was there I accompanied a team of British Army personnel on the ground where we discovered a facility capable of producing a high-level radiological weapon. The facility was neutralised, and a flight case of materials confiscated. We've now had the opportunity to analyse them.'

There was absolute silence around the room as Caroline continued.

'The case we removed contained a quantity of caesium-137. I'll try and keep the science simple, but what you need to know is this: it's highly toxic and has a half-life of just over thirty years. This makes it suitable for the production of a particularly devastating dirty bomb.'

The Director General interrupted. 'Let's have some specifics, Professor Stenton. When you say "particularly devastating", what exactly do you mean?'

'It's difficult to give an exact prediction. I would estimate that the quantity we confiscated would be sufficient to infect ten thousand people within a radius of about a mile. Of those, I would expect ten per cent fatalities within thirty days and fifty per cent within a year.' She let that sink in before continuing. 'Of the remainder, most of them would probably wish they were dead anyway. And with a thirty-year half-life, if somebody had successfully detonated such a bomb in a highly populated area, we would be feeling the aftershock for decades to

207

come. Small quantities of caesium-137 were released into the atmosphere after the Chernobyl disaster, and we all know what sort of effect *that* had.'

Another uncomfortable silence.

Bruce Sterne stood up again. 'Thank you, Caroline.' He looked around the room. 'I would like to state for the record, ladies and gentlemen, that a number of our special forces lost their lives in the process of capturing this material. Our debt to them, and to Professor Stenton, is greater than we perhaps realise.' Sterne looked as if he was waiting for some acknowledgement of this statement, but none came. With a slight shrug, he turned directly towards the Director General. 'There seems little doubt,' he said, 'that this is the terrorist threat of which our intelligence reports warned. Since it has been neutralised, I propose that we reduce the terrorism threat level from critical to severe.'

He sat down once more. There was a little hum of conversation from the assembled members of the JTAC, and their faces were substantially paler than they had been at the beginning of the meeting—the expressions, perhaps, of people who felt they'd just had a lucky escape. The Director General spoke up. 'Ladies and gentlemen,' he announced. 'I'm sure you'll all join me in thanking Professor Stenton for her work.'

The nodding of heads.

'Now that this threat has been dealt with,' Daniels continued, 'I see no reason not to downgrade the threat level. Perhaps I could have a show of hands for any of us who disagrees with this course of action.'

There were no raised hands. The members of the JTAC were all political creatures, and they knew as well as anyone how much easier a downgrading of the threat level would make their own lives.

'Good,' the DG said, his voice brisk. 'Then unless there's anything else, I'll inform the PM immediately.' He gathered the papers laid out on the table in front of him, gave a nod to the assembled company, and quickly left the room.

*      *      *

Back in the day, when Siobhan was being trained up in the Det, she'd had an instructor. He was a foul-mouthed bastard who for some reason had managed to sleep his way through at least half the females under his tutelage, and he never made it a secret that he'd like Siobhan to be another notch on his bedpost. She never succumbed, not only because the guy made her flesh creep, but also because it was in the early days with Jack, and her boyfriend would have nailed the instructor's bollocks to the floor if he thought he was messing with Siobhan. That was what Jack was like.

Still, say what you like about the instructor, he knew his stuff. Siobhan was more than happy to put up with his lechery if it meant she learned something. That was what *she* was like.

Siobhan found herself thinking of that instructor now. 'Surveillance,' he had told her, 'is boring. Fucking boring. But boredom's your biggest enemy. You get bored, you get careless. You get careless . . .' He'd made a gun shape with two fingers and thumb, then mimed shooting himself in

209

the head. 'And it would be a shame to be scraping *your* pretty little face off the pavement.'

Siobhan had never forgotten that. Since her days training in Hereford, she'd spent countless hours performing covert surveillance and she knew every trick in the book. Which was why she now found herself crouched in the boot of her old Volvo estate—a vehicle selected for no other reason than that it was perfect for a boot fit like this, with the back seats up and the space covered. Enough space for her to stay hidden, for her stash of different styles of clothes to help her blend in to whichever neighbourhood she was staking out, and for the briefcase opened up beside her, which contained a small radio receiver, a loudspeaker and a mess of wires like colourful spaghetti. Her torch was off, but light seeped in to the boot from the two peepholes that she had drilled into the number plate. At the end of the Troubles, the IRA had grown cute to boot fits like this and had started blowing up vehicles they only suspected of containing surveillance operatives. But those days were gone, which meant some of the old techniques could come back into play.

As she entered the fourth hour of surveillance outside the Horse and Three Feathers, she kept the instructor's words firmly in her mind. Under ordinary circumstances she'd have a partner, someone to share the duty with. But these circumstances weren't ordinary. Kieran's tip-off of a Drugs Squad police officer on Cormac's payroll meant she couldn't trust anybody on the force. Even if she could, she wouldn't. She knew what they thought of her—that life for her was just some long personal vendetta against the types who put Lily on the wrong path in the first place.

The very thought of Lily made her want to cry again. Alice's words resounded in her mind. *They ship them out. Africa, they say. Places where white girls fetch a price . . .*

She wanted to howl, but she tried to concentrate on the job in hand. All she could do for Lily right now was to blow a hole in the heroin trade that had dragged her down to God knew what depths. No matter how much she wanted to storm into that pub, put a Glock to O'Callaghan's head and tell him to talk, she knew that wasn't the right play. Siobhan needed leverage, otherwise she was helpless.

The loudspeaker crackled. This was old technology, but that was O'Callaghan through and through. Most dealers of his calibre had five or six mobile phones and discarded them on a regular basis. O'Callaghan was at the other end of the scale. As far as Siobhan could tell, he didn't use any mobile phones—or indeed any phones at all. To catch someone with such an old-fashioned way of doing business, you had to use old-fashioned policing. Siobhan could only hope Kieran's little bug would pay dividends.

Voices. Not for the first time that day, but up till now everything had been idle chit-chat. O'Callaghan was in the room—she'd established that much—and there was a woman called Betty who brought him teas and coffees. But that was it. Boring.

*You get bored, you get careless. You get careless . . .*

'Someone says he wants to see you.' Betty's voice on the loudspeaker. 'Foreign fella. Already told him to fuck off back to Dagoland, but he won't go.'

211

'Show him in, Betty. I'm expecting him.' O'Callaghan's voice was so soft that Siobhan had to strain to hear it.

The sound of someone entering the room.

'Leave us alone, Betty. No one to disturb us.'

Another pause. And then a new voice. No greetings. No pleasantries. Just straight down to business.

'The merchandise.' The newcomer spoke with the quiet precision of someone for whom English was not his first language. Whoever he was, he wasn't born and bred in Belfast. 'You are finding it satisfactory?'

'Yeah,' Cormac replied. His voice was just audible above the sudden crackling of the loudspeaker. 'The product's good. I'm surprised to see you here, though. I thought we agreed, minimal contact.'

'My presence makes you uncomfortable?'

'I like to keep my suppliers at arm's length. It's better for all of us.'

'Indeed. But there are some conversations that should be conducted face to face.' A shuffling sound. 'I am going away for a few days. Business abroad.'

'I heard something of the sort.'

'Good. Your next delivery is due very soon. I would like to receive my payment in advance.'

More crackling.

'That was never the deal,' Cormac said quickly. 'Cash on delivery. That's the way it works in these parts, my friend. Only way I can do it.'

'Mr O'Callaghan, you're a man of business. I am sure you understand that flexibility is a most important attribute in a businessman. I would like my money in advance, otherwise I will be forced to find another distributor.'

'You'll never find one. You know how good my distribution networks are. I can get product into every city in the UK within a day of receiving it. If you can't get the stuff on to the streets, it's worthless—'

'Mr O'Callaghan,' the stranger interrupted. 'I am supplying you with large quantities of very pure heroin at an extremely attractive rate.'

'You are that, my friend, you are that. But let's not forget that you're not the only one who's been supplying people with things. How's the white gold you've got stashed in a hole somewhere? Seeing to your needs, I hope . . .'

The stranger carried on as if he hadn't even heard O'Callaghan. 'There are plenty of other people who would be more than happy to take your place should you find my terms unacceptable. Since it is clear that you would prefer me to go elsewhere—'

'No . . .' O'Callaghan cut in. For the first time he sounded slightly hesitant. 'No. I'll get you your money. Just make sure the product arrives safely.'

'It will arrive just when you are expecting it.'

'Well that's something.'

'I have a final request, Mr O'Callaghan.' The newcomer's voice remained mild.

'You don't ask for much, do you?'

'Over the coming days, I will have some extra packages. I would like you to have them delivered to the mainland. I would, of course, expect to pay you a small fee—'

'Shit!' Suddenly, without warning, the speaker had fallen silent. Siobhan tapped it. Nothing. The feed was dead.

She had heard enough to realise she needed to know this guy's identity. She had to get out. Exiting a boot fit on your own was dangerous. If you had a partner, it was different—just drive somewhere out of sight. Siobhan didn't have that luxury. She looked through the peepholes. They gave her a limited view of the side street in which she'd parked. She gave it five seconds. No sign of anybody so she unlatched the boot from the inside, raised it slightly and slipped unnoticed out of the gap. Climbing into the driver's seat, she removed a shell-suit jacket and a baseball cap that she fitted over her blonde hair. For a run-down part of town like this, she needed to chav herself up.

The car was parked in a street running down the back of the pub; now she got out of the vehicle and sprinted round to the front. The place was a shithole—you could tell that just from the facade, with its blacked-out windows and rusting pub sign swinging gently in the breeze. She knew she could hardly walk in and demand to see the proprietor; but on the other side of the road there was a café. She went in, ordered a coffee and took a seat by the window.

The glass was smeared and greasy, but it gave her a direct view of the pub's entrance. By the time the coffee arrived, no one had emerged. It wasn't until her untouched drink was practically cold that the pub door swung open and a man emerged.

Siobhan's blood ran cold. The man's features were Middle Eastern. *The white gold you've got stashed in a hole somewhere.* She remembered what Alice had said and a sense of dread filled her veins. She also knew that this man's face was familiar. But where from?

She stood up, left a fiver on the table and walked out of the café. By the time she was on the pavement, she'd already removed her small digital camera from her jacket pocket. Her window of opportunity to get a snap of his face was tiny, so she started raising it to her eye.

At that exact moment, he turned to look at her. A look so chilling and intense that her arms fell to her side and she found herself just walking away. Siobhan was not easily spooked, but there was something about the way he had looked at her that made her want to get the hell out of there.

Twenty seconds later, when she glanced over her shoulder, the man was gone.

Siobhan's memory was very good. Well trained. Even now she kept up the memory exercises she used to perform when she was in the Det: Kim's game, remembering lists of random objects with unerring accuracy and speed; memorising number plates as she walked down the street; staring at photographs of major players so that she would recognise them instantly on sight.

The man who had walked out of the Horse and Three Feathers wasn't a major player. Not so far as Siobhan knew, anyway. That was why it had taken a moment for the penny to drop. But it had dropped now.

She knew who he was. And it didn't make sense. Which was why she sprinted to her car and burned the rubber back to her flat, where she would be able to check that her suspicion was right.

*     *     *

215

Siobhan burst into her flat and rushed into the living room, where her laptop was on one of the chairs. She booted it up and navigated through a few websites. It didn't take long to find his photograph.

She stared at the face gazing at her from the screen. There was no doubt about it. The Middle Eastern skin. The neatly trimmed beard. The little round glasses. That was him. That was *definitely* him.

But it made no sense. Because why, she asked herself, would Habib Khan, director of the Islamic Council for Peace and one of the most respected Muslims in the country, have any kind of dealings with a piece of shit like Cormac O'Callaghan?

# 1 JULY

# 12

'Heads up, Danny boy. It's your fancy girl.'

Frank Maloney's tie was fully done up, which meant it must be first thing in the morning. By lunchtime he'd have loosened it; by teatime he'd have stuffed it in the pocket of his crumpled suit. Come closing time, he'd have used it to wipe flecks of vomit from the corner of his mouth. It was no secret that Frank enjoyed a jar or two after work.

Danny looked up from his desk to see Siobhan Byrne walking purposefully through the office.

'Will you not be trying your luck then?' Frank persisted.

Danny ignored him.

'Ah, Danny boy. There was me thinking she was the love of your life. That you'd be taking her out, wining and dining her, whispering sweet words of love into her shell-likes. And then taking her back to your place to give her a face like a painter's radio—'

'Ah, shut the fuck up, Frank,' Danny interrupted him.

Frank shrugged. 'Your wish is my command, Danny boy. You know that.' His eyes followed Siobhan as she wove her way through the maze of desks in that enormous office, towards the glass-fronted room in which their DCI sat—as he always did—ploughing through file after file. Frank scratched his head so vigorously that little flakes fell on to the shoulders of his jacket; and he watched DI Byrne with such intensity that Danny was forced to wonder whether he himself harboured romantic feelings towards the woman . . .

*     *     *

Siobhan knocked on DCI Robertson's glass door. The DCI was an arsehole, with piggy little eyes, a jowly face and both the physique and the mentality of a man who spent too much time at his desk. Siobhan avoided contact with him as much as possible. But Jack hadn't called her back, and some things were too heavy for her to carry completely on her own. Having slept on it she'd decided this was one of them. The boss looked up, and was unable to hide his dismay at seeing Siobhan standing outside. But he gestured her in.

'Yes, DI Byrne. What is it?'

'Mind if I take a seat, sir?'

'Will this take long?'

'Not long, sir, no.' Siobhan sat opposite the DCI. 'I've been getting my teeth into Cormac O'Callaghan, sir,' she said.

'So I've heard. It's a waste of time and resources. We've had guys trying to pin him down for years, but it's like nailing jelly to a wall. I want you to lower your sights. Concentrate on more achievable goals.'

'I think I've stumbled on to something, sir,' she replied, ignoring his suggestion.

'I'm not interested in stumbles, DI Byrne. I'm interested in police work.'

Siobhan took a deep breath. Don't rise to it, she told herself. Keep calm. This is about Lily, nothing else. She handed him two pages that she'd printed out from her computer the night before. It was an

220

article about Habib Khan, his organisation and his forthcoming expedition to Somalia. DCI Robertson glanced at it. 'I saw this guy on the news,' he said. 'What about him?'

'He's been in Belfast.'

'So what?' Robertson handed the papers back to her. 'Last time I checked, that wasn't an off—'

'I saw him yesterday walking out of Cormac O'Callaghan's pub. I think he's involved in the O'Callaghan drug network.' She kept quiet about the reference to 'white gold'.

Silence. Robertson stared at her. Then he scraped his chair back, stood up and looked through his glass wall out on to the busy office beyond. For a moment it was almost as if he'd forgotten Siobhan was there. When he did speak, he sounded like he was doing his best to keep his voice slow and measured. 'DI Byrne,' he said. 'I know you have certain . . . certain *personal* issues to deal with.'

Siobhan looked down. 'That's got nothing to do—'

'*Damn it!*' her boss suddenly exploded. 'It's got *everything* to do with this. Look, detective, ever since you arrived here you've been a bloody liability. You see shadows at every corner and you refuse to work alongside the other officers in this department.'

Siobhan set her jaw. 'Do I have permission to interview Habib Khan, sir?'

'Of *course* you don't have fucking permission to interview him. Look who he is! Do you have any idea what sort of stink it would cause if we go harassing the guy on some trumped-up idiocy like this.' Robertson turned to look at her. His face was

221

red and, in the office, people were starting to take an interest in what was going on between them.

'I'm telling you, sir. I saw him—'

'Fine,' the DCI shouted. He stormed back to his seat, picked up the phone and dialled a number. 'This is Robertson,' he snapped. 'I need to know if there's any record of one Habib Khan entering Northern Ireland within the last week. Get back to me immediately.'

He replaced the handset, folded his arms and looked at Siobhan.

Siobhan looked back. She could feel her face moulding into an expression of disgust for this man. Sometimes she wished she could stop her emotions showing. Right now, she didn't care.

They sat in silence.

A minute passed.

Two.

And then the phone rang. The DCI picked it up. 'This is Robertson . . . You sure? OK . . . Good.' He hung up then gave Siobhan a level look.

'Not only has Habib Khan not travelled here in the last week, DI Byrne, our records suggest that he's never even *been* to Northern Ireland.'

Siobhan felt blood rushing to her skin. It wasn't embarrassment. It was anger. Frustration.

Robertson spoke again. 'Detective Inspector Byrne,' he said. 'You're clearly under some kind of emotional strain at the moment. Or maybe it's just your time of the month, I don't fucking know. I'm putting you on a four-week sabbatical. We'll re-assess the situation after that period of time with a view to moving you to less . . . less *stressful* duties.'

Siobhan stared at him. For a moment she didn't know what to say.

She stood up and her chair fell to its back. 'Fuck you, Robertson,' she hissed, before turning her back on him and stamping away.

Everyone who saw it happen marvelled afterwards that the glass wall of Robertson's office didn't shatter, so forcefully did DI Byrne slam the door as she left.

\*     \*     \*

After seeing Caroline walk up the steps of Thames House it had taken Jack three hours to get back to Hereford, then about ten minutes to get through the doors of the Spread Eagle. He wasn't exactly surprised she was on Five's payroll, but having it confirmed left a bitter taste in his mouth. He'd lost men on her account. Men with families who'd never know why their loved ones died. The thought made him want to kick the wall.

And so he'd started drinking, downing pints of Stella all that afternoon and most of the evening. He couldn't remember getting back home. It was almost midday when he woke up on his sofa with a head like a splintered bone and a mouth as dry as a shit in the desert. He showered, pulled on some fresh clothes and made hot coffee. It didn't make him feel much better.

In his bedroom the answering machine continued to glow, like a little beacon reminding him that he still had a call to make. Speaking to Siobhan still didn't rank high on his list of priorities, but what was it Red had said to him once? 'If you've got to eat a turd, no point staring at the fucker first.' He picked up his phone and dialled the number.

It rang three times. Four times. Jack felt relieved that it would probably go to voicemail. He could leave a message then switch off his phone. Job done.

But no such luck. A voice. 'Jack?'

She sounded breathless. On edge. So nothing new there. 'What's up, Siobhan? I got your message.'

'Where've you been?'

'Here and there.'

'Where are you now?'

Jack sighed. 'What is this? Twenty fucking questions?'

A pause. And then what sounded to an amazed Jack like a sob. From Siobhan? Christ, something must be wrong.

'What's the matter?' he demanded. 'What's happened?'

'Jack, I've got a lead on Lily. I think she might be alive . . .'

Siobhan carried on speaking, and Jack kept his phone to his ear. But he hardly heard a word. He was already heading out of the house on his way to the airport.

*       *       *

Jack drove blindly to Birmingham. He bought a ticket for the next plane to Belfast City Airport and didn't even return the meaningful smile the check-in girl gave him as he handed her his boarding card. 'Let me know if you need anything, Mr Harker,' she purred. Jack just took his seat.

And in Belfast, when everyone else was standing at the carousel for their luggage, he rushed straight through to the cab rank. He stared out the window of his taxi as his driver sped through the streets of the city.

Belfast. During the Troubles it had seemed to Jack like he would never leave the place. Even now he felt uneasy travelling through its streets unprotected—back then, he wouldn't so much as put his nose out the door without a Browning on his belt and a PPK strapped to his ankle. As a member of the Regiment, he'd have been a prime target for any Provo shooters—those fuckers would have done anything for an SAS pelt to show off in front of their mates—and there were certain parts of the city, especially West Belfast, where you just didn't go. Certain bars where you just didn't drink. Jack always had a cover story in case some suspicious IRA hood heard his accent and asked him what he was doing in the Province. For their purposes he was a BT engineer, over here on a six-month exchange. A reasonable cover story, but it was much better not to get into a situation where he had to explain himself in the first place.

The rules were the rules. Get it together with some chick on a night out and you never—*never*—went home with her on that first meeting, no matter *what* she promised to do for you. Get her name and address, or her car registration number, and put it through the police computer first. Only if she came up clean would you go back to her place next time you saw her. Ignore basic rules like that and the time would surely come when you found yourself sitting on the sofa while your honeytrap 'got herself ready', only to have a couple of Provos step into the room to hood you and blow your head off. It had happened to two of the green-army guys Jack knew, sent to meet their maker for the promise of a blowjob. The Regiment lads were bigger game for the Provos, and had to play it a bit smarter. One of Jack's mates picked up the niece of an IRA quartermaster one night. Good job he checked her out. She might have had great legs, but the relationship didn't.

They said Belfast was different now, but you don't shake off that kind of paranoia easily. Jack realised he had taken his place directly behind the driver's seat, not the passenger seat. Force of habit—he could quickly wrap the driver's seatbelt round his neck if things went pear-shaped.

The driver dropped him outside an apartment block overlooking the River Lagan. As he approached the building, he noticed an old bag lady on the pavement, her worldly belongings stuffed into a supermarket trolley. She had a battered wireless radio switched on, but it hadn't been tuned in properly and she was just listening to white noise. She gave Jack a look of intense suspicion that made him feel uncharacteristically uncomfortable.

It felt weird being here—the flat he'd shared with Siobhan when Lily was just a baby. He'd never forget the time he rocked up to find another man there. The fucker had left with a broken nose and a swelling between his legs very different to the one he'd been expecting. Even now the memory of it gave Jack a pang of irrational jealousy. He had never *wanted* to leave Siobhan, but she'd left him no choice.

He tried the main door, but it was shut and the intercom was fucked so he called Siobhan to say he was there. She came down to meet him.

Unlike Belfast, Siobhan never changed. The jeans, the leather jacket, the shoulder-length blonde hair. She hardly looked any different now to when they'd met all those years ago. A slight tightness around the eyes was all. A wariness. A sadness. As she opened the door, the bag lady barked something incoherent. Siobhan looked over his shoulder at her. 'She's always there,' she told him. 'Nowhere else to go. I give her a few quid sometimes. She just spends it on Cinzano.'

There was no greeting. No kiss on the cheek. Jack just followed her inside, up the stairwell and through Siobhan's front door.

The flat itself hadn't changed much. He scanned the familiar furniture, the framed picture on the wall that Lily had done when she was a toddler of her dad dressed in green and wearing a helmet. The whole place looked a bit shoddy, as though its owner had her mind on things other than interior design.

'You want a drink?' Siobhan asked.

Jack nodded and sat down as she poured two tumblers of Irish whiskey. The tumblers were empty before they spoke again.

'So what . . . ?' Jack said.

'A friend of hers turned up in the Royal. She had a picture of Lily in her pocket. I questioned her.' Siobhan closed her eyes. She was clearly finding it difficult to speak. 'She told me that Lily went with some guy. Some Asian or Middle Eastern guy. That he . . . that he gave her drugs in return for sex.'

Jack stood up. 'What's his name?'

'She didn't know.'

That wasn't good enough. 'She still there? I'll

talk to her myself. A few minutes with me and she might find she remembers after all.'

'Sit down, Jack,' Siobhan said peevishly. 'She's dead. She died just after I left.'

He stared angrily at her, then swore under his breath and turned to look out of the window.

An uncomfortable silence. Jack felt nauseous.

Siobhan rested her glass on top of her boxy old TV. 'I got myself suspended today. Well, as good as.'

'Join the club,' Jack said, but Siobhan continued as if she hadn't heard him.

'I tell you, Jack. You thought working for Five was a nightmare. These guys make them look like . . . ah, I don't know.' She waved one arm in the air in frustration. 'It's no wonder kids like Lily are killing themselves. There's more heroin on the streets of Belfast than there ever has been, but the Drugs Squad are half asleep.'

'It was your choice to move out of the Det, Siobhan.'

She gave him a sharp look. 'Give me a break, Jack. You wanted me out of there years ago. It's why you left us, isn't it?'

'I left,' Jack said quietly, 'because you couldn't keep your hands to yourself.'

Siobhan jutted her chin out at him. 'You were never there, Jack,' she said.

Jack shrugged. They'd had this conversation before and it always ended the same way. It wasn't something he felt like repeating now.

Siobhan paced the room, then turned to look at him. 'Listen, Jack. I think I might have a lead. The name Cormac O'Callaghan mean anything to you?'

228

Now *that* got Jack's attention.

O'Callaghan was one of those names any Regiment guy who'd served in the Province was unlikely to forget. Back in the early '90s, O'Callaghan's crew had been one of the PIRA's most feared nutting squads. The kind of punishments they dealt out to any of their fellow Republicans were brutal enough to make anyone feel queasy, but what the bastards did among themselves wasn't of much interest to Jack and his colleagues. O'Callaghan was on their radar for a very different reason: his men's penchant for nailing off-duty policemen when they were with their families on a Saturday afternoon. One of his lieutenants had mown down one poor sod in full view of about twenty witnesses when he was picking up his kid from football practice. By all accounts the lad had got to his knees and tried to stem the blood flowing from his dad's neck, and when it was clear the copper was dead, his son hadn't stopped screaming for an hour. None of the witnesses had dared say a word; at least not until Red had got his hands on one of them and encouraged him to reveal the name of the shooter. Red had tracked O'Callaghan's boy down, then driven the bastard over the border by himself—he wasn't the kind of guy to ask anyone else to do his dirty work, though he'd have had pretty much everyone in the Regiment queuing up to lend a hand—forced a confession out of him and put one in the back of the head. O'Callaghan, though, the ringleader, had gone to ground. The bastard knew what was good for him, and he knew what would happen if he ever crossed the path of a Blade.

'Yeah,' Jack said, his face dark. 'The name

229

means something to me. You know it does.'

'He's Belfast's Mr Heroin these days. The stuff that put Lily's friend in a hospital bed, you can bet your house it was part of his little enterprise. When they found her, they found a dead boyfriend in the same flat. He used to be part of O'Callaghan's crew, before he started using.'

'You know where O'Callaghan is?'

'Yeah.'

Jack started to move. 'All I need is an address. It's not too late to get him on to tomorrow morning's obituary pages.'

'For God's sake,' Siobhan snapped. 'Just sit down.'

A pause. Jack unclenched his teeth slightly, but he didn't take a seat.

'Things have moved on, Jack. You can't just stick these guys in a shallow grave and blame it on sectarianism. And anyway, killing Cormac O'Callaghan won't do anyone any good. Take him out of the picture, someone else from his organisation will just take his place.'

'That fucker's had a bullet with his name on it for a long time, Siobhan.'

'Look, Jack. I don't care about your Regiment bravado, OK? I care about our daughter. About finding her. Believe me, if I thought taking O'Callaghan out would achieve that, I'd do it myself.'

And the look on her face—half fury, half tears—gave Jack no cause to doubt it.

He got control of his anger. 'All right,' he said. 'So what *do* you want to do?'

'I've been trying to bring him down,' she replied. 'To get enough evidence against him to make him

230

start squealing. That way, I can dismantle the whole damn organisation, not just cut one head off the Hydra.'

'Well it sounds like you're in the right job, Siobhan. I don't see what I can do. I'm a soldier, not a copper. Why don't you just . . . I don't know.' He searched for the words. 'Work the case.'

'*Listen* to me, Jack, OK? Just *listen* to me.' Another deep breath. 'I've got a tout,' she said. 'O'Callaghan's nephew. One of the crew. He's come good with a few bits of intel. One of them is that we've got a nark in the squad. Could be anyone, I just don't know. And even if we didn't have a bent cop . . .'

She faltered.

'What?' Jack demanded.

'They think I'm flogging a dead horse, that there's no point going after O'Callaghan because he's the original Teflon don, all that lame shit. They think we should be putting our resources into the small fry—low-level dealers where we get a better chance of conviction, keep our numbers up. But that's *bullshit*.' She pronounced the last word as though she was spitting. 'Everyone knows why I joined the squad, Jack. I'm on some kind of personal vendetta. They think that because Lily went missing, I can't see the wood for the *fucking* trees.'

Silence.

And then, even though he knew what sort of reaction it would get, Jack spoke. 'Maybe they're right,' he said.

It was like taking the pin out of a fragmentation grenade: several seconds of ominous silence, and then an explosion. Siobhan picked up her empty

231

whiskey glass then threw it to the floor where it smashed into countless pieces. '*Jesus, Jack!*' she yelled. 'You're as bad as the rest of them. Of all people in the whole fucking world . . . *Lily's father* . . . Of all people, I thought *you'd* get it.'

'Get it?' Jack shouted back. 'Of course I fucking get it. You think I haven't thought about Lily every day since she went missing? You think it doesn't rip me apart too? But what are you going to do, Siobhan? Take on every drug dealer in Ireland? Every scumbag in the Province?'

'Of course not—'

'You know where I've just been? Afghanistan. Poppy fields as far as the eye can see. That's where you fight heroin, Siobhan. With guns and fast air. Not on the streets of Belfast with Provo touts—'

'Don't *give* me that shit, Jack. Just don't *give* me it. Guns and fast air? Is that your solution to everything? You know where I've been? In an O'Callaghan lock-up with a pile of guns, a pile of cash and enough drugs to put a hundred girls like Lily in the ground. You don't believe me? Go and look for yourself.' She stuck her hand into her back pocket and pulled out a scrap of paper, which in her fury she scrumpled up, and threw it at him like an unruly schoolkid. Jack just watched it fall to the carpet. 'You can go off playing soldiers all you like, Jack, but it's *here* where the real war is, not *fucking* Afghanistan.'

'You don't know *what's* happening in Afghanistan,' he shouted. But he knew Siobhan wasn't in the mood to start hearing about Regiment ops. She wasn't even listening any more. Her head was in her hands and though there was no sound of weeping, Jack could see her body shaking.

He swore under his breath. There was something about seeing Siobhan in tears that messed with him. He had to suppress the urge to put an arm around her, but he knew what sort of reaction that would get him. So he just tried to keep his cool and waited for her to raise her face to him once more. The skin around her eyes was streaked and red, and she looked at him with a kind of begging.

'Do you want to help me,' she asked, 'or don't you?'

Jack gave a deep sigh. He knew Siobhan. He knew she wouldn't let it lie until he'd heard her out. And even then . . . He helped himself to more whiskey. 'What I want,' he said, 'is to find Lily.'

Siobhan looked apologetically at the broken glass on the ground. 'I'm sorry about that,' she said.

Jack shrugged. 'It's your glass,' he replied. He waited a moment while she opened a wooden cabinet and pulled out a sheaf of papers. She flicked through them, pulled out one sheet and handed it to him. It was a printout from a news webpage containing the picture of a man Jack recognised—Middle Eastern origin, round glasses, a neat beard—but couldn't place. He read the news story underneath.

MUSLIM PEACE CAMPAIGNER TO TAKE ON THE TERRORISTS
Habib Khan, leader of the Islamic Council for Peace, has undertaken to visit the war-torn city of Mogadishu in an attempt to raise awareness of the dangers of fundamentalism within the UK's Islamic community. Somalia has no

functioning government, and as such is known to be a haven for Al Qaeda and other Islamist factions. In a statement, Khan expressed his hope that his trip 'will highlight the fact that those who threaten our peaceful way of life are no more than common criminals'. When asked whether he feared for his personal safety, he replied: 'I fear for the safety of us all if we do not unite to weed out terrorism.'

Jack handed the paper back to Siobhan. 'I saw this guy on TV,' he said. 'He's a fucking idiot. They'll make mincemeat out of him out there. But what the hell's he got to do with Lily?'

'Khan visited O'Callaghan yesterday. I bugged their conversation. He's O'Callaghan's supplier.'

Jack shook his head. 'For God's sake, Siobhan. It's obvious you've got the guy mixed up with someone else.'

Siobhan gave him a dangerous look. 'That's what my DCI said. But then he doesn't know me as well as you do. Do you *really* think I'd make a mistake like that?'

'He's just a peace campaigner. The guy might be naive, but that doesn't mean he's involved in all this shit.'

'Naive?' Siobhan scoffed. 'He's not naive, Jack. He's just got good cover. What do you expect him to have—a tattoo on his forehead saying "drug dealer"? I'm telling you: I heard him and I saw him. Khan's providing O'Callaghan with gear on the cheap, but he wants his money in advance before making this trip.'

'It'll cost him a fuck of a lot just to get the security around him he's going to need.'

'Whatever.' Siobhan dismissed Jack's comment. 'But there's something else. O'Callaghan said this thing to Khan. "How's the white gold you've got stashed in a hole somewhere? Seeing to your needs, I hope." Those exact words, Jack.'

She looked at him as though Jack should realise she'd just said something blindingly obvious. He stared at her blankly.

'White gold, Jack. They were talking about girls—*white* girls. Lily's friend told me that she and Lily were kept in a house where some "Paki" guy took a shine to her. She said that these people ship girls out to Africa where they fetch a price. Her boyfriend had links with the O'Callaghan crew. Don't you see? That's where Khan's going. Africa. What if he's the Paki guy she was talking about? What if he knows something about Lily? What if she's . . . Jesus, what if she's *out there*?'

Jack closed his eyes and pinched his forehead. 'Siobhan,' he said. 'You're putting two and two together and making five. White gold could mean anything.'

'Like what?'

He shrugged. 'Heroin? That's what you think their business is, after all.'

'It's not heroin, Jack. I could tell from their conversation. They were talking about girls. I *know* they were—'

'Christ, Siobhan,' Jack interrupted. 'You're not thinking straight. You're upset. You're clutching at straws.'

Her eyes flashed. 'No, Jack. I'm not.' She turned her back on him and looked through the window at the darkening Belfast skyline. 'I'm off the force for four weeks. After that, who knows? I can't do

235

anything here, so I've made a decision.'

She looked at him again, and a fire danced in her eyes.

'I'm going to follow him,' she said, turning away again. 'And I want you to come with me.'

She remained with her back to him.

Jack blinked. For a moment he didn't know what to say. He shook his head. 'Siobhan, have you got *any* idea what you're talking about? What do you think you're going to do—book an EasyJet flight to Mogadishu? Send your friends a postcard and fucking souvenir? Do you *know* what that shithole of a country is like?'

'Dangerous,' she said.

Jack shook his head. 'No,' he replied. 'Jumping out of a plane is dangerous. Running ex-Provo touts is dangerous. Mogadishu is fucking suicide. You've got a white face, Siobhan. They'd kill you before you'd even taken a few steps on Somali soil.'

'I can take care of myself, Jack.'

'You can take care of yourself in Belfast, sure. But Somalia? Fucking hell, Siobhan. Even the American army won't go near the place. You have *heard* of the Battle of Mogadishu? That little bit of business with the Black Hawk?'

'That's why I need you . . .'

But Jack was shaking his head. If there was one thing he knew about, this was it. 'Listen, Siobhan. If the Regiment was to do anything in Somalia— and trust me, they'd have to have a very fucking good reason in the first place—they'd send in half a squadron packing as much weaponry as they can carry and a swarm of choppers to get them in and out. You, me and a couple of handguns . . .' He shook his head again. 'Just forget it, all right? This stuff might sound good in your head, but it's not going to happen.'

'But—'

'No buts, Siobhan.' For a moment he felt like he was talking to a child. 'Look, Lily's missing. Maybe her friend was right. Maybe some fucking raghead *is* giving her drugs in return for sex.' He paused and drew a deep breath to control himself at the thought. 'If it's true, when I get my hands on this man I swear I'll rip him apart. You can help me do it. But you've got to choose your battles and right now you're chasing shadows. Habib Khan *isn't* who you think he is. He *doesn't* know Lily, he's *not* involved in drugs. If you start chasing him to Mogadishu, you won't find your daughter—you'll end up dead by the side of the road.'

'Fine,' Siobhan said. She refused to look directly at him. 'I guess I'll just sit here then, waiting for Lily to show up. Or not, as the case may be.'

Jack walked up to her. He grabbed her gently by the arm and she wriggled to get away, but he wouldn't let her. 'We're going to find her,' he said. 'We'll speak to this dead girl's friends; find out what they can tell us. When Khan gets back into the UK, I'll question the fucker. But we're not following him. It's the most dangerous country in the world, Siobhan. I'm not going with you, and you won't find anyone else to go either. At least, no one whose company is worth having. This is something I know about. Listen to me, and don't do anything stupid.'

She thinned her lips. 'I won't.'

'You promise? I don't want Lily to have to attend her mother's memorial service the moment she

237

shows up.'

That, at least, seemed to have an effect. Siobhan's brow furrowed. 'I promise,' she said quietly.

Jack nodded, then stepped back.

'You'd better go,' she told him.

'Yeah,' he replied. 'Yeah, all right. I'll call you tomorrow. We'll make a plan.'

'Whatever.' Siobhan was looking out of the window again, her shoulders slumped. Yet again, Jack felt a brief desire to go and put his arms around her, but he knew that was a road neither of them wanted to take. And so he stepped towards the main door and let himself out.

He glanced back once. Siobhan was still staring out of the window, her arms crossed and her legs slightly apart. It looked almost as if she was keeping watch over the whole city.

# 2 JULY

# 13

Salim Jamali smiled at his mother across the breakfast table. He poured Coco Pops into his bowl, followed by a slosh of milk. Most of his friends would be eating more traditional Pakistani food—mangoes, perhaps, or lassi—but not Salim. His late father and his mother had lived in North London all their lives, as had their parents before them. And while they observed some of the traditions of their homeland—visits to the mosque were occasional but not unknown—the Jamali household was in many ways as English as Buckingham Palace. Salim's mum wore jeans, and would much rather watch *The X Factor* than sit gossiping with some of the more traditional second-generation Pakistani women.

Salim picked at his Coco Pops. 'You need a good breakfast,' his mum said. 'You've got a busy day.'

He nodded and forced a spoonful down his throat. His mum, he reflected, didn't know how right she was.

In a way, it was all her fault. Kids had teased him all his life on account of his harelip that was so bad people turned their heads in the streets to stare at it. For the most part he'd learned to deal with that, but when some of the boys at his school had started teasing him, saying that his mother was a Western slut, Salim had found it hard to take. He had tried to fight back, but they were too many and he was too small. Perhaps that was why he had tried to make up for things by attending the mosque more often. He would tell his mum that he

241

was just going to the cinema, or to meet a friend, and she would believe him. In truth he was spending more and more time just off Finsbury Park, where he would hang out and chat with the young men who always seemed to be there. They didn't care that his face was deformed, or that he was small, or unpopular. Somehow he'd known his mum would not approve of him associating with them; but it gave him better standing in the playground. It stopped the teasing and the bullying.

And it was at the mosque that his real education had begun. There he had been persuaded—much to his mother's disappointment—to leave school. There he had learned what the duty of *true* Muslims was. It was the mosque boys who had explained to him that there were places in the country of his forefathers where young men like him could go, to be tutored in the skills of the jihadi. Special training camps, where he would be taught the skills he needed to fight the infidel. Salim had never been able to fight with anyone. Not successfully. The thought of being able to do so appealed to him. The day he had turned sixteen, he had, without his mother's knowledge, applied for a passport of his own. 'Keep it and wait,' the mosque boys had told him. 'They will let you know when you can travel to the camp.'

That had been seven months ago. A lifetime, in Salim's mind. The more he saw his mother embracing the ways of the West, the more he grew to loathe her. He couldn't wait to leave, but he was sensible enough not to let her suspect anything was afoot. Salim told her that he had found a job in a local garage, but she never seemed to notice the

242

absence of oil marks on his hands and clothes. And of course she never asked him for money towards the bills. When someone trusts you, he realised, you have a unique power over them.

Two days previously he had been given the word. One of the mosque boys—his name was Aamir—had handed him a ticket for Heathrow Airport to Islamabad. Somebody would meet him there and take him on to the training camp.

'What about my mother?' he'd asked.

Aamir had grinned. 'Don't worry about her. We'll take care of it.'

And now, as he finished his cereal, the passport and ticket felt strangely heavy in the inside of his jacket. He got up and kissed his mother on the cheek in the Western way that she expected.

'You seem tense, Salim. What's wrong?'

He refused to look her in the eye. 'Nothing's wrong.' And then, because it seemed like the obvious thing to say: 'I might be late back.'

She nodded, a look of quiet concern on her face, but didn't ask any more questions.

Salim left the house quickly, walked down the street and turned the corner, where a beaten-up old car was waiting for him. One of the mosque boys had offered to drive him to the airport and that was kind of him. It also meant Salim didn't see what happened just minutes after he had left the house. He was unaware of the knock on his mother's door, or of the two mosque boys—Aamir and one of his friends—who bundled into the house when she opened it, forced her into the front room and turned on the TV so that the neighbours wouldn't hear her screams. He didn't know that they had beaten her viciously, restraining their blows to below the neck so she wouldn't exhibit any bruises on her face, even though her belly and breasts were so brutalised that she squealed like a pig being led to slaughter. Salim had no idea that Aamir had then forced his mother to strip, or that they had then dragged her upstairs to the bathroom. He was ignorant of the fact that they had filled the bath with hot water and thrust her head below the surface, keeping it there for a full minute before allowing her a five-second breath and repeating the operation.

He was at the check-in desk when Aamir had said their first words to his mum. 'Salim is away for a month,' he hissed. 'If you tell anyone, we will come back and do this all over again. And if you even *think* about telling the police he is gone, we will see to it that he returns as an orphan.' They hadn't bothered to ask if she understood what they had said because they knew she was in no state to reply.

When Salim's plane took off from Terminal 3, his mother was curled up, naked and shaking on the bathroom floor.

*         *         *

The hotel Jack had chosen was central and expensive. In the basement there was a bar where he'd installed himself the moment he'd checked in and had started downing pints of black with the ferocity of a man having his last drink. If he'd expected the booze to soften the blow of the gruesome news about Lily, he was disappointed.

He had carried on drinking, only stumbling up to his room long after he was the last person in the

244

bar, and the barman had given up on the old meaningful looks. He had lain on his bed and, from his wallet, pulled out an old, dog-eared photograph. It showed him and Siobhan, with Lily between them. She was only three, and the photo had been taken on a summer's day when they'd driven up to Ballycastle and made sandcastles on the beach. You could see the blue and white surf in the background, and Lily's face was shining with childish pleasure. It seemed like a lifetime ago.

He woke up hungover and with the photo still lying on his chest. Having showered he left the hotel to find a café, where he wolfed down a big plate of ham, egg and chips and several cups of black coffee, before wandering around the town, marking time and getting his head in order. He was supposed to be in Hereford to meet the adjutant at 10.00 hrs the next day. He needed to get back, but he wanted to speak to Siobhan again first.

He called her. No answer—just her curt voicemail message. Mid-afternoon, he returned to the hotel and stayed in his room for an hour or two.

Just sitting.

And thinking.

He dialled Siobhan's number again.

Her phone started to ring this time.

And ring.

It was just before it clicked into voicemail that Jack realised what he was listening to. The ringtone. Not the standard two short rings, but different. A single tone, longer, and repeated.

Jack stared at the wall for a moment, listening to Siobhan's voice. An uneasy feeling rose in his

245

stomach. He knew what that single tone meant, of course. That the phone was ringing abroad.

'*Shit*,' he hissed. He was out of the room in three strides flat. Jack ran down the corridor, and the lift to the foyer couldn't move quickly enough for him. He burst out into the street, jumped into the nearest cab he could find and directed the driver to Siobhan's flat, cursing every time they hit a red light or got snarled up in traffic.

When they reached their destination, he shoved a handful of notes into the surprised cabby's hand and jumped out of the car. The old woman was there, with her supermarket trolley and her radio. Jack approached her and dropped a twenty in her trolley, keeping his breathing shallow because of the smell.

'Have you seen her?' he demanded. But the old woman just gave him a wild look, then started pushing the trolley away, muttering to herself.

Jack didn't even bother with the front entrance. Instead, he ran round to the back of the apartment block where a metal fire staircase stretched up, leading to a precarious iron balcony on each floor. Jack sprinted up, counting the floors as he went. Ten storeys up he walked along the balcony. He needed to pass five windows before he got to Siobhan's flat: he crouched down to avoid being seen by the occupants. But soon enough he came to a window that led on to Siobhan's kitchen. There were no lights on inside. It had an unoccupied air.

He looked over the balcony to check nobody was observing him. All clear. He removed his jacket, held it up in front of the kitchen window and punched it. The glass shattered and shards fell inwards into the sink. The window itself was locked, so Jack was forced to clear the remaining glass from around the frame and clamber in. He cut his hand, but barely noticed it.

It was gloomy inside, but Jack kept the lights switched off as he went from room to room. Everything about the place suggested that Siobhan had left in a hurry. In her bedroom, the cupboard doors were still open and there were clothes strewn on the bed. The broken whiskey glass that she had slammed on to the floor the previous night was still splintered over the carpet. He went into the bathroom. There was a removable panel at one end of the bath that you wouldn't see if you didn't know it was there. Jack did know. He felt behind it and his fingers touched the cold steel of the firearm that he knew she hid there whenever she was in the flat. It was a bad sign that it was still there.

Because the only time Siobhan *didn't* take that weapon with her was when she was catching a plane.

The sick feeling in his stomach grew worse.

He moved back into the main room. Her laptop was at an angle on the coffee table. He opened it up and switched it on. In less than a minute, he was reading her browsing history.

It didn't surprise him to see that she had been visiting airline websites.

He cursed under his breath, then opened up Siobhan's email. His eyes were instantly drawn to the two most recent messages. One from British Airways, confirming her on to a flight from Belfast to Paris via London. The second from Ethiopian Airlines, booking Siobhan on to a plane from Paris to Djibouti.

Jack consulted his mental map of Africa. Djibouti, the small country bordering the northern edge of Somalia. Jack had never been there, and he was positive Siobhan hadn't either. But he was equally positive that from there she'd be able to cross the border.

Fuck. Siobhan was good. One of the best even by the standards of the Det. No doubt about it. But this was too dangerous, even for her.

He looked at his watch. Just past six. From the flight times on Siobhan's computer, he could conclude that at that very moment she was somewhere in the air between Europe and East Africa.

Jack stared at the screen, stunned by her recklessness. He hadn't been exaggerating when he'd said that he wouldn't risk going to that part of the world without a crowd of heavily tooled-up Regiment guys. He hadn't been exaggerating when he told Siobhan that one glance of her white skin and they'd kill her—but probably not before they raped her first.

'*Damn it!*' he exploded, crashing his hand down on the laptop so that it slammed shut. He stood up and started prowling around the room, feeling that he'd like to start breaking things. He was angry with Siobhan; but he was angry with himself too. He remembered leaving the flat the night before, seeing her staring out over the city. Jack knew Siobhan well enough to realise that she wouldn't forget about her crazy idea just because he told her she should. That was like a red rag to a bull, and when Lily was involved . . .

It was starting to get dark outside. The River

Lagan snaked beneath him and the city lights were twinkling as Jack stood where Siobhan had stood, a solitary figure in the blackness, his broad shoulders hunched and his eyes hooded. Half of him wondered whether Siobhan had left those emails, so easily accessible, knowing Jack would read them. The laptop was, after all, uncharacteristically insecure. Or maybe she really had just left in a tearing hurry, because she knew that if Jack found out what she was doing, he'd try to stop her.

It didn't matter either way. Jack looked at his watch. He had to make a decision. Get back to Hereford and leave Siobhan to her fate, in the hope that her not inconsiderable training would be enough to keep her safe in Mogadishu. Or go after her. Stop her from running into trouble. And if she *did* run into trouble, get her out . . .

A little voice in his head spoke to him. She'd landed herself in this mess; she could get herself out. If he wasn't with the adjutant tomorrow morning, that was the end of his career. No question. And he wasn't supposed to give a shit about her any more. Remember?

Jack felt his lip curling in the darkness. It wasn't as easy as that, and really he knew that the decision he had to make was no decision at all. Siobhan, whether she meant to or not, had outmanoeuvred him. Just like she always did.

It had grown cold. The broken window was letting the elements in. Jack stayed where he was. His mind was churning. Working things out. Planning.

He could get to Djibouti the same way Siobhan had. That was the easy bit. Finding her would be more difficult; and finding her before she got transport into Somalia even more so. He knew nobody in-country and locating a fixer who could sort him out with the equipment he needed would take time. No. Following Siobhan to Djibouti would be pointless. Finding her in Mogadishu was riskier—but perhaps achievable. There were a limited number of places where Westerners could stay. Where *anyone* could stay. Yes, if he could make it into the Somali capital, he had a better chance of locating Siobhan and then getting her the hell out of there.

Jack sat himself down at the laptop again and brought up a map of East Africa. He picked up the shape of Somalia's angular coastline, then examined the borders. Djibouti to the north, Ethiopia to the west. Somalia's long western border was a violent badland populated by dissolute Ethiopian troops and African mercenaries who'd slaughter anyone if the price was right, or who got in the way of their primary objective of looting or raping. The Ethiopian border was Somalia's longest, and it was porous. With a decent fixer, an SAS unit and the appropriate weaponry, it could be crossed. But to try it alone would be stupidity.

Which left the southern border with Kenya—a country he knew well from a stint he'd spent there training Kenyan troops. He could be on a flight to Nairobi within hours, and the internal flight system was reasonable. All he needed then was a fixer. Someone discreet. Someone with the local knowledge that would enable him to get tooled up and in-country.

A face rose in his mind. It was deeply lined and

grizzled, the skin tanned like leather, the hair gun-metal grey and cropped—at least it had been last time Jack had seen it. Jack hadn't seen this man for years, but rumours of his whereabouts occasionally reached him. It wouldn't take long to find out if they were true. He scrolled through the contacts on his phone until he found the number he was looking for: Lew Miller, an ex-Delta Force operator who was now enjoying his retirement taking rich tourists game fishing off the west coast of Florida and fleecing them for the privilege. Lew never changed. Jack just hoped he was by his phone and not screwing whichever of his female clients were tanned and buxom enough to pass his undemanding criteria.

The phone rang several times before a voice answered. 'Jack fucking Harker,' it drawled. 'To what do I owe the goddamned pleasure?'

Jack didn't have time for small talk. 'I need a favour, Lew. Under the radar. Urgent.'

'I'm listening.'

'Markus Heller. He still got that set-up in Kenya?'

'Last I heard,' Lew said warily.

'Can you get me a number?'

A pause. 'Under the radar, huh?'

'Can you get it?'

'Call me in an hour.' A click, and Lew hung up.

Jack looked about. In the near darkness he would have to feel around for what he wanted, and his fingertips touched it soon enough. A crumpled piece of paper, the one Siobhan had thrown at him last night. When he unfurled it, he saw that it contained the scrawled address of a lock-up in West Belfast.

Jack memorised the address, then dropped the paper back on the floor and started searching the flat again. It didn't take long to locate Siobhan's car keys; and knowing her as he did, he realised that if he looked hard enough he'd find a set of picks and a tension wrench. They were in the cabinet from which Siobhan had brought out the papers on Habib Khan. He found something else there, too—something that almost made him smile. A thin torch with a piece of red lighting filter taped to the front. Jack pocketed his discoveries, then helped himself to Siobhan's M66 from under the bath. He noticed something else in the bathroom—an open packet of coloured contact lenses with one of the sachets missing. He had to hand it to Siobhan: she still knew what she was doing . . .

He left the flat by more conventional means. Outside, the old woman had her fist round a bottle of Thunderbird. She gave Jack a hard, unapologetic stare. He found Siobhan's car, kicked it into life and hit the road. Fifteen minutes later he was parked up a dark side street of a West Belfast estate.

Jack searched for the lock-up with a confidence bolstered by the weapon in his jacket. Once he had the place in his sights, he stopped and loitered in a dark corner. A couple of kids were playing footy, kicking the ball against the iron doors of the lock-ups so that they boomed with tinny thunder. Luckily they got bored after ten minutes and moved on, giving Jack a clear run at it.

He picked the lock in less than a minute.

Inside it was pitch-black. Jack was glad of Siobhan's torch. The red filter lit up the place without wrecking his night vision and he found what he wanted in no time at all. *A pile of cash and enough drugs to put a hundred girls like Lily in the ground.* That was what Siobhan had said he'd find and she wasn't wrong. To Jack it had all the hallmarks of an emergency stash, a place O'Callaghan could go when the shit hit the fan to supply himself with weaponry, cash and a means of making more. Jack ignored the guns and the drugs. All he wanted was the cash. He helped himself to two bundles of money—three or four G, he reckoned—and stuffed it in his pocket.

In Jack's experience, no one did anything for nothing. On overt or covert ops, he could expect to be given whatever funds he needed to grease whichever palms came his way. But this was different. Personal. Nobody was going to give him cash for such a trip, so it seemed only right that O'Callaghan should foot the bill.

Jack clutched the M66 as he stepped outside and locked the garage again.

A moment of doubt. Perhaps he should just alert the authorities, tell them about Siobhan. But what would they do? She'd travelled to Djibouti. That wasn't a crime. And start feeding them her fears about Habib Khan and he'd be laughed out of town.

No. This was his call. He ran back to Siobhan's car and headed towards the airport. As he neared the perimeter, he dialled Lew Miller again. His American friend was curt as he read out a number with a Kenyan prefix. 'You didn't get it from me, Jack. You got that?'

'Yeah, I got it.'

Once Lew was off the line, Jack thought of the

253

furrowed face again, and heard his laid-back, southern American accent almost as clearly as if the guy was standing next to him. Markus Heller. Formerly of A Squadron, Delta Force, now plying his trade in Africa. Would he help? Jack snorted. For a price, Markus Heller would help anyone.

Jack dialled the number. A low African voice answered. 'Rainbow Safaris.'

'Listen to me carefully,' Jack said. 'I need to speak to Markus Heller. Tell him it's Jack Harker and I need a favour.'

And he continued to drive towards the airport as he waited for his old friend to come on the line.

\*      \*      \*

Habib Khan was not a fool.

He would not be making this phone call from his flat; he wouldn't even be making it from the *vicinity* of his flat, preferring instead to take the pay-as-you-go mobile phone that he had bought under an assumed name to a quiet car park in the east of London, well away from any masts that would track the location of the call to his house. As he travelled there, he thought of O'Callaghan, who was similarly distrustful of telephones. Khan didn't like the man, didn't like his avarice. Everything O'Callaghan did, he did for money. Still, at least it meant he was loyal to something. Cormac O'Callaghan might be loathsome, but he had his uses. In the days to come, Khan knew he would prove to be invaluable, even though Cormac himself didn't realise it.

Other people were invaluable too, like the person he was about to call. It pleased him that

254

this person was not a slave to money. That their loyalties to his cause had more reliable, solid foundations. That they *believed*.

The voice was curt when it answered the phone. 'Yes?' It was a woman's voice.

'Is everything ready?' Khan asked.

A pause. 'I suppose so.'

'You don't sound sure.'

'I'm sure.'

Khan nodded in the darkness of his vehicle. 'Good. I fly to Paris tonight. The United Nations plane will drop me in Mogadishu tomorrow afternoon.'

'I don't see why I can't be on the same flight. It would be safer.'

'If you think about it,' Khan replied, 'as I'm sure you have, you will understand why. I will have to spend time with journalists when I arrive. If they see you there, they will want to know why. It is much better that you join me later.'

'And a lot more dangerous.'

'You will have security. It is already arranged. And besides, our objective is important. If we must endure hardship, it is of no importance. You understand that?'

A pause.

'Yes,' the voice replied. 'I understand that. You're sure nobody knows what you're doing?'

'Of course not,' Khan replied mildly. 'I know how people think. The bigger the lie you tell them, the more they are likely to believe it. I will be waiting for you in two nights' time at the Trust Hotel in Mogadishu. Until then, *Allahu Akbar*.'

'*Allahu Akbar*,' came the reply.

Khan smiled, hung up the phone and drove

255

away. He needed to be at the airport in a couple of hours, and there were still preparations to make.

# 3 JULY

# 14

07.30 hrs, local time.

The sun was already fierce and Siobhan Byrne was wet with sweat.

She had arrived in Djibouti just after nine the previous evening. On the plane from Paris she had locked herself in the toilet the moment the seatbelt lights had gone off. There she had inserted her brown contact lenses and smeared her face with fake tan that she'd bought at Charles de Gaulle and decanted into a small pot to get round the safety restrictions. By the time she'd got to Djibouti her eyes and skin were dark.

The airport was practically deserted, and the first thing she'd done was walk up to the Daallo Airlines counter. She knew from her research that this was the only airline operating to Somalia. The man at the desk was elderly, his curly hair short and grey. He wore thick spectacles and, to Siobhan's surprise, a Manchester United football shirt. He spoke no English, but they managed to converse using Siobhan's schoolgirl French. '*Le vol prochain à Mogadishu?*'

The man had raised an eyebrow at her. '*Vous y allez toute seule?*'

She nodded. '*Oui.*'

'*Ça n'est pas une bonne idée.*' Not a good idea? Siobhan was getting tired of people telling her that. '*Le vol prochain?*' she repeated.

It was with apparent reluctance that the man had sold her a ticket on the flight that left the following day, and his reaction had given Siobhan an uneasy feeling that lasted long after she had checked into a hotel in the European quarter of Djibouti City. Not one of the big-name places. If someone came looking for her, they'd try the Sheraton first, then work their way downwards. The place she had researched while she waited for her connecting flight back in Paris was something more modest. Unassuming. The building looked faintly colonial, with balconies and colonnades. It had the air of a place that was once desirable, but its splendour had faded. The beige exterior paint was peeling away and the arched wooden window frames were rotten. Siobhan wasn't used to Africa. She wasn't used to the shanties and the run-down vehicles and the strange looks, not all of them friendly. She wasn't used to the heat or the smells—a strange mixture of sewers festering in the heat, exhaust fumes and grilled meat from roadside stalls. And although the inside of her hotel was clean enough, the streets outside were filthy and rubbish-strewn.

As her taxi driver had driven her through some poor-looking places on the way to the European quarter, she found herself wishing that her handgun was in her jacket, not hidden behind the panels of her bath thousands of miles away.

Siobhan spent the night recovering from her journey on an uncomfortable bed underneath a circular ceiling fan that did little to keep her cool. Sleep had been impossible. Her mind had whirred as incessantly as the fans, and the recklessness of her actions surprised even her. In Belfast, this journey had seemed her only serious option; Jack's objections had sounded like the words of a coward. But she'd had time to reflect. Jack had his faults, but cowardice wasn't one of them. Perhaps she

260

should have listened.

But listened and done what? Sit around impotently and wait for Lily to show up—or not—when her only lead was slipping through her fingers? Doing nothing wasn't her style. As daylight arrived and the tinny sound of the call to prayer curled above the rooftops of the city, she managed to sideline her tiredness and her fear and concentrate on what she had to do. After an unappetising breakfast consisting of some kind of highly spiced meat stew, she headed out of the European quarter and found herself in a street of ramshackle market stalls. Everything was on sale here: bleating livestock allowed to roam the streets; unfamiliar vegetables; hunks of meat plastered in crawling flies; bunches of what she assumed was khat, the mildly hallucinogenic herb that practically everyone here chewed. Large, dirty umbrellas marked with logos for familiar drinks—Coca-Cola, Schweppes Indian Tonic Water—covered the market stalls to protect them from the sun's rays, and the air was thick with the smell of animal shit. People shouted in Arabic and French. Beggars—even they were chewing khat—lined the walls and the whole place was made more unpleasant by the ever-increasing heat.

Siobhan walked with as much confidence as she could. Although she had darkened her skin and her eyes, she was still wearing Western clothes, so she had to rely on her well-practised ability to disappear in a crowd. It was a state of mind—the moment you looked unsure of yourself, you'd stick out. And if that happened, she'd be surrounded by kids and beggars in an instant.

Siobhan needed clothes. She might not feel

entirely safe here in Djibouti, but she knew how much less safe she would be dressed like this over the border. So it was a relief when she saw what she wanted: a stall, presided over by a dark-skinned man so hunched up and wrinkled that he looked almost like a different species. He didn't have much to sell—a few brightly coloured shirts, some underpants, shoes that looked as if they'd already had several not-so-careful owners. And, at one end of his rickety old rail, what looked like a big sheet of black material, and a veil.

Siobhan pointed at them and nodded at the old man. He mumbled something she couldn't understand, so she just handed over a few notes. From the toothless grin he gave her, she assumed she'd overpaid, but that didn't matter. She took the material from the rack, folded it over her arm, then turned and hurried back to her hotel.

She locked herself in her room, then spread the black clothing out on her bed. Siobhan had never worn a burka, of course. In fact she'd never really seen one, and it took a while to work out how to put it on. It was too big, and she had to tie it in places to make it fit properly. Even in the supposedly air-conditioned hotel room, the extra layer of heavy clothing was almost unbearably hot and heavy. But at the very least the grille of the veil covered her face. Siobhan removed the headdress for now, then killed time in her room for a couple of hours before preparing to leave.

When she asked the guy at reception if he could organise a taxi back to the airport, he looked faintly amused before disappearing out into the street and coming back in with a thin-looking man chewing the ever-present khat. The taxi driver looked spaced out, but Siobhan wasn't in a position to argue. She climbed into the back of his cab and wasn't entirely surprised to see a hole in the floor that displayed the road below. The taxi driver jabbered away in Arabic all the way to the airport. It didn't seem to worry him that Siobhan said nothing.

The aircraft was already waiting to depart when she got to the airport, an Ilyushin Il-18 turboprop looking like something that might have flown behind the Iron Curtain thirty years previously. She put on her headdress before checking in, then walked to the departure gate.

There weren't many people waiting to take that trip to Mogadishu. Siobhan was one of only two women; the remaining men, about twenty of them, were without exception dark-skinned and lean— the kind of tough thinness that comes from hardship. A few carried briefcases—God only knew what business they were up to. Some of them had gathered into little groups, and within those groups a few men talked with animation. But the different groups eyed each other with suspicion, and Siobhan, despite her burka, or maybe because of it, drew some curious and hostile glances. These men clearly didn't trust strangers.

A flight attendant called them forwards. Siobhan allowed all the others to board first. That way she could be sure of getting a seat by herself. She didn't want people asking her questions, and not just because of the language barrier. It would be stupidity, she knew, to let anyone realise just how vulnerable she was. It was going to be difficult enough on the ground without letting her travelling companions know that she was a white

263

woman travelling on her own to the most dangerous country in the world.

Siobhan handed her ticket to the woman at the gate. She glanced at it, glanced at Siobhan, and then spoke. *'Attendez-vous, s'il-vous-plait.'* The woman took the ticket and the passport, then disappeared while Siobhan stood at the gate, feeling a hot surge of panic in her veins. What the hell was going on?

When the woman returned, she had two other men with her. Siobhan recognised one of them immediately—the grey hair and the Manchester United shirt of the man from the Daallo Airlines counter. The second stood out because he was white, and Siobhan immediately noticed a tattoo creeping below his sleeve on to his right hand. He had the physique of a rugby player, and the sweat on his brow made him look like he was in the middle of a match. As he walked right up to her, she noticed that his nose was squashed flat and he didn't smell too fresh.

He jerked his thumb towards the Man U fan. 'Bibi tells us you're getting on this flight by yourself.' He had a South African accent.

Siobhan surveyed them through the grille of her burka. 'Bibi talks too much,' she said.

The South African moved quickly. He grabbed one sleeve of Siobhan's robes and tugged it up, revealing a flash of white skin where she hadn't applied the fake tan. Her reaction was immediate. She grabbed his wrist in a fierce grip and pushed it away.

The man grinned. It wasn't a very nice look. 'I wouldn't mind betting, love,' he said, 'that there's a lot more beautiful white skin under those robes.'

He looked around. 'A lot of Kaffirs round here. Unless you're planning to get it together with one of them, I might be a better bet.'

He raised his hand again and made to lift her headdress.

'You even think about it,' Siobhan hissed, 'and I'll break your fingers.'

He paused. And then, clearly realising that she meant what she said, he lowered his hand again. 'Break my fingers,' he said, 'and I might not be able to pleasure you the way I'd like. You really thinking of getting on that plane?'

'I really am.'

'Don't.'

All of a sudden, the lasciviousness had fallen from his face.

'Who the hell are you?'

'Doesn't matter who I am, love. Let's just say I've made the trip a few times. Don't get on that plane.'

'Thanks for the advice.' Siobhan turned to the woman and held out one hand for her passport. She reluctantly handed it over.

A moment of silence. The South African leaned in even closer. 'You got American dollars?' he asked.

Siobhan nodded.

'When you land, don't even think of handing over your passport without a fifty-dollar bill. They won't let you in without a bribe, and it's not something you want to discuss with them, all right? Keep the rest of your money hidden in your shoe. At least that way they're less likely to take it off you while you're still alive.'

'Who's they?'

The man shook his head. 'Anyone, love. Anyone.

Have you ever handled a weapon?'

Siobhan sniffed. 'Now and then.'

'Buy one at the airport.'

'Who from?'

'Anybody. If you can, hire someone to look after you. Better still, hire several people. I don't move around the country without at least six guards. Make sure they're armed.'

'How do I know I can trust them?' Siobhan asked.

'You don't. But without them you'll be dead the moment you enter the capital. Before, probably. Keep the burka on. It won't stop you being robbed, but it might stop you being kidnapped, or shot on sight. There's only one safe place to stay in Mogadishu. It's called the Trust Hotel. It's where foreign journalists stay, and it has electricity and running water. If you've got any sense, you'll go straight there and not leave until you need to get out of the country. If you get there, make sure you get a room on the ground floor.'

'Why?'

'Because if the place gets hit by an artillery shell, you might escape.'

Siobhan nodded again. Despite herself, she felt a surge of gratitude towards this ugly man.

'Thank you,' she said.

The man shrugged again. 'You're not a journalist,' he said. 'If you were, you'd be taking the UN flight in. And you're not a pro, otherwise I wouldn't have to tell you this stuff. So whatever it is you're going to Mogadishu for, you need to ask yourself whether it's worth risking your life for. You'd be much safer coming back to my hotel with me.' He had reverted to his former self.

They stared at each other. Siobhan thought about O'Callaghan and Khan. Most of all, she thought about Lily.

'I don't want to keep the plane waiting,' she said.

Siobhan grabbed her passport and ticket, then turned her back on the others and started walking towards the aircraft. When she glanced over her shoulders, Bibi and the South African had gone.

## 15

Nairobi. Flight time from London, eight hours. An eight-hour journey to a different world.

From his cramped window seat on the 747, Jack saw the hazy Nairobi skyline shimmer in the late-afternoon sun and the city dust. As the plane circled in a holding pattern above the city, the captain announced that the passengers would be able to see Mount Kenya to the north, and Kilimanjaro to the south-east. Jack could also see the green, wooded districts that surrounded Nairobi. It was an impressive sight, but he knew from experience that those mountain regions and those woods hid more sinister backwaters. Nairobi presented to the world a face of prosperity and democracy, but that face hid the reality. Political corruption, widespread crime—Kenya wasn't the worst place in Africa, not by a mile, but like everywhere on the continent it had its problems. Step away from the comfortable tourist spots and you needed to be on your guard.

Jack wasn't heading to the tourist spots of Nairobi. In fact he wasn't heading to any spots.

Once he'd touched down and gone through security, he went straight to the departures area of the airport. It was busy and hot. Long queues snaked round the concourse; men and women gathered chaotically around the bureau de change; almost everyone seemed to have a cigarette in their mouth. Jack stood by a billboard that showed a giraffe with the skyline of Nairobi in the distance, and which announced in jolly red letters 'Kenya! Safari capital of the world!' He scanned the crowds, his eyes searching something out.

'My friend!'

A young black boy—he couldn't have been more than sixteen—was suddenly standing by him, grinning with a mouthful of large, yellow teeth. He held out a small wooden figure.

'My friend, this is for you. A gift for you, my friend!'

Jack ignored him. The boy took it in good spirit. He put one palm to his chest and grinned even wider. 'Oh!' he announced, like a ham actor on the stage. 'In Kenya, we are all friends. You must not turn your head away. Do not be hard like a coconut, my friend!'

Jack didn't listen to any more. He grabbed the kid by the front of his shirt and gave him a hard stare. The smile dropped from the boy's face.

'Go away,' Jack told him, before throwing him backwards. The boy managed to keep his balance, but scrambled away from Jack, all arms and legs, to where a small crowd of his peers were waiting. They gave him some unpleasant stares, but none of them looked like they were going to start tapping Jack for any cash.

He continued to scan over the heads of the

crowds on the concourse. Along the far wall he saw a line of booths, each with glowing signs advertising safaris in various parts of the country. Jack strode towards them and as he grew closer he examined each one. Most of them had two or three people standing by them, some of them white. One, at the end, attracted no one's interest. The sign above the booth read 'Rainbow Safaris. Discover the hidden beauty of Kenya at the Arawale Nature Reserve'. It was illustrated with indistinct pictures of lions, elephants and buffalo. Below the sign, sitting at the booth, was a bored-looking Kenyan. He didn't look much more animated when Jack approached him.

'Rainbow Safaris?'

The Kenyan nodded almost imperceptibly.

'When does the next excursion leave?'

'Full,' the Kenyan said.

'I didn't ask if it was full. I asked when it leaves. My name's Jack Harker.'

The name meant something to him. Markus had done his work. The man made a sucking sound with his teeth, then started writing out a ticket. 'One hour and a half, Mr Jack,' he said as he handed it over with a noticeable lack of enthusiasm. 'Have an enjoyable safari. I hope you find what you are looking for.'

Yeah, Jack thought as he walked away from the booth. Me too.

The aircraft was a twin prop. Jack didn't know how many flight hours the thing was built to manage in its lifetime, but he felt sure it had exceeded them a long time ago. Half the seats had been ripped out to make room for cargo, and that space was now filled with sealed wooden boxes containing God knew what.

The Kenyan who'd told him the plane was full hadn't been exaggerating. Jack was forced to use a spare cabin-crew seat, which didn't go down well with the crew themselves, who treated his lack of luggage and his sudden addition to the passenger list with suspicion. There were no other white faces on the plane, which made Jack suspect that not many of the passengers were heading off on safari. That made sense. There were other, more popular safari destinations in Kenya, and in any case not many foreigners would be keen to take an internal flight scheduled to land, as this one was, after dark.

They took off at 18.30 hrs, and the light was already beginning to fade as the old plane bumped its way through the air, heading east out of Nairobi and travelling a little more than an hour before it started to lose height in sudden, unprofessional lurches. The pilot, Jack decided, wasn't an expert. There were no trays of plastic food and complimentary coffee on this kind of flight. You just felt thankful to touch down in one piece.

Jack took his mind off it by thinking about Markus Heller. They went back a long way. Over the years, the Regiment and Delta Force had shared both personnel and information. Jack and Heller had been passing acquaintances on account of that, but it was in the aftermath of the invasion of Baghdad in 2003 that they really got to know each other. Both Heller and Jack had been seconded to Gray Fox—code name for the US's Intelligence Support Activity operations to locate Saddam Hussein. Iraqi militants had opened fire on them as they were closing in on a suspected hideaway on the outskirts of Samara and Heller had taken a round in the leg, straight through an artery on the inside of his thigh. He'd bled like a motherfucker and if Jack—or someone like him—hadn't been by his side, he'd have died there and then. But Jack had reacted quickly, fixing a tourniquet on Heller's leg while keeping the enemy at bay with covering fire. They'd got him out of there and into hospital in time for both his life and his leg to be saved, even though the long-term effects of his wound were enough to buy him a ticket out of the military that he didn't really want.

Jack would have done the same for anyone on his team, and they'd have done it for him. He neither asked for nor needed thanks for his actions. But Heller believed he owed him one. Big time. Trouble was, he was an unpredictable bastard—clever, ruthless, but also a Bible-basher who never seemed to have a problem resolving his religious beliefs with the fact that he killed people for a living. Maybe he was sanguine about sending them to meet their Maker; maybe it was more complicated than that. Didn't make him a bad soldier; it just meant he lived by a different code to the rest of them. Quite why Markus Heller had been filled with the desire to sell safaris in eastern Kenya, Jack didn't know. But with his background and his skills, he could hazard a pretty good guess . . .

It was fully dark now, and even though they were flying over land, Jack could see only the occasional lights from settlements dotted around that part of the country—parched terrain punctuated by forested areas. They came in to land after a ninety-minute flight. Jack had been on ops in Africa often enough to know what to expect of the airfield: a strip of hardened earth, some corrupt officials and little in the way of facilities.

He wasn't wrong. When the plane hit the ground it bumped and jolted against the potholed runway, causing both the passengers and the cargo to shake like a box of rattling bones. The engines screamed as the aircraft slowed down and stopped, abruptly, in the middle of nowhere.

The passengers filed out. A couple of old Land Rovers drove up, but they were for cargo and luggage, not people. The passengers were obliged to walk about 150 metres across the airfield towards a couple of low, shabby huts that passed as terminal buildings. The air here was humid and heavy, like a storm was coming. Jack felt himself sweating as he walked, a little separate from the others, away from the plane.

He was about twenty metres from the building when two men approached. They were broad-shouldered and flat-faced and Jack could instantly tell from the bulges under their shirts that they were tooled up. They didn't look like officials, but they blocked his way and stood menacingly close.

'Jack Harker?' one of them asked in a low voice.

Jack nodded.

'Mr Markus sent us. Our vehicle is this way.' He glanced to his right. In the darkness, Jack saw a Land Rover parked up just by the runway.

The vehicle was caked in dust and stank of diesel. Jack sat in the back. It was a silent journey. The roads were bad, and although the moon was full and bright it did little to penetrate the darkness all around. Jack could just make out some kind of vegetation on either side, but the road itself was baked hard. Nobody spoke. Jack saw the driver continually glancing in the rear-view mirror, the whites of his eyes glowing in the gloom as he looked at him with suspicion.

After about twenty slow, juddering minutes, Jack saw lights up ahead. A settlement of some kind. The headlamps from the truck lit up a small collection of wooden huts with thatched roofs. Jack knew these must be for tourists, because most Africans in this part of Kenya would be living in shacks. He saw a large sign that looked very similar to the one over the booth back in Nairobi. 'Rainbow Safaris'. In the centre of the huts there was a campfire, and Jack thought he could make out the silhouettes of people sitting around it.

The Land Rover came to a halt.

'Who are those people?' Jack asked

It was the driver who answered. 'Visitors to the safari,' he said in his deep, African accent.

'Is Markus with them?'

'No. There are buildings beyond the huts. That is where he stays. We must walk there.'

The people around the fire spoke in low voices. They appeared to be mostly white and male, and Jack thought he heard snatches of German in their conversation. But they didn't appear to notice the three of them walking round the huts until they came to an open space, beyond which there was a collection of uglier buildings with concrete walls, gently slanting corrugated iron roofs and an impressive network of aerials—including a small satellite—protruding from the top. The air was filled with the low hum of a generator, and from one of the buildings a light was shining.

273

'Is Markus in there?'

The men nodded.

They stepped across the open ground. The driver entered the building first, followed by his colleague. Jack heard them speak. 'Mr Markus? *Mr Markus*? Mr Markus, where are you?'

Footsteps behind him. Immediately Jack felt something hard and cold pressed against the back of his skull.

And then a voice. As southern as fried chicken.

'Here I am, boys,' it said. 'Now Jack, I don't want you to think it ain't a delight to see you. But I can't help thinking you've probably seen as much of this goddamn country as you want to. Now, this is just a wild stab in the dark, but I'm thinking you ain't here to be overwhelmed by the wonders of nature in all their glory. Would I be close to the mark?'

Jack turned around just as the man behind him was lowering his gun.

Markus Heller had changed. Back in Iraq he'd had short, steel-grey hair and a few days' growth on his tanned face. Now he had a grey beard and his hair, which was down to his shoulders, was held back by a red bandana. He wore khaki safari gear that suited him, but otherwise—with the exception of the matt-black Glock in his hand—he had the appearance of a hobo. It looked like he took a lot better care of his weapon than he did of himself.

A grin spread across his face. He raised a big hand and clasped Jack's left shoulder. 'Well you know what I say? Fuck the wonders of nature. Welcome to Africa, old friend.' His grin became broader. 'Welcome to Africa.'

# 16

'Do all your guests get the same kind of welcome?'
Jack asked, looking meaningfully at the Glock.

Markus looked mildly surprised. 'Sure hope not,'
he replied. 'Rainbow Safaris prides itself on
offering a first-class safari experience. Do I sound
kinda like an advertisement? But then . . .' Here he
smiled almost apologetically. 'But then not all our
guests are currently serving in the British SAS. You
*are* currently serving, right, Jack?'

Jack didn't answer and Markus nodded slowly.
'Absent without leave, huh? Hope you ain't trying
to get me into trouble.'

'I need help.'

'Unfortunately for you, Jack, these are not the
offices of the Kenyan Tourist Board.' He stepped
back a few paces, and Jack noticed that he still had
a pronounced limp.

'Not the sort of thing they can help me with,' he
said.

'And what makes you think I can, Jack?'

Jack shrugged. 'Regiment gossip. You know what
it is. You don't think you'd be able to set up shop
fifty miles from the Somali border without tongues
wagging in Hereford.' He glanced over his
shoulder and looked at the signalling aerials
jutting out from the top of the building.
'Impressive set-up,' he continued. 'A bit more than
I'd expect from, what is it you call yourself?
Rainbow Safaris?'

Heller's face remained expressionless.

'The thing I can't work out is who's paying you to

stay in this shithole. Delta? Their man on the ground in case they need to send a team over the border?'

Still no expression.

'CIA?'

A slight tightening around the eyes, and Jack gave an understanding nod. 'We've all got to earn a living,' he said, before slowly—so as not to make anyone nervy—putting his hand in his inside pocket and pulling out a bundle of O'Callaghan notes. Heller inclined his head. 'I need to get over the border,' Jack told him. 'Immediately. I need vehicles, I need weapons and I need them tonight.'

Heller seemed momentarily wrong-footed. 'Seems to me, Jack old buddy, that the Regiment are better placed to do that than I am.'

'Fuck the Regiment,' Jack said. 'This is personal. I don't want them finding out. Same goes for the Firm and the Cousins. Can you do it?'

Markus stared at him, then at the money, and behind those grey eyes Jack could see a world of suspicion. Finally, though, he seemed to come to a decision.

'Of course,' Markus said. And then, for the first time, he smiled. 'For the right price, and as long as the Lord wishes it, I can do anything. Let's go inside, Jack. Sounds like we have a few things to talk about.'

Markus's office was basic: a table, a telephone, a fridge full of local Tusker beer and a big metal cabinet along one wall. Markus cracked open a couple of cold beers while his flat-faced men stood guard outside.

'So the safari business is just a front,' Jack said.

'I guess you could say that,' Heller drawled. 'I

earn a few dimes from the business, keeps me outta trouble, but the real money's to be made from fixin'. You should consider getting into the game yourself. I could always use good men.'

'Maybe I'll think about it,' Jack lied. 'I could be in the market for a job soon.'

Heller raised an eyebrow, but didn't enquire further. He took another pull on his beer. 'Fuckin' Somalia!' he said suddenly. 'Eighteen years of civil war, no functioning government, thirty-six thousand IDPs and the aid agencies can't even deliver food aid because the fuckers shoot them if they try to step off their ships. You know, Jack, I got a pretty easy life out here. Now and then the CIA send a couple of scouts in-country, sniff around before reporting back that the place is still fucked up. But I got to tell you, it's not often I get someone wantin' to go into that piece-of-shit country off their own back. I don't suppose you want to share the reasons with an old friend.'

'Let's just call it woman trouble,' Jack replied.

Markus laughed. 'Hell, that's the worst kind. Say, whatever happened to that daughter of yours?'

Jack's face hardened and he downed his beer. 'Nothing to report,' he said.

Markus eyed him warily, but clearly got the hint. 'Whatever you say, Jack. So what's on your shopping list?'

'I need to get into Mogadishu, pull someone out and get them back.'

'You need a team on the ground?'

'I don't know,' Jack said. 'You got anyone you can trust?'

Heller laughed for second time. 'In Mogadishu? Hell no.'

'Sounds like I'll be going solo. What about weapons?'

'Weapons, my friend, we can do. He turned round and limped up to the metal cabinet. He unlocked it with a key kept round his neck, before opening the door and standing back like conjurer who had just performed a trick. The cabinet contained almost all the personal weaponry Jack could imagine. Assault rifles and submachine guns were neatly racked along the wall; beneath them were boxes of ammo, fragmentation grenades, flashbangs, night sights—the works. Credenhill wasn't much better kitted out than this Kenyan backwater.

'A lot of hardware for a safari operation,' Jack commented.

'It's very important,' Keller said piously, 'that we keep our customers safe.'

'With flashbangs?'

Keller laughed and took another pull on his beer. 'We've got a light aircraft,' he said. 'There's a storm comin' tonight. I'd say you'd be best leaving here just before dawn. There's a small airfield we use just outside the capital. We should be able to put you down there in about three hours.'

'What about a vehicle?'

'I'll make some calls now. I can arrange for someone to be at the airfield when you land. Can't promise what they'll bring you, but it'll hopefully be enough to get you into the town. You'll need to pay them with American dollars. You got any?'

Jack shook his head, so Markus pulled a briefcase from the cabinet. He clicked it open to reveal a stash of perfect, new US notes. He peeled off a wodge and handed them to Jack.'

'Not like you to throw your money about, Markus.'

'Neither a borrower nor a lender be, Jack. Anyways, ain't my money.' He winked at him. 'The Company understands that I occasionally need to spread the love, you understand me? And let me tell you: the greenback's the only thing out there that speaks louder than a 5.56.'

'Do you think your employers might come good with a bit of intel?'

'Depends what.'

'There's a guy called Habib Khan. He's some kind of peace activist, pulling a publicity stunt by going to Mogadishu. I need to know where I can find him.'

Markus gave him a sharp look. 'Thought you said it was woman trouble, Jack.'

'Where Khan goes, the woman won't be far behind.' His eyes darkened. 'It's complicated.'

Markus shrugged. 'I'll make the call, see what I can find out. Hope you're makin' yourself a buck or two going in there, Jack. And while we're on the subject of payment . . .'

'How much?' Jack demanded.

Markus squinted one eye and downed the rest of his beer, before smacking his lips with great satisfaction. 'Tell you what, buddy, I owe you one and I'm a man who likes to pay his debts. So here's what I suggest. That pile of UK banknotes you pulled out of your pocket, you leave them here. If you make it back from Mogadishu, they're all yours and I've returned that little favour I owe you. If not . . .' He inclined his head.

Jack stared at him. The implication of what he was saying wasn't lost on him. Markus was a

279

gambling man.

'How do I know you're not setting me up?'

Markus cast him a serious glance. 'Because I'm a man of my word, Jack. And because the good Lord above judges me by the choices I make.'

'I've seen good men be tempted by money before, Markus. Hope you don't mind if I feel a bit funny about leaving you here with the cash.'

'Leavin' me here? I don't think so, Jack. Ain't no one else round this place knows how to fly that bird but me. I'm going to put you on the ground. How long you need to do what you got to do?'

'I'm in and out. Twelve hours, max.'

'You got it. I'll put you on the ground in the morning, then wait at the airstrip. I'll give you till midnight. You back in that time, I fly you home. You a minute late, your goddamn carriage turns into a pumpkin. I'll know you're dead and I'm the hell out of there. We got a deal?'

Jack sniffed. Could he trust Markus? Truth was he didn't have a choice. He thought of Siobhan. God knows where she was now. Had she made it over the border from Djibouti? If so, was she safe? He felt a chill.

'We've got a deal,' he said.

'Hallelujah.' Heller stood aside and allowed Jack to approach the cabinet and start selecting his weapons.

'You good protecting yourself on the runway while I'm on the ground?' Jack asked.

For a moment, Markus didn't reply. Jack looked over his shoulder at him. The American's face was grim and serious. 'Destruction cometh,' he said in a low voice. 'And they shall seek peace, and there shall be none. Ezekiel, chapter 7, verse 25. Just

280

don't be late, huh?'

They stared at each other. Then Jack turned back to the cabinet and continued to select his tools.

*       *       *

Siobhan's plane came in to land just as the sun was setting. From her window, she could see the Somali coastline. It was stunning—holiday-brochure stuff with blue seas and golden sand. But beyond the beaches of Mogadishu lay the town itself. Even from the air, Siobhan could see how devastated it was—a mass graveyard of buildings as far as she could see, almost entirely demolished. A vast network of destruction. As she came in to land she saw the burnt-out wreckage of a Russian cargo plane at the end of the runway.

The Ilyushin Il-18 in which Siobhan was travelling wouldn't be staying on the ground for very long—just enough time to deposit its passengers and their luggage before taking to the air again. Back to safety.

The plane doors opened and the passengers spilled out.

The heat was the first thing Siobhan noticed as she stepped out of the air-conditioned cocoon of the aircraft. The second was the smell, a mixture of sea air and rotting debris, blown over from the fetid streets and sewers of the city.

And then she saw that this had clearly once been a big airfield, but now the terminal buildings and airport hangars were practically falling to the ground, surrounded by the kind of rubble that can only be caused by weaponry.

The passengers walked quickly—ran, almost—and Siobhan did the same, not towards one of these destroyed airport buildings, but to an area that was little more than a slab of concrete resting on eight metal pillars. Beneath the concrete roof were a collection of chairs and a single table. A man was sitting there. He had an assault rifle by his side on the table and a bandolier of ammo strapped round his chest. The passengers queued up in front of the table, with Siobhan at the end of the line. Up at the front there was much arguing, but Siobhan couldn't understand the language. Whatever the problems, they were all resolved in the same way: by handing over a few notes to the man at the desk.

Siobhan's turn came. The official—if that's what he was—looked her up and down with a sour smile that displayed yellow, tombstone teeth. The smile grew broader when he saw her UK passport with a fifty-dollar bill peeping out of the top. He slid the money out, pocketed it, but didn't return the passport immediately. He flicked through it with his fingers, not reading, but teasing.

Suddenly he barked a single word. From somewhere in the almost darkness around them, another man emerged. He was of a similar age to the official—perhaps in his twenties—and he wore a military jacket and a black and white keffiyeh round his neck. His rifle was strapped round his back, but in his fist there was a handgun. Siobhan recognised it instantly as a Makarov 9 mm semi-automatic, standard Soviet issue until the early nineties. She pointed at it. 'For me,' she said.

The two men looked at each other and started to laugh. An ugly sound. They stopped laughing, though, when Siobhan pulled out $200. The newcomer raised an eyebrow; moments later, the trade was complete. Siobhan had her weapon, the guy had his money. The loss of the handgun didn't worry him, however. He still had his assault rifle, after all.

In the distance there was a low rumbling. Something going down in the city. An explosion.

'You speak English?' Siobhan demanded of the two men.

It was the official who spoke. 'Maybe,' he said. His voice sounded too low for his thin body.

'I need someone to protect me. You understand?' Siobhan did what she could to stop her voice shaking.

The grin didn't leave the official's face. 'Protection, yes.'

'I can pay. I need to get into the city. The Trust Hotel. You know it?'

But all the official did was laugh again. A long, low laugh that had nothing to do with humour.

'Fine,' Siobhan said as she tucked the Makarov under her robes. 'You don't want my money . . .' She started to walk away.

When she thought about it afterwards, Siobhan realised that turning her back on them had been her first mistake. She heard a shuffling from behind and quickly spun round. The man from whom she had bought the gun had slung his assault rifle around from the back to the front, and even now he was flicking the safety switch and pointing it at Siobhan.

Her hand quickly dived under her robes for the Makarov, but the material—heavy and flowing—got in her way. Her stomach twisted with the

283

realisation that the guy had her in his sights now, and there was no doubting what he was about to do.

The burst of automatic fire rang across the airfield.

But it wasn't Siobhan who hit the ground. The seated official hadn't even bothered to lift up his gun. It was still lying on its side on the table, pointing at the other man, when he squeezed the trigger. The burst of rounds caused the rifle to rotate a few degrees as they slammed into the guy's belly, making his hands fly up from his own gun and his body jolt violently, like he was having a brief but intense seizure. An explosion of blood and he hit the ground, his left foot twitching and a deathly gurgling sound coming from his throat. Siobhan was glad she was wearing a veil. It meant the look of horror on her face was hidden.

A moment of silence. The official slid the weapon round on the table so that it was pointing at Siobhan. 'Maybe I kill you now,' he said.

Siobhan stood very still. 'If you were going to kill me, you'd have done it by now.'

She felt her clothes sucking up sweat from her body.

The man grinned again. 'I have four men. You pay them a hundred dollars each. Me, you pay two hundred. We take you where you want to go.'

On the ground, the wounded man breathed his last breath. It sounded like a ghost was escaping from his mouth.

'The Trust Hotel,' Siobhan repeated. 'You know it?'

The man shrugged. 'Of course.' From his pocket he pulled a mobile phone—a surprisingly modern

284

one. He dialled a number, gave a few short instructions and only seconds later Siobhan saw a pair of headlights approaching them at speed. An open-top truck screeched up to them. What type of vehicle it was, Siobhan couldn't tell. Sheets of steel had been welded to the side, into which small holes had been cut away, like peepholes. They weren't for anyone to look in, however. They were for guns to poke out.

Four men jumped out of the vehicle. They were all dressed much like the corpse on the ground: military camouflage jackets of varying degrees of disrepair and keffiyehs round their necks. They were very heavily armed: two of them carried assault rifles and ammo belts; one had a pistol in his hand and another on his belt; the driver carried nothing, but Siobhan could see the tip of an RPG pointing from the back of the truck. If it came down to it, there were more than enough weapons to go around.

The men glanced at the corpse by their feet. Their reaction shocked Siobhan even more than the killing: they wore expressions of casual boredom. These were clearly men for whom death was an everyday occurrence.

In the distance, another booming sound; and behind Siobhan, the noise of the Ilyushin taxiing to the end of the airstrip. She felt a moment of weakness as she realised that there really was no way out of here now.

The official started talking to his men and it wasn't long before they were arguing. It was the driver who was the most aggressive. He started waving his arms in the air, pointing at Siobhan and, as the sound of the aircraft speeding down the

285

runway began to deafen them, shouting at the top of his voice.

The official let him have his say. The driver was still shouting by the time the aircraft had taken off, clearly barking his objection to having anything to do with Siobhan. The others seemed torn, not knowing which side of the fence to fall on, and this only enraged the driver more. There was a wildness in his eyes that alarmed Siobhan, and she felt her right hand creeping into her robes almost as a matter of reflex, her fingers gripping the holster of her newly acquired Makarov.

And it was a good thing too.

The driver suddenly couldn't contain his anger. He strode towards Siobhan, his fists in the air and a snarl on his face. Siobhan didn't hesitate. She drew the Makarov from her robes and held it straight at the man's head.

He stopped. The anger didn't disappear from his expression, but at least he knew when he was staring death in the face.

'Tell him to step back,' Siobhan said.

The official translated her instruction, and the driver withdrew.

'I've made you my offer,' she continued. 'Do you want to take it, or shall I find someone else to do business with?'

The official grinned at her. He wasn't the only one to find this robed woman entertaining. All the others were smiling too. Except for the driver, of course. His eyes were firmly focused on the barrel of her handgun.

'We take you,' he announced. 'Get into the car.'

Siobhan shook her head. 'You first. All of you. I'll sit behind the driver. And you might as well tell

286

him that I'll have the gun pointed at the back of his seat. If I start to get nervous, I'll fire, and the bullet will go through his seat, through his back and probably through the steering column as well.'

'You must pay us our money first,' the official said.

'No way. I get to the hotel, *then* you get your money. And believe me, my friend, I *know* how to use this weapon. You can try to rob me if you want, but if you do, at least one of you will end up dead.'

She twitched her gun towards the armoured car. 'Move,' she said. 'Now.'

\*      \*      \*

The roads outside the airport were not designed for speed. That didn't stop the driver from putting his foot down. Siobhan knew why: fast-moving targets were more difficult to hit than slow ones.

There were no road markings. No signs. Just a network of dusty, well-travelled thoroughfares that bore all the scars of Somalia's embattled past. They barely passed a building that wasn't bombed out or burned down; piles of rubble outnumbered dwelling places a hundred to one; and she saw any number of small fires by the roadside, around which ragged people were clustered. More than once, Siobhan heard a loud bang, like a car engine backfiring. But she knew those sounds didn't come from engines. They came from guns.

Her companions had lost their smiles and their arrogance. They were sweating, concentrating, and their weapons were ready, poking through the cut-out holes of the armoured car. Only the driver was unarmed, and he sat low in his seat so that as much

287

of his body as possible was shielded by the chassis of the vehicle. Siobhan still didn't trust him and kept the Makarov firmly poked into his back.

The roadside buildings became more numerous, but no less devastated. Those buildings that were still intact were covered in graffiti. As the outskirts gave way to the city, Siobhan saw more and more people. They were all young men, dressed in an assortment of poor clothes and headgear. But what these people had failed to spend on their garments, they more than made up for on their weapons. As she peered round the back of the driver's seat, Siobhan couldn't see a single person not openly carrying a gun, and plenty of people carrying more than one. The men stood in groups, each group eyeing the others with suspicion.

The rotten smell grew stronger. The streets were littered with debris—rotting food, paper, hunks of metal and tyres. The outskirts of Mogadishu were behind them now; they were nearing the centre. It meant they couldn't travel so fast because the streets were smaller and more crowded. The number of fires didn't decrease—people just lit them seemingly at random by the road—and as Siobhan moved deeper into the city, she heard music blaring from unknown places. It was loud, Arabic in idiom, and somehow very threatening.

Not as threatening, though, as the looks they were attracting. Siobhan wouldn't have gone alone into those terrifying streets for any money in the world; but the presence of the armoured car drew a lot of attention. Hungry-looking eyes watched them pass, and Siobhan knew what thoughts were behind them: what is *that* vehicle carrying that is worthy of such protection?

The driver slammed on the breaks. 'What is it?' Siobhan demanded, her voice quavering.

Nobody answered. They didn't need to. Up ahead, maybe fifty metres away, there was a mob. They were moving up the road towards them, blocking the way. Siobhan could hear their shouts. Angry.

A weapon fired. The shouts swelled and the crowd continued to press towards them.

The driver didn't hesitate. He knocked the truck into reverse and hit the accelerator. The vehicle screamed backwards, and people in the street had to run out of its way because the driver sure as hell wasn't going to avoid them. *What's going on?* Siobhan screamed, but nobody answered because at that moment two rounds flew over her head. Instantly the air was alive with the sound of gunfire as her escorts opened up on the crowd. The mob faltered momentarily as two of their number fell to the ground, but they soon regrouped. By that time, however, the driver had put some more distance between them. They were at a crossroads now. The driver spun the wheel sharply to the left and the truck turned 180 degrees, kicking up a cloud of dust before they sped back in the opposite direction.

'What was that? *What the hell was that?*'

It was the official who spoke. From his position in the passenger seat he looked over his shoulder at her. 'That,' he said with a nasty leer, 'is Muqdisho.'

Siobhan's heart was pumping as they continued through the confusing network of streets that made up the capital. She was lost and terrified, not knowing if these men truly were taking her where she wanted to go, or if they were just heading for some out-of-the-way place where they could rob and either kill her or leave her alone on these streets, which would end up being the same thing. The gun felt sweaty in her palm, but she clutched it firmly anyway.

They continued to drive.

When they stopped again, it was outside a set of steel gates embedded in a thick, high wall marked with bullet holes. There were four guards, clearly Somali, wearing body armour and helmets, and they stood not outside the gates, but inside. Beyond them was a compound of white buildings. Unlike all the others Siobhan had seen so far, it was relatively unscarred. The main entrance was a dark archway, and all the windows were covered with steel bars. Anywhere else in the world this place would look forbidding, but here it looked like paradise, even if the guards did warily raise their weapons at the truck.

The official turned to look at her again. 'You pay us before you get out,' he instructed.

Siobhan narrowed her eyes. 'This is it?' she asked.

He nodded. 'You pay us before—'

'No,' she replied. 'You get out. Go to the gates. I'll pay you there.'

The official inclined his head but didn't argue. As the two of them left the truck, she felt the eyes of her travelling companions on her, but she hurried towards the gates. Once there, she removed her shoe and took out the bundle of notes that she'd stashed there. She counted out some notes, then handed them to the official. How he shared them out with the others was his own concern.

The man shoved them in his pocket and nodded at her. Something seemed to pass between them. 'Muqdisho,' he said, 'is not safe even for me.' He looked in through the gates of the Trust Hotel. 'You should not leave this place,' he said.

Siobhan looked at him from behind the black mask of her burka. 'I might not have a choice,' she murmured.

The official shrugged, then turned his back on her. He looked strangely vulnerable as he walked back to the armoured car, his rifle slung across his back. But Siobhan didn't feel inclined to watch him for long. From beneath her robes she pulled out her British passport and waved it at the guards. Their eyes widened slightly—it was clearly not what they expected to see from this burka-clad woman. But they opened the gates for her and let her in.

As Siobhan Byrne stepped over the threshold of the Trust Hotel, she removed her headdress for the first time since Djibouti; and as the gates shut behind her, she began to feel safe for the first time since she'd landed, though she knew this place was just a fragile bubble around which the whole city was burning and bleeding. She hurried towards the main hotel entrance, her whole body aching to get inside.

Past a gently swaying palm tree that stood sentinel in the courtyard.

Up the steps.

Through the door.

And then she stopped.

The reception room was large. Marble floors. Old mirrors on the wall. Plants in pots. But none of this caught her attention. Instead she was immediately transfixed by a small, neat figure at the long reception desk surrounded by four local bodyguards. He wore a dishdasha and had his back turned towards her so that his face was obscured. She recognised the voice, though, despite having only previously heard it over a crackly loudspeaker or on TV. It was quite distinct. That quiet, clipped, menacingly polite way of speaking.

'I expect journalists from your HornAfrik radio station here first thing in the morning,' he was telling the receptionist, speaking as though to a child. 'Please ensure that they are afforded all possible courtesy. In the afternoon, a colleague of mine will be arriving. I wish to know as soon as she is here. We will be leaving the hotel after dark . . . Yes, I do understand the risks involved, thank you for your concern . . . No, no, it will not be necessary for the hotel to arrange security. I have already seen to that. Thank you for your help. You are most kind.'

Siobhan waited, breathless, for Habib Khan to turn round.

Their eyes met instantly. Khan frowned, then quickly regained control of his expression. He stepped through his ring of close protection and walked towards her.

'Have we met before?' he asked politely.

Siobhan had to think fast. Their paths had crossed only once, outside O'Callaghan's pub; he had seen her for only a matter of seconds. Siobhan knew how people's memories worked. The chances of him placing her were small.

She put her hand out. His palm was sweaty. 'Alison Hoskins,' she simpered. 'Freelance

292

journalist. Perhaps you've seen me on TV.'

Khan smiled blandly. 'I don't really watch the television,' he said.

'Mr Khan, isn't it? I'm interested in your reasons for being here.'

'And I'm interested in yours, Miss Hoskins. It is a brave woman who travels here alone.'

'I had a UN escort. I won't be leaving this hotel.'

'You are sensible,' Khan said. 'I didn't notice you on the UN flight out here.'

'I've come direct from Washington,' Siobhan lied quickly. 'I wonder if I might have an interview.'

Khan seemed to relax. 'Unhappily, my dear, my time is taken up. Unlike you, I am unable to enjoy the hospitality of this place for much longer. Perhaps tomorrow morning I can find a few spare minutes . . .'

Siobhan simpered at him. 'That would be very kind, Mr Khan . . .'

But Khan was already turning his back. Siobhan could tell from his demeanour that he had already dismissed her as someone of no importance. He nodded at his men, then walked out of reception.

Siobhan exhaled deeply. Her head was spinning as she tried to piece together what she'd just learned. Khan had said he would be leaving tomorrow after dark. But he'd said more than that. A colleague was arriving. He wanted to know as soon as *she* was here. Siobhan remembered the words of the girl in the hospital bed. *They ship them out. Africa, they say. Places where white girls fetch a price . . .*

Where would Khan be taking this newcomer after sunset? Siobhan didn't know, but she had a pretty good hunch and she was damn well going to

293

find out.

She pulled herself up to her full height and checked in.

# 4 JULY

## 17

Jack managed two hours of sleep, lying on a hard bunk in one of the huts usually occupied by safari guests. It was still dark when Markus's voice woke him. 'Hands off cocks, on to socks,' the American drawled. 'We got to get going.'

Heavy with tiredness, Jack swung his legs off the bunk. Next to him was a pile of items he'd taken from Markus's stores. He took off his top and pulled on some body armour first. The plates were heavy, the material rough, but it felt like a second skin to him. Round his neck he looped a blade attached to a piece of cord so that it was hanging down his back, then he put his shirt on over the top. In most parts of the world, it was advisable to keep your weapons hidden. But Markus had told him that Somalia was different, that you'd attract attention if you *weren't* obviously tooled up. For this reason, he fixed his Colt M1911 45 mm in a holster round his waist. Jack had also selected a smaller snubnose .38, which he strapped to his lower leg underneath his trousers. American stash, American weapons.

It was in a canvas bag small enough to be slung over his shoulder that he stored his main weapon: a Colt Commando. He added a Claymore anti-personnel mine with its clacker and 100 metres of det cord, a small quantity of plastic explosive, plus two fragmentation grenades and ammo for the weapons. Markus had also given him a camera, which he slung over his shoulder. 'There ain't much in the way of authorities over there,' his fixer had said. 'But if you come across any, tell them you're a journalist. Grease their palms enough and they might decide to believe you.'

Outside he heard the sound of an engine starting. He left the hut and saw Markus behind the wheel of a 4 x 4, the headlamps bright in the darkness. Jack hurried up to it, took his place in the passenger seat and the former Delta man immediately hit the gas. He glanced sideways at Jack's bulky bag. 'Secret to a successful vacation,' he said. 'Preparation.'

'Where's your aircraft?'

'Ten minutes. Relax, buddy, and enjoy the journey.'

Markus's laid-back attitude was getting on Jack's nerves. 'Did you speak to your people?'

'Sure did. Seems your man flew in on a UN flight and has got himself holed up in the Trust Hotel. Good news for you. The hotel is kind of an anomaly—just about the only place in that piece-of-shit city where you don't have hoods with guns trying to put holes in you. Owner of the place pays off the leaders of the different warring factions. Keeps the place clean. Well, kinda. Ain't the Waldorf, but you weren't expecting room service, were you?'

'What about a vehicle?'

'I put the word out. There'll be someone at the airstrip to meet you.'

'Trustworthy?'

Markus snorted. 'What do you think I am, a fuckin' Avis rep?' On the dashboard he indicated what looked like two large mobile phones with thick sturdy aerials. Iridium sat phones. 'Take one of those babies,' he said. 'Number of the other one is scratched on the back. Means you can get in touch if the shit hits the fan.'

'They secure?' Jack asked.

Markus shrugged. 'Company says so. They're probably bullshitting, though. Don't use it if you don't have to, else you get me in the crap.'

06.30 hrs. Dawn was just beginning to creep into the air when they arrived at a nearby airfield. It was deserted apart from a couple of Kenyans smoking cigarettes by a small twin prop. As Markus stopped the car, the noise of the engine was replaced by the sound of a deafening dawn chorus: birds, of course, but also unfamiliar cries and shrieks from the surrounding countryside still blanketed in near blackness.

They approached the two men and Markus threw his car keys to one of them. 'She ready to fly, boys?'

They grinned widely and nodded.

By the time Jack and Markus were both sitting up front in the aircraft, they had about twenty metres visibility. Jack strapped himself in while Markus started up the engines and checked his instruments before handing him a set of shades. 'You'll need 'em,' he said. In a matter of minutes they were taxiing to the end of the runway. The plane turned and came to a halt. 'Ladies and gentlemen,' Markus announced. 'Welcome on board this flight to hell on earth. In the event of an emergency, say your fuckin' prayers.' He turned to Jack and winked. 'Happy fourth of July,' he said.

And with that, the aircraft gathered speed, lifted off and rose into the early morning African air.

The flight time was three hours. They flew in silence.

299

There was nothing to mark their crossing from Kenya to Somalia. Nothing to tell them they had passed over the border into the most dangerous country in the world. Beneath him, Jack saw the sun light up the African plains. He was glad of the shades as he surveyed beautiful patches of gold and green and brown, and to the east, the blue of the Indian Ocean.

It was only when they started to lose height that Markus spoke, and then only briefly. 'Fifteen minutes,' he said.

Jack looked out towards the horizon. In the distance he fancied he could see the edges of a built-up area, shimmering hazily by the ocean.

Mogadishu.

It looked so harmless from up here. Like it was asleep in the sun. Jack found himself wondering if Siobhan had made it there. And if she had, whether she was even still—

'We'll be getting in at a good time. The city tends to be relatively quiet before three p.m. After that, the technicals come out to play. When it gets dark, place is a goddamn war zone.'

Markus turned to look at him, a shrewd expression in his eyes.

'Ain't too late to turn back, my friend,' he said.

Jack didn't even answer.

The airfield where they touched down was as deserted as the one from which they had taken off. A single hut, but it had been burned out long ago. Certainly no officials. Just a vast expanse of low bushes surrounding a long strip of hard-baked earth on which the aircraft bounced and jolted as Markus brought it in to land. He taxied round to the side of the strip and they sat there while the

300

engines powered down.

Silence surrounded them. Silence and heat. The countryside was flat and bare, with just a few trees dotted around them. Up above, Jack saw two vultures circling. He set his jaw. They could circle all they liked. He wasn't carrion. Not yet.

'Welcome to Somalia,' Markus said, 'where the sun always shines.' He handed Jack a detailed satellite map of the area and showed him a circular pencil mark. 'You are here,' he said. 'Take it.'

Jack folded the map and put it into his canvas bag as a vehicle drove into view, emerging slowly out of a heat haze.

'Friends of ours?' Jack asked.

Markus shrugged. 'Hard to say.'

Jack wasn't taking any chances. He opened the side door of the aircraft, climbed out and then, using the door as cover, aimed his rifle in the direction of the approaching vehicle. It was a green Land Rover, probably thirty years old, with dust-caked windows and a canvas backing. It stopped twenty-five metres from the plane, and for a while Jack wondered if the driver was ever going to show himself.

After a minute or so, the driver's door opened and a man got out. He was young, maybe still a teenager, and he wore dark glasses, a black bandana and desert camo. The sleeves had been ripped off his jacket and round his left bicep he had tied a bandage which was bloodied and dirty. The wound, whatever it was, didn't seem to worry him. In his right hand was an AK-47, which he carried nonchalantly, the barrel pointing down at the ground.

'That your man?' Jack hissed at Markus.

'Could be,' the American replied. 'At least, he hasn't started shooting.'

Jack called out. *'Drop your weapon!'*

The kid just grinned and continued walking towards them.

*'Drop it!'* Jack repeated. *'Take another step forward and I'll kill you.'*

That brought him to a halt. The kid slowly bent his knees, then deposited the weapon on the ground.

*'Turn around!'*

Only when the kid was facing the truck did Jack emerge from the protection of the door. He strode quickly up to the newcomer, pulling his M1911 from its holster as he went. When he was behind the driver, he jabbed the butt of the pistol sharply into his cheek. 'You speak English?'

The kid nodded.

'Good. Word of advice. Do what you're told when I'm around if you want to make it till bedtime. Understand?'

Another nod.

'Get in the car. You're going to drive. I'm going to sit next to you. Walk.'

The kid, his arms still in the air, stepped towards the truck as Jack picked up his AK and looked over his shoulder at Markus. 'Midnight,' he called.

'Midnight, my friend,' Markus shouted back. 'And may the Lord guide you every step of the fuckin' way.'

\*      \*      \*

There was no air con in the Land Rover—just a flap above the dashboard that let in hot air. Jack and his driver sweated in the heat, breathing in the fumes of stinking petrol and oil from the jerrycans of fuel that were loaded in the back of the vehicle.

'What's your name?' Jack asked.

'Asad,' said the boy. He stank of sweat and had the habit of licking his lips quickly. It made him look anxious. Jack needed to get him onside.

'I'm going to the Trust Hotel. You know it?'

Asad nodded.

'You'd like enough money to take a girl there, right?'

Asad smiled. 'Yes, boss.'

Jack handed him a couple of notes. 'Stick with me,' he said, 'you'll get more. Every girl in Mogadishu will want to be with you.'

'Yes, boss,' Asad repeated.

They drove in silence.

Finally Asad spoke. 'In the back,' he said. 'A scarf. Cover your white skin. If someone sees it, they will kill you.'

It was Jack's turn to nod. He grabbed the keffiyeh that lay on the back seat and wrapped it round his head so that only his eyes were visible. It made the heat even less tolerable, but that was better than the alternative. When they approached a roadblock manned by three ragged-looking men, Asad gave an aggressive sneer. Jack pulled a couple of notes from his pocket. 'Pay them,' he said.

'It is not necess—'

'*Pay them.*'

Asad shrugged and when they stopped, he handed over the notes. The men were so surprised that the 'tax' had been paid without complaint, Asad was able to drive away quickly.

303

Jack had seen some war-blasted places in his time. Places where destruction was a matter of course. In Helmand, the deserted ruins of Now Zad were a brutal testament to the fighting that had gone on there; in Iraq, he'd wandered through villages where the Republican Guard had slaughtered all the inhabitants for some imagined slight against Saddam. But this was different. As the parched countryside gave way to the outskirts of Mogadishu, Jack saw women and children with ragged clothes and fearful eyes, bundled against piles of rubble that clearly had to make do as houses. The air stank of shit and rubbish and cordite, a thick, sickening stench. Every person he saw looked scared or aggressive or both. He saw children as young as ten or eleven carrying AK-47s, but as the sun was hot, there were few people moving around. Jack knew not to let that lull him into a false sense of security, however. It wouldn't take much for the sun-induced sleepiness to be disturbed. Still, it meant that Asad was able to drive quickly into the centre of Mogadishu, negotiating the confusing maze of streets in which Jack was immediately lost, and avoiding road-blocks and dangerous areas. Before long they had stopped outside the imposing gates and bullet-sprayed walls of the Trust Hotel.

'You pay me now?' the young Somali asked.

Jack fished out a hundred-dollar bill, which Asad grabbed quickly. Then he fished out two more and handed Asad his AK. 'See these?' he said, waving the notes under the kid's nose. 'I'm going into that hotel. I don't know how long I'll be—maybe ten minutes, maybe two hours, maybe more. This money is yours if the vehicle is still outside when I return. Understand?'

Asad licked his dry lips and looked nervously up and down the street. Two hundred bucks was a lot of money to him. He nodded. 'Yes, boss,' he said, touching the bloodied bandage on his arm almost instinctively.

Jack winked at him. 'Think of the girls,' he said.

Jack jumped down from the Land Rover and ran across the street, stopping outside the hotel gates. There were guards on the other side, wearing body armour and helmets. They looked edgy and had already raised their weapons in his direction. Jack peeled off the headscarf to reveal his white skin, then flashed his UK passport at them.

'Journalist,' he said.

'You have weapons?' one of them announced in a thick accent.

'No weapons,' Jack said.

'We must search you.'

Jack handed him money. 'You don't need to search me,' he said.

The guard grinned, revealing a mouthful of wonky yellow teeth. He opened the gates for him, then quickly closed them again. Jack crossed the large courtyard towards the main entrance of the building on the far side.

The reception of the Trust Hotel was a place of faded grandeur, but compared to the rest of the city, it was five star. A man sat at a wide wooden desk with an old computer and a telephone; behind him was a wide set of glass doors, and beyond that a swimming pool, entirely devoid of water. Jack strode straight up to the man.

'I need a room,' he said.

The man was wearing a Western-style suit with

no tie. He gave Jack a smile. Half his teeth were missing, and Jack noticed a nasty scar going from his jaw down his neck.

Checking in was slow. Jack refused to leave his passport, but the guy didn't seem to care, just so long as he saw the colour of his money, fifty bucks for the night. Once the receptionist had handed over the key, Jack looked all around him, then leaned over the desk and gave the guy his most winning smile.

'And now, my friend,' he said, 'I need a woman.'

The receptionist's toothless smile grew broader, bringing with it a cloud of halitosis that Jack ignored.

'Any white women staying here?'

The receptionist let out an unpleasant little giggle. 'You want *white* women?' he asked. 'I know a place. Not far from here. Very nice. Very young. They do everything you want, if you have . . .' He rubbed his fingers together to indicate cash.

Lily's face rose unbidden in his mind. Jack had to try very hard not to grab the guy by his throat. 'What about here?' he pressed. 'I don't want to leave. Are there any white women in the hotel?'

'Yes, boss,' he said. 'Maybe.' He raised an eyebrow. 'A guest.'

'What does she look like?' Jack asked.

The receptionist giggled again. 'Blonde hair,' he said. 'Like in the movies. Very nice.'

Jack laughed with him and nodded enthusiastically, then presented him with another note, which he slid into the top pocket of his jacket.

'What room number?' he whispered.

The receptionist glanced down at his pocket,

then gave Jack a meaningful look, so he stuffed another note in the jacket.

'Room three,' said the receptionist. 'That way. Very pretty, boss. You have nice time.'

He was still giggling to himself as Jack walked away.

*       *       *

Room 3.

The wooden door was scuffed and ill-fitting. Jack stood in the windowless corridor, breathing in the faintly antiseptic smell and listening for the sound of movement in the room. The pendant lights gave an electric flicker.

No sound.

He knocked on the door.

Footsteps.

He knocked again.

'Who is it?'

Siobhan's voice was wary. It was also very close.

'Open up, Siobhan.'

Even through the door he heard her sharp intake of breath.

A pause.

'Don't make me break it down,' Jack warned.

The door clicked open.

Siobhan had darkened her skin. She still looked exhausted. Black rings round her eyes, her hair matted and unkempt, her lips pale. She jutted out her chin at him, a strangely childlike gesture of defiance, but didn't say anything.

'I could have sworn,' Jack said, 'that last time we spoke you promised you weren't going to do anything stupid.'

307

She sniffed. 'I don't need your help, Jack.'

'Siobhan, let me in.'

She looked like she was considering it for a moment. Formulating a response. But after a second she just stepped aside. Jack entered the room and closed the door. There was a wooden wedge on the floor by his feet, which he jammed under the door. Wouldn't stop people from entering, but it would give him a few extra seconds if they tried.

Siobhan's room was basic. Just a bed with thin blankets and a sliding door leading to a bathroom of sorts. A circular fan hung from the ceiling, but it was either switched off or didn't work—the room was uncomfortably hot. Strewn on the bed were a set of black robes and a Makarov 9 mm, and by its side was a small case.

'How did you find me?' Siobhan asked.

'You're not the only person who can track people down, Siobhan. What the hell do you think you're playing at?'

Her lips thinned. 'I'm not *playing* at anything, Jack.'

He looked at the Makarov. 'Had to use it yet?'

'Not yet.'

'So you still got eight nine-millimetre rounds. Great. How do you reckon you're going to deal with the other few thousand of these fuckers who'll rape you and kill you the moment they see your white skin? This is Africa, you know, not Antrim.'

'I got this far, didn't I?'

'Congratulations. Now pack your bag. We're getting out of here.'

Siobhan shook her head. 'No,' she replied.

'I'm not fucking around, Siobhan. We're leav—'

'He's here, Jack. Khan's here.' Her eyes were ablaze.

'Good for him. I hope he has a great holiday. We're leaving.' He grabbed her by the arm and pushed her towards the bed; Siobhan used her free hand to swipe him a stinging blow across the face. Jack had to fight the urge to reciprocate.

They exchanged stares, both as determined as each other.

'Where is he?' Jack finally burst out. 'I'll put his bollocks in a vice, then we can leave.'

Siobhan shook her head. 'He's surrounded by muscle. You won't get close.' She took a deep breath, then spoke slowly, as if she was trying to keep her emotions under control. 'Khan's waiting for someone. A woman. They arrive this afternoon and tonight, after dark, they're travelling somewhere. I don't know where, but they have their own security. I'm going to follow them.'

'How?' Jack couldn't help himself from sounding sarcastic. 'You going to hitch a lift? Jesus, Siobhan, you've already seen what this place is like.'

'I'm not leaving, Jack. What if Khan leads us straight to Lily?'

'Lily's *not here*, Siobhan.'

'You don't *know* that. I'm not leaving this place till I've found out what he's up to.'

'Wrong.'

'Right.'

Jack shook his head. Then he bent down and pulled the snubnose from round his ankle. 'Wrong,' he repeated.

Siobhan gave him a scornful look. 'You didn't come this far to shoot me, Jack. Put it away.'

She was right, of course. Jack lowered the gun.

It all seemed too surreal, some kind of terrible dream.

'Siobhan, please . . .'

'I'm not leaving, Jack.' She gave him a direct look. 'You either stay with me, or you go home by yourself. Final answer.'

*Damn it.* Jack felt like exploding. Anyone else, he'd just remove them by force, shove them in Asad's truck and bundle them back out to the airfield. Why couldn't he do this with Siobhan? Why did she always manage to win their battles?

He heard himself speaking, almost as if someone else was in control of his voice, saying things he didn't want to say. Giving ground he didn't want to give. 'You still haven't told me how you're going to follow him.'

Siobhan gave him a sharp look, then opened the suitcase on to the bed. She pulled out a small object, no bigger than a fifty-pence piece. 'Tracking device,' she said. 'I'm going to plant it on him. Follow at a distance.'

'You got a vehicle?'

'Not yet,' she said. 'The hotel can supply security. I'll get them to hire something.' Siobhan's face was hard. Intractable. Jack could tell nothing would stop her from going through with it. The thought of her heading out of the hotel alone made him feel sick. He turned and stared at the door, his brow furrowed, before suddenly facing her again.

'All right,' he heard himself saying. 'I'll make you a deal. We follow Khan, you and me. I've got an aircraft waiting till midnight at an airfield two miles to the west of the city. If we're late, it leaves. If I come with you this evening, you've got to swear that you'll be on that plane with me.'

Siobhan narrowed her eyes. He could almost see her mind churning over.

'OK,' she said shortly. 'Deal.' There was the faint light of triumph in her face.

Jack picked up the tracking device and held it between his first finger and his thumb. 'There's no point putting this on Khan,' he said. 'You plant it on him now—'

'He changes his clothes half an hour later. Thanks for the lesson, Jack, but I'm not a Girl Guide. We need to get it on his vehicle.'

'Any ideas how you're going to do that?'

'A few. Leave it to me.'

Jack nodded. That was her area of expertise. 'You reckon he's not leaving till after dark?'

'That's what I heard him say.'

'Then we stay here till dusk. I've got a local kid looking after my vehicle. When the sun goes down, we'll move out to the Land Rover. As soon as he leaves we'll start tailing him.'

He turned his attention from the tracking device back to Siobhan. 'You got a GPS display?' She nodded her head and pulled a satnav-type box from her case. Jack nodded. It wouldn't work indoors, but once they were in the open the unit should give them a satellite fix on the tracker. 'That your only weapon?' he asked, pointing at the Makarov.

Siobhan nodded.

'Well keep it close.' He walked over to the other side of the room and pulled the frayed curtains closed. Then he took off his jacket and started unbuttoning his shirt.

'Jack, what are you doing?'

He didn't answer. He just peeled off his shirt to reveal the knife dangling down his back and his body armour, which he removed and handed to Siobhan.

'Put it on,' he said.

'Jack, I don't need—'

*'Put it on!'*

Siobhan bowed her head and picked up the waistcoat before walking with it to the other side of the bed. She turned her back to him, then removed her own jacket and white T-shirt. Jack couldn't stop himself looking at the thin straps of her bra pressing into the pale flesh of her back; couldn't stop himself taking in the familiar slant of her shoulders. She still looked good. Siobhan glanced back at him. It was only momentary, though. She pulled the heavy body armour over her head—it looked massive on her—then tied it at the sides and got dressed again. She gave Jack's bare chest an arch look. 'You trying to win me back?' she asked.

Jack didn't reply. The question made him uncomfortable and as he got dressed again, he couldn't shake a creeping sense of anxiety.

He knew this was stupid.

He knew they were asking for trouble.

He knew they were unprepared. Underplanned.

But he also knew Siobhan. Knew how fucking headstrong she was. He couldn't see what other option he had.

'I'm doing this for Lily, Jack,' she said in a quiet voice.

'I know,' he replied. 'But there are better ways to help her.'

'I have this image,' she said. 'I can't get rid of it.

Her in some kind of, I don't know, brothel. Men like Khan doing things to her.'

Jack put one finger over her lips.

'If we do find her,' Siobhan said, her voice on the brink of tears, 'we make it up to her, right?'

'Right.'

They bunked down and waited for the sun to set.


# 18


18.00 hrs.

It grew dark.

They'd known the sun was setting not only because of the darkness, but because of the sound of gunshots as the city around came to life. Or death. Explosions. Artillery. Fuck, Jack thought. It was like Helmand. Only in Helmand they had assets. Out here they had nothing.

'We need to go,' he said. 'Get ready.'

'I'm not going to wear my robes,' Siobhan told him. 'They're too heavy. They'll slow me down if it kicks off.'

Jack nodded and they started collecting their things. He checked his bag: grenades, ammo, Claymore, det cord, PE—everything was there. When they were ready, he stood in front of her and put his hands on her shoulders. 'Seriously, Siobhan,' he said. 'When we get out there, keep your head down and do what I say. I know you're good, but you're not trained for this kind of theatre. Agreed?'

'Agreed,' she said, before giving him a thin smile.

Outside the room, they strode side by side down

the corridor to reception. The toothless receptionist was still at his desk. He leered at Jack, who smiled back and gave him a discreet thumbs-up sign. The man's eyes sparkled. When he saw they were heading for the exit, though, his face fell. 'Where you go?' he called, alarmed.

They just kept walking towards the door. 'What was *he* so happy about?' Siobhan asked. Jack said nothing.

In the courtyard, the stench of the city hit them. Now that night was falling, the guards had moved themselves away from the gate and were standing in the protection of the wall. Jack walked up to them.

'Let us out,' he instructed.

The guards looked uneasy, but did as they were told. The moment Jack and Siobhan were on the street, however, they quickly locked the gates again.

The dusty green Land Rover was still parked up opposite the hotel. They hurried towards it. Asad sat in the driver's seat, his shades up on his forehead. The kid looked nervous, with a slightly wild look in his eyes.

'It is not safe to stay here after dark,' he hissed, and as if to reinforce his statement, there was an explosion nearby that caused a little shower of dust to fall from the bombed-out building next to them.

'Asad,' Jack said, 'I need to borrow your truck. Just till morning.'

Asad looked uncertain.

'I'll be back here at nine o'clock in the morning,' Jack lied. 'For you, two hundred dollars. Easy money.'

He handed over the notes. The battle between

cash and suspicion was written on the kid's face. Cash won. Two hundred bucks was probably more than the vehicle was worth anyway. 'Nine o'clock?' he said.

Jack nodded. 'Don't be late.' He watched as the kid climbed down from the Land Rover and disappeared down the street.

Jack turned to Siobhan.

'Get into the back seat,' he instructed. 'Lie down and keep your gun ready. People are more likely to come at us if they see a woman. You see a face that isn't mine, shoot it.'

Siobhan did as she was told.

Jack took the driver's seat. He drove slowly down the road, along the thick wall of the hotel on one side and the bombed-out remains on the other. After about thirty metres he stopped. He seized the Colt Commando in his right hand and the M1911 in the other before twisting his body round so that he could see the road behind him.

They waited.

The street was quiet. *They* were quiet. But just a few streets away the city was noisy. Bursts of gunshot; rumbles of explosive; indistinct metallic screeches; shouting. They'd only been there for ten minutes when a gang of fifteen people, some of them grown men, some of them little more than kids, approached. They were more heavily armed than the fucking Taliban—AKs, mostly, but one guy had an RPG launcher nonchalantly plonked on his shoulder. Jack was pleased that they were arguing among themselves because it meant they didn't notice him.

Half an hour passed. It grew fully dark. Jack's arms ached from holding the guns up and he was growing impatient. 'Where the fuck are they . . .'

'They'll come,' Siobhan said.

Two minutes later a vehicle turned into the top of the street. For now, Jack could see only the two headlamps, glowing in the darkness. They grew nearer, before coming to a stop outside the hotel gates. The headlamps dimmed to reveal the outline of the vehicle. It was a technical—an open-topped truck with a machine gun of some description mounted on the back. Jack could trace the outline of the gunner and could make out the heads of the other occupants—four, maybe five.

He watched carefully. Nobody got out. This truck wasn't dropping off. It was picking up. And from what he'd learned of Mogadishu, he realised that there weren't many people who'd be leaving this hotel after dark.

'They're here,' Jack said, his voice low. He heard Siobhan sitting up. 'You sure you know what you're doing?'

'I told you,' Siobhan said. 'Leave it to me. Just keep me covered.' She opened the door, stepped out into the street and started walking back to where the open-topped truck was parked, the tracking device secreted in the palm of her left hand.

Siobhan kept her head down as she approached the truck. The last thing she wanted to do was attract the attention of the six heavily armed Somalis in the technical. She was about ten metres away when the hotel gates opened and two figures appeared. One of them was Khan. He was dressed, as before, in a dishdasha, and he strode purposefully towards the technical. The second figure was clearly a woman. She wore loose robes that covered all her skin, and her head was wrapped in a headdress. She walked a little slower than Khan, with her head bowed. Then Khan barked an instruction at her, and she climbed up into the technical.

'Mr Khan!' Siobhan shouted. She was no more than five metres away from him now.

Khan looked round, alarmed, just as two of the men on the technical raised their rifles. When he saw it was Siobhan, a brief look of irritation crossed Khan's face, but he soon mastered it and raised his hand at the guards, who lowered their guns.

'Miss Hoskins . . .'

'Mr Khan, you said I could have an interview.'

'Now is not a good time, Miss Hoskins.'

She was right by the technical now. 'Perhaps I could come with you.' She gave him a dizzy smile.

Khan's face darkened.

'A photo, then.' She pulled her digital camera from her pocket. Khan immediately held up his hand to prevent her taking his picture. Siobhan shoved the camera into his fist. 'Then *you* take one of *me*. The papers will love it . . . very atmospheric . . .' She widened her eyes. 'All these guns!'

She had her back to the technical, leaning up against it with one hand behind her. It took only a second for her to attach the tiny magnetic device to the chassis of the vehicle. A good job too, because Khan was angry now. He threw the camera to the floor. 'Get away,' he whispered, a dangerous look in his eyes.

Siobhan feigned surprise. She staggered away from the technical as Khan hopped up. The guards grinned as the vehicle moved away, leaving

317

Siobhan alone at the gates.

She waited until it was out of sight, then sprinted back to the Land Rover. Jack had the GPS unit in front him.

'You got them?' Siobhan asked.

Jack pointed at a green blip on the unit. 'Yeah, I got them.' He handed the device back to Siobhan and turned the ignition.

'Let's go,' he said.

* * *

Jack drove with one hand on the steering wheel, one hand on the rifle. As they followed the signal through the maze-like grid of Mogadishu he raised the gun whenever he saw a group of more than three or four people or, less frequently, another vehicle. If anyone saw it, so much the better. Hopefully it meant they wouldn't fuck with him. Small fires lined the streets like pilot lights, ready to ignite the whole city if anyone switched on the gas. Jack felt sweat pouring down his grimy face, his whole body tense with watchfulness, his trigger finger taut.

'They're heading west,' Siobhan said.

Her voice was businesslike.

Only when they'd hit the outskirts of the city did Jack lower the rifle and concentrate more on the road. They passed several other technicals heading into Mogadishu, the open pick-ups crammed full of armed people and all the machine guns manned. Different factions, different clans, all congregating in the capital, drawn to it like wasps to poisonous honey. Put that kind of weaponry into the hands of lawless people—you didn't need to be a genius to work out what was going to happen.

The outskirts of the capital ebbed away. They found themselves on a single-track road, dark, potholed and bumpy.

'We're about five hundred metres behind them,' Siobhan said.

Jack nodded, then switched off the headlamps of the Land Rover in order to remain hidden if they got too close to the technical. Everything was plunged into darkness, and it took a good minute for his night vision to settle itself. Even then it was difficult to see the road ahead. Jack slowed down to avoid coming off the road: this wasn't somewhere he wanted to be waiting for a recovery vehicle.

Silence. Just the sound of the engine and the tyres crunching over the stony earth.

Suddenly, he caught sight of a flash of red up ahead. It disappeared momentarily, then came into view again. Rear lights.

'I've got a visual,' he said.

Siobhan peered over his shoulder. He could feel her hot breath against his neck. 'I got it,' she whispered.

'I'm going to hang back.'

Another five minutes of tense, careful travelling —during which the red lights disappeared once more a couple of hundred metres ahead. 'They've stopped,' Siobhan said. Jack slowed down, then directed the truck off the road on to a patch of dry mud at the side of a parched field. He hit the brakes. Sound travelled easily in these open plains, so he wanted to get the engine switched off as quickly as possible.

'We'll approach on foot,' he told Siobhan before handing her the keys to the Land Rover. 'Anything happens to me, get the hell back and drive.' He handed her Markus's map with the location of the airfield circled in pencil. 'The plane's waiting there until midnight. Guy called Markus. Tell him I said to get you out. Understood?'

'Midnight, Markus,' Siobhan repeated.

'When we get out of the vehicle we need to walk on opposite sides of the road, about fifteen metres apart. If we get too close, we're an easy target once we're seen. They'll take us out with one hit. You hear gunfire, voices, *anything*, hit the ground. Doesn't matter if it's a false alarm. You got your weapon ready?'

Siobhan held up the Makarov.

'Good. Don't be afraid to fire it, but don't unless you have to.'

'I'm competent with a weapon, Jack.'

'I know you are. Just don't waste ammo. Those fuckers up there will be armed to the teeth. If it comes to it, it's up to us to fight smarter. OK?'

'Sure.'

'Then let's move.'

They walked in silence. The ground was baked hard and stony; the only vegetation was low brush starved of water, side by side with the occasional hunk of jagged, rusted metal. Out here, away from the city, the sky overhead was breathtaking: no moon, but a riot of milky stars, a heavenly canopy over this hellish land. Jack held his rifle in his right hand and had the canvas ammo bag slung over his shoulder. There was no noise other than the crunch of their feet along the road. It was as if even the animals had deserted this benighted

320

place. Every twenty paces or so, he looked over his shoulder to check on Siobhan. She was always there, Makarov in hand, face set with concentration. It occurred to Jack that they worked well together, and there, under the African night sky, Jack felt an unexpected stab of regret. It was Siobhan's fault, not his, that they were no longer an item. He'd swept over his feelings with a brush of anger and resentment, but if it had truly been up to him . . .

He put those thoughts from his head. This was hardly the time or place.

The lights of the technical were switched off now, so judging its distance in the darkness was impossible. After about five minutes, however, his eyes started to make out something up ahead. Buildings—shacks, more like. Dilapidated. As they grew nearer, it became clear that they were on the edge of a village, or at least what had once been a village. Now it bore the scars of war, and Jack would have bet any money that it was unpopulated. Who could live among these scenes of almost post-nuclear destruction: craters in the earth, burned-out cars? As they regrouped behind a tumbledown wall Jack could see in a ditch behind them the gruesome figure of a corpse, its flesh now just a thin film over the bones, its limbs mangled and distorted. He didn't point it out to Siobhan, who was crossing the road to join him.

She was breathing heavily. He put one hand on her shoulder. 'You OK?' he whispered.

Siobhan nodded, but her face told a different story.

'Stay close to me,' he breathed. They weren't on open ground now. They could risk a little proximity. Jack advanced, with Siobhan a few steps behind him. As they moved forward, they used whatever they could for cover—rubble mounds, burned-out dwellings, old vehicles—which enabled them to advance in short, safe bursts. And as they advanced, they started to hear something: a low electrical hum that grew louder the more ground they covered.

Jack was peering out from behind a rusted old pickup with no tyres when he saw, fifteen metres away, a low building, just a single storey high and about twenty-five metres by twenty. What was startling, though, was not its size or its shape, but that it was intact. More than intact. It appeared to be fabricated from huge sheets of corrugated iron, and at the rough corners of the building little shards of light escaped into the darkness. The technical they'd been following was parked outside the front, just next to the large sliding door that was clearly the main entrance, and to one side of the wall there was a generator, gently vibrating, from which the humming sound came.

Jack and Siobhan looked at each other. 'That doesn't look like a brothel to me,' he murmured.

Just then there was a clattering sound as the door slid open. Bright light shone out and then a figure appeared in the doorway.

For a moment Jack thought he was hallucinating. He squinted at the figure, barely fifteen metres away, his brow furrowed as he tried to persuade himself that his brain was playing tricks.

But it wasn't. As the door slid shut and the figure lit a cigarette, Jack turned back to Siobhan. She could tell something was wrong. 'What is it?'

Jack didn't answer. He just clutched his rifle a

little more firmly. 'Wait there,' he instructed. Siobhan opened her mouth to argue, but a single look silenced her.

He had the advantage of the darkness, and as he crept out from behind the old vehicle, his feet barely made a sound. He circled round, approaching the building from one side, out of sight of the front. And once he'd reached the corrugated iron, he pressed his back against it and manoeuvred up to the corner of the structure.

He was less than five metres away from her. Close enough to hear her exhale, to smell the menthol smoke that she blew into the African night air. A million questions in his head needed answering now.

He extended his rifle, holding it out in front of him with a perfectly straight arm. Then he swung round the corner, advancing quickly. In just a few seconds the barrel of the gun was pressed against her temple.

The figure tensed up and dropped the cigarette. Her eyes rolled sideways, but she didn't dare move her head so she had no idea who was pressing the hard metal of an assault rifle against her head.

She started to shake. But that didn't have any effect on Jack. He was too busy thinking about the last few times he'd seen her.

In the Helmand cave, just before the Black Hawk went down.

At Bastion.

At her flat when they'd spent the night together.

Walking up the steps towards Five's offices at Thames House.

And now here. In the arid badlands of the world's most dangerous country, accompanying a man who had links to a former IRA drug dealer. None of it made any sense to Jack. She'd have to explain it for herself.

'Hello, Caroline,' he said.

Jack just managed to get his hand over her mouth before she was able to cry for help.


# 19


Caroline Stenton struggled. The rifle pressed against her head barely restrained the professor. Her arms and legs flailed and he had to use all his strength to drag her away from the building.

Gunshot.

Jack threw himself to the ground, and Caroline with him. He pressed himself down into the earth at the sound of more rounds being fired, like fireworks popping, but he soon realised that the guns were inside the building and not directed outside. So he dragged Caroline to her feet again and ran with her to behind the rusted vehicle where Siobhan was waiting. He threw the professor to the ground, pressed one foot roughly on to her ribcage, and aimed the rifle directly at her head.

She had an arrogant expression. But it fell momentarily away when she saw the look of fury on Jack's face.

'You remember the cave?' he hissed.

Caroline nodded.

'You saw the bodies?' He jerked his heel into her ribs again. 'You know I'll kill you and not even think about it?'

Caroline coughed in pain, but when she stopped there was a curious shining in her eyes. 'If I die,' she whispered, 'I will be accepted into the arms of Allah.'

'*What?*' Jack hissed. And then, as certain things slotted into place: 'You fucking bitch . . .'

'Who is she?' Siobhan demanded.

'Someone with a lot of explaining to do.' He knelt down, then roughly turned Caroline over on to her front and pressed her face in the dirt.

'Who's the baggage, Jack?' she said in a mocking tone of voice. 'Does she know about us?'

'Nothing to know,' Jack told her.

'Oh, Jack. Say it isn't so. You were so enthusiastic. You know, to keep my cover, I have to endure all sorts of hardships.' Her head was still sideways on the ground, but she managed to glance up at Siobhan. 'But some are harder than others—'

Jack had no desire to listen to this crap. He covered her mouth with one hand then grabbed her right wrist and yanked it up behind her back. She might not be scared of death, but pain . . .

Caroline's body tensed up, but with Jack's hand over her mouth she couldn't scream. Not loudly.

'You're going to talk,' he spat, 'and I'm going to listen. If I don't like what I hear, it's not Allah's arms you'll need to worry about. It's yours.' He removed his hand.

'They'll be looking for me,' she spluttered. 'Any minute.'

'Then you'd better be quick if you don't want to take a round in the crossfire. What's Khan doing in there? And what are *you* doing *here*?' He put a little more pressure on her twisted arm.

325

A sharp intake of breath. 'I work for him.'

'Doing what?' No reply. More pressure on the arm. *'Doing what?'*

'I advise British Intelligence.' There were tears in her voice as the words tumbled out. 'You're going to break my arm—'

'I'll break a lot more than your arm if you don't keep talking. What do you advise Five on?'

'Chemical . . .' She could hardly speak through the pain. 'Chemical and radiological warfare.'

'Dirty bombs?'

'If you like.'

His mind flashed back to Helmand.

'The flight case in the cave. What was it? *What the hell was it?*'

'Radioactive material.'

'A bomb?'

'Just the materials.'

'And Khan knew about it?' Jack felt like he was piecing together a jigsaw without knowing what picture it was supposed to make.

'Of *course* he knew about it,' Caroline said with contempt. And then, as Jack yanked her arm again, suddenly the words started to flow through her gritted teeth. 'What are you, Jack? A novice? You know that to hide something you have to show something. We *let* military intelligence find that place.'

'Why?' The arm was at breaking point. He yanked it a bit further.

'To put them off the scent,' she hissed. 'To make them feel like they were sitting comfortably. You really think that if they wanted to keep something a secret, they'd construct it under the noses of Coalition forces in Helmand Province? You really

326

think they're that stupid? The Helmand cave was a distraction to get the British and Americans to take their eyes off the ball, make it easier for the *real* device to pass over the borders.'

'And *you* passed on details of the cave raid. That's how the Taliban knew we were there.' Images in his mind of the Black Hawk going down. Of Red. It was all Jack could do to stop himself from nailing her right now.

Siobhan's voice from behind. 'Jack, what's going on? What are you two *talking* about?'

Jack just kept the pressure on Caroline's arm. 'What's going on in that building now? Why are you here?'

No answer at first. But then, when the pain grew too bad: 'A device,' she breathed. 'A dirty bomb. The real one. Khan's brought me out here because he needs to know it's properly constructed and primed.'

'What does this bomb do?'

'A small explosion,' she whimpered. 'It's what's in the bomb that causes the harm.'

'Enlighten me.'

'Let go of my arm first.' Her voice was barely audible.

Jack did nothing of the sort. He yanked the arm sharply.

'*Caesium-137*,' she gasped. 'Enough to infect several thousand people.'

'What does it do?'

'Kills a tenth of them within a month, half of them after a year . . .'

'And it's in there? In that building?'

'I've just examined it,' Caroline said. 'It's ready.'

'What's his target?'

327

'He hasn't told me. *He hasn't told me!*'

Silence. Caroline's body was shaking with the pain.

'Who's in there?' Jack demanded.

Her breathing was heavy. Fast. 'Khan,' she spat. 'His guards.'

'What about the people constructing the device?' But he answered his own question before Caroline had a chance. 'The gunshots . . .'

Jack's words seemed to give the professor a new surge of contempt. 'The bomb's made. And don't sound so disgusted, Captain Harker. Khan's men are only doing what you did in Helmand.'

Jack didn't even bother responding to that. His head rocked with this new information. He'd come out here on Siobhan's wild goose chase, but what they'd stumbled upon was something quite different.

'Jack?' Siobhan sounded scared. 'Tell me what's happening. What's this got to do with Lily?'

'Sounds like your friend Habib Khan's involved in more than hookers and heroin,' he spat. He turned his attention back to Caroline. 'How many people in there?' he demanded.

'I'm not telling you.'

Jack didn't waste any time. He relieved the pressure on the twisted arm, but the respite was only temporary. Covering Caroline's mouth again, he felt for her little finger. It was sweaty, but that didn't matter. One good yank and he heard the little bones splinter and snap. Jack allowed five seconds for the silent scream, then put his lips close to Caroline's ear. 'You've got nine more fingers,' he whispered threateningly. 'One for each time you fuck around with me. How many men has

Khan got?'

'Ten.'

'Armed?'

She nodded vigorously. Tearfully.

'With what?'

'I don't know. Guns.'

Immediately Jack started doing the calculations. Ten men plus Khan. If he had the element of surprise, he could down them with his assault rifle—the Colt Commando could spit out ten to twelve rounds a second. But the moment he stopped putting the pressure on Caroline, she would raise the alarm. He glanced up at Siobhan. She was competent with a weapon, no doubt about it. But stick her in the middle of a firefight like that? She'd agree to it, but he didn't want to put her in that kind of danger.

'Siobhan,' he hissed, 'you got the Makarov?'

'Sure.'

'Press it against the back of the professor's knee.'

She did as she was told.

'Right, ladies. Here's what's going to happen. If Caroline makes a fucking sound, you kneecap her.'

'Painful,' Siobhan observed in a bland voice.

'That's the idea. I'm going in. Listen for shots. If I'm not back out thirty seconds after they start, put one in her head and fucking swastika it back to the Land Rover. You need to get to Markus as fast as possible and tell him what's happening. He'll get you out of here, and he'll know what to do.'

'What about you?'

'If I'm more than thirty seconds, I won't be needing a plane out,' he said.

Jack stood up and Siobhan immediately took his place by Caroline's shivering body and gouged the barrel of her Makarov deep into the back of the woman's knee. One thing Jack could be sure of was that if it came down to it, Siobhan would act.

He checked his weapon, then squinted at the building. The main entrance was the only visible way in. If he slid the door open, they would assume it was Caroline and as he'd be standing in the dark he'd have a momentary advantage. If everything went to plan, the occupants of the building wouldn't realise he was hostile until he started firing, and by then it would be too late.

He turned to Siobhan. She was looking up at him, anxiety in her face. 'Be careful,' she whispered.

'Remember. Thirty seconds.'

He stood up again and prepared to cover the fifteen metres of open ground between them and the building.

But the preparations didn't last long.

If Jack had hit the ground two seconds later, he'd have been dead. Two technicals suddenly skidded round from the far side of the building, their machine guns pumping randomly into the air; above the sound of the weaponry, the vicious shouting of the shooters. Only when they'd come to a halt did they switch their headlamps on, and by that time Jack was hugging the dirt as several rounds ricocheted with metallic sparks off the rusted vehicle.

Silence.

There was another burst of random fire that missed them only by chance. Jack realised they'd been seen. '*Shit*,' he hissed. Their options were limited. Emerge from behind the vehicle and they'd be lit up like bunnies in a headlight. Jack could try to pick off the top-gunners, but he'd be blinded by the lights, and to fire a gun would just reveal their position.

A loudspeaker. Through it, an African voice. Deep. Resonant. *'Show yourselves. If we see weapons, we will fire. You have twenty seconds.'*

Jack and Siobhan looked at each other. She still had her gun pressed to Caroline's knee.

*'Fifteen seconds.'*

'If we show ourselves, they'll shoot,' Siobhan said.

'Maybe,' Jack replied. He was desperately trying to think of a way out. But he could read the situation well enough. There wasn't one.

'We could use her as a hostage,' Siobhan suggested, desperation in her voice, but Jack shook his head.

'Trust me,' he said. 'They'll just kill her.'

'They won't kill *me*,' Caroline interrupted with scorn.

'Shut the fuck up or I will.'

*'Ten seconds.'*

Jack thrust his rifle and the canvas bag under the vehicle. 'Hold on to your weapon. I'll go out first. If they start shooting, use the rifle.'

*'Five seconds.'*

He stood up. Then, with his hands in the air, he stepped out into the beams of light.

It was almost a surprise that there was no gunfire to mow him down; just two silhouettes, approaching from in front of the technicals. Jack was able to make out their bandoliers and rifles. By the time they were no longer silhouettes but actual figures that he could see and smell and fear, Siobhan had joined him, her hands in the air too.

And only then did Caroline start to scream. Half pain, half fury—a million miles from the woman Jack had spent the night with, what seemed like a century ago. 'Tell Khan to kill them!' she yelled, as the Somali guards held them at gunpoint. 'Tell Khan to damn well *kill* them!'

The inside of the iron building was a contrast to the outside. There was no proper flooring, so the ground was still little more than dusty earth, but the bright white lights powered by the rumbling generator made the place seem strangely modern. Along one side of the wall were crates of bottled water; and just beyond them, a couple of low mattresses and a rusted old refrigerator. On the opposite wall were jerrycans of fuel, presumably to replenish the generator, and the pungent smell of the fumes penetrated the air. In the middle of the room, scientific instruments that meant nothing to Jack were laid out on metal tables, and a silver flight case, no different to the one he'd seen in Helmand, lying on its side.

And at the far end of the building, by the wall, were a number of bodies. It was impossible to say quite how many because they had fallen in a mangled heap, but Jack estimated nine or ten Africans. It was obvious that they'd been lined up before being shot. On the wall above them was a poster. The one concession this place had to homeliness. It showed Emmanuel Adebayor, in his Manchester City strip. The African footballer smiled brightly over this scene of unspeakable carnage. In the wall beyond the corpses, to the right of Adebayor, there was another door. It was through there that the guards must have exited to get their technicals.

Standing by the flight case was Habib Khan. His dishdasha was pure white, apart from a splash of red across the chest that looked as if someone had flicked paint at it. Two men stood on either side of him—heavily armed Somalis, each of them a good head taller than Khan himself.

There were other guards, too. Ten of them in all, as Caroline had said. Six had hustled Jack and Siobhan into the building and even now were forcing them up against the left-hand wall and telling them to keep their hands on their heads before retreating. Two more stood on either side of the main door, and just in front of them was Caroline. She cradled her broken finger in her good hand, her face was even paler than usual and her eyes contained more venom than Jack had ever seen.

There was an ominous silence in the building. Khan removed his little round spectacles, buffed them on the material of his robes, then replaced them on his nose and peered, owl-like, at them.

'I already know Miss Hoskins of course,' he said in quiet, precise tones, 'but I imagine that is an assumed name. I will require you to tell me who you are, and for whom you work.'

Jack didn't say a word. Nor did Siobhan. They just stared defiantly at him.

Khan raised an eyebrow. 'It would be boring if I had to force this information out of you,' he observed.

'You don't need to.' It was Caroline who spoke, through gritted teeth as she tried to master the pain in her hand.

Khan looked sharply at her. 'What do you mean?'

333

'I know him. We met in Afghanistan. His name is Captain Jack Harker and he's a member of the SAS. He was part of the unit that shut down the other operation.'

Khan's eyes narrowed. 'Indeed . . .'

Jack jutted his chin out. 'There's a special-forces backup unit on its way,' he said. 'Any minute. You're fucked, Khan. It's over.'

'He's lying,' Caroline interrupted. 'They interrogated me. They knew nothing about what was going on here . . .'

But Khan had raised one hand to silence her, and Caroline's voice petered out. He stepped a few paces closer to Jack and Siobhan, then eyed them carefully, as if he were examining an item for purchase. His face grew shrewd and eventually he shook his head. 'No,' he breathed. 'You would not be here with a mere woman if it were in an . . .' He searched for the words. 'An *official* capacity.'

'They're chancers,' Caroline raged. 'They don't know what they've stumbled upon.'

'Perhaps,' Khan said. 'Perhaps not.'

'What's your target, Khan?' Jack demanded. 'London? New York?'

Khan remained silent, but a mysterious look crossed his face. He turned and walked back towards the flight case.

Suddenly Siobhan's voice echoed off the metal walls of the building. 'Where is she, Khan?' she asked.

Khan stopped, then turned again. It was impossible to read his expression. 'Where is who, my dear?' he asked.

Siobhan's eyes were burning. 'Lily Byrne. I know you've got her and she's all we want. Where is she?'

An agonising pause. And then, slowly, Khan's lips creased into an incredulous smile. 'You have come all this way for *her*?' he demanded.

Jack felt his insides crunch up. Khan wasn't even denying it. Everything else faded into the background—Caroline, the device, everything. *'What did you say?'* he hissed.

Khan looked from one to the other, his eyes cruel and bright. 'You thought I would bring that girl to *this* place? You have followed me just for *her*?'

'Don't listen to them,' Caroline interrupted. 'They know about the device. They're just trying to—'

*'Quiet!'* Khan approached Siobhan and inclined his head. 'And why are you so interested in my pretty white whore?' he whispered.

Jack couldn't help himself. He went for Khan, but instantly Khan's guards stepped forwards, their guns trained on him. Jack stopped and raised his hands.

'I am astonished,' said Khan, 'that anyone would risk their lives for that wretched creature.'

'You'd be surprised just what I'd do for her,' Jack said.

'Then you waste your time. Western women, with their appetites and their needs, are little more than animals. Like bitches on heat. But she is worse than most. Worse than a dog.' His eyes shone as he taunted them. 'She is dirty,' he gloated. *'Filthy.* She *begs* me and my soldiers to favour her in return for the drugs that she cannot live without.'

Jack felt surrounded by a hot haze of rage.

335

'Where is she?' he breathed.

'Imprisoned,' Khan smiled. 'Alone. If she isn't dead now, she will be soon. I do not plan to return to her.' He stepped closer to Jack. 'Perhaps you don't believe what I say about white women,' he breathed, his lips thin with contempt. 'Perhaps you require a demonstration?'

He turned again and walked away from them, then barked an instruction in Arabic. The two guards standing by the main door stepped inside and approached the flight case. One of them picked it up and walked out with the device, while the other stuck close to him, his weapon primed. Khan continued to speak to the remaining guards. Five of them nodded with unpleasant grins on their faces; the other three closed up around Khan.

'Professor Stenton,' he announced. 'Please join our friends by the wall.'

A look of confusion crossed her pained face. 'But I'm coming with you—'

'*Now!*' Khan said, and to reinforce his instruction one of the men approached and pushed her over towards Jack and Siobhan. She fell to the ground between them.

'What's going on?' she demanded.

But Khan and his guards were already moving towards the exit. As he stood by the door, he looked at Jack. 'I have places to be. These men—' he indicated the five Somali guards who were left '—have served me well. I have instructed them that they may have their fun with the girls before they kill you all. They are simple men, after all— but they too have appetites. I don't know what Lily Byrne is to you. I don't really care. But think of her while you watch, because it is no more than what she does back in London. I hope you enjoy the spectacle.'

Khan's eyes flashed—the eyes of a madman. He strode out of the building, his three guards surrounding him, while the others kept their guns trained on Jack and Siobhan. 'Habib!' Stenton shouted. '*Habib!* Don't you dare . . . How could you . . .' Nobody paid her any attention. From outside, there was the sound of a vehicle moving away.

And then silence. Both outside and inside the building.

Jack immediately started working out his options. His snubnose was still secreted round his ankle, but that only gave him six rounds. And even if he went for it, they'd mow him down in an instant if they saw him move. They were outnumbered and out-armed. He exchanged a glance with Siobhan. Unless they could raise some kind of distraction, they didn't stand a fucking chance . . .

Stenton was shaking. 'Let me go! Let me out of here!' The five Somali guards ignored her. They were all dressed similarly: ragged jeans, dirty T-shirts, black and white keffiyehs wrapped round their necks. One of them stepped forward. He had sallow, sunken eyes, a dead expression and a rank smell. He looked first at Caroline.

Then he looked at Siobhan. He smiled.

It was Siobhan whom he selected.

The sallow-eyed man pointed his gun at her, then flicked it to indicate that she should walk to the end of the room where the dead bodies lay. She gave him a hateful look. But her only option, for now, was to comply.

Siobhan moved slowly to the end of the room, the gunman right behind her. He gave a harsh-sounding instruction. She stopped and turned to him. Anyone who saw her would think she was scared. No doubt she was. But Jack knew her well and saw something else. Her palms were open; her legs were slightly apart to keep her balance. And when she glanced briefly at him, he understood and nodded imperceptibly: she was choosing her moment carefully, and he needed to be ready.

The other guards still had their guns trained on Jack and Caroline, whose body was shaking, although it was impossible to tell if this was a result of the pain in her finger, Khan's betrayal or fear at the agony and humiliation to come. Their attention, though, was elsewhere. They were watching to see what would happen at the end of the room, in anticipation of their own turn . . .

The sallow-faced gunman used his firearm to prod Siobhan's breasts. She gave him a defiant stare, and he looked over his shoulder to leer at his companions.

That was his mistake.

Siobhan moved like lightning. With one hand she yanked the firearm upwards, then lifted her right leg to knee her would-be rapist in the groin. He groaned and bent double just as he discharged his weapon. A burst of fire echoed around the building—first the noise of discharge, then the tinny sound of the rounds ricocheting from the metal roof. The remaining guards looked at each other.

It was that second that gave Siobhan and Jack the time they needed.

Siobhan crooked one arm round the neck of her man, then spun him round so that he was facing the others. He was still carrying his weapon, so she stretched out her free arm and pulled his finger back against the trigger. Rounds sprayed across the room, hitting one of the guards in the chest, and forcing another to run for the door.

Jack hit the floor, rolling the couple of metres over towards the man Siobhan had downed just as a spray of rounds hit the wall behind him. Caroline wasn't so lucky. She screamed as a stray round caught her squarely in the thigh, spraying blood over the floor. The remaining guards didn't bother finishing her off. They knew Jack was the threat. They were a couple of metres apart, five metres from Jack and bearing down on him.

Jack pulled his snubnose from his ankle just as a burst missed him by inches as he rolled away. It took less than a second to aim the revolver and fire two rounds, both entering the foreheads of the two guards and killing them outright.

Jack tried to take everything in. There was screaming from Caroline; the remaining guard was leaving the building; but there was also scuffling from the back of the building, and he knew what that meant. He pushed himself up to his feet, spun round and saw Siobhan struggling with the sallow-faced gunman. She still had her arm round his throat and his eyes were bulging; but he was clearly stronger than he looked and had managed to move his weapon so that it was almost pointing over his shoulder.

Jack launched himself, swinging his legs over the metal table and running towards them. The man's eyes widened and he moved his rifle forward again. But before he could fire at Jack, Siobhan yanked him to the right so that his bullets again sprayed against the metal wall.

And then Jack was on him. He put the snubnose to the Somali's head, and fired. There was an explosion of red blood, white bone and slushy grey brain matter that spattered over Siobhan, Jack and the picture of Adebayor on the wall.

Outside there was the noise of another truck starting. 'He's getting away!' Siobhan shouted. Jack was halfway across the room before the dead man had even slumped to the floor. He ignored Caroline's howls of pain, but by the time he was outside, the technical was twenty metres away. Jack got down on one knee and into the firing position. He had three rounds left, but only needed two to take out the back tyres of the vehicle.

Siobhan's voice from the door: 'We need him alive, Jack! He can lead us to Khan!'

He was already on it, bearing down quickly on the technical, his revolver arm stretched out in front, a single round left. The final Somali guard, however, scrambled quickly into the back of the technical where a GPMG was mounted on a sturdy tripod.

Jack was ten metres away. The GPMG was loaded and the guard was pointing it towards him. Jack hissed with frustration. He had to take him out, now, otherwise he was a goner.

He squeezed the trigger and the snubnose fired; but at that moment—more by luck, it seemed, than by design—the guard moved out of the way and the round flew harmlessly into the air beyond him.

Jack froze. The guard was grinning, his teeth as

yellow as his eyes. He clearly knew he had the upper hand. Even if Jack dived or ran, the spray from the GPMG would follow him.

A burst of fire. Jack felt the rounds—not hitting his body, but whizzing only a couple of inches away from his shoulder. And they weren't coming from the gimpy, but from behind. They caught the guard on the side of the head and he slumped into the back of the technical with the groan of a dying man.

A deadly silence filled the air. Jack looked back. Siobhan was at the entrance to the building. Still pressed into her shoulder was one of the guards' AK-47s. She lowered it, then joined him.

'Nice shot,' Jack said.

Siobhan didn't reply. They stood there for a moment, breathless, bloodied and shocked. And then the quiet was shattered by a terrible scream. A scream of pain. Without saying a word, they ran back into the building where they saw Caroline, her face contorted. She was on her side, clutching her thigh. Siobhan knelt by her and lifted up her robes. The bare leg was pissing blood. Jack had seen a lot of bad wounds in his time. This was one of them.

'She needs treatment,' Siobhan said abruptly.

'Fuck it,' Jack replied. 'She doesn't need the kind of treatment I want to give her and we don't have time. We can make it back to the airfield if we leave now.'

'Holy mother of God, Jack,' Siobhan muttered, and she removed her jacket.

'Get away from me!' Caroline shouted, but Siobhan ignored the instruction. Instead she wrapped the sleeve of her jacket round the patient's thigh.

'This is going to hurt,' she said without emotion, then instantly tightened the makeshift bandage and pressed down on the bleeding wound. Caroline's scream was barely human, but Siobhan's face remained unmoved, as though she hadn't even heard it. She kept the pressure on, ignoring the blood that was seeping around the leather of her jacket and through the gaps in her fingers.

Jack stood over them. There were plenty of loaded weapons in the building, and all he wanted to do was unload them into the professor.

Caroline saw the look on his face. She closed her eyes and started muttering something. Jack strained to make out what it was. *'Allahu Akbar . . . Allahu Akbar . . .'*

'Don't even think about it Jack,' Siobhan hissed.

'You don't know what she's responsible for.'

'I don't *care* what she's responsible for. *Think!* She's our only link to Khan. We need to find out what she knows.'

Jack scowled. He knew she was right. He checked his watch. 22.36 hrs. 'I'm going to recce,' he said. He walked outside and started prowling around the area. The technical was fucked. He climbed up into the back and over the body of the dead guard to examine the machine gun: it seemed to be in working order, but there was only a single ammo belt. It would give them a few bursts of defensive fire if they needed it. But with blown-out tyres, the vehicle was as good as useless.

While Siobhan continued to treat Caroline, Jack recouped the Colt, the Makarov and the canvas bag containing his supplies and Siobhan's GPS

342

from their hiding place beneath the rusted truck. When he returned, the professor was pale-faced and shaking, but she wasn't bleeding so badly, and she was conscious.

'She's stabilising,' Siobhan said.

'Give me a minute with her,' Jack told her.

'No way. We need her alive, Jack. Without her—'

'I'm not going to kill her. Just ask her a few questions is all. Get outside.'

'I'm—'

'*Get outside . . .*'

'Fine.' Siobhan stood up and stomped out of the building like a teenager.

Jack knelt down beside Caroline. 'Changed your mind about your boyfriend?' he asked.

'He's not my boyfriend,' she spat.

'I guess that's why he left you here with me.'

'Whatever he does, he does for the greater good.'

Jack ignored that. 'Here's what's going to happen. You're going to tell me where he's going with that bomb. What's his target?'

'Go to hell, Harker.'

He inclined his head. And then, with no warning at all, he slammed his fist down on Caroline's wound. She didn't even scream this time, the pain was so much—just a strangely silent intake of breath as her body shuddered and tears came to her eyes.

'Where's he taking it?'

'I . . . I don't know . . .'

Another slam on the wound. Her body convulsed.

'*Where's he taking it?*'

Caroline struggled to get the words out. '*I don't*

343

know . . . *I swear I don't know . . . He said it was better that way . . . Please don't hit me again . . .'* She continued to shake.

Jack stood, leaving her on the ground—she wasn't going anywhere without their help, anyway—and walked outside. Siobhan was standing five metres from the door, her head in her hands, her shoulders shaking. After what they'd just heard about Lily, he didn't blame her for crying. Under different circumstances, he might have cried himself. But there wasn't time for that. Not if they were going to act on the information they had.

'Khan hasn't told her anything.'

She looked at him, her face tear-stained. 'How do you know?'

Jack gave her a dark look. 'You get a feel for these things.'

Siobhan closed her eyes briefly. 'We need to get her out of here,' she said quietly. 'Back to the UK. She's our only witness to what Khan's up to. Nobody's going to accept a word of this without her. And if we don't find Khan . . .'

Jack looked away. 'This vehicle's useless,' he said. 'I need to check on our Land Rover. You wait here. Try to keep her conscious.'

Siobhan nodded. She handed over the keys and the two of them went their separate ways, her towards the supine and shaking body of the professor, Jack towards their vehicle.

He just prayed it was in some kind of state to use.

*     *     *

The technical that carried Khan and his men bumped and jolted over the shoddy track that passed as a road.

'Slow down,' he shouted in Arabic. 'Be careful of the case!'

The driver didn't acknowledge hearing him, so Khan grabbed a pistol from the lap of the guard sitting next to him on the rear seat and held it to the man's head. *'Slow down.'*

The driver hit the brakes and the jolting reduced.

Khan wiped the sweat from his brow, then cleaned his glasses again on his now filthy dishdasha. The arrival of his unexpected guests had shaken him. He needed a clear head if his carefully laid plans were to be executed without complication. He had made a mistake, he realised, letting the guards have their way with the women. It had been done in anger. He should have just killed them.

He turned to his neighbour. 'Get on the phone,' he said. 'If Harker and the women are not dead, they should be killed immediately.'

The guard nodded. He pulled out a mobile phone and dialled a number.

No answer.

He gave Khan a glance and tried one of the other men. 'They are not answering,' he said.

Khan frowned. He knew what it meant.

'The prisoners are still alive,' he said. 'Our men are dead. Call the others. Instruct them to meet us as quickly as possible. One vehicle can take me and the case on to safety.' He pointed a finger around the men in the technical. 'The rest of you must return with a convoy and eliminate Stenton,

Harker and the woman. They mustn't leave that place alive.'

The guard nodded. He pulled out a mobile phone, dialled a number and started to speak.

*     *     *

It took five minutes for Jack to run the kilometre or so of dry, stony terrain to where they had parked the Land Rover. It was a mess. The windows had been smashed out, the tyres blown away and the chassis ripped. Jack could only assume that Khan and his men had shot it up with the machine gun from their technical as they passed. Whatever the truth, one thing was clear— they weren't going anywhere in that vehicle. Jack cursed under his breath, then ran back to the deserted village. Before he returned to Siobhan, though, he searched the area. It was a scene of devastation. The shacks and shanties that passed for houses were burned out and deserted; looters had picked the whole place clean. In the back of his mind he'd entertained the thought that he might find a serviceable vehicle. That, he now realised, was wishful fucking thinking.

He found Siobhan still crouched down by Caroline. He could tell by the look she gave him that the professor was in a bad way.

'The vehicle's fucked.'

'The dead guards,' Siobhan said. 'Their phones have been ringing.'

'Shit,' Jack muttered.

Caroline groaned and her eyes rolled.

'We've *got* to get her out of here,' Siobhan told him.

Jack turned away and checked his watch. 23.00 hrs. Markus would fly at midnight. Even with a vehicle it was tight. But in the middle of nowhere in the middle of the night without a ride—it wasn't exactly like they could call a cab. He had to think of another way to—

'Jack.' Siobhan interrupted his train of thought. He turned round. She had the GPS cupped in her hands and was staring at it with anxiety written all over her face. 'Jack, you need to look at this.'

He joined her in staring at the screen.

There was no mistaking it. The green dot was moving, not away from them this time. Towards them. They were no more than five klicks away.

Jack kept staring at the dot. It continued to blink silently but inexorably in their direction. There was no way Khan would be bringing the device anywhere near them. It meant only one thing. They'd dropped him off somewhere and now they were returning to take care of unfinished business. They knew who Jack was and what he was capable of; they knew the guards whose job had been to finish them off weren't answering their phones. Chances were they were returning with reinforcements.

'Jesus, Jack. What are we going to do?'

Jack stared out into the darkness. He couldn't defend this place alone. Not by himself. Not with the assets at his disposal. The dead guards had assault rifles, but he could only fire one at a time. The machine gun on the technical could take out a truck, two at a push. But once he was out of ammo, the truth was that they'd be sitting ducks. They had two options. To run, and take their chances in the night. Or . . .

347

He looked around for his canvas bag. It was on the ground just a couple of metres from where Caroline lay trembling. Rummaging inside it, Jack pulled out the sat phone Markus had given him. He turned to Siobhan, who was still carrying the GPS. 'I need our coordinates,' he instructed.

It took a matter of seconds for Siobhan to run outside, then return and hand him the unit, which now displayed their latitude and longitude coordinates. He nodded at her, then checked the number scratched on the back of his sat phone and dialled it.

Markus answered immediately. 'Jack, buddy, I'm getting nervous. Give me some good news.'

'Negative,' Jack replied. He strode away from the two women. 'Markus, we've got ourselves a situation . . .'

# 20

Jack looked at the GPS. The enemy were four klicks away. 'We need to get Stenton on to the technical,' he said.

Caroline howled as they picked her up, Jack lifting her beneath the arms and Siobhan taking her feet. They manoeuvred her into the passenger seat, where she slouched listlessly. Jack climbed into the back, picked up the lifeless body of the Somali guard and threw it over the side. It crunched as it hit the ground. 'Take his place,' he told Siobhan as he jumped behind the steering wheel. 'The tyres are fucked, but it's only about five hundred metres up to the main road.'

Jack floored it. It was a bumpy ride and it got worse the further they travelled and the more the wheels distorted against the rubble-strewn ground. Caroline shrieked more than once as her wound bashed against the side of the vehicle. He could smell the engine getting hot but that didn't matter: once they got to the road they weren't going far.

Once he was on the main road, Jack drove a further 500 metres up to their Land Rover, where he stopped and transferred the jerrycans of petrol and bottles of engine oil into the back of the technical. He continued another 100 metres before driving a little way off the road and coming to a halt. He clambered into the back of the technical, then felt for the clamp that attached the machine gun to its tripod. He undid it. His muscles burned as he lifted the heavy weapon off the truck, then he used the integrated bipod to set it up on a level patch of baked mud by the road, facing north.

He pointed at Caroline. 'Help me get her out,' he said. Together they laid the shivering woman on the ground behind the truck. Even if he'd felt any, there wouldn't be time for sympathy. 'Stay with her,' he told Siobhan. 'Keep behind the truck. It's the only cover we've got.'

'What are you going to do?'

Jack glanced at the flashing light on the GPS. Three klicks. Jesus, they were getting here more quickly than he'd expected.

'Roadworks,' he said, handing her the GPS. 'Update me on their location.'

He slung his canvas bag over his shoulder, then took one of the jerrycans of petrol and a bottle of engine oil from the back of the technical and ran with them north up the road, away from the village and in the direction from which the enemy would arrive. A couple of hundred metres and he stopped in the middle of the road, knelt down and poured the bottle of oil into the jerrycan of petrol. Out of his holdall he took the Claymore he'd taken from Markus's supplies, which he fixed to the jerrycan using his plastic explosive. His bag on his shoulder, he unwound the Claymore's det cord back down the road and to the side, laying the clacker on the ground ready for when he needed it. He sprinted back to the technical, jumped up on to the top of it, raised his hand and felt for the wind. There wasn't much, but as far as he could tell the dry breeze was blowing in his direction from the village.

'*Two klicks, Jack!*' Siobhan's voice was tense.

He pulled out another can of diesel, sprinkled a line of it for a couple of metres down their side of the road, then ran fifty metres towards the village and poured another line. He repeated the process until there were five lines of diesel stretching out along the road and the jerrycan was empty.

'*Jack!*' Siobhan's voice travelled across the open ground. '*They're coming! I can see them!*'

He looked up. Headlamps wobbling in the distance. Several sets. It was impossible to gauge their distance accurately in the dark, but it was no more than 1,500 metres. Khan's men were returning mob-handed. Jack took a lighter from his bag and lit the strip of diesel he was standing by, then ran back towards the technical, lighting each of the remaining four as he went.

The headlamps were getting nearer, and Jack knew that although the lines of flame extending down the road were designed to be seen from the air, the occupants of the approaching trucks might be able to see them too. They could open fire at any moment.

Jack sprinted back to where the women were taking cover behind the technical and got back on the sat phone. When Markus answered, he could barely hear the American's voice over the sound of the plane's engines. 'Jack, where in the hell are you?'

'Small fires,' Jack shouted. 'One every fifty metres, port side of the landing strip as you're bearing south. Enemy one klick to the north. I'm expecting to draw fire.'

A pause. The throbbing of the engines over the phone. And then . . .

*'Got you . . . Am I landing into the wind?'*

'Roger that.' Jack checked the headlamps. 'Get down here quickly, Markus, and kill your lights. It's about to go noisy.'

*'Keep the line open!'* Markus shouted back. *'I'm coming in steep.'*

Jack slipped the sat phone into his pocket, turned to Siobhan and pointed to the road. 'He'll hit ground any minute. When he does, he'll slow down along the road, then turn back to pick us up.' He looked down at Caroline, who was barely awake now. 'Can you get her on to the plane by yourself?'

Siobhan nodded. 'But what about you. What about *them*?'

Jack narrowed his eyes. 'I'll be on the plane as quickly as I can. Just concentrate on yourself, OK?' And with that he ran back along the road to where the Claymore clacker was resting, then he hunkered down by the detonator so that his profile

351

was out of sight.

A sound. Engines. Up in the air. Jack couldn't see Markus approaching, but he could hear him. The same couldn't be said for the trucks. They were close now. Five hundred metres, maybe less. Jack and the enemy were now well within range of each other. He counted their headlamps. Five sets. Five vehicles. If each one was tooled up with a gimpy, it was a lot of firepower.

He fixed his eyes on the Claymore and the jerrycan. In the darkness, they were small enough not to be seen until the convoy was upon them. He hoped.

The sound of the trucks' engines merged with the buzzing of the aircraft. Jack estimated that they were 300 metres away now, and 100 from the booby trap.

Fifty metres.

A dark shadow overhead. The plane's engines were roaring and Jack could see its silhouette fifty feet above the convoy, coming in to land.

Twenty-five metres to the booby trap.

Fifteen.

Ten.

The front truck was about a metre from the Claymore when Jack activated the clacker. There was a loud clap as the mine detonated, followed immediately by a second booming noise and a flash that was the jerrycan igniting and exploding. The lead vehicle slammed to a halt, one of its front wheels raised slightly in the air. Jack could tell it was an open-top truck, and he watched with grim satisfaction as the oil he had mixed in with the fuel sprayed on to the passengers. Thick and burning, it would stick to their skin and set fire to their clothes.

The convoy stopped. Jack couldn't hear screams above the sound of Markus's aircraft, which was just now hitting the ground, but he could see panicked, burning figures moving around, jumping out of the lead truck and rolling on the ground to extinguish the flames. He got to his feet and sprinted back to the technical, accompanied by the whining sound of Markus decelerating down the road some seventy-five metres away. He pulled the sat phone from his pocket. *'Hurry up!'* he yelled. *'Fucking hurry up!'*

Jack took up position behind the machine gun. With limited ammo, he needed to choose his moment carefully. The convoy, if they had any sense, would advance gingerly in case the road ahead had been mined further. They didn't know Jack only had a single Claymore.

A hundred metres away the plane was turning. It started to trundle back in their direction.

*'Get ready to load!'* Jack shouted at Siobhan. He didn't need to: she already had Caroline over her shoulder and was still standing behind the technical for protection. Up ahead, the convoy was still stalled, but that wouldn't last for long.

The plane was practically alongside them when the first bullets landed. They came from one of the convoy, and landed five metres short of the aircraft. Jack didn't hesitate. He fired a short burst from the machine gun that battered his ears like deafening thunder. Up ahead, he thought he saw sparks as the rounds made contact with one of the vehicles, just as he heard the sound of empty shells clattering to the ground. His instinct was to follow it up with a second burst, but his ammo was limited: he had to pace himself.

The aircraft made a tight turning circle so that it was facing back into the wind. A door swung open.

'Go!' Jack shouted. *'Go!'*

He released another burst to cover Siobhan as she ran to the plane with Caroline still over her shoulder.

This time, though, the enemy fought back.

A burst of rounds slammed into the front of the technical—the enemy hadn't realized he'd moved the gimpy from the vehicle. Jack returned fire then looked over his shoulder. Siobhan and Caroline were in the aircraft now, and there was a high-pitched screaming from the engines—Markus was clearly revving the plane to fuck with the brakes on, ready to accelerate down the road . . .

A voice over the sat phone. Markus. *'Get in, Jack! If they hit the plane, we're—'*

Jack didn't hear the rest of the sentence. It was drowned out as he fired the final few rounds of his ammo belt towards the convoy. One of the headlamps faded, and he thought he saw the windscreen of the same vehicle shattering. No time to check whether he'd nailed anyone: he pushed himself up and sprinted towards the aircraft.

Jack jumped into the cabin. He slammed the door behind and was immediately thrown to the ground again as Markus suddenly released the brakes and the aircraft shot down the road like a stone from a catapult. He pushed himself up. There was the sound of gunfire over the noise of the engines, and through the window he could just make out the faded lines of burning diesel speeding past.

Nothing more he could do now. Just hope and

354

pray Markus could get the bird into the air before their attackers managed to land a round anywhere on the aircraft.

A deafening roar from the engines.

The bird jolted and bumped on the makeshift runway.

And then, suddenly, everything went smooth. Weightless. The bird kept low—no more than five metres from the ground.

And then: *'Hold the fuck on!'*

The aircraft banked hard and to the left. The engines continued to scream as they suddenly—and steeply—gained height.

The sound of the enemy's guns had receded. Now there was just the continuing noise of the engines, and Markus's tense voice shouting above it.

*'Jack, old buddy!'* he screamed, even as he concentrated on controlling the aircraft. *'I always thought you were a fucking psychopath. I don't want you to think I ain't grateful for what you did back in Iraq, but I think we can safely say my debt to you is paid in fucking full! Agreed?'*

Yeah, Jack thought to himself, sweat pouring from his body and his heart thumping with adrenaline and exertion. Fucking agreed.

\*    \*    \*

The engines were quieter now. A steady, even throb. As the plane hummed its way back towards the Kenyan border, Jack sat up front next to Markus, who concentrated intently on the instruments in front of him while Siobhan tended to Caroline in the back. Not that there was much

355

for her to do. The professor was unconscious and needed a surgeon. Proper medical care. 'I know a guy,' Markus had said. 'There's morphine and antibiotics back at the camp. We just need to get her on the ground.'

'How long?' Jack asked him.

'Two hours, minimum.' Time was running out.

It was running out in other ways too. Khan had his device, and he had Lily. Jack thumped the side of the plane in anger and frustration. Where and when he intended to detonate his dirty bomb was anyone's guess. Whatever happened, Jack *had* to get his hands on Khan. But he was a clever bastard. The world saw him as a peacemaker. A force for good. Like he had a bulletproof jacket of respectability. Without proof, nobody would believe what Jack and Siobhan knew about him.

The proof they had was Caroline Stenton. Jack tried to get everything he'd learned about her straight in his head. She advised Five on radiological weapons but she was in Khan's pocket. A fundamentalist convert. A wolf in sheep's clothing. She was complicit in the intelligence that a dirty bomb was being manufactured in Helmand and that it had been destroyed. But now the real thing had been made in Somalia.

And what about Farzad Haq? Was his ambush anything to do with this? Had Caroline been feeding him information about where and when the unit would be going in? Jack scowled. Whatever the truth, she was implicated. It felt wrong that they should be hurrying to save her life, but they needed to get crucial info out of her just as soon as she was stable enough to talk.

To be persuaded.

To be—

'Jack.' It was Siobhan's voice. Tired, but something else too. He looked over his shoulder to see her gazing back at him. Her face was white.

'What is it?'

Siobhan looked down at the professor. Her body was perfectly still and Jack knew exactly what Siobhan was going to tell him.

'She's dead,' she said.

# 5 JULY

# 21

The vehicle carrying Habib Khan moved swiftly.

Khan himself sat in the back seat with the silver flight case next to it. One hand was resting lightly on the case, the other held a mobile phone to his ear. He listened to the voice at the other end.

'They got away.'

'All of them?'

'All of them. They had an aircraft.'

His eyes narrowed and he hung up without another word. This news angered him, but as he turned it round in his mind he realised he should not be unduly worried. They were idiots. They had stumbled upon him in an attempt to find the girl. And as he thought about the girl, his cheek twitched. He wondered what Harker and the woman wanted with her. Not that it really mattered. He hadn't been lying when he said she was probably dead by now. Dead or driven to madness by withdrawal symptoms from the drugs she needed to function. He thought of the things she had let him do to her for those drugs—things no Muslim woman would ever allow. And he wasn't the only one who had taken advantage of her. There were British men who had helped Khan, men whose allegiance could not be assured on account of their faith. They had to be rewarded in other ways—some with money, others with the filthy, broken body of a drug addict who would let them do anything as long as she knew where her next hit was coming from. In Khan's preparations for the events of the next three days, young Lily

Byrne had been more useful than she would ever know . . .

He snapped his mind back to the events of two hours ago. Stenton knew very little of his plans; and he could easily put out the word that she and this Jack Harker should be eliminated as soon as they set foot back in the UK. There was really no way anybody could prevent what was going to happen.

They continued to drive westwards through the night.

When they finally stopped, Khan alighted from the truck, then gave a quiet instruction to one of his entourage to remove the case. Once outside the vehicle, it was with a certain satisfaction that he saw the aircraft waiting for him, its engines already whirring and its lights glowing in the night air.

'Load the case, please,' he said. His man carried out the instruction while Khan looked around. They had driven for two hours through the night to get to this airfield. His heavily armed entourage would easily have dealt with anything they might have come across before they reached this deserted, desolate spot, but Allah had been with them and they had avoided any trouble.

And now? Now it was time to leave Somalia. But there was still much to do. Still many preparations to make.

He approached the aircraft. It was a small machine, propeller-driven with just a single pilot— a former commercial pilot from the Middle East whose services and discretion could now be acquired for a price. Money, of course, was immaterial to Khan. He took his cut of

362

O'Callaghan's drugs funds in Belfast in order to keep the man professional, to make sure that he didn't get sloppy, but his real finances came from elsewhere.

He climbed into the plane and took a seat next to where the flight case had been carefully strapped in. 'I am ready,' he told the pilot, who nodded, then knocked the plane into motion. It sped down the runway before rising effortlessly into the air.

Khan gazed out of the window, staring at the occasional lights below him. And as time passed and the sun lit up the African plains, he gazed at these too and smiled. Africa was vast. You could hide anything there. *Do* anything. Africa had always been a playground for the Arabs. The preparations that had been made here on his account had gone well. Very well.

The next phase, though, was complicated. It needed a great deal of care. Everything had to go smoothly. But Khan was confident that all would run as it should.

He looked at his watch, an inexpensive Seiko that he had bought in London. 05.30 hrs, East Africa time. In West Africa, where he was headed, it would be only 02.30. It would take them a few hours to cross the continent, however. A few hours of relative peace before his operations began again.

Habib Khan sat back in his seat and closed his eyes. Now, he decided, would be a very good time to sleep.

\*       \*       \*

Salim Jamali could *not* sleep. He was too excited for that.

Since leaving London he felt as though his eyes had been opened. As though he had passed through a gateway into a magical new world. His flight from Heathrow had taken him directly to Islamabad where a young man called Mahmood of approximately his own age, and who reminded him very much of Aamir back at the mosque, had met him at the airport. Mahmood had embraced him like a brother, then taken him to a house in the heart of that beautiful and verdant city. The heat was intense, even at night-time; but the house in question offered a cool courtyard where his hosts—men of faith whose eyes shone with enthusiastic welcome—had given him water to drink and fruit to eat, and answered all his questions. No, they told him with indulgent smiles, he could not expect the training camp to be nearly so comfortable as this. They would expect him to work hard. To learn fast. But he would be among like-minded men. People willing—eager—to fight for what they believed in. Yes, they would give him weapons training, but more than that. By the end of his time in the camp he would be proficient in bomb-making and surveillance. All the skills of the successful jihadi. And when the time had come for him to sleep, they had shown him to a mattress with clean white sheets. 'Sleep well,' they had said. 'Tomorrow will be a long journey.'

It had, indeed, been long. At dawn Salim, Mahmood and two others had loaded their things into a Land Rover and headed out of Islamabad and into the country beyond. It hadn't taken long for the heat to start punishing them, and Salim

364

sweated profusely in that moving oven, which jolted his body around on a road that displayed an increasing level of disrepair as their journey wore on. When his companions shared water from a plastic bottle, he would have liked some too, but they declined to pass him any. It was important, Mahmood told him, that he learn how to endure certain hardships. This was the beginning of his training.

Aamir had warned him that it wouldn't be easy, and Salim was eager to do well. He nodded, closed his mouth and weathered the heat.

The scenery around him changed. First the busy outskirts of the city melted away, then came the countryside and finally, after many hours of travelling, the mountains up ahead. The sight of them gave Salim a thrill, because he knew that was where they were headed.

They spent that night in the foothills, camping under the stars by an open fire that Salim himself had built, hoping to impress the others. And the following day they had continued their journey, up the winding roads that led deep into the mountains, then down confusing networks of paths that were barely suitable for their vehicle, until that evening they came to a little village. It consisted of a few simple dwellings whose walls were constructed of mud baked hard in the fierce sun. A thin dog roamed outside, and a couple of men in robes appeared in doorways. Salim could see no women, and certainly no children.

'Is this the place?' he asked.

'Yes,' Mahmood nodded. 'This is the place.'

'Where do I go?'

They led him to one of the huts. It was dark

inside, and it didn't smell too good. Unlike the bed in which he'd slept in Islamabad, the mattress here was dusty and stained, with no sheets. There was nothing else in there.

'Sleep here tonight,' Mahmood told him. 'At dawn, someone is coming to see you.'

'Who?' Salim asked.

But Mahmood had just smiled. 'You will see, my friend,' he said. 'Sleep well. Tomorrow is an important day.'

But Salim didn't sleep. He lay on that filthy mattress, wearing nothing but his jeans in the heat, listening to the sounds outside: men talking in low voices; animals snuffling. Occasionally there was the noise of an aircraft overhead. He remembered reading that the Americans patrolled this area with drones and occasionally launched attacks on Taliban and Al Qaeda bases. In the corner of his mind it occurred to him that as he was in one of those places now, perhaps he should be scared.

But he wasn't scared. He was excited. Excited to be part of something. Excited by the challenges to come.

It was just before dawn that he heard the sound of a vehicle arriving. Voices outside. Salim sat up on his mattress, excited like a child. More voices. And then a light creeping under the thin wooden door to his hut.

The door opened, and a figure stood there. In his hand was an electric lantern, which lit up the hut but meant that Salim could see only the newcomer's silhouette. For a moment he felt scared of the sinister figure. But then he reminded himself why he was here. That he had been looking forward to this moment. He stood up and took a step forward.

'My name is Salim,' he said.

The figure stepped inside. 'Salim Jamali?' he asked in a thin, slightly reedy voice as he put the lantern on the ground in the middle of the room. Salim could see him better now, could make out his black beard flecked with grey, his dark brown eyes. It was not, he had to admit, a friendly face.

'Yes,' he replied.

'From London?'

'That's right.'

The newcomer nodded. 'I am pleased to see you here,' he said, and Salim felt a sense of relief. 'Come closer.'

Salim approached his new friend, his eyes bright.

He didn't see the knife, so he had no way of knowing that the blade was five inches long and with cruel hooks jutting back towards the handle. As it punctured his skin and slid with ease into his belly, he didn't fully realise what was happening. It felt rather as if he had been punched in the stomach, and because he couldn't understand why this man would do that, he gave him a perplexed look.

The real pain only kicked in as the man slid the blade upwards, butchering the centre of his torso with one easy slice. Salim tried to cry out, but there was no breath in his lungs; he tried to struggle, but the strength in his arms deserted him. As his attacker removed the blade, the jagged edge started to bring with it his minced internal organs. One of the hooks caught on the underside of his ribcage, and the man was obliged to free it with a particularly robust yank.

But by that time, Salim Jamali's life was ebbing

fast. He collapsed to the floor, his fingers weakly splayed round the guts that had spilled out of his fresh wound. As he looked up, he could just make out the figure of the man standing over him. He was still holding up the knife. A gobbet of Salim's internal flesh hung from one of the hooks, and the blade was covered in blood that dripped down on to the man's hand.

And it was that hand, in the final moments of Salim's life, that he focused upon. Even as the dim light grew dimmer and the awful pain started to dissolve into an overwhelming tiredness, he realised that there was something strange about it.

Something different.

He tried to speak again, but all that came was a mouthful of blood, foaming over his lips and down his chin.

The man wasn't looking at him; he was gazing at the bloodied knife, turning it round in his hand. And as the hand turned, Salim saw what was different. The fingers. He counted them precisely, like a child counting sheep at bedtime. One. Two. Three. Four.

His eyes closed. His hands fell to his side. Blood continued to ooze from the gaping wound in his stomach. But by now Salim Jamali was dead.

Farzad Haq wiped his knife on the corpse's jeans, then stepped over it towards the mattress. There was a small holdall here, and he started rummaging around in it. He found nothing of any real interest—just a few clothes—and it didn't take more than a few seconds for him to locate what he was really after: the return section of the young man's ticket and a UK passport, its thick red binding shiny and new.

Haq flicked through the passport, pausing only to look briefly at the photograph, which seemed to highlight Jamali's cleft lip. Then, without a second look at his victim's bleeding body, he stepped outside.

The men were waiting for him near the hut around a small fire, on which they had set an old kettle. In the half-light of the dawn the flames flickered around the metal. One of the men—about the same age as Salim Jamali—approached him. 'My name is Mahmood,' he said.

Haq handed him the passport. 'You know what to do?'

Mahmood nodded and walked away with the document. Haq sat quietly by the fire.

Forty-five minutes later, Mahmood returned. He handed over the passport and Haq flicked through it, checking the details.

The name: Salim Jamali.

Nationality: British Citizen.

The biometric data: all intact.

There were just two differences. The date of birth had been subtly changed and the photograph on the final page showed not the young man who was even now being embraced by the arms of God. It showed the features of his murderer, Farzad Haq, a man who knew he was high up on the so-called Terrorist Screening Database no-fly list, but who now had everything he needed to enter the UK.

\*       \*       \*

Habib Khan's plane followed the dawn as it headed west over the African continent.

369

Beneath him, Ethiopia came and went, then Sudan. They passed over Chad, where the extended dawn became morning, then over Niger and Mali before losing height over the featureless desert of Mauritania and coming in to land on the coast of Western Sahara. It was 10.30 hrs local time when they hit the tarmac and as the aircraft decelerated on the runway and Khan looked out of the window, he could hardly believe that they had crossed an entire continent, so similar was this abandoned airstrip to the one from which they'd departed eight hours earlier.

The state of Western Sahara was not so lawless as Somalia, of course, but it was still a disputed state and vast swathes of this desert land were devoid of anything approaching order or authority. It meant that crossing its border and landing without interference were straightforward.

The aircraft came to a halt near a small, sandstone-coloured domed building, twice the height of a man and four times as wide. Parked outside the structure was a very old truck, in the back of which sat two men. Their skin was much darker than that of the Somalis, their faces less emaciated—plump, almost. Like the East Africans, these two wore heavy clothing despite the furnace-like heat, but the clothes were more colourful—tie-dyed shirts and bright trousers. They were both smoking cigarettes. Only when the plane doors opened and Khan stepped out did they even acknowledge its existence, but once they did, they worked with sudden and surprising efficiency, jumping down and, without even being asked, carefully carrying the flight case down from the aircraft and into the back of the truck.

Khan didn't say a word to the pilot, nor to the two men, as he stepped up to the passenger seat of the truck. One of the two men retook his position out back; the other took the steering wheel; and within minutes of having landed, Habib Khan was leaving the airstrip and travelling down a long straight road surrounded by clay-coloured desert sands that shimmered in the heat.

He was relieved when, after half an hour of silent, sweltering travel, he saw the blue of the ocean sparkling in the distance. The driver smelled of sweat and dirt, and made an unpleasant companion. The road led them into a small settlement—nothing more than four or five huts and a rickety pier that protruded about fifty metres out to sea.

And at the end of the pier was a boat.

By any standards of the wealthy it wasn't a particularly impressive-looking vessel. The best that could be said of it was that it was seaworthy. But that didn't stop it from being an object of considerable interest to the small crowd—mostly children, but also a few adults—who had congregated at the shore end of the pier to gawp at it. They were paying the boat so much attention that two of the crew had seen fit to stand guard— well armed—at the far end of the pier to deter any opportunists. They were wise to have done so. As Khan stepped through the crowd, flanked by his two companions—one of whom was carrying the flight case—he sensed undercurrents. Even the children were restless. The sooner he loaded the device on to the boat, the better. He walked swiftly down the pier.

The armed guards were expecting him, of

course. They stood aside as Khan and his companions approached the boat to be met by the skipper. He was a lanky man, with greased-back red hair and freckles on his white skin. He nodded at the man carrying the flight case and allowed him to step on board.

'Down below,' he instructed. 'They'll show you where to put it.'

The man disappeared and the skipper looked towards Khan.

'You won't be late?' Khan enquired. 'You understand that your payment depends on my package arriving on time?'

'Don't worry about it, my friend.' The man had a pronounced Irish accent. 'The weather conditions are fine and this little baby's a lot faster than she looks. We'll hit land early, if anything. O'Callaghan's boys will be waiting for us, you can be sure of that.' He looked pointedly towards the crowd on the shore. 'If it's all the same with you, though, we'll be making a move. We don't want the natives getting ugly, now do we?'

'Indeed not,' Khan replied mildly. 'But before you go, a word of advice.'

'Go ahead. I always listen to advice, even if I don't always take it.'

'You would be wise,' Khan said in a flat voice, 'to take *this* advice. I understand that you and your men might be inquisitive types. But do not let that inquisitive nature get the better of you. This is not O'Callaghan's regular commodity. It would be extremely foolish for you to open that case, or to tinker with it in any way.'

The skipper gave him a sharp look. 'Care to tell me what we're transporting?'

372

'No,' Khan said. 'I do not. But I trust you will heed my warning and reflect on the fact that you are being well paid for this small voyage.' He looked over his shoulder at the crowd. 'It would be a good idea if you left now,' he said. 'You can never tell what is just around the corner in these parts of the world.'

And without another word Khan turned and walked back down the pier. By the time he hit the shore the boat was slipping away, and the crowd had already lost interest.

It took three hours for Khan's companions to take him from the village with the pier to the city of Dakhla. Three long, hot hours across arid and featureless terrain that rolled out as far as he could see. More than once, the driver had to stop and pour bottled water into the engine's steaming radiator. 'You are sure the vehicle will get us there?' Khan asked when it happened for the second time, unable to hide the anxiety he felt. The man just grunted and continued to pour the water.

It was late in the afternoon when the relentless sand gave way to a smattering of buildings, the total absence of life to the occasional black-clothed Bedouin and their thin, filthy-looking livestock. Khan knew that these buildings must indicate the outskirts of Dakhla: this country was so sparsely populated that you were only likely to come across settlements on the edges of what passed as cities. They would not be travelling, however, into the city itself. Khan had no business there. Instead, their tedious, uncomfortable road took them to the airport on the edges of the city— a busier place than the strips he had been used to over the last twenty-four hours, but still a poor shadow of the major hubs of the First World.

The airport was made up of a number of modern concrete blocks surrounded by a perimeter road that was newly tarmacked. There were lorries driving up and down, and the occasional run-down white minibus full of passengers that wouldn't have looked out of place in any African city. By the side of this road was a hotel. This too was made of concrete. Two palm trees had been planted outside, perhaps in an attempt to make it look a little more welcoming. The driver parked outside, then escorted Khan into the hotel where the reception was cavernous and entirely empty apart from the receptionist. Khan's driver spoke to this man, who glanced with suspicion at Khan and his dirty, blood-spattered dishdasha, but immediately handed over a key. Moments later they were walking into a first-floor room that overlooked an aircraft hangar and was, by any standards, basic.

'Wait outside,' Khan told the driver.

Once he was alone in the room, he unpacked his bag and checked the contents. Everything he needed was there. Khan removed his stained dishdasha, then stepped underneath the weak trickle of the shower in the adjoining room. Once he had cleansed himself of the blood, sweat and dirt that covered his body, he stood in front of the mirror and rubbed shaving foam into his neat beard. It felt strange to hold a razor and know that he was about to remove the beard that had covered his face since he was old enough to grow one, but that was precisely what he did, scraping away the whiskers in short, determined strokes.

Once he had removed the beard, he returned to

the bedroom, leaving his round spectacles by the sink. He wouldn't be needing those any more. He dried his naked body, then started to get dressed—not back into his dirty *dishdasha*, but into the new jeans, T-shirt and trainers that had been in the bag.

His transformation was complete. There was no need for him to look in the mirror. With no beard, no glasses and new clothes, he knew he would be unrecognisable.

A mobile phone lay on the bed. He picked it up and dialled a number he knew by heart: the commander of a small cell in London who was ready to do anything Khan needed.

'It is me,' he said when the call was answered.

No reply.

'All is going well,' he said. 'But I must ask you to do something. There is a man called Jack Harker. Find out who he is and where he lives. Watch his house. Watch the airports. And when—if—he returns home, eliminate him. If there is a woman with him, kill her too. The same goes for Caroline Stenton, should she return.'

There was no acknowledgement, but Khan wasn't expecting one. He threw the handset back on the bed, then picked up the final item he had unpacked. A passport—not British, but German, in the fake name of Arif Samaha. Not even a forgery; it had been newly issued by the German passport office and would allow him free travel from Western Sahara into Morocco.

And from Morocco, it was just a short flight back into Heathrow.

To all intents and purposes, he had left Habib Khan back in Somalia, hidden in the backwaters, negotiating with so-called terrorists. 'Arif Samaha', on the other hand, had other plans. He would be safely in the UK by the following day.

## 22

A pall of thin drizzle hung over Belfast. Fat Betty wiped a clammy rag over the surface of the bar, which didn't so much clean it as redistribute the grease. A few old men huddled in the dark corners of the pub, nursing pints that had already lasted them most of the afternoon.

The door opened and a man entered. He was young—mid-twenties, probably—and lanky. He had loosened his tie a couple of inches, and had the collar of his jacket pulled up over his head to protect him from the rain. Once inside, he pulled the jacket back down, looked around the gloomy pub, then approached the bar.

Fat Betty pretended not to notice him and continued wiping.

'Cormac in?' the young man asked.

Fat Betty stopped wiping and gave him a jowly stare. 'Tell you what, sunshine. Why don't you take your pretty little arse and fuck off out of it.'

Wipe wipe.

The young man took a seat. 'You see now,' he said, 'I could do that, sure I could. But then you'd have to tell him you sent me away, and I really don't think he'd be very pleased with that.'

'What's your name?'

'Danny,' the young man said.

A look of suspicion fell over Betty's face.

'Danny, hey?'

'You've heard of me. I'm flattered.'

'Don't be, sunshine. In my book, there's only one thing worse than a copper, and that's a bent copper.'

She turned her back on him and disappeared into the room behind the bar. Moments later she returned and lifted up the bar flap. She didn't speak; she just gave him a curt nod to indicate he should go through.

'There's nothing quite like service with a smile,' Danny murmured as he squeezed past. 'It warms the heart on a day like this.'

*      *      *

Cormac O'Callaghan sat where he always sat. He gazed at the policeman as he entered. There were no greetings. No pleasantries. 'You're an expensive man to have on the books, young Danny,' he said. 'And I've not heard from you for what, two weeks? I've been beginning to wonder if you're really worth the money.'

Danny shrugged. 'I can't just wander down here any time of the day, you know. And what with your aversion to the telephone—'

'Why don't you just sit down and tell me what you've got for me.'

Danny took a seat opposite O'Callaghan. 'Let's just say,' the policeman noted, 'that you don't have a whole lot to worry about in the Belfast police department.'

O'Callaghan remained expressionless. 'What do you mean?'

'Just what I say.' Danny looked around. 'Any

chance of a drink round here. It's a pub, isn't it?'

O'Callaghan gave him a bleak look, and Danny didn't push it. 'Whatever,' he murmured. 'You've got one less of us to worry about, anyway.'

'I don't like talking in riddles, young Danny.' His words were mild, his tone wasn't, and Danny was prudent enough to pick up on it.

'Four days ago,' he said. 'Colleague by the name of Siobhan Byrne got suspended. Saw her with my own eyes having a ding-dong with the DCI.'

'Police officers come and go,' O'Callaghan said. 'What's this got to do with me?'

'Well, according to my mate Frank—Frank Maloney, he's my partner you know, old-timer, bit of a lush but knows what's going on in the department—she was given the old heave-ho for spending too much time sniffing around you.' Danny grinned. 'You're off limits, it seems. No realistic hope of a conviction. The word from on high is that we have to bludgeon the dealers at street level—make our arrest rates look rosy. What is it, man? You don't exactly look overjoyed now.'

Danny was right. O'Callaghan's face remained hard. 'What did you say this girl's name was?'

'Siobhan Byrne.' He slipped his hand into the inside pocket of his jacket and pulled out a few crumpled sheets of paper, which he handed to O'Callaghan. 'Frank told me she used to be with the Det. Doesn't really mean fuck all to me, but then he's more your generation, if you know what I mean.'

O'Callaghan did. Very well.

'I thought you'd be pleased,' Danny said sarcastically, then immediately regretted it.

The older man didn't reply. Danny shrugged,

stood up and left the room.

Cormac sat perfectly still, his fingers pressed together as though in prayer. He closed his eyes and thought. That wet-behind-the-ears copper might not be impressed that his suspended colleague was an alumnus of 14 Company, but O'Callaghan was minded to take it more seriously. He'd had enough run-ins with those bastards during the Troubles to know that he'd be stupid not to take them seriously. The police—the ones like Danny—were idiots, everyone knew that. But the Det? No. If one of their number was on to him, it was cause for concern, not least because he knew their tactics: surveillance and informants. There was nothing they liked better than a tout. O'Callaghan was mistrustful by nature, but he knew that if a former Det officer was on the scene, he needed to play his cards even closer to his chest, to find out just what she had on him. And he needed to do it himself.

O'Callaghan studied the pieces of paper Danny had given him. There was a grainy picture of Byrne, and a brief CV that made no mention of her time in 14 Company. There was also an address. O'Callaghan memorised it, then threw the sheets back down on the table.

And then he stood up.

Fat Betty looked surprised when he emerged behind the bar. 'I'll be going out now, Betty,' he said and her surprise only increased. This was an unexpected occurrence.

'When will you be back?' she asked.

Cormac shrugged. 'I don't rightly know, Betty,' he said. 'I don't rightly know.'

An hour later he was standing by the River Lagan, outside Siobhan Byrne's apartment block, looking up. An old woman with a shopping trolley stood nearby, staring at him as she listened to the crackling sounds coming from a radio set. O'Callaghan ignored her and stepped towards the entrance of the block. There was a vast set of intercom buttons. He pressed the one marked with Byrne's flat number and waited for a reply. None came.

He moved round to the back of the block. There were stairs here, tall metal ones. O'Callaghan counted the floors as he climbed them, stopping every minute or so to catch his breath. He was wheezing heavily by the time he got to the tenth floor, where he pressed himself against the wall to catch his breath. As he stood there, looking along the balcony that stretched past the windows of the flats on this floor, he noticed that one of them was broken open. He hurried over to it and looked inside.

There were no lights on, and rain had seeped into the kitchen. It looked to him like the window had been broken for some time and nobody had thought to fix it up. Still, it saved him a job, and he squeezed through the opening with difficulty—his joints were not supple, and he scratched the back of his hand on a jagged piece of glass. Then he moved swiftly through the flat and bolted the front door from the inside.

Once secure, he started to look around carefully. It was Siobhan Byrne's flat all right—he could tell by a framed photograph of her with some man and a young girl—and it had all the signs of having been left in a hurry. The broken window was more of a mystery. The place didn't look like it had been burgled, and Cormac did what he could not to leave any hint of his own presence as he meticulously started going through the owner's effects.

An hour passed. Two. O'Callaghan remained patient as he looked through the drawers in her bedroom and the cupboards in her kitchen. He looked under the bed and behind the sofa. He even opened up the laptop on the coffee table, but those machines were too modern for him. He considered taking it to see if it contained any information that might be useful.

He was almost ready to give up and leave when he saw it: a small scrap of paper crumpled up on the floor. He picked it up and unfolded it. The address scrawled on the piece of paper was familiar, of course, but it was not that which filled his blood with a sudden chill; it was the fact that it was in his own handwriting.

He remembered writing it, of course. And he remembered whom he had given it to.

O'Callaghan shut his eyes. It was always the way. You looked all around for the disloyal and untrustworthy, and they were right under your nose all the time.

He put the scrap of paper in his pocket, left the flat, then crossed the city to the location of the lock-up. It was dark and deserted here, as always, and he used one of the many keys on his keyring to unlock it. A quick search of the cache revealed all he needed to know. The weapons were all there and intact. But the money was light. About £4,000 light. There was only one person who knew about this cache. Either he had stolen money from it, or he had given its location up to the police, or both.

Cormac O'Callaghan left the cache and locked up behind him. There was no doubt about where he needed to go next.

*       *       *

It had been a pleasant afternoon. Kieran had taken little Jackie, his four-year-old boy, to the Dunville playground where he'd had fun on the swings and screamed down the slide. When it started to rain, Kieran had taken him to McDonald's in Donegall Place for a Happy Meal—his favourite treat. And now, back home, Janice was giving Jackie a bath while Kieran sat in front of *The Weakest Link*, a whiskey in his hand, his pouch of baccy by his side and his feet up on the coffee table. He had just taken his final swig and was preparing to roll another tab when the doorbell rang.

'Get that, will you?' Kieran shouted at his wife. Janice, of course, knew better than to complain that her hands were full. Division of labour was division of labour. She had her jobs; he had his. But he listened to the sound of her coming downstairs, opening the door, and greeting their visitor with what sounded like enthusiasm but which Kieran—knowing her well—recognised as something else.

'Cormac! What a lovely surprise. Come on in, won't you?'

Kieran's blood ran cold. Cormac never visited people. *Never*. They went to him—either at the

382

Horse and Three Feathers, for business, or at a restaurant, for pleasure, although Kieran suspected that his uncle didn't really make much distinction between the two.

He stood up just as another pair of feet thundered down the stairs. 'Uncle Cormac!' little Jackie shouted, and from his vantage point in the front room, Kieran could just see the newcomer in the hallway, bending down to ruffle Jackie's hair and give him a lollipop. Then he stood up and looked through the door towards Kieran.

'I'll be needing to have a word with your da, young Jackie,' Cormac said. 'Why don't you and your ma just pop upstairs for a while?' He made his suggestion with a certain authority that it was impossible to refuse. Janice and Jackie immediately disappeared.

'Come on through, Cormac,' Kieran called, doing what he could to sound welcoming. 'What'll it be? Whiskey?'

His uncle didn't answer. He stood in the doorway and stared at Kieran. His heavy overcoat made him look bigger than he was, and his bushy eyebrows were furrowed.

'Will you not sit down, Cormac?' Kieran suggested, pointing at the comfortable chair that he had just vacated by the gas fire.

Still no reply.

Kieran switched off the TV. He heard himself chattering over the silence. 'Little Jackie will have been pleased to see you. Always asking where his uncle Cormac is. Doesn't *stop* asking. He's like a—'

'Does the name Siobhan Byrne mean anything to you, lad?' Cormac asked in barely more than a whisper.

Kieran tried not to let any guilt show in his face, forcing his features instead into an expression of bewilderment. 'Who?' he asked. 'No. Who is she?' He couldn't quite bring himself to look in Cormac's eyes as he spoke.

Cormac walked slowly into the room. 'Why don't *you* sit down, now, Kieran?'

'No, really, I'm—'

'Sit down, Kieran.' A soft, sing-song voice. Like a hypnotist.

Kieran took a seat.

A pause.

'How's Mikey?'

'Not so good, Cormac. I fucked him up proper, like you told me. He might lose the leg.'

Cormac inclined his head. 'A shame,' he observed. 'Mikey's a nice lad. But it would be a disaster for us all, wouldn't it now, Kieran, if we weren't careful about security. If we didn't make sure we knew who our friends were, and our enemies.'

Silence.

'Would you agree with that, Kieran?'

'Sure, Cormac,' he replied in a low voice. 'Sure I would.'

The sound of Jackie's laughing drifted down from upstairs.

'I'll ask you again, Kieran. Does the name Siobhan Byrne mean anything to you? *Detective* Siobhan Byrne.'

'I told you, Cormac. I've never heard of her.' But he could feel the colour draining from his face as his uncle continued to stare at him with that flinty look.

384

'Would you like to know where I've just been, Kieran?' he asked.

Kieran nodded mutely.

'The lock-up. You know, where you picked up the tools to deal with Mikey.'

Kieran swallowed hard.

'I couldn't help noticing, lad, that the money stash was short. To the tune of four G.'

'That wasn't me, Cormac,' Kieran burst out with relief. Of this, at least, he knew he could speak honestly. 'I wouldn't touch your money, you know that—'

'Ah, I thought I *did* know that, lad. Until today, I thought I did. But you see, here's the thing. You were the only person that knew about that stash. So either you took the money yourself, or you told someone where it was.'

Kieran's limbs felt heavy with dread. He couldn't shake the feeling that his uncle was playing with him, like a cat with a mouse. He'd seen that happen before, and the mouse always ended up dead.

'Maybe someone just knocked it off,' he suggested, his voice cracking as he spoke. 'You know, kids or something.'

'Maybe they did. Maybe they just took the four G and left the rest—not to mention the weapons—and locked the door properly behind them like the good little children that they are. Does that sound likely to you, Kieran?'

He could do nothing but shake his head.

'So the question is this. Why would I be nosing around that cache if I wasn't suspicious about something in the first place? Can you think why that would be?'

He shook his head even as a wave of nausea crashed over him. He watched, in slow-motion horror, as his uncle put a hand into his pocket and withdrew a small scrap of paper, which he dropped into Kieran's lap, like he was throwing a piece of loose change to a beggar.

Kieran looked at the paper. He knew what it was, of course. But the question was—

'Where did I get it? That's what you're thinking, isn't it, lad? Well let me put you out of your misery. I found it on the floor of Detective Siobhan Byrne's flat. Now wouldn't you say that's an amazing coincidence?' He looked around the room. 'Shall I pour you one of those whiskeys now, lad? Or have you got the bollocks to tell me what the fuck has been going on without any Dutch courage?'

Kieran swallowed. He felt sweat soaking into the back of his shirt. More laughter from Jackie upstairs.

'She had me over a barrel, Cormac,' he whispered. 'Threatened me with enough chokey to keep me going till retirement. I couldn't do it to little Jackie.' And then he buried his head in his hands. 'Don't do it here,' he breathed. 'Not in front of my family. I'll come quietly, but at least grant me that, Cormac.'

He didn't dare look up.

It was a full minute until Cormac spoke. 'You realise, lad, that if it was anyone else, you'd already be dead.'

Kieran removed his hands from his face and stared at his uncle.

'It's only out of respect for your father that you're still sitting there.'

'Thank you, Cormac . . .' It was all he could think of to say.

'Don't thank me yet, you little rat. You're not out of the woods yet.'

'I'll do anything, Cormac. Whatever you say.'

His uncle sniffed disdainfully. 'So you will, lad. So you will. So here's what's going to happen. You're going to arrange a little meeting with our inquisitive detective. We're going to find out what she knows, and then *you* are going to put a bullet in her pretty little skull.' He knelt down so that his eyes were at Kieran's level. 'And make no mistake about it, lad. You put one foot wrong and it won't be *your* funeral Janice will be arranging. It'll be young Jackie's.'

He stood up and walked out of the room. 'I'll be showing myself out now, Janice,' he called up the stairs, before opening the door, stepping outside, and shutting it quietly behind him.

\*     \*     \*

Jack and Markus stood by a hole in the ground. It had taken them an hour and a half to dig it and they were sweating from the effort. And lying at the bottom of the hole was Caroline Stenton's corpse.

They had taken it where no one would see them—a parched, treeless wasteland a couple of miles from Markus's safari base, far away from any casual observers. 'If it was down to the natives,' he told Jack, 'they wouldn't bother burying her. Plenty of wild animals roaming around—a mouthful of her would be like a Big Mac and fucking fries for them. Too goddamn risky, though.

387

Fine if she was black, but the authorities get jumpy when white bodies turn up.' He grinned at Jack. 'And I reckon the Company might have something to say about it, if the eyes of the world suddenly turn to my little operation here.'

They started shovelling dirt back into the hole.

'Jack, buddy,' Markus said when they were finished, 'I don't know what you've got yourself into. Ain't none of my business. But if this is your idea of woman trouble . . .'

They walked away from the grave. Jack didn't answer his American friend.

'Done a bit of research of my own since we landed. Hell, Jack, don't give me that kind of look. Some fucker tries to shoot me out of the air, I want to know who they are. I kept it under the radar, OK? Friend of mine over at Langley. Trustworthy. Got him to pull up everything he could on this Habib Khan fella.'

Jack looked at him. 'And?'

'Drew a blank. No priors, no nothing. He's of no interest whatsoever to the Company.'

Jack remembered something Siobhan had said back in Belfast. *He's just got good cover.* 'That figures,' he said. He glanced back at the grave, then continued walking away without regret. Some people weren't worthy of it.

By now it was dark. Since touching down back in Kenya, Jack and Siobhan had spent the time recovering. Siobhan had slept; when she hadn't slept, she'd been silent. Jack had let her be. He knew her well, and he knew she'd talk when she wanted to.

Markus drove them back to the Safari. 'You've got an hour,' he said. 'Plane back to Nairobi leaves

388

at 21.00. You should be there in time to get the red-eye back to London.'

Jack nodded, then went to find Siobhan.

She was still in the hut where they'd been sleeping and she looked fucked. Red eyes, bags under them and the thousand-yard stare he recognised from the faces of any number of men in the field. But Siobhan was as good an operator as the Det ever had. Close-quarter battle didn't faze her and Jack knew she wasn't traumatised by the firefight. It was Lily.

She was sitting on the edge of the bed and barely reacted as Jack walked in. He sat down next to her.

'You all right?'

Siobhan barely nodded.

'You did well back there,' he said. 'Kept your head. I've seen a lot of guys lose it under fire, but—'

'Do you think she's still alive?' she whispered. Her voice was hoarse.

'Siobhan—'

*'Do you think she's still alive?'*

A horrible silence.

'I don't know,' Jack said. 'But if she is, I'm going to find her.'

They sat in silence. Siobhan rested her head against him. It was comforting, and Jack moved one arm around her shoulders. She felt impossibly slight in his broad arms, and her body felt like it fitted snugly into his, like they were two pieces of a jigsaw puzzle.

'We'll be back in the UK tomorrow,' Jack said. 'Khan's got my name, so I need to keep under the radar, but you can go straight to Belfast. Wait for me there. You should be safe—he doesn't know who you are.'

'What about you?'

'I'm going to stay in London for a bit. Do some snooping. Khan's playing the authorities like an instrument, just like Stenton was. We need their help. They're not going to pull the big guns out just to find Lily, but if they think there's going to be a terrorist strike, they will. If we're going to find him, we need to get them to take us seriously, to show them that he's not what they think he is.'

'How?'

A pause.

'I don't know.' He kept his voice level. He could lie to most people easily, but Siobhan wasn't one of them.

'I still think we should tell someone now.'

'Tell them what? That a guy the whole world thinks is a peace campaigner is actually a terrorist fuck? That a brainiac who advises Five is some kind of closet fundamentalist?' He corrected himself: '*Was* some kind of closet fundamentalist. Think about it, Siobhan. Khan took a UN flight into Mogadishu. All the agencies will have details of who was on that plane, so as far as they're concerned, he'll still be somewhere in Somalia until they take him out again. He's got it all figured.' His face darkened. 'As for us, I was sent home from the Stan for laying in to some Rupert. I've missed my disciplinary with the adjutant. My name's shit and I'm as good as fired. Next thing, I come up with some bullshit about how they've been played and I'm the only one who knows what's going down. Same with you—you saw what happened when you tried to finger Khan.'

'What happens if he gets that device into the

390

country?'

'We don't even know that the UK's his target,' Jack replied. 'Even if it is, it's going to take him a while to import it. You can't just fly into Heathrow with something like that in your suitcase. If I draw a blank, we'll do it your way, I promise. But I know how the security services work. They get intelligence of a hundred threats a week. Unless I can give them something more concrete . . .'

Silence.

'What have you done with the body?' she asked.

'It's dealt with.'

He felt her go a little bit tense. 'Was it true?' she asked in a small voice. 'What she said, about you and her.'

'Forget about it.'

Siobhan remained pressed close to him. 'When this is over,' she said, 'when we find Lily, maybe we should . . .'

'What?'

'I don't know. Give it a go. I mean, another go. For her sake. And for us.'

Jack didn't reply. He couldn't find the words. They just sat there quietly for a few more minutes, then he unfurled his arm and stood up. 'We need to get ready to leave,' he said.

Siobhan looked away. Soon she got to her feet and started to gather her things. Jack watched from the edge of his vision. She still had that faraway look.

Shell-shocked.

Numb.

Haunted.

He couldn't help thinking that she looked like a woman for whom both the past and the future held things too terrible even to contemplate. And as she continued to get herself ready, Jack even felt a little guilty that he'd not been quite honest with her.

He knew what his next move was; he just didn't want Siobhan to find out just yet.

# 6 JULY

## 23

04.00 hrs.

On the southern coast of Ireland, dawn was still an hour away. In a shingle-strewn bay, no wider than an articulated lorry and with needle-sharp rocks on two sides, five men stood in the darkness. They wore heavy coats against the early-morning chill, and their cigarettes glowed as they inhaled. None of them spoke. They just looked out to sea where, in the distance, they could see a dot of light.

It approached quickly. They always did, these vessels. Their skippers knew the timings of the coastguard's patrols. And even if the coastguard changed schedule, by the time they were noticed, the vessels had made anchor, dumped their cargo, then chuntered back off into the night. There was never any trouble. This stretch of the Atlantic off the southern Irish coastline was dotted with sea traffic 24/7. It was impossible to police effectively.

'Moving faster than most,' a voice said. Sam Delaney was an old hand. He'd been part of the O'Callaghan crew for as long as there had *been* a crew, and the others looked up to him.

'Why's that then?'

Sam glanced over at young Leo Mackay. This was only his second run, and he sounded on edge.

'No reason, Leo. No reason. One speed's as good as another. Don't you worry your head about it, lad.'

They went back to smoking their cigarettes.

Fifteen minutes later, the vessel had stopped. It was about thirty metres out and had hauled anchor. The five men watched as a smaller launch was lowered into the water, and two crew members embarked and headed towards them.

'Help them in, Leo,' Sam instructed.

Leo looked at the others, but they clearly weren't about to get themselves wet to help the new boy; the younger man sighed, dropped his ciggy on the beach, then waded out into the chilly waters as the launch came in to land. He grabbed the boat's stern and pulled it across the hissing shingle.

'All yours,' one of the men in the boat said. 'And we won't be sad to see the back of it.'

Leo looked into the boat. It contained nothing but a metal flight case—quite different to the wooden pallet of narcotics he was expecting to see. 'What the fuck's this?' he asked. And then, over his shoulder at his colleagues, *'What the fuck's this?'*

'Just bring it ashore, lad,' Sam called out.

Leo did as he was told. The case was heavy, but not so heavy that he couldn't carry it single-handed. He hauled it to shore as the launch retreated without a word from the crew, then laid it on the beach. The five of them stood around and looked at it.

'If that's a shipment of H,' one of them said, 'I'm a monkey's ball sacks.'

'What is it then?' Leo asked.

'Not for us to know,' Sam replied. 'Get the fucker loaded up.'

They weren't by nature a mutinous crew, but there was a definite sense of reluctance.

'Maybe we should open it,' Leo said. 'Take a look.'

'Maybe we should at that,' another man said.

Sam Delaney wasn't having it. 'For fuck's sake, you lot. Have you forgotten who you damn well work for? Have you forgotten what happened to Mikey Elliott? And he was one of Cormac's rude boys. You reckon he'd think twice about fucking any of you lot up if you start messing with his shipments? Especially you, Leo Mackay. Carry on with this sort of shit, it'll be the Paralympics for you, if you're lucky.'

He looked at each of them in turn. A flat, flinty look that wouldn't tolerate any bullshit. 'Get it loaded up,' he said. 'Now.'

Leo did what he had to do. He bent over, picked up the case, and with the rest of them trailing behind, carried it off the beach, up a small winding track and into the back of a waiting Ford Transit. He and two of the others accompanied it in the back, while Sam and the remaining man went up front.

Sam checked his watch. 04.17. He'd be over the border by midday and at Larne Harbour on the east coast of Northern Ireland by early afternoon. They'd hand the consignment over—whatever the fuck it was—and it would be on its way to the mainland without anybody being the wiser.

He shook his head. The sooner Cormac stopped these non-standard deliveries, the happier he'd be. This was the second one in the last week and the guys were getting suspicious. Hell, *he* was getting suspicious. Packages of heroin off the boat were two a penny for the guys, but if these curious shipments continued, his threats regarding Cormac's retribution wouldn't be enough to stop them poking their noses in.

He turned to the man behind the wheel. 'Let's

go,' he said. 'Don't drive too quickly. We don't want to be picked up.'

His colleague looked at him. 'Sure, Sam, you talk as if I've never done this before.' And with that, he turned the ignition key and drove steadily off into the early morning.

*　　　　*　　　　*

'Gentlemen, let's see your imagery.'

Brad Joseph was clean-cut and sharp-suited, his hair slicked back and his ever-present shades hanging by a cord around his neck. He'd flown in from Washington three days earlier, heading up the sixteen-man advance team from the President's Secret Service detail. He sensed that the two Brits sitting with him in the slightly shabby ground-floor office of Scotland Yard resented his presence, even if they were too professional to say anything. But that didn't matter one little bit to Brad Joseph. He was well used to it.

Bill Oliver, i/c the British Police's Diplomatic Protection Group, was a quietly spoken man in his mid-fifties with a receding hairline and the remnants of a Cockney accent. He clicked a button on the laptop in front of him—Brad couldn't help noticing that it was a lot older and clunkier than the machines they were used to in Washington. Up on the wall appeared a large satellite image of the Greater London area. Superimposed in red was a dotted line leading from a point on the western part of the map, directly to a central location.

'As we agreed,' Bill Oliver said, 'RAF Northolt is the most secure location for Air Force One to fly in to. We can seal it off and, unlike at the

398

commercial airports, we can divert all other incoming flights elsewhere.'

'And,' Brad stepped in, 'it's nearby, in case of emergency.'

Bill Oliver scratched his bald patch, raised an eyebrow at the interruption, then nodded. 'That too,' he said. 'This shows the most direct flightline from RAF Northolt in to the helipad at Buckingham Palace.'

Brad interrupted again. 'You understand that Marine One flies with two decoy choppers and they'll choose their own flight path in to the palace?'

Bill nodded. He pressed the button on the laptop and another image appeared—the same map, but with a different route marked—this time a solid red line. It led from Buckingham Palace, along Birdcage Walk, round Parliament Square and into the Houses of Parliament. 'And this is the most direct route from Buck House to Westminster.'

'Buck House?'

Bill smiled. 'Buckingham Palace, Brad.'

'I take it your teams have secured the route?'

Oliver pressed another button and the image changed: the bottom panel of a lamp post, with a plastic cord tied round it. 'We've sealed all the lamp posts and manholes, emptied and sealed all bins and postboxes. Parking restrictions are in force from today until you leave—any unauthorised stopping along these routes and the vehicles get towed away immediately. We also have four teams of Metropolitan Police outriders ready to escort the President wherever he goes.'

Brad interrupted again. 'It's fully understood, I hope, that the President will have his own close protection and counter-attack team at all times.' He set his face into a look of implacability. It was amazing how often foreign police teams got rubbed up the wrong way about this. Most figures of any kind of diplomatic importance could expect local bodyguarding teams; but not the President of the United States. Secret Service wouldn't be letting anybody else close to him. And while most foreign security teams knew they had to surrender their weapons when they arrived in-country, the President's close protection would keep their Glocks, Berettas and MP5 Kurzs firmly on their persons, no matter what; while the CAT's armour-plated 4 x 4s, MP5s, G3s and UMPs had already been airlifted into Northolt ready for the President's arrival.

Bill Oliver nodded. 'Understood,' he said. 'We'll leave everything else to the President's close protection and CAT team. Our outriders will just make sure that the path of traffic is cleared for the, er . . .' The policeman's eyes sparkled for the first time, and a ghost of a smile flickered across his lips.

'The Beast,' Brad said in a voice devoid of irony. The British could laugh all they wanted, but there was no doubting that the Secret Service felt a hell of sight more comfortable now that the President was able to travel in the world's most secure armoured car. The Beast—Cadillac One to Brad and his colleagues—was an awesome machine. It could take hits from small arms fire, the tyres worked even when they were flat, and the vehicle could be completely sealed with its own oxygen supply in the event of a chemical attack. It wasn't so much a car as a moving fortress, and even as they spoke a C-17 Globemaster was transporting that fortress across the Atlantic so that it could be waiting for the President at Buckingham Palace when he arrived.

'Oh yeah,' murmured Oliver. 'The Beast.' He brought up another picture on the screen. London again, this time with two locations marked: the residence of the American ambassador, Nathaniel Gresham, in Regent's Park, where the President would be staying the night; and Buckingham Palace again, where he would be having a lunchtime audience with the Queen on 8 July, before Marine One returned him to RAF Northolt. There Air Force One would be waiting to transport him back to Washington. Brad Joseph would never have admitted it in front of his British counterparts, but that moment couldn't come soon enough. Back home, it was easy to keep him safe; the moment he went walkabout, every goddamn eventuality had to be accounted for.

'Routes to and from the Embassy and Buckingham Palace secured?'

Oliver nodded.

'And do we have alternative evacuation routes from all the President's locations back to Marine One at Buckingham Palace?'

Again the policeman nodded, and over the course of several more pictures he explained the emergency extraction routes. 'We'll leave your people to decide which priority to give the evacuation routes. Just let us know which ones you're likely to use for preference.'

'Negative,' Brad stated, and he ignored the widening of Bill Oliver's eyes. 'Secret Service will keep the evacuation route priority classified.' And

401

before the police officer could make any complaint, he turned to the other man sitting in the room.

David Colley hadn't said a word. He'd just sat there, expressionless, in his grey suit and sober tie. As a representative of MI5, the nitty-gritty of the President's movements were not his immediate concern. He was here to give Brad an intelligence briefing. Even though the Security Service and the CIA were constantly liaising over the President's visit, it was important that the guys on the ground should have some face time. Brad knew Dave Colley from previous assignments. For a spook, he was OK. Brad kind of liked him, and trusted his judgement.

'So, Dave. No alarm bells ringing over at Thames House?'

Colley inclined his head. 'There's always alarm bells,' he said soberly. 'The skill's in judging which ones to listen to and which ones to ignore.'

Brad smiled for the first time in the whole meeting. 'My line of work, Dave, you react to every goddamn alarm bell you hear.'

Colley shrugged. 'In that case, Brad, you should call the whole thing off. Anniversary of the London bombings, your man should be safely tucked up in the Oval Office.'

'Ain't that the truth,' Brad agreed. 'Look, we know the score. This is party time for every wannabe Al Qaeda nut in the UK. We get the same shit on 9/11. But you get even a sniff of anything we need to take seriously—'

'You'll be the first to know, Brad. Meantime...' He slid a thin file across the table. 'That's a precis of any relevant intelligence. It won't take you long to read.'

The Secret Service operative nodded. 'Well, gentlemen,' he said, taking the file and standing up, 'thank you for your time and your cooperation. Bill, you'll pass the imagery on to my people? And we'll stay in constant touch between now and when Air Force One flies on the morning of the eighth. You have my cell, right?'

'Of course,' Oliver and Colley said in unison.

'Now if you'll excuse me, my team needs to recce these routes and arrange our OPs around the President's stop-off points. Don't want any big-game hunters taking pot shots at the Beast, huh?'

He winked at them, then turned and left, leaving the two British men to exchange a raised eyebrow before they themselves continued about their business.

\*         \*         \*

Nairobi to London. Nine hours. Jack used the remainder of the O'Callaghan notes to book them into first class, where the safari clothes they'd borrowed from Markus raised some eyebrows, but they were too exhausted to pay any attention to that and just used the flight to sleep.

It was just before 6 a.m. when they emerged through the cloud cover to see the patchwork fields of southern England as the plane made its approach to Heathrow. As the remainder of the passengers waited for their luggage, Jack and Siobhan walked wordlessly through passport control. Out on the concourse, they stood awkwardly.

'You'll be careful, won't you?' Siobhan said.

403

Jack didn't need to reply. 'Get on the next flight,' he said. 'Go straight to the flat and don't do anything until you hear from me. OK?'

'OK.' No aggression now. No argument. Siobhan had learned her lesson. He hoped. 'But don't go dark on me, Jack.' She looked up at him. 'I'm scared.'

'I'll call you as soon as I know anything. Any problems call me immediately.' He gave her his mobile number, which she put on to speed dial. Then he handed over her car keys and a crumpled ticket. 'It's parked at the airport,' he said. 'Your weapon is in the glove compartment. I had to break your kitchen window to get in.' Jack smiled for what seemed like the first time in days. 'Sorry about that.'

Siobhan smiled back and he kissed her lightly on the top of her head. The kiss seemed to surprise her, but she didn't look displeased. She squeezed his hand, then turned and disappeared into the crowd.

Jack watched her go, then followed her from a distance. He watched as she approached the BMI ticket desk; when she turned away five minutes later, she was holding a ticket. She'd booked herself on to a flight and was now heading towards the check-in desk.

Jack walked up to the BMI desk. An attractive brunette with large eyes and full lips smiled up at him. 'When's the next flight to Belfast?' he asked.

She checked her terminal. 'I can just get you on the ten-thirty. After that, I'm afraid, it's the three p.m.'

That was all he needed to know. Siobhan would be on the first flight, and he wanted to get to

Belfast without her realising. So the 15.00 hrs it was. 'I'll take a seat on the three o'clock,' he replied, handing over his credit card.

Once he had his ticket, Jack headed to the retail area of the terminal where he bought himself a full set of clean clothes before leaving the building and checking in to a hotel for a couple of hours. He showered off the dirt, put on the new clothes and left Markus's safari gear in the bin. They still had the faint reek of Africa about them. He was glad to be rid of it.

With time still to kill, he lay on the bed, closed his eyes and straightened his head. Everything was so confusing. Upside down. He needed to clear his thoughts and plan his next move.

Maybe he was wrong to pull the wool over Siobhan's eyes. He admired her for her determination, but now wasn't the time for her to stop him doing what needed to be done. There was only one lead he could follow. One person he knew of who could give him anything on Khan. That person was Cormac O'Callaghan, and Jack couldn't be sure that Siobhan wouldn't try to stop him making contact with the PIRA bastard. She would do anything to find Lily and he could tell she didn't fully agree with his strategy to go it alone. Truth was, he couldn't risk her getting in the way. Let the authorities question O'Callaghan and they'd play it by the book. It would take too long. If Jack was going to do anything, he needed to work quickly. Without interference.

His strategy was clear. Raid the O'Callaghan lock-up for a weapon, then hit some of the bars of Belfast that were once Republican hang-outs. If he asked the right questions of the right people, he'd soon be able to track O'Callaghan down. And he didn't mind admitting to himself that once he had the bastard in his hands, he'd almost enjoy the process of extracting every last bit of information from him. Cormac O'Callaghan might hold the key to preventing a major terrorist attack; he might give Jack a lead on where his daughter was; but when it came to answering for his crimes, he had a lot of back payments to make. Jack was perfectly happy to act as banker.

He looked at his watch. 12.30 hrs. Siobhan would have landed now. With any luck she'd have taken his advice and headed home to lie low. Unwanted, the question she'd asked him back at Markus's popped into his head. About them getting together again. He put it from his mind. When this was all over, when he had held Lily in his arms and seen that she was safe, maybe he could think about it. But until then . . .

Jack left the hotel then returned to the terminal to check in.

*　　　*　　　*

Siobhan walked across the concourse of Belfast International in a daze. In a corner of her mind she remembered what Jack used to be like when he came home from ops. Distracted—like the world he had just left was the real one, and this was a fake. In her dazed state she took a while to find her car and she drove on autopilot. She couldn't think right and she needed to sleep. To recuperate. Jack had told her to go home, and she planned to do exactly that.

It was chilly back at the flat because of the

406

broken window, but she was too overcome with exhaustion and emotion to do anything about it; instead she headed straight for the bedroom, plugged her mobile phone in to charge, then climbed, fully dressed, into bed. She was asleep in seconds.

It was the mobile that woke her, painfully puncturing her sleep like a knife piercing flesh. She rolled over and fumbled with it. 'Yeah . . . hello . . . who's this?' It was a chore just to get the words out.

'It's me.'

She shook her head and tried to place the voice. Male. Surly. She recognised it, but her exhaustion got in the way of pinpointing who it was.

'I know a lot of "me's",' she murmured.

A pause. 'And there was me thinking I was important to the pigs.'

'Kieran?'

'I've been trying to get hold of you.'

'I've been out of town for a bit,' Siobhan said, sitting up on the side of the bed. 'What's up?'

'Clever old Kieran's got something for you.' He sounded terribly pleased with himself.

'What?'

'Not on the phone.'

Siobhan shrugged, even though there was no one to see it. 'All right then. The usual place.'

'No,' Kieran said quickly. 'Not there. That's no good. I've got something to show you.'

She stood up. 'What?' she demanded.

But Kieran remained enigmatic. 'You want Cormac,' he said, 'I'll give you Cormac. On a fucking plate. You only have to meet with me. Once I've shown you what I've got to show, I won't

407

need to look at your ugly pig face ever again.'

'All right, all right.' She felt uncharacteristically wrong-footed. 'Where are you now?'

She listened carefully as he gave her directions to the outskirts of Crossgar, a village thirty miles to the south of Belfast. 'There's an old farm there,' he said. 'Deserted. I'll be waiting for you in the barn. I think you'll have a nice surprise when you get here.'

Siobhan hesitated for a moment. 'Forget it, Kieran,' she decided finally. 'If we're meeting, I name the place.'

'The place,' Kieran replied, 'is the important thing.'

'What do you mean?'

There was a pause. Siobhan half imagined Kieran looking over his shoulder. 'It's a stash,' he said quietly. 'Dug into the ground. Street value a couple of hundred G. And the barn's Cormac's. You can trace it to him. He's got sloppy.'

Siobhan paused, turning it over in her mind, trying to think several moves ahead. Cormac was their only lead to Khan. Frankly she didn't care about the drugs any more, but if she could use Kieran's info as leverage, maybe she could find out something about Lily . . .

'I've heard whisperings they're moving it tonight,' said Kieran, 'and the chances of Cormac fucking up again—'

'All right,' she heard herself reply. 'I'll be there in an hour. This had better be worth it, Kieran.'

A minute later she was walking out of the flat. On the street, the old bag lady was there with her supermarket trolley. Her eyes were bloodshot and wary; she spoke, but Siobhan didn't hear what she said as she strode round to where her car was parked.

She sat behind the wheel, one hand on the ignition keys, and stared through the windscreen. It was late afternoon and everything around her was grey: the tower block, the pavement, the stooped old man walking towards her. Through her dazed numbness she heard Jack's voice. *Go straight to the flat and don't do anything until you hear from me.*

She should go back. She knew it. God knows how many SOPs she was breaking. But somehow she couldn't make herself do it. Call it arrogance, call it determination, call it desperation, call it what you like. Siobhan could no more ignore a bite like this than she could stop breathing. But that didn't mean she couldn't take precautions. She found her M66, which Jack had left in the glove compartment, then pulled her phone from her jacket. She held her finger on the number 1 and speed-dialled Jack. There was no ringing tone as it clicked automatically on to his voicemail. *This is Jack, leave a message.*

'Jack, it's me. It's Siobhan. I know you told me to stay at home, but something's come up. I need to visit my O'Callaghan tout . . .' She recited the directions Kieran had given her. 'Just in case, you know . . . you need to find me. And Jack . . .' She paused, then spoke quickly. 'Jack, I meant what I said. I want you to come back. I want us to try again.'

Siobhan hung up immediately and felt her heart racing, her skin flushing. She tucked the phone back into her jacket, turned the key and pulled away.

Kieran's directions were good. She took the A7 south of Belfast and it was a little before 5 p.m. when she pulled off a country lane on to a track marked 'Not Suitable for Vehicles' and stopped about 100 metres from a cluster of disused farm outbuildings. She switched off the engine.

Silence.

Through the windscreen she could see an old tractor missing one of its wheels, and she had a sudden flashback to the rusted vehicle she and Jack had used for cover in Somalia. Apart from that, just beyond it, there was only one other car—a silver Alfa Romeo that positively gleamed in comparison with the mud-caked outbuildings as the setting sun glowed against its paintwork.

Siobhan stepped out of the car with the firearm in her right hand and scanned the area. No sign of anyone. If that was Kieran's car—and she had to assume that it was—he must be inside one of the buildings, and she recognised the ramshackle barn from his description. She started to walk towards it.

Siobhan stopped by the old tractor and looked around again. Still no one.

A rook called somewhere nearby, shattering the silence.

Siobhan stepped out from behind the tractor and approached the entrance to the barn.

The big door was open—not fully, but enough for her to peer into the gloom inside, and it took a moment for her eyes to adapt. The first thing she saw was Kieran. He was alone, standing in the centre of the large open space, wearing his strangely unfashionable clothes—a patterned jumper and ill-fitting jeans. He hadn't noticed her

410

yet, but he looked anxious as he stepped from one foot to the other and blew into his hands even though it wasn't all that cold. The barn itself was full of junk—old tyres, tractor attachments, rusting bits of farmyard machinery and hand tools, even a few bales of hay—and it was immediately obvious that nobody had paid this place any attention for a very long time.

Siobhan raised her gun.

'This had better be good, Kieran,' she called, and the tout appeared to jump. He looked in her direction; the moment he saw the gun he put his hands in the air.

'Oh,' he said. 'Sure. I think it'll be good. For everyone, you know.' He licked his lips and looked at the gun. 'There's no need for that, now is there?'

Siobhan hesitated. There was something about him. Something different. It wasn't just that he was on edge—that was to be expected. It was something else. Siobhan's senses screamed at her to abort.

'I'm leaving,' she said.

*'I don't think you are, now.'*

The voice didn't come from Kieran. It came from behind, and it caused all the warmth to drain from Siobhan's blood just as she felt something hard at the back of her head.

'Drop the weapon and kick it away.'

She had no choice but to obey.

'I know who you are,' the voice continued. 'If you do a single thing to make me nervous, I'll kill you without a second thought. Take five steps forward and turn around slowly.'

Siobhan did as she was told. A figure was

standing there, no more than three metres away. He wore a heavy coat, but his body was as thin as the lines on his face; his hair was bushy and so were his eyebrows. There was a cruel scar running from one corner of his mouth up into his cheek, but it wasn't half so cruel as the chilling look in his eyes as he aimed a sawn-off shotgun directly at Siobhan's stomach.

She recognised Cormac O'Callaghan, of course. How could she not? And how, she wondered in a moment of clarity, could she not have realised what she was walking into?

'Step backwards,' he told her.

Kieran had moved closer; he bent down to pick up her M66. For a moment she considered going for him, but she knew Cormac O'Callaghan meant what he said.

'Keep going,' Cormac instructed in just a whisper. He bore down on her as she continued to step backwards into the barn. 'Stop,' he said when she was in the middle.

They were both in her view now, standing next to each other about ten metres away, guns raised in her direction.

'You'll do exactly what I say,' Cormac hissed. 'You fuck me around, lady, and you'll get one in the head before you know it. Empty your pockets slowly and drop everything you're carrying on the ground.'

Siobhan's limbs would barely obey the instructions her brain was giving them. She removed her car keys from her pocket, dropped them in the dirt, and then took her mobile phone from her jacket.

'Easy,' Kieran said, as she started to bring it out;

when he saw it wasn't a weapon, relief was clear on his face.

'Drop it,' Cormac said.

Siobhan stared directly at him. Anything to stop his attention wandering to the phone itself. While it was still between her fingertips, she squeezed the '1' button. She heard the sound of the phone dialling Jack's number, but it was too faint for the others to hear at a distance. Lowering her arm, she dropped the mobile next to her keys, making sure that it landed mouthpiece side upwards.

'You don't want to go down the path of shooting a cop, do you now, Cormac?' she said, in a voice that she hoped was both confident and loud enough to be heard over the phone.

'To be honest,' O'Callaghan replied, 'I think you'd be surprised at what I'd be prepared to do to you.' He turned to Kieran and nodded. 'Go ahead,' he said.

Siobhan Byrne could feel her jugular pulsating as the tout started walking towards her.

\*　　　\*　　　\*

Jack had been on the ground in Belfast for thirty minutes, but he was still inside the terminal building queuing up to hire a vehicle, and the queue was moving impossibly slowly. It was all he could do to stop himself from barging through the lot of them to get to the front. It was more to distract himself than for any other reason that he took his phone from his pocket and switched it on. He waited a moment to get a signal, then saw that a voicemail was waiting for him. It had been left just under an hour ago.

Siobhan's voice, and it made his stomach go heavy. *Jack, it's me. It's Siobhan. I know you told me to stay at home, but . . .*

He listened to the message and when it was finished he cursed under his breath. What was it with her? Why the fuck couldn't she just do what she was told? He counted the people in front of him. Six of them. He walked up to the front of the queue. 'Look, mate,' he said to the guy up front, 'I'm in a real hurry. Could I just—'

'We're all in a hurry, pal . . .' and the fucker turned his back on him.

Jack saw red. But just as he was about to escalate the argument, he felt his phone vibrate in his hand. Siobhan's number. He pressed a button to answer.

'Siobhan, where the *fuck*—'

But Siobhan didn't answer. Not at first. There was just a crackling sound, confused and incomprehensible. When he did hear her voice it was distant. Faint. Above the noise of the airport terminal he could barely hear what she was saying. *You don't want to . . . shooting a cop . . . Cormac.*

He suddenly felt nauseous. What was going on? What the *hell* was going on? 'Siobhan!' he barked down the phone. '*Siobhan!*'

No answer. He looked around in frustration: he'd be here for hours if he carried on queuing, so he ran out of the terminal building, his phone still pressed against his ear.

The drop-off area was busy, but for now Jack ignored the cars parked with their engines running and their doors open. Instead he looked up and spotted a line of white security cameras attached five metres up on the terminal wall at intervals of ten metres. The three nearest cameras were

414

angled towards him; after that the angle changed as they pointed in the opposite direction—which meant there was a blind spot. Jack positioned himself there, all the while listening to the ominous silence on his phone.

It took two minutes for a suitable opportunity to present itself. A black Renault Mégane pulled up by the kerb and a young man with a goatee climbed out, leaving the driver's door open. From the other side a red-headed woman emerged and shut the passenger door behind her. There was no one in the back seat. The woman went off to get a trolley while the man opened up the boot and removed one suitcase and a laptop bag. Thirty seconds later the woman returned with her trolley.

Jack stepped forwards as the man hauled the suitcase on to the trolley; neither the man nor his partner noticed him walk behind them as they embraced. And because the woman had her eyes shut, she didn't see him slip behind the wheel.

Jack quietly shut the door and pulled out. He accelerated to 15 m.p.h.—fast enough that the car's owner wouldn't be able to catch him up; not so fast that he'd draw attention to himself. He kept his eyes on the rear-view mirror: the man only noticed what had happened once Jack had travelled the thirty-odd metres to the end of the drop-off area. He swung the car round to the right and only then did he take the phone out of his pocket, switch it on to speakerphone and prop it up on the dashboard before navigating towards the exit.

As he drove he heard voices. They were muffled and indistinct, but he could tell aggression when he heard it. The sound made his skin prickle and

415

he increased his speed without even thinking about it. He wanted to burn the road, but he couldn't risk being stopped; it was all he could do to keep his speed down. He went through Siobhan's directions in his head. Crossgar was thirty minutes away; twenty if he could floor it once he hit the A7.

He tried not to panic. To keep his head clear. His eyes on the road and his ears on the phone.

He had just left the airport perimeter when he heard the shot. It was almost as if the bullet had entered his own body.

And when he heard the scream, it felt as if he himself had just been ripped apart . . .

*       *       *

The first thing they did was force her to remove her clothes. 'I've always loved a striptease,' Kieran said. 'But couldn't you just do it with a bit more feeling, now?'

As she stood naked and trembling, he sidled up to her—close enough for her to smell the cigarettes on his breath and see the tiny little hairs sprouting on the bridge of his nose. 'You know,' he said in that reedy voice of his, 'I just can't decide what to do first. Fuck you, or kill you.'

Siobhan just closed her eyes. She wished it could be over. Now.

'Maybe I could do both,' he whispered. 'You know, fuck you first, *then* kill you. I'm a bit worried that I might not be able to get wood, but maybe if you'd just talk dirty to me for a while . . .' He walked round behind her and she felt the steel of his gun pressed against one of her buttocks. 'But then, like I told you first time we met, you're not

416

really my type.' He pressed the gun a bit harder, and she staggered forward involuntarily. There was the sound of laughter—Kieran's laughter—but when she opened her eyes, it was Cormac she saw, his gun still pointing directly at her, and there was no smile in *his* expression. He had the eyes of a snake.

'Tie her,' he said.

There were three posts in the middle of the barn, thick, solid structures that supported the rafters. Kieran approached a couple of the hay bales and, with a pocket knife, cut one of the plastic strips that bound them together. He pushed Siobhan up to one of the posts and started to tie her using the strip. The plastic cut sharply into her skin where it made contact around her neck, her breasts, her belly and her ankles. She did what she could not to make the pain show, but it was impossible and a whimper of discomfort escaped her throat. Once Kieran had tied the strip tightly behind the post, he moved round to her front, squeezed her cheeks between the fingers of his right hand, then cupped his left between her legs. She felt a finger, and struggled to get away, but of course she was going nowhere, and her attempts simply encouraged Kieran to grip harder—with both hands.

'Stand away, lad.' Cormac's voice was still deathly quiet.

Kieran gave her a nasty leer, then a final, rough grope; but he clearly knew to obey his uncle. He stepped back, then took his place a few metres to his uncle's right where he removed a pouch of baccy from his coat and expertly rolled and lit himself a cigarette. Cormac raised his sawn-off and aimed it casually at Siobhan. Her body started to tremble violently—a terrified, humiliated mess.

Silence in the barn. The two men stared balefully at her.

'*Please . . .*' she whispered.

A smile twitched on Cormac's face. 'Please what?'

'*I have a daughter who needs me. Please don't . . .*'

'Well, you see, lass—we have a lot to talk about, don't we now?'

Siobhan stared at him in horror.

'But I can't help thinking some conversations are best had just between the two of us.'

As he spoke, Cormac O'Callaghan turned ninety degrees to his right, so that the sawn-off was pointing at his nephew, who was just taking a drag on his roll-up. It took a moment for Kieran to work out what was happening; a moment for the unpleasant, gloating look on his face to switch first to an expression of confusion, and then to one of alarm as he staggered backwards, away from his uncle.

'Jesus, Cormac,' he whispered, his voice suddenly hoarse. 'I did what you asked, didn't I?'

'That you did, Kieran.' He didn't move the barrel of the gun away from his nephew.

'I'm family,' he rasped.

'Indeed you are, Kieran. And you know, that's what makes it all the worse.'

He fired.

The noise of the gun echoed round the barn, and caused a number of birds roosting in the rafters to flock up and squawk. Siobhan screamed, simply unable to help herself. Kieran himself didn't fall to the ground. Not at first. He bent over, clutching his stomach as though somebody had winded him

418

with a solid punch. He opened his mouth as if to speak, but no words came; just a sudden, vicious torrent of blood and foam.

A strangled noise.

Only then did he tumble, twitching, to the floor.

\*　　　\*　　　\*

The sound of Siobhan's scream rang in Jack's ears. He burned through the outskirts of Belfast on the A55, not caring now whether he was bringing attention to himself as he ran red lights and only narrowly avoided collisions using his skill behind the wheel. And in a horrible kind of way, the silence that followed was even worse than the scream itself. What the hell was going on at the other end of the phone? *What the hell was going on?* He lifted the handset and put it to his ear. Maybe, *maybe*, he could make something out. A voice. Male. But even without the sound of the car engine it would have been too muffled to hear.

Jack slung the phone back on the dashboard and increased his speed. He had Siobhan's directions firmly in his head and he drove with his foot to the floor.

\*　　　\*　　　\*

Kieran's body was twitching. Siobhan couldn't tell if he was dead yet, but if he wasn't, he soon would be.

Cormac approached her. If he felt any remorse at killing his nephew, it didn't show on his face. 'He was a wrong 'un,' the old man whispered. 'It was stupid of him to think I wouldn't find out.

419

Stupid of you, too.' He looked her up and down the length of her naked body, then pressed the sawn-off into the flesh of her belly. 'You're going to tell me everything you know about me,' he said. 'Otherwise the next few minutes are going to be very nasty for you.'

Siobhan closed her eyes. 'Go to hell,' she hissed.

'Yes,' Cormac replied, with not even a hint of irony, 'I imagine I probably will. Who knows, maybe I'll see you there. We can chat about the old times round the fire. But you know what, lass? When you know you're going to hell, it's very liberating. Means you don't have to worry so much about what you do in *this* life.'

He gave her a bland smile, then lay his gun on the ground and walked to the side of the barn where he had stashed an old leather sports bag. Cormac fished around inside the bag, then returned with a battered metal dog bowl and a one-litre plastic bottle containing a clear liquid. He poured the liquid into the bowl. 'My dog died ten years ago,' he said as the liquid glugged out of the bottle. 'I couldn't bring myself to throw the bowl away. I'm a sentimental old thing . . .' He placed the full bowl at Siobhan's feet and pulled a lighter from his pocket.

'*Don't*,' she whispered. '*Please. I don't care about you . . . I don't care about the drugs . . .*'

But O'Callaghan wasn't listening. He made a flame, then touched the dog bowl.

The fuel, whatever it was, didn't erupt. It ignited gently—a blue and orange flame that grew no higher than six inches. But that was high enough. It started to singe the skin on the side of Siobhan's naked left leg. She gasped and gritted her teeth.

'*Put it out,*' she begged, just as the acrid stench of her own burning flesh reached her nose.

O'Callaghan just looked on without expression.

'Please . . .'

The skin was fizzing and blistering. She could hear it.

'*Please . . .*'

'I don't think so, lass—' O'Callaghan started to say, but he didn't finish his sentence. Siobhan had started screaming. The voice didn't even sound like hers. More like that of an animal. And once it started, a little part of her mind wondered if it would ever stop.

\*        \*        \*

The second scream Jack heard was worse than the first. A million times worse. He knew what pain sounded like, and that was it. It continued for more than a minute.

He was on the A7 now, only five miles from Crossgar, tipping 100 with his heart in his throat. He told himself that the scream meant that at least she hadn't been killed outright.

Yet.

That wasn't much consolation.

It was all he could do to stop himself from shouting out too, in panic and frustration. In fear at the thought of what was happening to Siobhan.

He kept his foot on the accelerator, and his gaze on the road.

\*        \*        \*

Siobhan had never known agony like it. Vaguely,

she was aware that O'Callaghan had thrown his heavy overcoat over the flames to extinguish them; that she'd stopped screaming, and that noise had been replaced by short, desperate gasps of hyperventilating pain.

'What do you have on me?' O'Callaghan demanded. He seemed quite unmoved by her agony.

Siobhan clenched her teeth. She wished she was stronger, that she could withstand this. But she knew she couldn't. She knew she didn't have any option other than to talk.

'Khan,' she breathed. 'I know about Khan. I followed him.' As she spoke, she was looking at O'Callaghan, and she saw an expression of surprise pass over his lined face. 'He's got my daughter. He's a terrorist.' Even through her pain, she knew it sounded feeble.

'It's my experience,' O'Callaghan hissed, 'that one man's terrorist is another man's—'

'You don't know what you're talking about,' Siobhan interrupted. 'He's got a chemical weapon, a dirty bomb, enough to kill thousands. I don't know what his target is. I don't even know which country, but . . .'

She couldn't speak any more. It was just too much. The nausea was almost as bad as the pain in her leg and she thought she was going to vomit. O'Callaghan, though, looked almost thoughtful, as though this new piece of intelligence had explained something to him.

He narrowed his eyes. Contemplation. The sound of Siobhan's renewed gasping filled the air.

Cormac O'Callaghan turned back to her. His eyes, suddenly, were fierce. Fiery. He aimed his shotgun at Siobhan's pelvis and inclined his head slightly like a man curious to observe the effects of what he was about to do.

'Where is Khan now?'

'I don't know.'

It wasn't the answer he wanted to hear. Or maybe it was.

Without another second's hesitation he put a flame to the dog bowl again.

\*     \*     \*

When the screams returned, they pierced Jack's core.

The hedgerow whizzed past him in a blur. He passed a car coming in the other direction that was forced to swerve into a ditch. Jack didn't care. Horrific images had filled his head. He pushed them away. There was no space for them. He had to concentrate on what was important. Getting there quickly.

Getting there in time . . .

\*     \*     \*

Cormac O'Callaghan deadened the flames again. He had long grown immune to the sight and sound of people suffering. He knew of his reputation, of course—that he enjoyed inflicting pain—and was perfectly happy to foster it. But the truth was he felt nothing. As a younger man he had done terrible things to people, more to see if he could stir up some sort of feeling in himself than anything else. It never did.

So it was that the sight of this naked, burned,

brutalised cop failed to move him; her screams, growing increasingly hoarse by the minute, barely attracted his attention; the stink of her burning skin and her blood failed to nauseate him. It would have been the same even if his mind hadn't been on other things.

Like Khan.

For months now, he'd been wondering why the man had been supplying him with high-quality heroin at such a low rate. Truth was, Habib Khan could have named his price and O'Callaghan would most likely have paid it. There had to be an ulterior motive, and Cormac wasn't so stupid that he didn't realise Khan's 'additional' packages, smuggled in on the southern Irish coast, over the border into Northern Ireland then across to the mainland by sea, were something to do with it. But what the pig had just told him made the pennies drop . . .

He turned back to look at her. She was a mess, no two ways about it. Strapped to that post, with flames licking up her legs and hair straggling over her agonised face, she reminded him of figures he had seen as a child, etched on the stained-glass windows of the churches his mother had dragged him to on Sundays. The young Cormac had never known who those figures represented, and as an adult he'd never been inclined to find out.

Khan was a clever guy. Everyone thought he was a goody-fucking-two-shoes, and Cormac had always assumed that this was just a front for his drug business. If what the cop was saying was right, though, he had bigger interests.

Bigger plans.

It didn't matter to Cormac O'Callaghan what

they were. His only concern was that the drugs kept coming. And if this pig was on Khan's case, if she had something on him . . . well then, she was a threat to Cormac's business. To his livelihood.

And that wasn't something he could allow to continue.

She was murmuring something. At first he tried to work out what it was. Perhaps it was of interest. He thought he caught a single word.

'Lily', maybe.

He smiled. The woman had said Khan had her daughter and a face rose in his mind: pale, thin, with greasy mousy hair and black rings round her eyes. Khan had wanted a girl when they first met, and O'Callaghan of all people was in a position to supply him with one of the helpless junkies that littered the streets of Belfast. Her name had been Lily.

He walked up to the whimpering woman and put his lips to her ears. 'She's all fucked up,' he whispered. 'And I mean that literally.'

The woman tried to say something, but the words didn't come. She was clearly on the way out.

There was no point prolonging it. She needed to be dead. He retrieved his gun from the floor, then placed it against her head. He looked away, not because he was disgusted, but to avoid the spatter.

And then he fired.

At the sound of the gunshot, the pigeons in the rafters flocked up in a cloud yet again.

# 24

Jack saw Siobhan's car thirty metres up ahead; and beyond it, the barn. He stopped the car and approached by foot, running quickly but quietly, driven by panic, past an old tractor and up to the big main barn, where he stopped by the half-open door, mastered his heavy breathing, and peered inside.

He would never, he knew, be able to forget the scene that awaited him.

There was a body on the floor away to his right. Impossible to tell who it was, but he was male and still had a half-smoked cigarette in his hand. Along one side of the barn, against some hay bales and with his back to him, was another man, stooping slightly as he put something into a small bag. But it was neither of these two people that commanded Jack's attention. His eyes were glued to the horror in the centre of the barn.

Siobhan was tied naked to a post. At least, he thought it was Siobhan. Half her head was blown away, and her legs were charred and blistered. Her skin was spattered with blood and although her body was still upright, it had the appalling limpness of the newly dead.

Jack felt his strength momentarily desert him. The world seemed to spin, and as he pressed his back up against the outside wall of the barn he struggled to keep his balance. He drew a deep breath, steadying himself, absorbing the shock like a boxer taking a punch.

And then he felt all his emotions turn to anger.

More than anger. A kind of blind, all-consuming rage that filled every cell of his body. All self-control left him. He turned into the doorway and burst into the barn.

By now the stooped figure had turned. He was a thin-looking man with a deeply lined face, a full head of hair, unruly eyebrows and a scar leading from the side of his mouth across one cheek. Jack knew the face. It was imprinted on his mind from his time in the Province, the result of having studied any number of photographs of the fucker back in the days of the Provisional IRA. He looked older now, of course, but there was no doubt in Jack's mind that this was Cormac O'Callaghan himself.

When O'Callaghan saw Jack, his eyes widened, and he tried to open the bag he was carrying. But he didn't have nearly enough time as the Regiment man bore down on him like a tank, covering the ten metres between them in a second. Jack grabbed him by the neck, then threw him to the ground with a single, brutal thrust.

For an old guy, O'Callaghan scrambled to his feet remarkably quickly, and rather than try to get away from Jack, he continued to fumble with the zip of his bag. Jack went for it, launching himself at his enemy again, swiping the bag from his hands and then cracking it against the side of the man's skull. The hard metal of the concealed sawn-off knocked O'Callaghan to the ground for a second time, creating a red welt on the side of his face. He didn't move. Unconscious. How long for, it was impossible to tell.

Jack opened the bag. Inside he found the shotgun, the cross-bolt safety in front of its trigger

427

switched on. He knocked it off, but then looked around him. Two bodies. Two shots. If there were cartridges in the weapon, they'd both been spent. He turned it round, held on to the barrel and started pummelling O'Callaghan's unconscious body with the butt. He was going to kill the bastard right now.

But something stopped him.

Jack looked over his shoulder, and the sight of Siobhan's trussed-up corpse was once more like a corkscrew in his stomach. Jesus, he'd seen enough deaths in his time, but this was different.

He turned back to O'Callaghan, ready to finish him off.

But he stopped again. It was almost as if there was a presence in the room. Siobhan, holding him back. What would she tell him to do? Avenge her? No. She'd want to question him. Find out what he knew. *Do it, Jack.* He could almost hear her voice in his head. *Work it properly. Find Lily. For me.*

He strode up to O'Callaghan and booted him hard in the stomach to keep him out of action a while longer. He walked up to Siobhan and quickly untied her, carefully laying her body on the ground. Only then did he return to O'Callaghan, dragging him to another of the posts, forcing him up on to two feet and then tying him up in just the same way that Siobhan had been bound. O'Callaghan was conscious now and he tried to struggle—but he was no match for Jack's strength, or his fury, or his determination.

No match at all.

When he was bound and immobile, Jack stood with his face only inches away from O'Callaghan.

'Here's the problem, O'Callaghan,' he growled.

'I don't think you're nearly scared enough of me yet, so we're going to do something to make that change.'

Cormac didn't reply, but the wildness behind his eyes was eloquent enough.

Jack looked around, then jogged to the far end of the barn. There was an old tool here, some kind of scythe, rusty, with a long wooden handle. He leaned it up against the wall, then brought his foot down against it until the handle snapped. Smaller. More manageable. He carried it back to where his victim was waiting.

O'Callaghan's eyes darted between Jack's face and the rusty blade.

'Which side?' Jack mused. 'The left?' He waved the blade just in front of O'Callaghan's shoulder. 'Or the right?' He moved it to the other side of his body. 'Left or right?' he murmured to himself. 'Left or right?'

A pause. And then, suddenly . . .

'I'd say, *left*.'

Jack's arm moved quickly and with great force. He skewered the old blade into the area between O'Callaghan's left shoulder and his torso. O'Callaghan shrieked with agony, even more so when Jack twisted the blade like he was rotating a spit. There wasn't much blood, but there would be if he removed the blade, and Jack didn't want the bastard bleeding to death. Not yet.

'Who killed her?' he demanded. 'You or him?' He indicated the dead male body on the floor.

'*He did*,' O'Callaghan hissed. '*He was going to do me too, so I took him out.*'

Jack gave him a sad kind of look. 'Seems you're still not scared enough,' he said. 'You're lying to me.'

'*I'm not lying . . . I'm not . . .*'

'If he was going to take you out, he'd have done you first. I mean, I know he's a Mick and everything, but he can't be *that* stupid.'

Cormac just looked at him in terror.

Jack turned his back and scanned the barn, doing what he could to stop his gaze falling on Siobhan's body. There were three or four old tyres over in the corner. He ran to them, lifted one up and carried it to where O'Callaghan was tied. He threw it at his feet, then lifted the man's legs and inserted them into the hole of the tyre.

There was something else that had caught his eye, too. A big, industrial-grade strimmer, petrol-driven. He dragged that over to the post.

'Jesus, man,' O'Callaghan breathed, looking at the machinery with wild eyes. Jack ignored him. When he was close enough, he opened up the strimmer's petrol tank. It was half full. Jack upturned it, sloshing two-stroke and oil all over the tyre, the ground inside it and the bottom of O'Callaghan's trousers.

'Now then,' he said, as though to himself. 'What do I need next?' And then, as if it had suddenly come to him: 'Of course!' He went over to the male body and removed the half-smoked cigarette from his fingers, which he waved in O'Callaghan's direction. 'Where there's smoke,' he announced, before rummaging through the corpse's pockets and pulling out a half-full box of Swan Vestas, 'there's fire.'

He returned to O'Callaghan, lit a match and waved it around.

'Here's what's going to happen,' he said. 'You're

430

going to tell me everything you know about Habib Khan.'

Through his fear and wincing pain, O'Callaghan just managed to nod.

'The bitch knew more about him than I did.'

Jack's eyes narrowed. 'You call her that again,' he said, 'and it'll be the last thing you say.'

O'Callaghan looked like he believed him.

'Khan's been using me,' he breathed. 'He knows I've got importation lines set up. For the drugs. I've greased the right palms, you know. I can get anything anywhere without the authorities knowing about it. He supplies me with cheap heroin.' His face screwed up as a new wave of pain spread from the blade. 'To start with, I thought that was it, but a few days ago he sent something else into the country. Boxes. I don't know what they are. Nothing to do with me. I just see that they get shipped where he wants them.'

'And where *does* he want them?'

O'Callaghan hesitated, so Jack lit another match.

'The mainland,' he said quickly. 'A boat to Stranraer. The boxes get picked up there. I don't know who by . . .'

'You'll have to do better than that, you piece of shit.'

*'I don't know who by! I swear to God, man—I don't know who by!'*

'When was the last package. *When was it?*'

O'Callaghan's eyes were rolling. 'Today,' he whispered. 'It's too late. It's already gone to the mainland.' And then, a faint grin. 'It's too goddamn late,' he said.

Jack didn't know what it was that tipped him over the edge. Siobhan's death? Maybe.

Frustration? Perhaps it was just the look on O'Callaghan's face which, despite everything, was arrogant.

He did it without thinking—lit a third match and threw it down at the fuel-soaked tyre.

The fuel ignited slowly—a low, blue flame that oozed around the area. O'Callaghan's eyes stopped rolling when he realised what Jack had done. He opened his mouth just as the bottom of his trousers started to curl and smoke. But no words came out.

Jack watched the rubber start to singe and blister. Tendrils of thick, black smoke started to billow from it, filling the air with a disgustingly acrid smell that caught in the back of the throat. O'Callaghan started to squeal as the flesh on his leg burned, but the squeals turned to a strangled, coughing noise as the smoke entered his respiratory system. 'Please,' he barked. 'I've got money . . . I'll give you anything . . .'

The tyre was burning hard now, the flames licking up O'Callaghan's body.

'She asked about the girl . . .' the Irishman shouted. '*I know where she is . . .*'

That got Jack's attention. 'Then you'd better start talking,' he said over the crackling of the flames.

'*Let me out first . . .*'

Jack shook his head and the terror in O'Callaghan's eyes doubled. The bastard was lying. It was obvious. If he truly knew where Lily was, he'd be screaming it to the fucking rafters.

Strangled noises from O'Callaghan's throat echoed round the barn but Jack was deaf to them. He just stared, unable to stop thinking of Red, all the way back in Helmand, and the manner of *his* death. O'Callaghan didn't know Jack's friend. He'd never heard of him. But he was part of Khan's conspiracy, and he was just as responsible for that death as anyone else.

But that, of course, wasn't the only reason why Jack wanted him dead.

He turned and, very slowly, walked over to Siobhan's body.

He knelt beside her and put one hand on the side of her face that hadn't been shot away. It was as cold as his heart.

All of a sudden, nothing seemed real.

Jack knew it was stupid, but he felt he wanted to say something to her. But no words came. More desperate squeals from behind him, and the crackle of flames. Jack barely heard them. All his attention was on Siobhan.

'*I'm going to stop this happening,*' he heard himself whisper, his voice choked. '*I promise you I'm going to stop this happening. And Lily . . .*'

He tried to think of a promise he could make about their daughter, but he couldn't.

The flames roared behind him, and so did O'Callaghan. Like an animal in pain. Which he was. Jack didn't move his hand from Siobhan's bloodied cheek.

He stayed like that for a full minute. Then he moved over to where her clothes were piled in a heap. In her khaki jacket was a dark purple wallet. He looked inside. Some money. A few credit cards. And a photograph. He recognised it. It was exactly the same picture he carried around in his own wallet, taken all those years ago on the beach in Ballycastle. Siobhan's hair was blowing in the wind. So was Lily's. They looked happy. Jack had no idea that Siobhan had carried this photograph too. No idea that day was imprinted on her memory as firmly as it was on his.

He stared at the photograph, then down at Siobhan's brutalised corpse. Then he cast a final glance over at O'Callaghan. The man was enshrouded in flames now, his charred body barely visible as the fire spread up the length of the wooden post, licking towards the rafters. He could see the skin on his face blistering and starting to peel. He wanted to feel good that he'd avenged Siobhan, but he didn't.

The fire was going to spread—it was out of control and the birds in the rafters were starting to squawk in panic. It wouldn't take long for someone to see the smoke and alert the emergency services, and this wasn't the sort of scene he'd be able to explain to a few Northern Ireland Old Bill. And so, with one final, anguished look at the mother of his child, he ran from the barn, slipping out of the main entrance and heading back to his stolen vehicle. Three deaths and an arson. They'd be erecting a perimeter around the place as soon as they could, and Jack needed to be beyond it. If he could get the car back to the airport, he hoped people would put its theft down to a couple of joyriding kids and not investigate too much further.

He turned the car round and drove. At no point did he look back in the mirror, so he never saw the roof of the barn catch alight and then fall in, creating an enormous funeral pyre.

# 7 JULY

## 25

04.30 hrs.

The sun had yet to rise, but Special Agent Brad Joseph was already up. He stood at the window of his room in the Four Seasons Hotel, looking down on to the night lights of London. From here he could see the bridges over the river and the dome of St Paul's Cathedral in the distance. Even he had to admit it was an impressive sight. Busy, yet somehow peaceful.

He was glad of this moment of quiet. Glad to have these few minutes to get his head in order. Presidential visits like today's were finely tuned affairs. A whole raft of standard operating procedures were in place, designed to ensure the President's safety. Every single member of his security team was as familiar with these SOPs as with their own names, but Brad knew that sometimes familiarity could be dangerous. It could lull you into a false sense of security. His job was to make sure that didn't happen. He knew that there were plenty of Secret Service operatives who considered him a jobsworth, but it made no difference to him. Rather that, he thought to himself, than give free rein to some wannabe Lee Harvey Oswald.

He took himself through the details of the President's movements, looking for any weak links he might have missed. There was none. Not now that they had the Beast. They could move him round London in absolute safety, no matter what happened. That, at least, was a relief.

He turned from the window, took his firearm from the bedside table and placed it in its holster. He looked at the clock. 04.58 hrs. Today would be a long day. It would be a relief when the President arrived safely at the Houses of Parliament a little after 18.00 hrs. It would be even more of a relief when today was safely consigned to history.

Brad collected his cellphone and key card, then left the room. It was time, he decided, to go to work.

*     *     *

06.00 hrs. Hereford.

Jack stood at the end of his street in the dim lamplight.

The previous twelve hours had passed in a blur. It had taken him half an hour to get back to the airport, where he kept his profile low and his mind alert. But there was a constant mental distraction.

Siobhan. Dead.

Every time he thought of it, it was like a knife in his guts.

He relived O'Callaghan's death, but it didn't help. Siobhan would be mad at him. He could hear her now. *He was our lead, Jack. Our only lead. And you—*

He pushed the imaginary reprimand from his mind. He'd fucked up. He knew that. But there was no point beating himself up about it. Khan's dirty bomb was in England. He knew he had to do something about it.

But what? The question had burned in his brain on the night flight back to Birmingham. Go to the authorities, tell them everything? No way. He knew how they worked. The police would take Siobhan's killing as sectarian, and they'd be more interested in quizzing Jack about the dead bodies that were sticking to him than listening to his theories about terrorist attacks. And the date wasn't lost on him either. One day until the anniversary of 7/7—party time for every nutcase and bogus caller in the country. The security services would be overwhelmed by people seeing shadows. If anyone was going to take Jack seriously, he needed evidence. But all the evidence that crossed his path had an unfortunate habit of ending up dead.

By the time he landed, though, he'd come to a decision.

Khan knew who he was, and he knew Jack was on to him. That put Jack himself in a position of danger. But maybe it also gave him an advantage. If Habib Khan had a hit list, Jack was on the top of it. And although, being Regiment, it wasn't easy to track him down, it wasn't impossible. Not if you had resources. And so, Jack had one last throw of the dice. One last avenue to follow. If Khan had a contract on him, he needed to put himself in harm's way. Wait for the bullet to come to him. Khan wouldn't use some random shooter, someone untrustworthy—he was too clever for that. Whoever he sent would be part of his operation. And that would make them—as Siobhan would have it—a lead.

Which was why he found himself back home. In Hereford. Jack knew only too well that the easiest place to hit someone was at home when they were feeling secure and comfortable. And from what he'd learned about the man, Habib Khan would know that too.

There weren't many people about at this time. An old guy walking his dog. The postman. Jack didn't trust either of them, and he waited for both to conclude their business in his street before walking down the road. As he approached the house, he paid diligent attention to the curtains in the windows of the houses opposite. Jack was never around enough to know his neighbours or anything about them, but he saw their curtains were all closed apart from two. These windows opened out on to rooms that had their lights on. No sniper worth their salt would be hiding out where they were lit up, so Jack felt reasonably safe hurrying up to his front door and letting himself in.

It was cold in his flat, and gloomy. Jack didn't turn the lights on, though. That would be like a beacon to anybody awaiting his arrival, and he didn't want to shine a beacon until he was ready to do so. He moved from room to room, checking for anything suspicious. There was nothing. At least, nothing that he could see. The flat was empty.

There were two entrances, front and back. The front door opened out on to the street, the back on to a small, overgrown garden whose rear wall was shared with the garden of an opposing house. If Jack was trying to gain entry, that was the way he'd come. His garden was uncared for, and easy to hide in. You could gain access to it, then break in the back door without raising the suspicion of anyone in the street. But as far as he could tell, there was no sign of anyone.

The back door led directly into Jack's bedroom, where his Bergan was still lying on his bed.

Underneath the Ikea bedside table he had stashed a handgun. He took it now, then switched on the bedside light. He saw the answering machine flashing. Four messages. He turned down the volume and listened to them. The first two were from Bill Parker, the adjutant's clerk, politely asking where he was. The third was from the adjutant, who was less polite. 'I don't know where the hell you are, Harker, but—' Jack pressed a button and moved on to the next message. It was blank. Just a click as someone hung up the phone. It had been left at 22.38 the previous evening. Jack didn't have much doubt that it was someone checking to see if he was in . . .

He returned to the corridor that led from the bedroom up to the front door. Here he waited. Weapon primed. When his man came, he'd come hard and fast. It was the only way in confined quarters like this. Jack pushed all thoughts of yesterday's events from his mind. Time to grieve later. For now, he needed to keep his focus because if—when—his shooter came, Jack had to be ready for him.

*　　　*　　　*

12.38 hrs.

The doorbell rang.

Jack jumped. It seemed unnaturally loud in the silence of the flat, and his first instinct was to ignore it. But something changed his mind. He'd already seen the postman that morning, and nobody else would be ringing on his door at this time of day. He approached the front door. It was solid wood, with a small peephole at eye-level.

441

Keeping his gun ready, Jack looked out.

There was a kid on the doorstep. Probably a teenager, but only just. Baggy jeans. IPod earphones hanging over the front of his T-shirt. Gum in his mouth. Jack opened the door a little, keeping his weapon concealed, and gave him an enquiring glance.

'Wash your car, mate?' the kid asked in a West Country accent. 'Fiver.'

Jack shook his head. 'Try next door,' he said.

The kid shrugged. 'Yeah. All right.' He stepped backwards and didn't take his eyes off Jack until he'd shut the door again. Jack looked through the peephole just in time to see the lad running back down the street and out of his vision.

One thing was for sure: the kid hadn't tried the neighbours.

\*     \*     \*

Aamir Hussein wished he could return to London. He missed the mosque, and these Hereford streets were unfamiliar to him. He wasn't all that keen on the clothes he was wearing to make himself blend in—white trainers, khaki combats and a hooded top. But he had his instructions and he was glad, at least, to put some of his training into action. He sat on the bench of an empty bus shelter and watched as the kid with the baggy trousers ran up to him.

'He's there,' the kid said breathlessly. 'He answered the door. He's in.'

Aamir felt a little surge of relief. He removed a twenty-pound note from his pocket and handed it to the kid.

'*Twenty*?' the boy protested.

Aamir shrugged and handed over another note. The kid had earned it, after all, knocking on his target's door every few hours for the whole of the previous day and again just now, then running back to report on his progress.

'You can go now,' Aamir said. 'I don't need you any more.'

The kid slunk off.

Avoiding the gaze of the other pedestrians— mums with pushchairs—Aamir started to walk towards his target's house. Jack Harker, his name was. Aamir knew nothing else about him. It didn't matter. When you had a gun in your hand, one man was very like another. And the gun Aamir carried was powerful enough for him to deal with any problems he might encounter: a .500 Smith & Wesson Magnum revolver. Its barrel was too long to keep in his belt, so he had it strapped across the front of his body in a holster specifically designed for the task. And he knew that the .50-calibre rounds that were loaded inside would put a hole in almost anything he cared to point it at.

He surveyed the main entrance from a distance. A solid-wood door and a small, concrete front yard with a low brick wall and no gate. He could be through that door and into the flat in no time at all; and once inside, with the element of surprise, his target wouldn't stand a chance.

Aamir smiled to himself. What he was about to do would be an act of jihad. But that didn't mean he couldn't enjoy it. He put his hand into his jacket, curled his fingers round the handle of his Magnum, then loosened it in his holster.

And then he strode across the road to Jack

Harker's front door.

He was fully prepared to shoot it in. By the time the shots were reported he'd be long gone, after all. When he was about a metre away from the door, however, he stopped. And blinked. It was ever so slightly ajar.

Aamir shook his head. The guy hadn't closed it properly. The way some people went about their daily lives, he thought to himself, it was almost as if they *wanted* to get killed.

He pulled the gun from its holster and used it to poke the door open. The hallway light was on. Aamir stepped inside. Then he stood and listened.

A stillness. If there was anybody moving about in this flat, they were as stealthy as a cat.

Aamir closed the door gently behind him, then stepped further down the hallway. He stopped again. Listened.

It took a moment for him to identify the sound he could hear: a constant hissing that came from a room off the hallway, ahead and to the left, whose door was half open. When he realised what it was, though, he blinked again.

A shower.

Harker was actually taking a shower.

Aamir's grin became broader. This would be like shooting fish in a barrel. He raised the Magnum slightly and stepped towards the door. It took only a gentle poke for the door to swing fully open and for Aamir to see what was in the room: a bath, a toilet, a sink. And in the corner, a rectangular shower unit, fully closed, with thick frosted glass; and the unmistakable outline of a person inside.

He raised his gun a little higher. One shot would probably do it, but two in quick succession would

444

be safer: one to shatter the glass, the second to make sure the target was dead.

Steam billowed from the top of the shower.

He fired. Once. Twice.

It all happened so quickly. The moment the first round made contact with the shower screen, it shattered and crashed to the floor. What it revealed, however, was not a person, but a beige raincoat suspended from the shower rose. Aamir didn't realise what he was looking at until the second round had thumped harmlessly into the raincoat and shattered the white tiles behind it; but by that time it was too late. Someone behind him had wrapped a thin cord round his neck and was already pulling it hard.

His arms flailed as he tried to raise his gun hand up and shoot randomly behind him, but his assailant quickly grabbed his wrist and knocked it against the door frame so sharply that he thought he felt his wrist breaking. The gun fell to the ground and he tried to cry out, but the cord round his neck meant no sound came other than a strangled gasp.

He felt faint. The room began to spin. As his legs gave way beneath him, he felt himself being lowered to the ground, but by the time his head touched the floor he had already passed out.

When Aamir woke up, he had no way of telling how long he'd been out. Not very, he suspected. The first thing he noticed was the burning sensation around his throat; he groaned, and as he did so, he realised that a gag had been tied round his mouth. He opened his eyes to find himself lying down. It took a moment to work out that he was in the bath, fully clad, with his hands tied behind him and his ankles bound. The blinds were closed and the radio was on. A memory flashed across his eyes: it had occurred only a few days previously, when he had been beating Salim Jamali's mother. Aamir had turned on the TV then, to stop the neighbours hearing her screams. Now, he realised, someone else was taking similar precautions.

That someone was standing by the bath looking down at him. The sight of him made Aamir's blood freeze. His face was expressionless. Aamir didn't need to guess who it was, of course, and he stared at Jack Harker, the man he'd been sent to kill.

Harker didn't move. Not for a minute or two. *The World at One* wittered on in the background. Aamir began to wonder if he was seeing things. If the motionless figure hulking above him was just a hallucination. It was only when Harker eventually bent slightly towards him that he noticed what he was carrying.

An ordinary kitchen tea towel.

Harker bent down further and ripped the gag from his mouth. Aamir gasped just as his captor laid the tea towel over his face. 'What are you doing?' he whispered, but his voice was drowned out by the sudden sound of the shower. He felt his combats moisten. The water was cold at first, but it soon became stingingly hot and Harker didn't keep it aimed at his trousers. He moved it up to his face.

It took only a second or two for the tea towel to become saturated. Aamir tried to breathe, but his mouth didn't suck in any air—just the damp material. After only a few seconds his lungs started to burn through lack of oxygen. He tried to move his head to one side in order to allow a little air to enter the corner of his mouth, but that didn't work.

He was panicking now, and he tried to sit up. All he got was a boot in the chest. The sensation of drowning continued. He desperately tried to breathe in. He started to become dizzy . . . he thought he was dying . . .

Suddenly, Harker ripped the tea towel from his face and directed the shower jet to the bottom of the bath. Aamir gasped in a noisy lungful of breath, and then another. He felt almost grateful to his assailant for giving him the opportunity to breathe.

'Who sent you?' They were the first words Harker had spoken to him. His voice was a low growl, and it was full of intention.

'I don't know,' he whispered.

Which wasn't the answer Harker wanted to hear. He draped the tea towel over Aamir's face again, and repeated the process.

It was worse this time. Aamir's lungs were already feeling bruised by the first session. Now they screamed for oxygen, but this second bout lasted longer than the first. How long, he couldn't have said. It seemed like an age of agony.

When Harker finally removed the tea towel, Aamir was almost unconscious. He choked and gasped for breath while Harker stood over him, silent. Only when his breathing achieved some semblance of normality did Harker finally speak.

'If you make me do it again, the cloth's not coming off. Don't make the mistake of not believing me.'

Aamir shook his head violently.

'Who sent you?'

He started to shake. 'I swear, I do not know.'

Harker shrugged, then reached for the shower hose. Immediately, Aamir felt a warm sensation spread through his already wet trousers as he lost control of his bladder, and he heard himself squealing. '*I swear it . . . I do not know his name. He calls me with instructions. I call him when they are carried out. I swear on the life of the Prophet . . . I am telling you the truth . . .*'

He stared, wild-eyed, at Harker, who surveyed him with a bland look on his face.

'If you'd killed me, what would you have done?'

'Called a number. Told him you were dead. Then gone back to London.'

'The person who gave you these instructions, what are his plans?'

Aamir shook his head again. 'I don't know. *I swear I don't know.* I was to kill you, and if there was someone with you called Caroline Stenton, or another woman, I was to kill her too . . .'

Silence. Harker looked like he was concentrating. Working things out in his mind.

The radio babbled in the background. A woman's voice, cheerful, even chirpy. Aamir found himself focusing on it—a way of distracting himself from the monster in front of him.

'*Preparations are underway for the President of the United States' visit this evening to a dinner at the Houses of Parliament, where he is expected to give a speech. This controversial announcement has angered the relatives of some 7/7 victims, who believe that the President's arrival has directed attention away from the memory of the fallen. But in a statement, Downing Street has denied it is ignoring the concerns of the victims' families, saying, "The*

448

*Prime Minister believes that standing alongside our allies on this day shows to those who would attack our people that we have strength in unity . . .'"*

Jack Harker was staring at the radio. Then he bent down again. Quickly. Aamir jumped, his nerves shredded. To his surprise, however—and, he supposed, his relief—Harker pulled him out of the bath.

'Untie me,' Aamir begged. 'It hurts.'

'Not as much as it will if you don't shut the fuck up.' Harker picked up a mobile phone from the top of the toilet cistern. 'Yours?' he demanded.

Aamir nodded. Harker had obviously removed it while he was unconscious. Now he grabbed him by the scruff of his neck and dragged him out of the bathroom, into the hallway and out the front door.

There were children playing on the pavement, kicking a ball around. As soon as they saw the two men erupt from the flat, they ran off. Harker didn't appear remotely concerned that they'd seen him dragging a soaked, bound man out of his flat. He just bundled Aamir, face downwards, into the back seat of his car, then took his place behind the wheel and flicked on the central locking.

'Where are we going?' Aamir demanded. 'Where are you taking me?'

Harker didn't answer him. He just started the engine and drove.

# 26

13.42 hrs.

Jack burned through the streets of Hereford. He knew the route he was taking—he could have driven it blindfolded. He kept one eye on the rear-view mirror just in case the fucker in the back tried anything on.

SAS HQ never changed. The vast former RAF training centre was as drab and utilitarian as ever. If you didn't know what it was, you'd walk right on past, in the hope of finding somewhere more interesting. Jack sped round the perimeter road; when he reached the main entrance, he came to a sudden halt and waved his military ID at the MoD policeman at the gate. The guy recognised him: he opened the barrier and let him through.

There were designated parking places at the base. Jack didn't bother with them. He just stopped his car in the middle of the tarmac courtyard in front of the main building, then loosened the knots around his hostage's ankles before dragging him out of the back. The little shit could *try* to run, he figured, but one shout from Jack and he wouldn't get very far. Not here.

'That way,' Jack said, pointing up at the main building, and he pushed the hit man towards it.

Inside the building, a group of lads Jack knew saw him and gave a low ironic cheer—news of his little disagreement with the goon back in the Stan had obviously travelled. Jack ignored them. He dragged his man through a network of corridors until he came to a door. He didn't knock. He just

450

burst straight in.

There were three men in the little office. Jack recognised only one of them: Elliott Carver, CO of 22 SAS. He was a big man, with steely-grey hair and a square jaw. Carver had seen it all in his time with the Regiment, and Jack liked him. When the CO glanced up and saw him, however, he didn't exactly look full of the joys.

'Jack, what the hell . . .' He looked from the soldier to the hostage, then back again.

'We need to talk,' Jack said. He looked at the two men who were sitting on the other side of Carver's desk. They wore suits and didn't have the bearing of military men. Spooks, Jack assumed, but he wasn't going to spill his load in front of them. 'Alone, boss. It's important.'

Carver's face was a thunderstorm. 'I'm busy, Jack.'

Jack turned his back on him, walked up to one of the suits, hauled him to his feet and then threw him out of the door. He looked at the second man. 'You,' he growled. 'Out.'

The guy scurried away. Jack shut the door after him then pushed his hostage down on to one of the newly vacated seats.

'Christ's sake, Jack. You're ten feet deep in the shit and a cunt hair away from being fired. What the hell are you playing at?'

Jack ignored the CO and turned his attention to the hostage. 'Tell him what your orders were,' he said.

The hostage looked fearfully at Jack. 'To kill you,' he replied. His voice cracked.

'Jack, what's going on?'

'Get a couple of the guys to watch him. Then I'll

451

tell you.'

The CO stared at him, like he was staring at a madman.

'Elliott,' Jack snapped. 'How long have I been with the Regiment?'

'Twenty years . . . more . . . I don't know.'

'Then give me ten minutes of your time. If you still think I'm a lunatic, you can have me in the fucking nick. I won't put up a fight.'

The CO narrowed his eyes and nodded slowly. 'All right,' he said, the reluctance clear in his voice. He picked up a phone on his desk and dialled a single number. 'I just hope you don't make me fucking regret this.'

Jack hoped that, too.

Carver gave a short instruction into the phone. Moments later there was a knock on the door and two Regiment guys appeared. Jack didn't recognise one of them, but the other was Fly Forsyth, one of Jack's unit from the Stan who, along with his cousin Dunc, had chaperoned him back to the UK. He gave Jack a mystified look.

'Look after our friend,' the CO instructed. They led the hit man out of the room without any kind of ceremony, then closed the door behind them.

'Ten minutes, Jack. Make it good.'

Jack took a deep breath. And then he started to speak. He took it slowly. Carefully. From the beginning. He told Carver about Siobhan, her lead on O'Callaghan and the girl that had ended up in hospital. He explained about Khan, how Siobhan had followed him to Mogadishu, and why; that he'd followed her and what they'd discovered about their daughter, and about the dirty bomb. He forced himself to keep his voice steady as he explained to his boss about the call he'd received from Siobhan, what he'd heard and what he'd found in that barn outside Belfast. And while he didn't go into detail about the manner of O'Callaghan's death, he didn't shy away from explaining that the piece of shit had gone the way of the dodo.

Carver listened intently, his face expressionless. He didn't say a word as Jack was speaking, and even when Jack had finished he remained silent for a good minute or two, though now there was a frown of concentration on his forehead.

'You should have come to me with this earlier,' he said finally.

'I couldn't, boss. Think about it. Until Mogadishu, I didn't know anything. And after Mogadishu, my leads kept disappearing.'

'You could have brought in O'Callaghan.'

Jack glanced at the floor. 'I fucked up,' he admitted. Then he jutted his chin out at the CO. He knew Carver wouldn't hold it against him. It was a Blade rule: admit to your cock-ups and there was no comeback. Total indemnity. When the shit hit the fan, there wasn't time for the blame game. 'You should have seen what he did to her,' he added in a quiet voice. 'You'd have done the same, boss. Any of us would.'

'I remember her,' Carver said. 'She was a good lass.' And as far as commiserations went, that was it. There was no time for them.

Jack said, 'You know about the President.'

Carver gave a curt nod. 'Fucking dickhead politicians. Today of all days . . .'

'Get our man to make the call to his employer,' Jack urged. 'To tell them I'm dead. GCHQ can listen in. If it's Khan who answers, Five should be able to match his voice with our records. Even if it's not, GCHQ can try to use the number to triangulate the position of the phone. You can send in a unit to go after them.'

Carver stood up. Say what you like about the guy, he knew how to make a decision. 'I'll get it in motion,' he said in a curt voice.

'Boss, Khan knows where my daughter is. When you find him, you've got to get a location out of him, let me go in to find her.'

A brief, tense silence. Jack knew he was asking a lot; but even though the CO was a boss, underneath it all he was still a Blade. He had to let him do this.

But Carver shook his head. 'No can do, Jack . . .'

'Boss—'

Carver held up one hand. 'You saw Khan two days ago. You can ID him. I'm attaching you to the Special Projects team. You want to know where your daughter is? When you find Khan you can ask him yourself. I'll make sure there's a team on standby to retrieve her the moment you get an address.'

They stared at each other.

'All right,' Jack said quietly.

Carver nodded. 'One more thing, Jack,' he said. 'This isn't a free pass for you. I'm under pressure to deliver your head on a plate. So no fuck-ups. You've run out of credit.'

\*     \*     \*

14.45 hrs.

David Colley, the MI5 representative who had

454

been the main point of contact with Brad Joseph and the Secret Service, cut through the busy corridors of Thames House like the bow of a fast ship cutting through the waves. His mouth was dry and he could feel sweat running down the back of his neck. It was like one of those dreams when you have to be somewhere, but can't move fast enough.

The Director General's secretary looked up in surprise as he burst into her room.

'I need to see him,' he said.

'I'm sorry, Mr Colley, he's—'

'*NOW!*' Colley roared.

The secretary gulped, then disappeared into the DG's room; seconds later she was ushering him in.

Jonathan Daniels looked tired. He was reading reports over the top of a pair of half-moon glasses; when he saw Colley, however, he dropped the papers on to his desk. 'What is it, David?'

'Ops room at Hereford, sir.' Brisk and to the point, Colley relayed everything he knew.

Daniels got to his feet. 'Habib Khan?' He was incredulous. 'They've got to be out of their fucking minds. Have we got anything on him?'

'Nothing, sir. Squeaky clean.'

'And this Harker fellow. I know the name—isn't he the one that laid in to our man Willoughby?'

'Yes, sir. But just because he rubbed Willoughby up the wrong way, it doesn't mean we should discount everything the man's telling us.'

'Have they made the call yet?'

'Not yet, sir. The GCHQ boys are setting it up now. The Special Projects team at Hereford are on standby and we've given CO19 the nod. And sir, I need to inform the Americans. Do I have your permission?'

Daniels didn't answer immediately. He turned back to his desk and pressed a button on his handset. The secretary's voice came over the loudspeaker. 'I need the Prime Minister,' he instructed. 'Now.'

'I'll wait outside, sir,' Colley offered.

'No.' The DG shook his head. 'Stay here.'

An awkward silence while they waited for the call to go through.

*'Prime Minister's office. Please hold, Mr Daniels.'*

And then, a moment later, a familiar voice came over the loudspeaker. 'Jonathan, I'm rather busy. What can I do for—'

'We've got a problem, Prime Minister,' Daniels interrupted, and he proceeded to tell the top man the bare bones of what Colley had just relayed to him. When he had finished, he didn't wait for the PM's reaction. 'I need your permission to inform the Americans, sir. The President hasn't landed yet—'

'*No!*' the PM said.

'Prime Minister, I hardly need remind you that this is a credible threat.'

'Of course, of course, of course.' The PM's voice came over the loudspeaker unnaturally loudly. 'But I'm right in saying, am I not, Jonathan, that there's no intelligence to suggest that this is an attack specifically aimed at the President?'

'Not specifically . . .'

'And is it not policy to ensure that all threats are confirmed by at least two sources?'

'Yes, Prime Minister, but—'

'No buts, Jonathan. Inform the Americans that we have low-level intelligence about a possible threat and that we're doing everything necessary to

456

counter it. Nothing more. The politics are very delicate at the moment, Jonathan. Don't let me down. We *are* doing everything necessary to counter it, aren't we?'

Daniels and Colley exchanged a long look. 'Yes, Prime Minister,' Daniels said. 'Everything we can.'

*    *    *

15.20 hrs.

'Brad, it's Dave Colley, Thames House.'

'I'm hearing you, Dave. What's happening?'

'Something's come up on the radar. I wanted to keep you in the loop.'

'Serious, Dave?'

A pause.

'Low-level intelligence. Unreliable source. We're following it up but our analysts don't expect it to lead anywhere. Our people are talking, but I thought I'd let you know personally.'

Another pause.

'I need details, Dave.'

'I don't even have them. I've delegated this down. Like I say, it's low-level. Your guys will fill you in if you need chapter and verse.'

'Dave, you sound tense.'

'Not tense, Brad. Just busy.'

'Then I'll leave you to it.'

'Thank you. I'll keep you posted.'

'Just one thing, Dave.'

'Yep?'

'We go back a whiles, huh? If there was anything I needed to know, you'd tell me, right?'

A final pause.

'Right, Brad. Look, I've got to go.'

457

'Me too, Dave. Me too.'

*      *      *

15.23 hrs

Brad Joseph pressed a button on his cellphone, then stared at it for a while. He was standing in a wood-panelled room in the Houses of Parliament that the British had given over to the Secret Service and at that very moment there were at least another eight men in there, all of them wearing black suits and each with a coiled earpiece attached to one side of his head. None of them appeared to be at all impressed by the magnificent stained-glass windows looking out on to the river beyond. They were all too preoccupied for that.

Brad remained perfectly still. Colley's call made him uneasy. Hell, everything made him uneasy these days, but this especially. His British colleague had sounded concerned. And if he was concerned, Brad should be too.

He dialled another number. 'Get me Air Force One,' he instructed. 'I need to speak to the Chief of Staff.'

A thirty-second pause, and then a familiar voice came on the line. 'Yeah?'

'Sir, this is Brad Joseph.'

'What is it, Brad?'

'I just took a call, sir, from a contact at MI5. They're getting a bit antsy about something.'

'What are you trying to tell me, Brad?'

Brad thought for a moment. What *was* he trying to tell the President's Chief of Staff—and by extension, the President himself.

'I think we should abort, sir. Cancel the event.

Something doesn't feel right.'

A brief silence. Brad could almost see the Chief of Staff's faintly patronising politician's smile. 'Relax, Brad,' he said. 'The British have already made our people aware of their concerns. They're not taking it seriously. Believe me, they're puppies. They wouldn't dare let this go ahead if there was a real problem. The President has instructed that we proceed.'

'But sir—'

'I gotta go, Brad. See you on the ground.'

The Chief of Staff hung up, leaving Brad to stare at his cell once more.

*     *     *

16.00 hrs.

In the operations room in the basement of Thames House, electronic maps glowed on the walls, and banks of technicians sat at computer terminals. Ordinarily, there was a low blur of steady conversation in this room twenty-four hours a day. But not now. Everybody was silent, their attention clearly focused on what they were doing.

A woman in her mid-forties approached Colley. 'GCHQ have put the mobile-phone company that issued the number on alert. As long as the phone's switched on, they should be able to start locating it any minute now. They'll be piping the information directly through to us.'

'How accurate can you be?' Colley demanded.

'Hard to say, sir. If the phone is switched on and in a service area, it'll be wirelessly communicating with at least one mobile mast. But that will only give us a very rough area.'

'Enough to send a team in?'

459

'No, sir. You're talking two to three square miles. But depending on the phone's location, it could be communicating with more than one mast. We get *three* masts, we can triangulate. As soon as we do that, we can pinpoint the location to a fifty-metre radius.'

'OK. What's your name?'

'Jackie, sir.'

'Let me know the minute you've got anything, Jackie.'

The woman nodded and went back to work. Two minutes later, Colley heard her voice from the other side of the room. 'We've got a fix. Coming up on screen now.'

Colley looked up at the main wall in front of him. An enlarged map of London appeared, several metres square. And superimposed on to it, a big red circle centred on an area of south-east London. 'Single mast,' the woman announced. 'Bermondsey area.'

Colley found himself involuntarily shaking his head. The circle reached as far north as the river, as far south as New Cross. To locate one mobile phone in that area in the time they had was impossible. He cursed.

The woman's voice again. 'Sir, we have an estimate of the kill zone based on what we know about the device from Hereford.'

Colley blinked. 'Go ahead.'

The screen changed. The red circle was still there, but this time it was superimposed with a larger circle, shaded in blue. This blue area covered most of the eastern half of London.

*Ten per cent fatalities in a month; half within a year.*

With a sickening twist in his stomach, it came home to Colley what they were talking about. Thousands of deaths.

A thick silence penetrated the room.

'It's an estimate,' Jackie stated, as if that made things better. 'Based on what we know about the device—'

'How long till we can make the call?' Colley demanded.

A young man with thick-rimmed glasses and prematurely thinning hair answered. 'We've sourced a recording of Habib Khan's voice for the comparison, sir,' he said as he continued to type into his terminal. 'It's an extract from a TV appearance he made on *Question Time* about three months—'

'I don't need to know what it is, man,' Colley interrupted. 'Just tell me how long until we're ready to get an ID match.'

'We're about three minutes away, sir.'

'Inform Hereford. Get them on standby.'

'Yes, sir,' came another voice from behind him.

Colley looked back up at the screen. The red circle pulsated slightly. He tried to look for the positives. There weren't many: just that the area covered by the kill zone didn't include Westminster.

At least, not yet . . .

\*　　　\*　　　\*

16.05 hrs.

The ops room at Hereford was smaller than that at Thames House, but it was no less full of activity. Fifteen men from the Special Projects team, plus

461

four helicopter flight crew, had congregated and were tensely waiting for their instructions. Like Jack, they had already tooled themselves up. Each man carried an MP5 and a Sig 226 in expectation of close-quarter battle, and they were dressed in digital camo, body armour and armoured helmets. In addition, they all wore abseil and radio harnesses, and they all had bags with NBC suits and SF10 respirator masks slung across their arms.

The ops officer dotted around like a pinball, anxious to issue instructions but not knowing yet what the instructions were. Everyone knew, though, that it wasn't a matter of *when* the SP team were to be inserted, but where and how.

The hit man was ushered in. They'd got a name off him now—Aamir Hussein—and the fucker looked terrified. His eyes darted around at all the grim-faced men in this large, busy room; when they fell on Jack he became twice as scared, and that suited Jack down to the ground.

The ops officer's voice above the hubbub. 'Word from Five,' he shouted. 'GCHQ are online. Make the call.'

Elliott Carver approached Jack. It was rare for the CO to take an operational role, and Jack knew a chaperone when he saw one, but there was no time to feel sore about that. 'Follow me, Jack,' he said. 'We'll do it together.'

Jack nodded, then roughly grabbed Aamir's arm and followed the CO to a nearby room. It was quiet here. It needed to be. Any telltale noises in the background and they'd give the game away. There were several wooden chairs in the room: Jack pushed Aamir onto one of them, but he and Carver remained standing. Jack towered over the hit man and handed him back his mobile phone.

'You fuck this up,' he said, 'I'm going to hurt you. You know I will, don't you?'

Aamir nodded vigorously.

'You're going to make the call,' he said. 'You'll say exactly these words: "Is that you?" If he doesn't reply, you repeat those words until he does. Then you say, "It's Aamir, Harker's dead." If I hear you say anything else I'll assume you're delivering a covert distress call and by the time I've finished with you, you'll be begging to climb back into my bath again. Do you understand?'

Aamir nodded.

'Say, "I understand".'

'I understand.'

Jack and Carver exchanged a look.

'Do it,' Jack said.

\*       \*       \*

16.10 hrs.

Back at Thames House, everyone had focused their attention on the young technician with the thin hair. He looked nervous—no doubt because he had not only David Colley but also the newly arrived Director General standing over his shoulder.

From the terminal came the sound of a dialling tone, then the unsteady beeps of a number being dialled.

It felt as if the whole room was holding its breath.

A ringtone.

'Answer it,' Colley muttered.

Two rings.

463

Three rings.

Four.

A click. Then a generic voicemail message.

Colley swore. 'Get on to Hereford,' he instructed. 'Tell them to try again.'

A minute's pause.

The dialling tone returned.

The phone rang.

Voicemail again.

The men and women in the operations room started to murmur. They were long enough in the tooth to know when an operation was going pear-shaped.

'Quiet!' Colley shouted. 'Go again!'

He was chewing on the corner of his lower lip now, his eyes fixed on the technician's screen. Once more there was a dialling tone. A ring.

Once.

Twice.

And then a voice.

*'Yes?'*

A wave formation appeared on the technician's screen; the young man started typing furiously into his keyboard. 'Matching now,' he breathed.

*'Is that you?'* A second voice, sounding a bit nervous.

Silence.

*'Is that you?'* the second voice repeated.

Silence.

*'Harker is dead.'*

Another silence. And then . . .

*'Do not return home. Avoid London, and you will survive to continue the fight.'*

A click.

'Have you got a match?' Colley demanded

immediately.

The technician continued to type.

Silence in the room.

And then the young man spoke.

'It's a match,' he stated. 'The guy on the phone is Habib Khan.'

Colley felt a chill run through his veins. 'Get back on to Hereford,' he instructed in a loud voice that cracked slightly. 'I need that unit in London and I need it here now.'

*     *     *

16.20 hrs.

Hereford ops room. The call came through. Carver gave the instruction. 'Special Projects team, immediate action. Jack, give them the low-down.'

Jack raised his voice and spoke briskly. 'Our target is one Habib Khan. We've reason to believe he's carrying a dirty bomb and our best guess is he's using it to target the President at Westminster this evening. President or not, the device is capable of spreading enough contaminants to infect several thousand people within a radius of one mile, killing ten per cent within a month, up to half within a year.'

He surveyed the team. Their grim faces mirrored the horror of what he was describing.

'Our best intelligence is that the device is packed in a metal flight case, about the size of a small suitcase. Method of detonation is unknown, but if we get into close quarters with it, we need to be aware that a stray round could cause it to explode. We're using frangible ammunition, but even so we need to keep discharges to a minimum. And we want to take Khan alive if possible.' Jack and the CO exchanged a look.

The ops officer spoke up. 'Khan is in the general area of south-east London. He's not near enough to where the President's going to be to launch a direct attack, though, so we're assuming that he'll be on the move before long. That should help us narrow down his location, assuming he keeps his phone switched on. You'll be set down at the heliport near Battersea to await further movement orders there. We'll be in constant comms with the ops room at Thames House. Any questions?'

One guy put his hand up. 'Why the hell don't they extract the President?' he asked.

'Good question,' the ops officer said with a dark frown. 'Can't fucking answer it.'

'All right,' Carver interrupted. 'You'll get further instructions on the ground. *Move!*'

The ops room started to swarm once more with activity.

'Jack!' Carver called.

He'd been heading for the door, but he turned to see the CO gesturing at him, so he approached his boss. Carver tapped two fingers on his skull. 'Head, Jack,' he said. 'Not heart. Remember what's at stake. Thousands of people, not just one. Isolate the device first, then you can question him. Now's not the time to get personal.'

Jack sniffed. 'Roger that, boss.'

On the southern boundary of RAF Credenhill, two Agusta A109 helicopters were loaded and ready to fly, rotary blades spinning. The men of the Special Projects team ran towards them, heads bowed, then bundled in, eight soldiers and two flight crew to an aircraft. Jack's was the first to leave the ground, gaining height quickly before spinning mid-air and, its tail slightly raised, accelerating eastwards towards London.

Jack checked his kit, his weapons and the contents of his ops waistcoat before fitting his earpiece. The sound of conversation from the ops room filled his senses. *Estimated flight time, fifty-eight minutes. Police liaison waiting at landing zone. Await further instructions on the ground.*

'Who's the raghead with the phone, Jack?' a voice shouted over the noise of the engines. Jack looked up. It was Fly Forsyth.

'Just some dickhead who thought the world would be a better place without Jack Harker in it.'

Fly grinned. 'Who hired him? Ex-girlfriend?'

Jack forced himself to smile and Fly noticed how strained it was. 'Maybe it was the adjutant,' he joked to relieve the tension. 'Jack, care to share how you know so much about our target?'

'Not really.' The guys seemed to accept that.

Jack looked out of the window at the patchwork countryside speeding below. A memory flashed across his mind: the sandy view from the Black Hawk in Helmand, just moments before it went down. He pushed it away. He had to keep his mind on the job in hand. Dwell too much on the last few days and he wouldn't just be ineffective. He'd be a liability.

Silence in the heli. There was none of the usual pre-op banter. Just eight men carefully preparing themselves and their kit. Everyone seemed to understand that the situation they were heading into was serious.

The sort of operation from which they could very well not return.

## 27

17.01 hrs.

Thames House. David Colley looked up at the enlarged map of London. The red circle continued to pulsate.

'CO19 teams in place,' a voice called. 'Target's location perimeter secured.'

Colley took a deep breath. It was all very well putting armed police around the area of Bermondsey defined by the red circle, but they all knew it would be the easiest job in the world for Khan to slip through such a cordon. There simply weren't enough CO19 officers to secure an area like that effectively. Lack§ of personnel wasn't their only problem, though. If Khan got even a whiff that they were on to him, he might be encouraged to detonate his device early. Even if he was nowhere near the President when it happened, the death toll would be devastating. They had to keep this covert until the very last minute. Only when they had a precise location could they hit him hard and fast.

Time passed. A strange sense of helplessness descended upon the ops room.

'What if he knows we're tracking him?' the DG asked. 'What if he's left his phone somewhere just to put us off the track.'

Colley turned to his boss. The balance of power seemed to have shifted, and Daniels was giving the impression of being entirely in Colley's hands.

'Then we're in trouble,' he said. 'But we know he was with the phone when they made the call from

Hereford fifty minutes ago. That's something.'

They continued to wait.

A sudden blur of voices. The red circle had disappeared. Within seconds, another one started to glow on the map of London. It had moved. Its centre was about half a mile further north of the previous circle.

*'He's moving!'*

The ops room was alive again.

'Sir!' a voice called across the room. It was Jackie, and she was gesturing to Colley. He strode over to her.

'What is it, Jackie?'

'The fix, sir. His phone's connecting to two mobile masts.' She pointed up at the screen. A second circle had appeared. 'Where the two circles intersect, that's where the phone's broadcasting from.'

Colley looked at the elliptical shape. It crossed the River Thames between Southwark Park and Shadwell.

'Is he heading for the river?'

'Hard to say, sir.' And as she spoke, the shaded blue area of the kill zone moved half a mile further north.

Colley raised his voice. 'Inform CO19 of the new location,' he instructed. 'And make sure they're discreet.'

'We could close the river,' the DG suggested from over Colley's shoulder.

Colley shook his head. 'It would alert him.' He addressed Jackie again. 'Do we have satellite tracking on his possible locations?'

She nodded. 'Yes, sir. We have people examining them in real time.'

'Good. Speak to Hereford. Tell them there's a possibility that he's heading for the Thames.'

He looked back up at the map. The red circles were like eyes, glowing at him balefully. Colley stared back at them.

'Where are you, Khan?' he said under his breath. 'Where the *hell* are you?'

\*       \*       \*

17.28 hrs.

'*RAF Northolt. RAF Northolt. This is Air Force One.*'

'*Copy, Air Force One.*'

'*Requesting permission to land.*'

'*Go ahead, Air Force One. You have full clearance.*'

Sean Barclay looked out from the control tower at Northolt. The evening sky was still a rich, cloudless blue. Perfect weather for the President's arrival. Sean's line of sight was clear. The airspace had been emptied of traffic for the arrival of Air Force One—regular holding patterns changed, military flights diverted to Brize Norton or elsewhere. And although he couldn't yet see the President's aircraft in the distance, his screen told him that it would be only a couple of minutes before he saw the blue and white Boeing 747 emerge from the hazy skies in the distance.

From his vantage point, he glanced down to the ground. Bloody Yanks, he thought to himself. They'd taken the whole place over. The previous day, a Globemaster had arrived with the President's limousine—the Beast—which two Secret Service drivers had immediately taken off

470

site to Buckingham Palace. Now there were three identical US Marine Corps helicopters, with Secret Service personnel swarming round them like bluebottles.

Sean shook his head. Talk about over the top. Yesterday, one of these Secret Service guys had taken him to one side to explain that they'd chosen him to guide Air Force One down, like it was some great privilege. They'd run background checks on him, and Sean couldn't help wondering why, if he and his colleagues were all trusted by the British Army, they couldn't just be trusted by the Yanks. The agent had then explained to him certain security precautions. Secret Service—*not* RAF personnel—would escort the President directly to one of the helicopters. Once he was on board, all three choppers would take to the air. Whichever of them carried the President would be given the call sign Marine One.

'You go to all this trouble every time the President takes a trip?' Sean had asked.

The Secret Service man's face had remained impassive. 'When the President takes a trip,' he'd said, 'it ain't just a trip.'

No shit, Sean thought to himself now as he continued to look out of the control tower. This was, quite literally, a military operation.

He squinted back up into the sky. Far away, he thought he saw a dot of light appearing from the distance. He glanced down at his screen. The green dot with the President's call sign and altitude had entered that part of the screen that included Sean's field of vision.

Air Force One was coming in to land.

17.32 hrs.

From the window of the Agusta, Jack saw the western outskirts of London come into view. Somewhere over Wormwood Scrubs Park they started to lose height, continuing across the urban sprawl to Hyde Park, where they veered more sharply to the south before coming in to land in the drab surroundings of the London Heliport just west of Battersea, and bang on the south bank of the Thames. The helipad was surrounded by police liaison vehicles and other unmarked cars. As the two Agustas touched down and the Regiment unit spilled out on to the ground, Jack took in the ten or so people waiting for them around the helipad—some of them uniformed police officers, others in suits he assumed to be a mixture of plainclothes and MI5. 'Who's in charge?' he shouted above the noise of the chopper's blades.

An armed police officer stepped forward. 'We think he's on the river. Hereford have requested police dive teams meet your guys with equipment. They'll be here within a minute.' He pointed at the water where, among the many boats passing up and down the Thames, a long vessel covered with dirty, multicoloured cargo boxes was drifting up towards the bank. 'Your transport,' stated the police officer.

Jack didn't need to hear any more. He turned back to the unit who had assembled in a group a little way from the two helis. *Dive team!* he shouted.

Six of the guys—all of them members of Boat

Troop—immediately peeled off from the others and ran towards him. At that moment, an unmarked white Transit van screamed on to the helipad. The moment it stopped, two men jumped out of the front, opened up the rear doors and started unloading equipment on to the tarmac.

Jack and the rest of the Boat Troop guys ran up to them. 'Get changed!' he shouted. 'Intel suggests the target's on the river.'

There was no fucking around. All seven of them stripped out of their operational clothing and started changing into the dive gear. The black drysuits went on first, followed by tight neoprene hoods and black boots; after this second skin went their ops waistcoats and firearms, followed by a weight belt to ensure they kept well hidden under the surface. Each man attached a dive mask with a Dräger rebreather and a matt black oxygen canister. These compact, closed-circuit rebreathers would allow them to swim shallow without any telltale air bubbles rising to the surface. Each man took a black swim board, which had a large, illuminated compass that they would be able to see in the murky waters of the Thames, along with a depth gauge and a luminous timer; plus the various other bits of kit they needed for the covert boarding of a hostile vessel.

Jack and the others carried their military fins—into which they would be able to fit their boots directly—and ran to the water's edge. They tumbled in and swam to the nearby cargo vessel. They boarded, then hid among the cargo boxes.

There was no need to make contact with the skipper: Jack knew that the vessel's regular captain would have been replaced by a professional. Their priority now was to keep out of sight until they got the go order. And that was out of his hands.

The boat started moving, surprisingly quickly, up the river towards the centre of London.

*     *     *

17.40 hrs.

From his vantage point in the control tower, Sean Barclay watched the slick choreography of a presidential arrival. Air Force One had barely come to a halt before the RAF ground crew had pushed the steps up to the plane and a group of people—Sean assumed that the President was in the middle of them, but he couldn't see his face no matter how hard he peered—swept down to the waiting helicopters.

The middle of the three aircraft was designated Marine One. Once the entourage had boarded, however, all three rose into the air at the same time. Sean watched them carefully. They were barely thirty metres in the air before they performed a swift, skilful switch: Marine One swapped with the aircraft to its right, while the third rose above the other two before sandwiching itself between them. He remembered a game his great-uncle used to play with him when he was a kid: the old man would put a fifty-pence piece under one of three cups, then slide the cups around in a steady but confusing pattern. If Sean managed to locate the fifty pence, he was allowed to keep it. He never did.

He felt like that now—bemused as the three helicopters continued to rise out of sight, realising that he had already lost track of which one carried

474

the world's most powerful man.

And then they were gone.

Air Force One taxied over to another part of the airfield to be refuelled. Sean shrugged. He was obliged to remain here for the rest of the evening, but there would be no more flights into RAF Northolt tonight.

'Excitement's over for one day,' he muttered to himself as he prepared for the boring hours ahead . . .

\*       \*       \*

18.00 hrs.

'He's moving again!'

The two red circles on the map in the Thames House operations room had faded away. Colley stared at it, waiting for Khan's location to reappear.

'Three masts!' Jackie called. 'We've got three masts!'

As she spoke, three red circles appeared on the map. The area of intersection was concentrated firmly on the river between Westminster and Waterloo Bridge, and the blue kill zone had moved west, its boundary just touching Westminster Bridge.

'Alert Hereford,' Colley instructed. 'Let the dive teams know we've narrowed it down. What's the satellite imagery telling us? Can we identify Khan's boat? Can we tell which way he's moving?'

A tense pause.

'Negative, sir. There's too much river traffic—we have sixty-three vessels in the area. It could be any of them.'

'*Shit,*' Colley muttered.

The DG spoke up. 'Where's the President now?'

A voice from the other end of the room: 'Limousine One has just left Buckingham Palace. Estimated time to Westminster seven minutes.'

'Damn it!' Daniels shouted. '*Damn it!*'

The DG fumed and started pacing round the ops room. He felt entirely helpless, and it wasn't a feeling he liked. And he was so hung up in his own panic that he didn't notice Dave Colley walk out, fingering his mobile phone.

\*     \*     \*

18.02 hrs.

Jack remained hunkered down, hidden behind the containers on the cargo vessel that was transporting him along the river. A voice in his earpiece. Hereford ops room. '*Target's location between Westminster and Waterloo Bridge. Do you copy?*'

'Copy that,' Jack replied. 'Do you have a precise fix?'

'*Negative. They're working on it, Jack.*'

Then they'd better work on it a bit harder, Jack thought, as the cargo vessel continued to course downstream.

\*     \*     \*

18.03 hrs.

The block of caesium-137 was encased in lead. Three wires protruded from the lead casing, leading to a complicated mess of more wires and plastic explosive. All this within a metal flight case whose lid was now open and which was sitting on a table within the cabin of the *Guinevere*—an old, unassuming boat with a blue hull and white cabin, part of the busy river traffic approaching Westminster Bridge, which was thirty metres away, and counting.

Habib Khan looked down on the device, and his eyes shone.

On the right-hand side of the explosives was an unassuming metal lever. It was in the up position, and Khan could not help allowing his hand to hover above it. The hand, he noticed, was shaking slightly. That was to be expected, he told himself. Everything for which he had worked for so long— so *long*—was on the verge of fruition.

Next to the flight case was a phone. Its large screen displayed a website and at the top of the page were the words PRESIDENTIAL VISIT: LIVE TEXT UPDATES. Khan's eyes scanned the most recent update. THE PRESIDENTIAL MOTORCADE IS MOVING SLOWLY UP BIRDCAGE WALK . . .

He smiled. Only a few more minutes. Give the President time to reach Parliament and then . . .

He looked up. The skipper of the boat—a young Middle Eastern man with a full beard and greased-back hair—had his back to him and was concentrating on steering the vehicle towards their location.

'You are ready?' he asked. 'You are ready to give your life for the Prophet?'

The skipper looked over his shoulder. Like Khan, he had fervour in his brown eyes. 'I am ready,' he said in a clear voice. 'God willing, they will not find us before the time is right. God willing, we will not fail.'

An enigmatic look crossed Khan's face. 'We will not fail,' he said quietly. 'It is impossible.'

He turned his attention back to the device while the boat continued to drift upriver. It was almost as an afterthought that he switched off his phone.

\*       \*       \*

18.05 hrs.

Brad Joseph stood on a balcony at the corner of the Houses of Parliament. From here, he could see diagonally across Parliament Square, which was now cordoned off and lined with police as they waited for the President to arrive. He didn't mind admitting to himself that it gave him a good feeling to see the brisk efficiency with which the whole operation was playing out. He took a deep breath as he drank in the pleasant sight of the evening sun on the green-leaved trees of the square; and he felt a small thrill as, at the furthest corner, the first sight of the presidential motorcade—two police outriders in luminous yellow jackets—came into view.

And then his cellphone rang.

Brad looked at his screen, then frowned. Dave Colley. What the hell did he want?

He clicked a button and answered the call.

\*       \*       \*

18.06 hrs.

David Colley stood in the corridor outside the ops room, his phone pressed to his ear. Brad's American drawl came on to the line. 'Dave, what can I do you for?'

478

'We never had this conversation, Brad.'

A pause.

'What you got for me, Dave?'

Colley took a deep breath. If word of what he was about to do got out to anyone, his job was history. But if he didn't, history could change anyway. Sometimes, you just had to do the right thing . . .

'Get your man out of London. Evacuate him now. We've got some nutter planning a spectacular and the PM's got his head in the sand. We haven't got a handle on it and the shit's about to hit.'

Another pause. And then . . .

'Thank you, Dave.'

Brad hung up just as Dave Colley slumped against a wall. In the back of his mind he considered getting the hell out of there, vacating the area himself, but he soon vetoed that thought. He knew where his duty lay, and that was here in the basement of Thames House.

He straightened himself up and returned to the operations room.

\*         \*         \*


18.07 hrs.

Brad Joseph didn't hesitate for a second. In the far corner of Parliament Square, the nose of the Beast, flying two miniature Union Jacks on its bonnet, as was the tradition, was just peeping into view.

He raised his wrist to his mouth and spoke clearly into his microphone. *'We got a Category One alert. Evacuate the President now. REPEAT— EVACUATE THE PRESIDENT NOW!'*

When David Colley returned to the ops room, everything was in chaos. The DG was framed by the enlarged map of London, but its three pulsating circles had disappeared and there was a wild look in his eyes. He barked at him across the room. 'We've lost the signal. The motorcade's turning round. What's happening? The PM's going to shit on us from a height. *Damn it, Colley! What's happening?*'

Colley ignored him, because just as the DG was losing it in front of half of Five's operational staff, Jackie was striding up to him. 'Sir,' she said sharply. 'I think we've got him.'

# 28

Colley blinked, then quickly followed Jackie back to her station where she had satellite images on two separate screens. She pointed at the left-hand one. 'This was taken fifteen minutes ago and covers the area Khan's phone was transmitting from.' She moved her attention to the right-hand screen. 'This was taken two minutes ago, just before we lost the signal. There's only two vessels that appear in both images. One's a covert police boat. The other one's this.' She clicked a button on her keyboard, and a blurred, grainy, bird's-eye image appeared.

Colley felt his mouth go dry. 'Have we . . .'

'Police teams on the bank are scoping it now, sir.

As soon as they have a description and a—'

She stopped, held up one finger and listened into her headset.

'Vessel's name is *Guinevere*,' she reported. 'It's moved away from the traffic flow and come to a halt ten metres south of Westminster Bridge. Details are being relayed to the dive team now.'

They looked at each other. Both of them knew that they'd done everything they could. It was out of their hands now.

\*          \*          \*

Hidden among the multicoloured cargo boxes, Jack couldn't tell which part of the river they had reached. All he knew was that the boat was beginning to slow down.

Suddenly his earpiece burst into life. *'We have a fix. Repeat, we have a fix.'*

Jack raised a hand and caught the attention of the rest of the team, but they'd heard the communication too and had already turned to look at him.

The vessel was practically still now. Further instructions over the comms. *'Dive team, on my command enter the water to starboard. Approach at a bearing of two hundred and fifty degrees. Allowing for the movement of the current you should reach the target in approximately one hundred and twenty-five seconds. The vessel is named* Guinevere, *blue freeboard, white cabin. We have eyes on—two crew in the cabin. Do you copy?'*

Jack looked around at his team. They all gave the thumbs-up. 'Copy that,' he replied.

*'Entry in sixty seconds. Repeat, entry in sixty*

481

seconds. *The President is being evacuated to Northolt, repeat, Marine One is about to fly.'*

The team was already moving, emerging from their covert positions behind the cargo units. If the instruction was to enter the water to starboard, that meant the target vessel was stationed to port side. They could submerge themselves without being seen.

'*T minus forty seconds.'*

Along with the others, Jack attended to his swim board, setting the thick, black rotational dial to a bearing of 250 degrees and illuminating the backlight. Up here, you couldn't tell the difference. Underwater, it would be like a beacon leading him onwards.

Leading him to Khan.

'When we get there,' he told the unit, 'Khan's mine.'

'*T minus twenty seconds.'* The vessel was still moving, but very slowly now. Jack switched his timer to count 120 seconds, then the eight of them crouched by the edge of the platform, facing inwards. Jack checked that his dive helmet and rebreather were properly fitted, and that his weapons were properly attached to his person.

'*T minus five seconds. Four. Three. Two. One. Go! Go! Go!'*

Jack tumbled backwards, and he sensed the others doing the same.

A splash.

Darkness.

He felt his body righting itself in the water. Everything around him was murky. Dark. Visibility, one to two metres, max. Jack knew the others were around him, but he couldn't fully

482

make them out—they were like shadows in the twilight. His eyes sought out the glowing compass of the swim board that he now held out in front of him. He was on a bearing of 100 degrees, so he spun his body round until he was facing the right direction.

He turned on the timer. And then he started kicking his flippers. Steadily. Rhythmically.

Habib Khan, he told himself, was only metres away.

*       *       *

The Beast roared back up Birdcage Walk. The police outriders had their sirens blaring and the President's counter-attack team stood sentinel by their 4 x 4s, MP5s on full display as they surveyed the surrounding area with grim, implacable faces.

The gates to Buckingham Palace were already wide open, and the motorcade sped through it, swinging round the side of the great building and hurtling towards the three waiting helicopters, whose blades were already spinning in preparation for the off. The Beast skidded to a halt, but the doors didn't open until members of the CAT team surrounded the limousine and formed a protective corridor between the rear door and the nearest of the three choppers. One of the CAT team opened the back door of the limo and, without even the pretence of presidential reverence, yelled at the top of his voice. '*Into the chopper! Get into the chopper! Now!*'

A figure emerged—tall, lanky almost, with short hair and dark skin. His head bowed, he ran towards the helicopter and jumped up into Marine

One, quickly followed by two of his guards.

The door slammed shut. In a moment of perfect choreography, all three choppers rose into the air at precisely the same time. They were no higher than the top of Buckingham Palace when they performed their intricate switching. Moments later, they did it again. Only someone who had seen the President enter his chopper and had then carefully watched the switching pattern would know which aircraft contained him, and by the time the three helis had started moving north-west across London, it was impossible to say which was Marine One, and which were the decoys.

\*           \*           \*

Jack's timer counted down in the gloom. Three seconds.

Two seconds.

One.

Suddenly, up ahead, there was the hull of a vessel. He swam towards it. Seconds later he became aware of the others, huddled around it and manoeuvring themselves towards the stern.

He pulled himself towards the surface— gradually, so as not to make a noise when he emerged. As he came up into the open air, he was aware of Westminster Bridge hulking above them ten to fifteen metres away.

The team worked silently, but with swift skill. While the others boarded, two of the men would stay in the water to provide covering fire if necessary. So they peeled off while the remaining six prepared to board. First off, the washing line: they fixed magnets to the tatty paintwork of the blue hull, allowing them to strip themselves of their masks, Drägers, fins and weight belts and attach this unneeded gear to the boat. Once they'd done that, one of the lads produced a telescopic pole, while another started to unfurl a rolled-up rope ladder. The top end of the ladder, which had two hooks on each side, was fitted to the end of the pole; as the pole was extended, the ladder continued to unfurl completely until they were able to hook it over the side of the boat, towards the stern. All this took less than thirty seconds.

Jack took to the ladder first and started climbing up the freeboard. As he emerged from the water, he felt the water draining not only off his body, but also out of his weapon. He moved quickly. Just as his head was about to appear over the edge of the boat he stopped and took a deep breath. Then he peered over.

The first thing he checked was that there was nobody on deck to spot him. It was empty. The cabin was painted white and was entirely surrounded by deck. There were windows all around, but they were sufficiently high for him to be able to crouch underneath them. He didn't hesitate a second longer. He swung his legs over the side and landed silently on deck. He moved towards the walls of the cabin where he stayed under the windows. He unclipped his MP5 and waited for the remaining five members of the boarding team to join him. They were up and over in seconds.

Jack made a quick hand gesture to indicate that three of the team should move round to the other side of the cabin. He waited two seconds for them to get into position, then, still crouching, he crept round to the entrance of the cabin. He removed a flashbang from his ops waistcoat, and held up three fingers to his opposite number on the other side of the door.

Two fingers.

One.

Jack pulled the pin, pushed the door open and hurled it through. A sudden, ear-blistering crack and a flash of light—enough to disorientate anyone who wasn't used to it. Jack and his team *were* used to it, though. By the time the grenade had exploded, Jack was inside, moving through the cabin with all the force and anger of a tsunami.

His eyes zeroed in on Khan. The fucker might have shaved off his beard, but Jack would recognise that face anywhere. As he stormed towards him, his MP5 pointing directly at his enemy's head, he felt a sudden burst of anger and hatred surging through his veins. He wanted to roar, to make him feel tenfold every ounce of pain he was carrying with him on account of Siobhan's death. To make the bastard *suffer*.

Khan must have seen that in him. Or maybe other things were going through his twisted mind. Either way, in the split second it took for Jack to be upon him, a fierce, insane look burned behind his eyes. He was standing over a metal flight case—Jack recognised it easily enough. It was open, and Khan's arm was hovering over it.

He lowered his hand.

Jack launched himself through the air. Khan crashed to the ground, his thin body crushed by Jack's enormous bulk. Jack put the MP5 against his skull, and was a nanosecond away from firing it and spraying the cunt's brains all over the interior of the cabin. But at the last moment he stopped himself. He looked over his shoulder. The second member of the crew was on the floor with three of the team suppressing him. The remaining two SAS men were hulking above Jack, MP5s trained on Khan.

'*Target secure!*' he spoke into his comms. '*Target secure! We've got the device and we've got Khan. Send in the choppers to extract!*'

And then he looked down at Khan.

The man was gazing up at him. There appeared to be a flicker of a smile on his lips, like he was too crazy to know what was happening. It was too much for Jack. Rage took hold of him. He dropped his MP5 on the ground, and started to pummel Khan's face with his fist until the bastard's nose was broken and his features were mashed and bloody.

And even then the fucker wouldn't stop smiling.

He grabbed him by the throat. 'You're going to tell me where the girl is,' he hissed. '*Now.*'

Khan did nothing but smile, so Jack squeezed at his jugular.

'The girl,' Khan croaked, 'is not important.'

'She's important to me. You've got ten seconds to tell me where she is.'

Khan stared at him. There was something calculating behind his eyes. 'Yes,' he breathed. 'Go and find her. Kane Road, Tottenham. House number sixty-seven. In the basement.'

Jack immediately spoke into his radio, repeating the address. 'Tell Carver,' he instructed. 'Tell him to send a team in now . . .'

He turned his attention back to Khan, but found he couldn't look at his face any more, so he turned

487

him on to his front and Plasticuffed his hands behind his back. 'If you're lying to me, Khan, I swear to God you'll wish you'd never been born.'

'I think,' Khan replied, 'that is most unlikely.'

Jack paused, his eyes boring into the back of Khan's head. The man sounded like he knew something. He stood up and put a boot on his neck, then looked around. The inside of the boat was strangely still.

Strangely calm.

It was over. They'd captured Khan. They'd captured the device. London was safe. A team was on its way to get his daughter.

Why, then, did Jack feel that something wasn't quite right?

\*　　　\*　　　\*

Thames House operations room. *'Target acquired, target acquired. The dive team have Khan. The device is secured. Bomb disposal on their way.'*

A cheer went up. High fives from the technicians. David Colley's voice above the hubbub: 'Keep your minds on the job, damn it. *Keep your minds on the job!'*

But nothing he said could dispel the atmosphere of relief that had suddenly descended on the room.

\*　　　\*　　　\*

It took about two minutes before one of the Agustas was hovering over the boat. Jack pulled the Plasticuffed Khan by the scruff of his neck, then forced him out of the cabin and on to the deck. The dirty water of the Thames sprayed over them in the wake of the chopper's downdraught; Khan faced the spray with his eyes open.

A rope tumbled from the Agusta. At the end of it were two blue harnesses with metal links. Khan didn't even put up a fight as Jack strapped him into one of them; and as the loadie in the chopper winched them both up, his body remained limp and submissive.

As soon as they were in the body of the chopper, Jack unclipped them both, then looked out to check that everything else was happening as it should. The second Agusta was getting into position to winch up the boat's skipper; and he saw three RIBs cutting their way through the Thames towards the vessel—bomb disposal guys, no doubt, there to work their magic with the device.

He turned his attention back to Khan, put one hand on his shoulder, then kicked him in the right knee so that he collapsed like a house of cards in a hurricane. The Agusta veered off to the right. Jack didn't know what their destination was: a facility somewhere, he supposed, where Khan could be questioned. No good cop, bad cop routine for him. It would be bad cop all the way, and Jack hoped he'd get the chance to ask a few questions of his own.

Fly was on board. Apart from him, just the pilot. Jack's colleague gave him a look. 'Easy, Jack. He's not going anywhere. They'll want him in one piece when he lands.'

Jack barely heard him. He knelt down where Khan was lying, grabbed his hair and whispered into his ear. 'It's over, Khan. You're fucked.'

And again, a smile played around Khan's lips. 'It is not over, Jack Harker,' he whispered. 'It has

489

only just begun.'

'What's he saying, Jack?' Fly shouted over the noise of the aircraft.

Jack held up one hand. 'What do you mean?' he asked sharply.

Khan just smiled again, a smile that filled Jack with such fury that he unclipped his MP5, then pulled Khan to his feet and hauled him to the still-open door of the Agusta. Jack pushed him so that he was teetering on the brink of the helicopter, then placed the MP5 against the back of his head. 'The safety's off and it's fully loaded,' he roared as the river snaked beneath them. 'Tell me what you're talking about!'

'*Go ahead and shoot me!*' Khan yelled above the wind. '*It is all you can do, and I woke up this morning expecting to die!*'

Jack felt his finger twitching. He wanted the satisfaction of feeling the rounds pump into the fucker's body; of seeing him fall dead into the river below. But something stopped him. He pulled Khan back again, then whacked his weapon against the man's face. A satisfying crack of breaking bone; a flash of blood; Khan fell to the floor once more. Jack could sense that Fly was unsure whether to restrain him or not; but for now, his fellow soldier was giving him the benefit of the doubt.

Khan's blood was flowing freely, but still he seemed unmoved. 'Without your gun,' he smirked, 'you are nothing.'

Jack felt fire in his veins. He beat Khan's head once more with the metal of his MP5. More blood. This time, Khan's eyes remained closed and he took a deep breath, as though absorbing the pain.

Finally he spoke again. Jack had to strain his ears to hear him. 'Without your gun,' he repeated, 'you are nothing.' Another deep breath. 'A long time ago, my grandfather taught me something. It is with your weapon that you win the battle, he said, but with your mind that you win the war.'

Jack stared at him. Khan's words seemed to glow like coals in the air, and his smirk grew wider.

'What did you say?'

'You think that with your weapons you can do anything, but you do not use your *minds*,' Khan hissed.

Jack continued to stare.

The fire in his veins had turned to ice.

Khan's words had taken him back. It was only days previously, but it seemed like a lifetime. He was imprisoned in a dark room, having been captured in the heart of enemy territory in Afghanistan. A man was talking to him. He stank of greasy sweat, wore desert camo. And he was missing a finger on one hand. In his mind, Jack could see him as clearly as he could see Habib Khan in front of him. And he could hear his voice, too.

*When I was very small, my grandfather told me something. I have never forgotten it. It is with your weapons that you win the battle, but with your mind that you win the war. And that is why this war, for you, is already lost.*

Farzad Haq's words echoed in his mind as the helicopter swerved again. Jack looked in horror at Khan. At the smile of satisfaction that remained on his head even though the blood continued to drench it.

And then he was elsewhere. The ops centre in

491

Bastion. That goon Willoughby showing off his intel.

*When the Iraqis invaded Iran later that year, Haq's younger brother was killed by Saddam's forces . . . he's obsessed with our American cousins. Blames them for supporting the Iraqi regime that killed his brother. There's a videotape somewhere in the archives of him promising to eliminate any American he comes across, just like they killed Adel.*

Adel . . .

*A long time ago, my grandfather taught me something . . .*

Farzad Haq's younger brother wasn't dead at all. He was very much alive. And he was lying on the floor of the Agusta as it continued to speed through London airspace.

Jack looked at him.

'Your name is Adel.' It wasn't a question. It was a statement of fact.

Khan's eyes opened. He blinked rapidly because of the blood flowing over his brow. 'You're too late,' he hissed.

But Jack's mind was racing ahead. Pieces of a jigsaw puzzle that had been floating around in his head suddenly started dropping into place.

O'Callaghan's importation line. The old man had admitted, just before Jack dealt with him, that Khan had sent a number of packages into the country that weren't related to the O'Callaghan drugs operation.

*Boxes. I don't know what they are. Nothing to do with me. I just see that they get shipped where he wants them.*

Jack was hitting the Taliban stronghold in Afghanistan, fast-roping into the compound where

492

Haq had held him captive. But he hadn't been after Haq himself. He'd been after something else.

'*The Stingers . . .*'

A look of triumph in Khan's eyes.

'*Jack!*' Fly shouted. '*What the hell's going on?*'

Jack's brow was furrowed. A final memory shunted through his brain. He was in a helicopter. Not an Agusta, this time, but a Black Hawk. It was making a fast extraction, away from the kill zone in the Helmand desert, north above the cliff that was home to the cave system they'd just hit.

But on top of the cliff there were enemy.

Waiting for them.

Lying in ambush.

Ready to bring the chopper down.

These were Haq's tactics. This was the way he fought his wars. And he was doing it again.

Now.

Time slowed down.

Jack pushed himself up on his feet. He turned to face the front of the chopper. The pilot was wearing a helmet and headphones. Jack switched his radio on. He didn't know who was listening in, but he shouted anyway.

'*TURN THE CHOPPER ROUND!*' he yelled at the top of his voice, feeling his throat rip as he did so. '*IT'S AN AMBUSH. IT'S A FUCKING AMBUSH! TURN THE CHOPPER ROUND! THEY'RE ABOUT TO TAKE OUT THE PRESIDENT!*'

# 29

It was not in Farzad Haq's nature to smile often. But he did so now, like his brother—a brief flicker as he gazed upwards.

There were few people enjoying the evening air in Hillingdon Park—just a couple of dog walkers and, loitering around a litter-strewn bandstand about 200 metres from where he was standing, some youths smoking cigarettes, or more likely something stronger.

Haq himself was standing next to a battered white van that was parked just by an old cricket pavilion. The numbers on the scoreboard were faded; some of them hung at an angle by only a single hinge. There was obscene graffiti on the wall. It was clear that nobody had used this pavilion for months, perhaps even years. Which was why it had proved to be the perfect hiding place for the missiles once they had completed their long journey from Helmand to the southern tip of Ireland and into the UK. Adel had set things up well. Very well. Farzad felt a sense of pride in his younger brother.

How pleased, he thought to himself, Grandfather would have been.

The sky opened up above him. A vast, clear expanse. Here, on the perimeter of RAF Northolt, one would not usually have to wait long to see an aircraft. But today, the British and the Americans had cleared the skies. It was predictable of them. Foolish. But Haq wasn't going to complain about that. Especially now that he saw, in the distance, three dots approaching in the sky.

'It is time!' he shouted.

Two other men appeared from inside the pavilion. They were young, but had the serious expressions of older men. And they carried their weapons with them.

The Stinger systems were bulky, but light. A thick tube, a little over a metre and a half long, with a sight mounted on the top and the firing mechanics underneath. They were already loaded. One of the men handed his weapon to Farzad Haq, before returning indoors and appearing with the third.

All three of them now looked into the sky.

The three dots were coming gradually closer, swapping positions as they approached like dancing birds.

Farzad felt an unfamiliar pang of regret. He wished Adel could be here to witness the fruition of their carefully laid plan. But that couldn't be. For him, there would have been only two possible outcomes. Either he had managed to detonate his chemical weapon and was even now enjoying the embrace of God while the radiation spread around the centre of London, infecting its infidel citizens and causing the President's helicopters to use their well-documented operating procedures and evacuate their way into Farzad's trap. Or, he had been discovered and the Americans, in their cowardice, had evacuated the President anyway. Whichever of the two outcomes had materialised, the Americans would have had only one option: to airlift the President to where Air Force One was waiting. And Adel had known, from his meeting with the foolish American ambassador, that it was waiting at Northolt.

The plan had been simple in its conception but complicated in its execution. The three birds dotting their way towards him, however, meant they had succeeded.

Haq raised the viewfinder to his eye and the others did the same. Three minutes, he estimated. Three minutes and it would all be over.

A voice. 'What in the blazes do you think you're doing?'

Haq lowered the Stinger system. A man had approached. He was old, maybe seventy, with a small dog on a lead and a sturdy walking stick in the other hand. His wrinkled face was angry. Haq put the weapon on the ground, then plunged his hand inside his jacket and withdrew a handgun. The old man's eyes widened and he took a step backwards. Haq didn't hesitate for a moment. A single shot, aimed precisely at the man's forehead. The top half of his head blew away, rendering him unrecognisable, and the force of the round flung him to the floor. The little dog started to whimper and paw at his dead master; almost as an afterthought, Haq dispatched the animal too.

The youths at the bandstand ran away as Haq raised the Stinger system once more. He wasn't worried about the police—they wouldn't be here in time. Marine One and its two decoys came into view on the high-powered scope. Which was which, Farzad couldn't tell. But it didn't matter. Three helicopters. Three Stingers.

The President was coming.

The world was about to change.

'On my instruction, lock on to the aircraft as we arranged,' he said.

The helicopters continued to approach.

*     *     *

The noise in Jack's earpiece was a riot of confusion. *'Turn the President round!'* he yelled. *'Turn him round!'*

'Negative,' a voice crackled in his ear. 'Secret Service are evacuating him.'

Jack cursed. 'Then turn us round! Get us into Marine One's airspace!'

A pause. Then . . .

'No can do, Jack. It's a no-fly zone for anyone except—'

Jack had stopped listening. He bustled to the front of the chopper. *'Northolt!'* he yelled. *'Fly to Northolt!'*

The chopper swerved, following Jack's instruction. As it did so, the pilot's voice came over the comms. 'What the hell's going on?'

Jack was crazed. Confused. Without even thinking, he pressed his MP5 against the pilot's helmet. *'Northolt!'* he screamed.

'Jesus, Jack!' Fly shouted. 'He's doing what you wanted!'

Jack moved his weapon round to point at Fly, who had already started to raise his own MP5. *'Don't fucking move, Fly,'* he shouted. *'I mean it. Don't fucking move.'*

Fly lowered his gun. He licked his dry lips slightly, obviously about to say something. To talk the sense into Jack that he so obviously needed.

He never got the chance.

Habib Khan didn't care that Jack had a submachine gun in his fist. He had already pushed

497

himself up and was even now preparing to launch himself at his captor. Jack opened his mouth to warn him off, but Khan's body slammed against his. What the man was trying to achieve, Jack didn't know. His puny, Plasticuffed frame was never going to be up to the task of fighting him. Jack swatted him away and Khan fell by the open doorway before pushing himself up on his feet again and, with a wild, insane look on his bloodied face, taking another step inwards.

It was almost a reflex action that caused Jack to shoot him; and although it all happened with sudden, brutal speed, every millisecond seemed long and drawn out. The burst of fire from his gun slammed directly into Khan's body. A sudden explosion of red burst from the cavity of his chest, and the force of the ammunition knocked him backwards.

Khan staggered, buffeted by the wind and the movement of the chopper. He teetered on the brink of the doorway.

And then he fell into the almost darkness, slipping silently from Jack's sight and plunging to the ground below.

Jack didn't even have time to be pleased that he was dead. Just as Khan disappeared, he felt Fly's weapon pressed against his neck. *'Get on the fucking floor, Jack. Now. I mean it. You're out of control . . .'*

'The President!' Jack roared. *'They're targeting the Pre—'*

He didn't finish, because Fly used all his strength to press him to the ground. Jack was sideways on, looking out of the chopper door, a boot on his back and an MP5 pointed at his head.

The chopper swerved, back on to its previous bearing.

'You've got to believe me!' he shouted over the thunder of the helicopter. *'You've got to believe me!'*

And then he fell silent. Because in the distance he saw a sight that made it feel like all the blood had drained from his body.

It didn't last long. Not long at all. A brief flash, exploding in the evening sky with a sudden orange glow.

*'Jesus!'* Fly shouted. *'What the fuck was that?'*

Jack didn't answer. He couldn't.

He just watched as the glow faded as quickly as it had come, back into nothingness.

*     *     *

The birds had continued to dance, but now they were settling as they started to lose height on their descent into RAF Northolt. They were close, and Farzad Haq had all his attention on the westernmost helicopter. He trusted that his two accomplices would each have locked on to the others. They had their instructions and they were scared of him. Fear was a great motivator. 'Activate the weapons!' he instructed in his harshly accented English.

He pushed the activation lever on his own weapon forward. A click, and then a spinning noise as the weapon warmed up.

They were close now. Maybe a kilometre away, as the crow flies. Maybe slightly further.

Which of these little birds, he wondered, carried his hated target? He privately wished it was the one *he* would shoot down, but he understood that this was something he could never know.

No matter. As long as all three were destroyed.

He kept the chopper in his sight.

'Acquire the target!'

His launch system locked on, and a loud tone indicated that the missile had a good lock on the infrared being emitted by the aircraft he was tracking.

It flew closer.

*For you, Grandfather*, he said silently in his head. *And for you, Adel.*

He could hear the choppers now.

'Fire!' he commanded.

It was so simple. Like flicking a switch.

Each of the three Stingers flew from their launch systems at immense speed. Farzad Haq staggered backwards and lowered the device in time to see the missiles shed their launch engines and swerve towards the choppers with astonishing accuracy.

He watched as the rocket engines shot like fireworks in the evening sky. The missiles kept true to their targets. Even when the pilots of the helicopters realised what was happening and swerved sharply, veering away from their close-cluster formation like a flower spreading its petals, the Stingers kept on track—changing their bearing to follow each twist and turn the pilots made.

His grandfather's voice echoed down the years and resounded in his head. *The time will come when all who are true to the Prophet will be called to rise up and fight against them . . . Will you be ready to answer the call?*

'I will be ready,' he muttered to himself. And with wonder etched on his face, and triumph burning through his veins, Farzad Haq's eyes

500

feasted on the moment of impact.

The three helicopters exploded at almost the same time. The noise was deafening—the dreadful thunder of God's wrath. It vibrated through Haq's body, shook the earth and numbed his ears. He relished every moment.

Three massive fireballs ripped the fabric of the sky. They hung in the air, billowing and scorching, before merging into one great rain cloud of burning debris, scattering its load of searing metal, blazing fuel and human flesh on to the earth below.

# EPILOGUE

All the airports were shut, all flights grounded. The underground stations were surrounded by throngs of armed police; pubs were filled with loud-mouthed experts on international relations. Bin Laden's name was mentioned in every other sentence, but nobody really knew what they were talking about.

There was barely a house in England—in the world—with a television set that didn't have it switched on; no news networks had footage of Marine One going down, so they replayed scenes of the twin towers instead. In America, men and women wept for their fallen President. In Africa too. They would always remember where they were when they heard the news. Ashen-faced politicians of all nations made statements condemning the act, declaring a renewed war on terror. Nobody admitted that terror had won.

Jack Harker was aware of none of this. The minute Marine One had taken the hit, Hereford had ordered the Agusta to land. The pilot had radioed for backup to help with the crazy Regiment soldier who'd lost it and pulled a gun on him, and as soon as they'd touched down on the helipad that crowned a tall building in the city, CO19 officers were waiting for them. Fly had disarmed Jack, who in any case wasn't inclined to put up a fight any more. CO19 cuffed him and led him into a waiting car. The air seemed to be filled with the sirens of a thousand police cars as they'd taken him through panic-ridden streets to Paddington Green, where they unceremoniously hurled him into a cell and told him to wait.

There was a bed, a mattress and a stinking bog with no seat and piss-stains round the porcelain. Jack had ignored them all, slumping instead into one corner, clutching his knees and staring, numb, into the middle distance.

Just after midnight, there was a voice outside the cell. 'Open it.'

Jack blinked and looked through the bars. Elliott Carver was there. The CO of 22 SAS looked like he'd aged several years in the few hours since Jack had seen him last—dark rings under his eyes and a greyness about his skin. An officer opened the door and Carver stepped in.

'Leave us alone,' he told the cop. Only when they could talk without being heard did he continue. 'Khan pulled a secreted weapon and was going to take out the pilot. That's why you shot him. Got it?'

'Did you find Lily?' Jack asked. It was the only thing he cared about now.

Carver ignored the question. 'You're fucking lucky I got to Fly and the crew before anyone else did, Jack, otherwise you'd be celebrating your next birthday in jail. After what's gone down tonight they'll be queuing up to find scapegoats and you'll be at the top of everyone's list. You need to tell me every last thing and then we'll sort out your story, chapter and fucking verse. Not now.' He shook his head as Jack started to speak. 'In the car back to Hereford. Get moving.'

'Did you find Lily?'

Carver closed his eyes. 'Yeah, Jack. We found

her.'

Jack stared at him, preparing himself for the worst.

'She was where Khan said she'd be. She's alive, Jack, but she's not pretty.'

Jack felt his lips thinning. 'I want to see her.'

'Not yet.'

'Damn it, boss.' Jack exploded.

Carver raised his voice. 'Get to the car. It's an order, Jack.'

Jack felt the muscles in his face tensing up. 'All right,' he said finally. 'Let's go.'

In the car, Jack didn't hold back and Carver didn't say a word until he'd finished. Even then he was silent for several minutes as he digested it all. 'You're telling me that Habib Khan was Farzad Haq's brother, and they've been planning this whole spectacular together?'

Jack nodded. 'It was an ambush, plain and simple. If the dirty bomb went off, all well and good. But the main thing was to force the President into the kill zone, and then . . .' He inclined his head slightly. 'Did they get Haq?'

Carver shook his head. 'By the time we got to the Stinger launch area, he'd got away. Every set of eyes in the country is looking for him, but—'

'They won't find him,' Jack said quietly. He didn't know how he knew. He just knew.

'The suits will be at Hereford before you know it,' Carver told him. 'British and Yank. We need to work out what you're going to tell them.'

'Fuck it,' Jack replied. 'I'll tell them the truth.'

'You killed O'Callaghan and Khan,' Carver said sharply. 'And if they want to put Caroline Stenton on you, they'd do it in an instant. They'll say you

504

knew who Khan was before we mounted the op and that you withheld the information. The Yanks would love to pin all this on a rogue SAS agent. Takes the heat off them.'

Jack shrugged. 'Fine.'

'Don't be stupid, Jack. They'll chew you up.'

Jack turned to his boss and gave him a dark look. 'Let them try,' he said.

'No,' the CO said. 'I won't. And if you want to see your daughter again, neither will you.'

A pause.

'Jack,' Carver said finally. 'Nobody else is ever going to say this, but well done. London owes you.'

'Is that an official backslap?'

'You know it isn't.'

They sat in silence for the rest of the journey.

*       *       *

There was no time to rest. Carver and Jack headed straight for the CO's office where they sat down and worked on Jack's story. No lawyers, no nobody. Just the two of them. They excised all mention of O'Callaghan and Caroline Stenton and tweaked the rest of it so that Jack came up smelling not of roses, but less strongly of shit. And then Carver had done the official debrief. On tape. On the record.

They'd only just finished when there was a knock on the door. 'Visitors, boss. Secret Service. CIA. The lot.'

Carver gave Jack a cool look. 'I'll deal with them,' he said. 'You need to leave.' He took a piece of paper and scribbled an address on it. 'I think you've got somewhere to be.'

505

'Yeah,' Jack replied. 'As it happens, I do.'

'Then go. Now.'

Jack stood up. But before he left, he turned to Carver. 'Thank you, boss.'

'Go,' the CO repeated.

In the corridor, he heard American voices. They were abrupt and accompanied by footsteps. Opposite the CO's office was a briefing room. Jack slipped inside and put his ear to the closed door. The footsteps grew closer and then he heard Carver's voice. 'Come inside, gentlemen.'

He gave it a minute, then left the room. He could hear conversation inside the CO's office, and he stopped for a moment to listen.

'. . . I am responsible for the men under my command, and I will debrief them. If you've got a problem with that . . .'

Jack didn't need to hear any more. He hurried down the corridor and minutes later he was slipping silently out of RAF Credenhill. He didn't know when, or if, he would return.

\* \* \*

The scrap of paper Carver had given him carried the address of a hospital ward deep in the belly of University College Hospital. Jack drove to London at full speed, but it was still the slowest and saddest journey of his life.

The ward was a small room, with only enough space for four beds, each of which was sectioned off with frayed floral curtains. The whole place stank of hospital food and disinfectant. The young police officer who had escorted Jack there nodded at a female doctor in a white coat and half-moon glasses. The doctor approached. She had a serious, thin-lipped expression.

'You need to brace yourself,' she said. 'She's in a bad way.'

Jack nodded, and the doctor led him to one of the sets of curtains. She peered behind it, then held it open for him to approach.

The girl in the bed looked pale and desperately thin. There was a saline drip hanging from a stand and attached intravenously to the back of her hand, and an oxygen mask over her nose and mouth. Her eyes were closed and the skin on her face was purple and mottled. It was a face that had taken repeated beatings; the bruises extended down her neck and below the collar of her hospital gown. Her mousy hair was greasy and scraggly. She looked human, but only just.

'Lily,' Jack breathed.

Her eyes opened. At first there was nothing behind them. Just a blank, unknowing expression. But after a few seconds they widened, and their red rims started to ooze tears.

'Dad?' she asked. Her voice was weak.

There was a seat by the bed. Jack sat down and took his daughter by the hand. The skin was dry and cold.

'I thought I'd never see you again,' Lily said. 'I thought I was going to die. I thought he would . . .'

'You don't need to worry about him any more,' Jack said. He thought of Khan, falling dead from the Agusta. There was no satisfaction.

Lily closed her eyes. 'They made me do things . . .' she breathed.

Jack felt he should say something, but the words stuck in his throat. He squeezed her hand a little

507

tighter.

They sat in silence together. Father and daughter. The world could burn around them. It had already started. So what.

He knew she would ask the question sooner or later. It came sooner.

'Where's Mum?'

The words were like daggers. Jack hung his head. He took a deep breath. And then he looked his daughter in the eye, and told her.

**Fact**

During the Second Gulf War, a compromised SBS unit abandoned a stash of equipment, including a number of Stinger missiles, which are thought to have been stolen by enemy forces.

**Fact**

At the time of writing, it is estimated that each year approximately seventy sources of radioactive isotopes, suitable for acts of radiological terror, go missing in Europe alone.